DEMONS BANE

The Half-Blood Chronicles

J.R. Smith

This book is dedicated to my wonderful husband and daughters. Thank you for always believing and going along with me on this crazy adventure

Prologue

The King paced his war room like a restless lion itching for a battle. What was taking the seer so long? His anger mounted with each passing second. The rest of the castle was as silent as a tomb. The servants scurried like frightened mice to their quarters praying not to incur his majesty's wrath. Only his personal butler remained nearby, as silent and immovable as a statue. Perhaps if he didn't move or make a sound he would live through the night. It was clear the King had gone mad. Everyone in the castle knew this to be true, but no one dared to speak of it.

The King's third wife had died in childbirth three months prior taking the baby with her. There was no heir to the throne and the King was no longer a young man. There had been rumors in the court and whispers, talk that the death of his three wives were not natural. Some whispered of murder and sacrifice. For three days the King had been secluded in a dark room with no windows refusing food and drink, refusing to speak to anyone. When he emerged, his eyes were wild and darting. He spoke like a man possessed or paranoid beyond reason. He had demanded the seer be summoned and began dismissing his advisors. He prowled around the castle and lashed out at anyone who attracted his attention. Some servants had fled, only to be hunted down and killed. The rest scurried to avoid his notice and wrath. The castle had turned from a place of joy to a place of darkness and torment. May the Gods have mercy on them all.

The door to the room quietly drifted open admitting the old seer into the room. The King spun on his heels, piercing the old woman to the wall with his glare. The silence was deafening, the tension growing to unbearable portions. The King's booming voice shattered the icy cold silence causing the servant and seer to quake in fear.

"Well, old woman, what do the spirits say? Out with it!"

"Your majesty I can only say what they show and that isn't very clear." Her fragile voice quaked with each word, her bent frame crumpling underneath the King's terrible scrutiny.

"Tell me crone or your next visit will be with the executioner!"

"Of course, your majesty, as you wish. The time of separation is ending. Soon the races will unite bringing forth the age of half-bloods. When the races of elf and man unite, your time on the throne will be finite. The half-elf race will be born, going where none will roam conquering the unknown and finally sitting the throne."

"WHAT?! No half-blood mongrel will take my throne!"

"Your majesty, there are many ways this can be interpreted. Perhaps it means that the half-elf will do you a great service and in return you will name him as heir. This doesn't have to be negative…"

"SILENCE!! Leave hag before I decide to end your existence for possessing this knowledge!

You will tell no one of what you have seen, am I clear?"

"Of course, your majesty, I reveal nothing." The bent old woman turned to leave with a speed only fear could incite, but as she reached for the doorknob her body crumbled to ash without a sound.

"Correct hag, you will reveal nothing." With a twist of his hand the ashes were swept up in a gust of wind and blown out the nearest window. "They haven't united yet, so there is time. Tomorrow I will send emissaries to instill fear and hatred between the races. Then I will see to ensuring no half-blood child lives to fulfill this prophecy." With a confident smile spreading across his face, the King glided out of the room and up to his chambers. Only his forgotten personal butler remained behind, quietly weeping for the loss of the woman and the terror gripping his heart. He could not stay, that was clear. He would have to leave before the morning and pray the King wouldn't remember his presence here tonight. If he did… shouldn't think of such things. He would just have to get away as quickly as possible and find someone who would be able to keep the prophecy alive. There were lords that were secretly against the King. If he could get to them and pass the word before the King's assassins found him, then perhaps there was a ray of light. The prophecy was their only hope….

Chapter 1

The spring festival was a time of joy, hope, and rebirth. Everyone in the village was helping to prepare for the celebration. Decorations were hung everywhere, colorful streamers and lanterns lined the main street. All the store fronts had placed decorated tables and chairs outside of their windows. Laurelie skipped up and down the street in her new white dress, dancing and singing with the other children. Her parents owned the village bakery and had shooed her outdoors while they finished the cakes and pastries to bring to the festival.

The day was perfect. The musicians were warming up their instruments and beginning to play some light tunes, while the younger maidens of the village began dancing around the May pole giggling and gossiping. Laurel saw her father and mother bringing out the cakes and setting them on the tables. She giggled as a group of villagers began crowding around the table hungrily gaping at the delectable treats and complimenting her father on the extravagance of his contribution. She loved how he always laughed heartily and humbly accepted their praises. It was no secret that her father was considered one of the best bakers in the land. In fact, several high lords sent their most trusted emissaries to request cakes from her father.

Laurel quickly left what she was doing to help her parents, running into the bakery and grabbing a tray of pastries to bring out. She wasn't strong enough to carry out the multi-layered cakes, but the pastry trays she could manage, as long as she didn't rush.

"Laurel, you need not help with the trays. It is a day of celebration. You should be with your friends and enjoying the day."

"I know father, but if I help then you can begin enjoying the day all the sooner." Her father ran his hand through her long white-blonde hair chuckling to himself and shaking his head.

"Very well, I accept your help. Now let us get these other trays laid out so that I may ask your mother for a dance."

Giggling, Laurel ran back inside and grabbed another tray. Within minutes they had all of the trays laid out and the villagers had started partaking of the sweets. Laurel watched as her father bowed deeply to her mother, taking her hand and asking her for a dance. Others might laugh at her parents' romantic notions, but Laurel was always warmed inside by their love for each other.

A sudden scream from the edge of town broke the entrancing moment as it sent men running towards the commotion. Laurel's eyes followed the flood of villagers, leaving her frozen with terror as she beheld a blood red cloud descending upon her village. Laurel was jerked into action as her father grabbed her arm and shoved her into the bakery, dragging her to the back of the house. Everything was happening so fast…. why? Laurel could hear the screams of her friends and neighbors, and the roar of whatever was out there.

Day had turned to night, as her father shoved the bookshelf away from the wall and opened a secret panel hidden behind. Where did that come from? When did her father put that there? Laurel could hear her mother crying softly in the background as she grabbed something from a nearby cupboard. Her father was telling her something, but Laurel just couldn't focus. What was he saying? He was taking her down a set of dark stairs and into another room. The walls were covered with strange markings. There was a mat on the floor and crates with dried meats and fruits. Were they going to hide in here?

"Laurelie, are you listening?" Her father's voice was frightened and desperate. Laurel looked at him in confusion, her father wasn't afraid of anything.

"Are we going to hide in here from whatever is happening?" She watched as her father closed his eyes and sighed.

"I wish there was more time, but there just isn't. This has to stop and you are the only hope of stopping this. You are stronger than you realize my dearest. Trust in yourself, have faith in the Gods, and find your way. Whatever you hear, stay in here. The runes should keep you safe. Remember that we love you." Laurel could barely breathe as her father pulled her into a strong, safe hug for the last time. Tears streamed down her face as her mother joined the hug.

"Toran, give her the amulet. It's the only identification she'll have. It's the only way they'll know she's your daughter." Her mother turned from her father to embrace Laurel holding her tightly to her. "My dearest daughter, I wish I could watch you grow, but remember that what we do now, we do so that you may live. Stay strong, never give up, and trust in your heart. I love you and I wouldn't change a moment of our lives together. May the Goddess protect you." Her mother removed the chain she always wore from her neck and placed it over Laurel's head. At the end of the chain was a medallion symbolizing the Goddess of Nature, Gaia.

"Lily, it's time. Laurel, this amulet is our family's crest. When you have grown, take it to the Elves in Laurendale. They will know what this means, and they will help you. Goodbye my princess. Do not forget who you are." With that her father made some motions with his hand and his appearance melted from that of a human to that of an Elf. Laurel stood in shock, not fully understanding what was happening. How could she? She was only eight! This couldn't be happening!

With another wave of his hands the runes in the room began to glow softly. Then her parents took each other's hands and walked out of the room barring it from the outside. Only then did Laurel realize what was happening. Only then did she realize the sacrifice her parents were about to make. When the roaring ripped through her home, Laurel ran to the door and began pounding on the door with her fists. She never heard her parents scream; she heard nothing but that terrible hollow roar.

Then the room began shaking, as if whatever was making that sound was trying to rip the room apart. Its howling was thunderous and painful. Laurel cowered in the far corner of the room, curled into a ball on the mat, her mother's holy symbol and her father's amulet clenched tightly in her small fists. Silence finally gripped the tiny room, leaving Laurel weeping and exhausted. Slowly she allowed herself to relax enough to lay down, trembling and alone for the first time in her life. With a sudden deathly howl, the door ripped from its frame and the blood red cloud seeped into the room bathing everything crimson.

Laurel froze, her back pressed tightly against the wall, her breath coming in short quick gasps. She watched horrified as the cloud coalesced into the form of a demonic face, its hollow eyes boring into her soul. Slowly it glided across the room, its tendrils reaching towards her. Just as it was about to wrap itself around her the holy symbol around her neck began to glow brightening the room in its white warm light. Its brightness grew in intensity until Laurel was forced to close her eyes. She could hear the entity screaming in pain as it tried to flee the holy glow of the medallion. Then…

Laurel woke with a start, gasping for breath and drenched in her own sweat. It was that time of the year again, the anniversary of her parents' and village's deaths. Every year she was plagued by the memory of that day playing out in her dreams for the week leading up to the day of the blood storm. It had never come back, in all her years playing at being a human, the demon storm had never returned. Her village became something of legend, the lost city, at least that was what the locals called it.

Every year treasure crazed fools came to Vale Ridge trying to find clues to the lost city's whereabouts. Little did they know the town was just over the Shadow Mountains, in the caldera on the other side. The journey however was a very dangerous one. The mountains were filled with hidden gullies, swamps, and treacherous cliffs. They were inhabited by goblins, trolls, giant lizards, horrible misshapen creatures, warped creations of the magic used to raise the mountains from the plains, the plains that used to lead to her home. Every year, a couple of days before the anniversary of the destruction, Laurel made the treacherous journey alone. Every year, she took time off of work and quietly slipped out of town before sunrise. Every year she spent a day in her lost town waiting to confront the demon that took everything from her. Now, it was time once again to pack and leave on her annual pilgrimage.

She put on her dress and pulled her blonde hair into a mess of loose curls on top of her head. Her ears she hid with putty that matched her skin tone and a few tendrils of hair hanging down. People saw what they wanted to see, and no one expected to see a half-elf. She made her way to the Swan and Dragon Inn, where she worked as a serving girl. What fools would she meet today? She smiled as she wondered how much gold they would offer this year for any information about the lost city. She wouldn't take their gold, but she would send them on a wild goose chase in the wrong direction. They would travel for weeks through barren wastes until they came to an abandoned salt mining camp that was no longer on the map. With any luck they would come away from the experience wiser and alive.

She walked into an inn crowded with adventurers, villagers, and smoke. Bartholomew, the inn keeper, was a man almost as wide as he was tall, usually with a jolly smile and kerchief in hand, to wipe sweat away from his brow, as he bustled around the room. Today, however, he was hurrying around with a grimace plastered on his face, shouting orders and harrying the other girls.

"Laurel!! Where have you been?"

"This is my…."

"Never mind, never mind…. We have customers everywhere, guardsmen filling the rooms, and the King's personal advisor arriving tomorrow!!! We need to get all these people taken care of and out of here! Quickly, quickly girl, get your apron on and start serving. I want this lot cleaned out before the advanced guard gets here!"

"Of course, sir, I'll be but a moment…. Why is the King's advisor coming here, anyway?"

"He's heard that there is someone here who knows the way to the lost city and they want to find the person and discover if it's true. Now don't bother me girl, there is too much work to be done." Bartholomew quickly slipped away through the crowd to attend to a man in armor who looked rather important.

Quickly Laurel danced through the crowd and donned her apron. The sooner she got everyone served and out of here, the sooner she would be free to get away from here. The King's advisor was coming here? If they found her.... Best to leave that thought unfinished. She had to get out of here before the advance guard's arrival or she would be trapped here. With luck and faith the goddess would protect her, and she would be able to escape before the cage was dropped on her.

Laurel moved with the grace of a swan as she sped around the room taking orders, delivering food and drink, and answering questions. A few times she was groped by some guards, but that was nothing new. She would always giggle, blush and spin out of their grasp, playing the shy and demure damsel. As the day wore on the crowd began to dwindle. Those that sought the town were keeping their questions to vague hints for information, leaving her free to feign ignorance. As the inn emptied out, the excitement of the new arrivals dwindling, Laurel took stock of who was left.

There were several guardsmen still drinking their ale at the counter, a few townspeople taking their dinners and fishing for gossip, and at a table in a dark corner two young men. One of the young men was dressed too fine to be of common blood, although he was trying to play at it. His chestnut hair was cut to his shoulders and held back by a leather tie, exposing his strong chin and piercing blue eyes. His shoulders were broad and his tunic left the impression of strong and chiseled muscles beneath. He would be handsome if not for the brooding expression set on his face. His friend was just as muscular, but with a mischievous twinkle to his green eyes. His red hair was also cut to his shoulders, but it hung loose and wild, as if he had just rolled out of bed.

Laurel felt herself drawn to the one with chestnut hair; she had a need to learn more about him. Casually, she made her way over to them, checking on everyone she passed and tending to the other patrons' needs as she went. She knew she shouldn't be doing this. She had plans to make if she was going to get out of town tonight. Still…. Laurel took a breath and finally walked over to them.

"Hello, welcome to the Swan and Dragon, can I get you anything?" The red head raised his eyebrows and smiled playfully at her.

"How about some time alone with you?" He slipped his hand around her waist and pulled her closer. She smiled and blushed coyly as she extricated herself from his grip.

"Enough Bane! We are here for a reason and it's not for you to get laid!"

Bane leaned back in his chair putting his hands up in a defensive gesture and laughing heartily. "All well and good Kale, but maybe you should try asking for the information you're seeking instead of staring at everyone like you're going to kill them. Just saying…."

Kale, the chestnut-haired young man, sighed and closed his eyes. He ran his large hand across his forehead rubbing his temples as he shook his head. Laurel couldn't explain it, but she wanted to reach out and soothe his pain. Whatever information he needed she knew she would give it to him.

"I know, Bane, I know. I'm just not sure who to ask without raising suspicion." Suddenly, he looked up, his gaze piercing into Laurel's soul. "Perhaps you…. Do you know how we can find information about the village of Soldar?"

Laurel could only stare at him in shock. No one had ever spoken the name of her hometown. No one remembered its name, yet… he knew… he remembered…. How was that possible? She caught her breath and quickly dropped her gaze from his piercing eyes. A plan, she needed a plan… a guide. She would have to be quick and quiet.

"Meet me out back, after my day is done… that will be in one more hour. I'll tell you what I can then. Make sure you are not followed, please." Then with a laugh that didn't reach her eyes she turned and went back into the kitchen. Tonight she would meet with them and tell them of a guide. Then she would go home change into her woodland clothing and meet them outside the town as the cloaked, mute, ranger who would take them to Soldar. It was time.

Chapter 2

Kale had grown up the son of a noble. His mother had died many years ago… painfully and slowly. She had been a seer, though no one had known that except her husband and son. Her final vision had killed her, a blood storm that had wiped out an entire town. Kale had taken her hands as she screamed in agony, consumed by her vision. In that moment, he had witnessed the same atrocity his mother was experiencing. It had been horrible, a small town covered in blood and gore. The villagers' bodies had been thrown every which way, many torn limb from limb. A red cloud with a hideous face formed inside it howled and laughed as it ripped through every building, every hiding place. It pulled everyone out into the open where it devoured them.

"Go to Soldar, my son. Find her. Find the one that can end this. She is your destiny." Kale still remembered those last words of his mother. Find her, but who? Who was this girl he was supposed to find? How could she stop this? And how was he supposed to find her? He was only a boy… he could barely hold a sword.

Bane's hearty laugh followed by a girl's giggle brought him out of his morbid reverie. He looked up and saw her. She was beautiful. Her platinum blonde hair was piled up on her head in a cascade of curls that fell to just below her shoulders. Her blue eyes glimmered in the candlelight showing a soul filled with joy and pain. He almost lost his breath. Had she said her name?

Maybe… maybe she was the one he was supposed to find. He wouldn't mind her being his destiny.

When she answered his question about Soldar, pain had flashed through her eyes… an intense look of suffering, loss, and fear. She was the one, she had to be. Of course he would meet her tonight, there was no question about it. She would help him find that monster and destroy it, although what a tavern girl could do against such a formidable enemy was beyond him. Perhaps she was just meant to guide him to it, and then he would be able to destroy it… maybe.

After forty more minutes he nudged Bane and the two of them left the inn, presumably to get some fresh air. Guards patrolled the streets in small groups, scanning the faces of the town's people. This meeting was going to be more dangerous than he had expected. Why did the King have to have his suspicions raised now and why here?

Over the past several generations, the royal family had become increasingly monstrous. With laws against magic, interracial relationships and town meetings, the current King had everyone jumping at shadows and suspicious of any outsiders. The elves and dwarves had isolated themselves to the west and north creating an impenetrable wall severing Kallihan's ties with its neighboring countries. Death squads enforced the laws, searching out and killing anyone who demonstrated magical talent… regardless of age.

As a noble, he had been tested at birth and found free of the curse… but he wasn't. When he was ten, he began to notice little things happening around him. Small animals would approach him, strong desires would be fulfilled, and he could read the runic script he had found in his mother's hidden library. When his father discovered the truth about his son a few years later, he warned Kale to never let anyone know what he could do.

His father had explained to him, in gruesome detail, the consequences of manifesting magical talent. He had also confided stories and rumors about the King, such as sacrifices and bargains with demons. Some said the King hadn't aged in many years… although those who spread such rumors were quickly silenced. It had been because of the King's harsh laws, rumors and corruption in the military and government, and his promise to his mother that Kale and Bane had left their service.

Like all noble sons, he had been forced to attend military school and serve for one year in the King's military. His father had paid to have Bane attend the academy with him, so he would have a trusted friend and companion at the school. The more Kale and Bane had seen, the more they began to question their King and those that served him. In the end it came down to one question. How could he serve a man whom he didn't trust or believe in? A cough roused him from his thoughts.

"You came. I wasn't sure with all the soldiers around if you would show or not." Kale extended his hand to the young maiden before him.

"You know its name. No one remembers its name anymore. I can't tell you how to get there, but I know it exists." Her voice was quivering and soft, almost as if she were a rabbit ready to bolt.

"You have to be able to tell us something." He tried to keep his voice steady and calm, but his frustration was fighting what little composure he had left.

"I said I can't take you, but…" She looked around nervously, checking the shadows. "I know someone who can, a guide. The person is a ranger, small and mute, but well-traveled and an apt fighter. The ranger can take you to where you seek, but you must go tonight under the cover of darkness. Be at the South gate two hours before dawn. Take this…" She placed a wooden coin into Kale's hand. Its surface was well worn, but a carving of a tree was still apparent on it. "Give this to your guide, it means you can be trusted. Now I must go. If we're spotted… it's the end of me." Kale quickly grabbed her arm before she could leave.

"What's your name? Please, tell me." His eyes looked deeply into the two perfectly blue pools of her eyes, willing her to trust him. He watched as she wet her lips nervously before looking away.

"My name is Laurel. Now please, I must go… may the Gods protect you." As quickly and silently as she came, she was gone. Bane placed his hand on Kale's shoulder.

"If we're going to be at the South Gate two hours before dawn, we had better get packed and get some sleep. Come on, it doesn't look like you're going to have any company in bed tonight anyway. By the way… I saw her first." With a chuckle, Bane clapped an arm around Kale's shoulder, and they strode back towards the inn like two men who had experienced a good time at the local brothel and were ready for some sleep. No one stopped them and they were able to get everything packed and ready to go before falling into a deep sleep.

    Two hours before dawn found Kale and Bane hiding in the shadows of some trees near the South Gate. A light tap on their shoulders sent both men spinning, weapons in hand. In one quick, blinding movement their swords were knocked from their hands and they found themselves on their backsides looking up at a cloaked figure. The man's face was hidden within the shadows of his hood. He was small, but agile and quiet. This had to be the guide Laurel had spoken of. Kale took the wooden coin from his pocket and held it up to the cloaked figure.

    "Laurel said you could take us to Soldar. I need to go there. I need to know what happened. I need to stop it." Kale watched the figure before him carefully, not daring to move. While a staff couldn't run him through, it could definitely ruin his day or kill him with the proper strike. The silent man extended a gloved hand to help them up. Then he turned and strode into the woods to the South.

    Kale and Bane looked at each other then back where the man had gone. Were they supposed to follow? Bane shrugged and then headed off into the woods. Kale took one last look at the town they were leaving. He would come back for her, that he promised himself. Then he followed after the others partly jogging to catch up.

They traveled for what seemed like hours. The forest was so densely packed that barely any light made it through the canopy to the floor. Every so often the ranger would motion for them to stop, heading off into the underbrush like a shadow. In those moments, it felt like hours before he would return, motioning for them to follow once more. Kale and Bane's military training had prepared them for intense physical exertion, but this was different. The dense underbrush was sometimes so thick they would have to climb under, on their stomachs, or over risking entanglement and injury. Twice they skirted swamps that would have left them soaked and trapped.

Finally, the ranger motioned for them to stop near a rock outcropping. He began setting up camp, a sign the two young men could finally collapse on the ground in exhaustion. Conversation was limited, and because the ranger was mute, Kale was left to asking yes or no questions to try and discover more about their silent guide. By the time he laid down to sleep, Kale had learned that his companion had lived in Soldar, was a worshipper of the Goddess Gaia, and most likely elven. No other man would be of such a small frame, and it would explain why he chose to remain cloaked, even at night. When Kale laid down, he was left with a disquieted longing for Laurel and an urgency to find Soldar before the King's men could find him.

That night, Kale's dreams were filled with the beautiful girl from the tavern, the King's death squads, and a blood red cloud bent on their destruction. His sleep was restless and draining as he rescued Laurel from one danger to only lose her to another. He couldn't get her out of his mind. If he went back for her, would he only be putting her in greater danger? Were his dreams trying to tell him that he would be her death if he went back for her? Were his dreams telling him she would die if he didn't go back for her? Answers, he needed answers not more questions. He needed her... but why? He was shaken awake, at dawn, by their silent ranger. Kale sluggishly arose to a packed camp and a concerned Bane at his side. How could he have overslept? He must look completely incompetent. Maybe it was a good thing Laurel wasn't there to witness his blunders. Gathering up the last of his belongings and rolling his shoulders, Kale hefted his pack onto his back with a sigh. This was going to be a long day.

Chapter 3

Laurel woke them at dawn. It was still a hike to get to the village and she had to get to its outskirts today. Tomorrow morning they would enter the town and she would begin her silent vigil for the day. She would let the two young men wander around and look to their hearts content, but they would need to be gone by dark…. The dark brought out the specters and shadows that haunted the village.

The human named Kale had slept fitfully all night. She had kept watch through most of it, only nodding off for short stints from time to time. On a number of occasions, she had wanted to go to him and sooth his forehead, but what if he had woken up… she couldn't risk being discovered for who she really was. Still…she wanted to connect to him… there was something about him, something that almost felt like a memory or dream. It drew her to him.

His friend, Bane, however had slept like a log oblivious to anything happening around him. It was possible a battle could have broken out and he would have slept through it. At one point a leaf had fallen on his face and he didn't even flinch. How could anyone sleep that heavily? He had awoken just before the sun and without word made short work of packing up the camp. Afterward he sat vigil over Kale until his fitful sleep had come to an end. He was a good and loyal friend, something to be admired. She wondered what that would be like… to have someone that loyal and caring at her side. Laurel shook her head ruefully; this was going to be a long day.

By mid-morning they had reached the peaks of the mountain range and could look down into the circular valley below. It was possible to just make out the small village in the center. She motioned for the two young men to look at the surrounding slopes. Then she motioned for quiet. It may look like everything was easy going from here on in, but she knew better. This was the most dangerous part of the journey. If they were lucky, they would be able to slip past any goblin sentries and avoid detection by the berserkers. Even the goblins feared the berserkers, horribly misshapen creatures formed when the mountains were. They were the combination of several creatures that had been magically merged together. Berserkers were mindless monsters whose only thoughts were of their next meal. Laurel had only come across them twice, once on her first journey to Soldar and again when she was a bit older. The first time she had been lucky enough to hide up a tree, the second she had been horrified to find them devouring one of their own. She had been lucky each time, and had escaped their notice, otherwise she would have been their next meal. She shuddered inwardly at the memory of those encounters, she still had nightmares dealing with them.

Quietly she led the two young men down the mountainside. They traveled as quietly as possible, cringing at each snap of a twig and rustle of branches. More than once, Laurel had wanted to hit the two men… no, not men, boys for making so much racket. They would be lucky to get to the bottom without the entire mountain coming down on them at this rate. Only twice did they have to stop and hide as goblin patrols swept through the area. Both times Laurel had hidden Kale and Bane and then led the patrols off in opposite directions. Once she had been lucky enough to lead them towards a berserker napping under a ledge. She didn't stay to see the outcome of that meeting. It most likely wouldn't end well for the goblins. Once she knew the area was clear, she would return to grab them and continue quietly down the mountainside; never speaking, never revealing her true identity.

By late afternoon, she was able to breathe a sigh of relief as they reached the base of the mountain. She had them keep moving for another couple of hours before calling a halt to their journey. The woods they were in would mask their location, and besides, nothing from the mountain ever came this close to the town. There was a darkness in the town… a curse. Here they would be safe, for the night at least. After setting up camp and getting a fire going with some dead fall, Laurel scouted the surrounding area and managed to gather some fresh berries and apples to add to their dinners. By the time she had returned, Kale and Bane had put a small pot of water on to boil and were adding dried meat, wild onions, and rice. She laid down her cache of berries and apples near the two before grabbing an apple and starting to munch on it.

"I had no idea this journey would be so dangerous. If it hadn't been for you, friend, I don't think we would have made it. Thank you. How did you lose those goblins anyway?" Kale offered her a bowl of the makeshift soup as he spoke. She just shook her head and shrugged. He kept trying to trick her into talking, but she wasn't so foolish. He was a smart one though. She would have to be careful not to give anything away. She would be glad when she was rid of the two of them... almost.

"I still say we could have taken them. What's a few more dead goblins? I don't see why we had to hide." Laurel shook her head and smacked Bane on the back of his head, a reprimand for being stupid. "Hey, ow, what was that for?"

Kale started laughing heartily.

"Perhaps he thinks you need your brain jogged a bit. If we had started fighting the sound of the battle would have brought the rest. Sometimes, Bane, I wonder if we went to the same military academy." Kale's laughter was cut short by unearthly wails of torment and spine-tingling howls of madness.

They all looked up towards the surrounding mountains, each inching ever so closer to the warmth of the fire and each other. Night descended quickly wrapping them in a dark blanket of uncertainty and fear. As the three companions settled down into their bedrolls for the night, each thought of the day to come and what horrors still awaited them.

Laurel watched Kale and Bane drift off into uneasy sleep. Whether they were really asleep or just trying to rest was uncertain, but she knew there would be little to no sleep tonight for her. The sounds of battle and death cries echoed around the valley as goblins and berserkers fought for dominance of the mountains. Would their fight finally bring them down onto the floor of the valley, or would their battle cut off the only ways out of this place for their small group? Laurel's mind raced with possibilities and potential escape routes. From the sounds of the battle, there would be no way for them to go back the way they had come. The goblins would be patrolling that place with higher numbers and more awareness. They would have to travel another way… one she was less certain of. Perhaps they should chance the swamps upon returning… the way was more dangerous, but it was unlikely the goblins would travel there. The carnivorous lizard people, and their giant lizards, who inhabited the swamp, would most likely find the three of them a tasty snack best eaten while still kicking.

More chills spread throughout Laurel's body. How would she get them out of here? How would she get these two naïve boys back to the relative safety of civilization? Would they be content to just go on their way after seeing this place? Would they want to know more? How many more questions would they ask? Amid all the questions plaguing her mind, Laurel's eyes drifted shut sending her into dreams of her past…

Her father was baking in the kitchen again. The smells of cakes, pies and pastries filled the small store. Her mother was up front taking orders and making sure everyone had what they desired. Watching the two of them work was like watching a pair of dancers moving effortlessly in time with a beautiful song. In those days her mother often sang songs quietly to herself as she attended to the day's tasks, always smiling, always happy.

Laurel sighed contentedly. Life couldn't possibly be better than this. The bell on the front door rang and a tall man with dark hair and a fine cloak came into the store. Her mother smiled and went to greet him. Behind him was a boy about Laurel's age and a woman with beautiful long blonde hair to her waist. Fairer in hair than his father the boy stood proudly by looking up at his mother on occasion with a mischievous smile on his face. A young Laurel walked over to him and smiled politely, dipping into a quick curtsy.

"Hello. Are you here to place an order or pick up one?" The boy looked at his mother, who nodded at him with a smile.

"We're picking up a cake for my birthday party. Our cook says that your father is the best baker in all of Kallihan. Is that true?" He tilted his head looking at her with a look of suspicion. Laurel giggled at his seriousness, and bit her lower lip shyly. Why was she acting this way? She was never shy around boys.

"It's true. We have some extra cupcakes if you would like to try one… for proof of course." The boy looked once more at his mother who smiled lovingly down at him and winked. He quickly turned to Laurel and nodded his head, a broad smile spreading across his face. She took his hand and walked him over to the counter where she picked up a chocolate cupcake with blue and silver frosting on it.

"Thank you." He smiled warmly at her before taking a bite of the sweet confection. Laurel felt a warmness spreading throughout her body as she watched him eat the cupcake with relish and surprise. "This is amazing! It's the best cupcake I've ever had! Could I have another one?" A deep cough from behind him made the boy jump and stare sheepishly at the ground. His father shook his head before turning back to the conversation he was having with Laurel's father. Both men looked rather amused by the situation, perhaps Laurel could ask her father about it later, if he wasn't too busy preparing for the festival.

"Well, maybe not a cupcake, but here… I can give you a cookie." The boy smiled at her as he accepted the cookie. She watched with delight as he carefully wrapped the cookie up and placed it in an inner pocket of his cloak.

"I'll save it for the ride home. Maybe you could come to my party… it's going to be mostly boys, but I'll make sure none of them bother you. You could be my escort… or I could be your escort." He smiled at her with pride and courage. Laurel could only bite her lower lip and look at her father hopefully since both fathers were watching the two young ones. Her father shook his head sadly.

"I'm sorry my lord, but that won't be possible. The spring festival is about to begin and we have much to do to get ready for it. Perhaps another time, after the festival, we will be able to come and visit. I'll make sure to make a batch of chocolate cupcakes to bring." The boy's face lit up like a solstice tree filled with candles.

"You don't have to bring cupcakes, Toran, but I would definitely be glad to have you and your family visit. It would give Kaleford someone other than Bane to talk to, and I think a girl's influence would be good for the boy." Both fathers laughed and shook hands.

"Well, I don't see how we could refuse such an invitation. How about I write to you after the celebration and we will see if we can work something out?"

"That would be fine. I'll tell the staff to get the guest house prepared. I look forward to having your family stay with us for a time. It's been too long." Laurel felt a jolt of shock as she watched the two men shake hands and continue their jovial conversation.

Laurel awoke with a start... Kaleford, Bane... Kale and Bane. Was Kale the same boy she met as a child in her parent's shop? Could it just be coincidence? Kale was hardened, dark and brooding. He held a look of sadness that never quite left his eyes... eyes that pierced into her soul and made her want to.... No, they couldn't be the same, she wouldn't believe it.

Laurel looked at the world around her. The darkness of night was starting to give way to the gray of early morning. Quietly, Laurel arose and began stirring the embers of their dying fire back to life. She looked once more at the sleeping form of

Kale. This couldn't be just coincidence. Why had their fathers wanted them to meet and spend time together? Kale was a noble and she was just the daughter of a baker... wasn't she? She felt in her pocket for the amulet her father had given her. Its metal was warm and comforting in her hand. How much information had her parents withheld from her? Would she ever know the truth?

Silently, she refocused on the fire as the two men began to stir. Today was the day. She could feel it. Today, Laurel would take her place of silent vigil and wait once more for her elusive enemy to show itself. Today her town would finally be avenged... or she would die trying.

Chapter 4

When Kale had awoken, their ranger friend had already coaxed the fire back to life and was packing up camp. It had been a long night filled with terrifying sounds and painful memories… except for one. Last night he had remembered he had been to Soldar before, once when he was a small child. His parents had insisted on traveling to the small town to purchase a cake for his birthday party. At the time he thought it was stupid. Why travel all that way to buy a cake when their cook was an excellent baker? When they had arrived however, he had met this young girl, about his age, who made the sun smile. It was the first time he had ever found a girl interesting, the first time he had been curious about one. Before that time girls had just been an annoyance, but after her…. Why had he forgotten about her and Soldar? Maybe because of what had happened after they returned home. It had been the first time he remembered seeing a death squad… it had been a nightmare.

One year later, his mother had fallen ill. It had been the first day of the Spring Festival; the whole city was decorated for it. His mother was lying in bed, feverish and incoherent. He had refused to go to the festival, even though his father had insisted on it. He had spent the morning and early afternoon by his mother's bedside, reading and talking softly to her. Kale spoke of the girl from the bakery and how she had made him feel. He spoke of the festival and what was probably happening there. He had spoken of everything but his worries for his mother.

As the day progressed her condition worsened. Kale could only watch and pray. His father had told him not to touch her. He had told him to let her rest and not disturb her. Kale couldn't abide by those rules any longer. He took his mother's hand and collapsed next to her as he was swept up in horrible visions of Soldar being destroyed. He had no idea how long he had been like this, but when he regained his senses, his mother was laying calmly in bed, her hand gently stroking his head. She smiled weakly at him then imparted the words that would direct the rest of his life.

"Kale, my precious son, it is to you I leave a terrible responsibility. When you are old enough, you must find Soldar and the girl that will end this. You have already met her, but soon you will forget her. When you meet again and find Soldar, you will remember all. Until that time, grow strong my son... strong in love and in courage. Now before I fade away...go to my wardrobe and you will find a box in a hidden floor panel." Kale had heeded her words and quickly went to the wardrobe, tears streaming down his pale face. He found the box without trouble and brought it back to her. "Good... Inside you will find a book... this book will teach you the language of runes. Learn them well... they will help you later when you have grown. Do not tell anyone you have this book. Do not show it to anyone. This is a secret you must keep always. Your very life depends upon it. I love you Kale… my precious…boy…"

Kale wiped a stray tear from his face as he remembered those last moments. All of it had been for this. Now he had found Soldar, and the entire memory had returned. Laurel must have been the girl from his memory. She had to be the one he remembered. She had survived… somehow, she had survived, and he had left her in that town to face the King's soldiers and possible imprisonment if they discovered she had aided those seeking Soldar. He was such a fool. How could he have left her to such a fate? Whatever happened here, he would go back to the town and find her. There could be no question now… he would rescue Laurel from those monsters and take her away to safety, but first he had to finish here.

Standing, Kale picked up his bedroll and began helping with the clean-up of camp. Bane had his gear already packed and was starting to put out what was left of the fire. Their ranger friend had already left camp, presumably to scout ahead. Just as they finished picking up the camp site the ranger returned and motioned them to follow. Before the sun had even risen above the mountain peaks, the three travelers were staring silently at the remains of Soldar.

Kale and Bane stood in shocked silence as they tried to process what they were looking at. Many of the buildings were still standing, the remains of the festival decorations hanging from buildings, ragged and torn. There were still the stains of blood splattered on most of the buildings.

Kale's mind raced with questions. Why had Soldar been attacked like this? Who had sent that cloud to destroy these innocent people? Was it sent by man or demon? How did Laurel survive this devastation?

Kale was startled out of his mental ranting by Bane's hand coming down on his shoulder. He turned towards Bane and then followed his gaze back towards the center of town. Their ranger friend was walking swiftly down the center of the road towards a wooden post. An old, withered wreath hung from a hook at the top of the post. As the ranger approached, he reached up and removed the decrepit wreath, dropping it to the ground and then pulling a fresh wreath out from under his cloak, he placed it on the now empty hook. Kale wondered again how the ranger was tied to this village. Did he travel here regularly to replace the wreath? If so, why?

Kale nudged Bane and they started to head towards the ranger, who had now taken up a kneeling position in front of the post. His head was bowed as if in prayer for the deceased. Kale stopped short of the scene; he really didn't want to disturb him if he was in some form of ritual prayer. Looking around the remains of the town, Kale found himself drawn to one dilapidated building in particular.

The doors and windows had been destroyed long ago, but the main structure was still intact. The familiarity of the place became gradually clearer as Kale approached the time-worn and broken building. This was the building of the baker and his family… the place he had come as a child with his family. This had been *her* home, the girl who had awoken his heart all those years ago. The bakery part of the house was completely destroyed, but the house portion was still surprisingly intact. He was standing in the remains of her childhood. The walls were stained red with the suffering of her parents' last moments.

Slowly he walked around looking at the odds and ends from her life. In one corner was a broken-up rocking chair, in another was a broken bookshelf; some of the books still scattered on one of the slanted shelves and on the floor around it. Kale reached down and picked up a particularly rotten looking book. As he held it in his hand, the mildew and rot faded away to reveal a pristine green cover with gold inlay. As he opened the book, the pages began filling with countless magical runes.

Kale began reading in rapt fascination, turning one page after another in rapid succession. The book was filled with spells, potions, and magical theory. Kale looked around at the surrounding room quickly as he realized it was an instructional book, meant to teach its reader about magic. This was forbidden literature. Possessing this book was a crime punishable by death… or worse. Laurel's father or mother must have been a practitioner… his parents had said they were good friends… his father had known. Kale stumbled backwards several steps before landing in a rickety chair that gave way under his sudden weight.

Crashing to the floor, Kale sat stunned by his sudden realization.

Quickly he closed the book, ready to toss it to the side, when he noticed an emblem on the front cover. As he touched the emblem, it rose out of the cover and became an amulet he could grab hold of. Slowly he turned his hand over and looked at the amulet in his hand. It was circular with many interweaving silver and gold parts that resembled ropes. He knew they were forming a pattern, but what it meant he had no idea. A familiar voice shook him from his reverie.

"My son… I knew you would find this place and Laurel. The amulet is a gift from Laurel's father, Toran, and myself. You are a wizard, a very powerful one. You are descended from a long line of powerful wizards, but you are special. You must unite with Laurel and protect her. What she is trying to do alone is impossible. Only together can the two of you fight the growing darkness, defeating the King and his demon master. You must free our country and save our people. That is your destiny my son. That is what you were born to do." Kale shook his head, squeezing his eyes shut. It couldn't be his mother, she was gone, dead and buried in the family crypt. As he opened his eyes, he gasped and jumped back at the sight of her semi-transparent form standing before him.

"You can't be my mother… you can't!"

"Oh Kale, do you not believe your own eyes? I am your mother, here only temporarily to warn you and help."

"Warn about what?" Kale took a few more steps backwards, breathing slowly to calm himself.

"To warn you about what you face and give you the amulet and book. They will guide you, if you let them…." The ghost of his mother looked around quickly, a worried expression growing on her beautiful face. "There's no more time! Kale, put the amulet around your neck, it will protect you until you know more about what you are. You must be quick! Get Laurel and run! Run home as quickly as you can! Your father will help you. It's coming! Quickly… you must go now!!" The image vanished as quickly as it had appeared, her voice echoing in his heart and head. Kale felt his heart racing. What was coming? He put the amulet around his neck, and stashing the book inside his pack, he ran outside to get the others.

In the distance a developing storm was moving in their direction swallowing the midday sun. Their ranger had taken a stance in the middle of town, his quarter staff in front of him ready for battle. Bane was running towards him yelling and pointing at the growing storm, but Kale couldn't hear what he was saying. The wind was whipping through the town in great gusts that carried his words away. Then Kale turned once more to the storm, fear gripping his heart as he drew his sword…possibly for the last time. The clouds were blood red… and a face was beginning to form on its surface. Kale raced towards the ranger, Bane close behind, as a particularly strong gust blew the ranger's hood from his… her head. The ranger was a girl, and not just any girl, but Laurel! Her blonde hair whipped in the wind giving her a wild, untamed beauty. Kale almost tripped from the shock of what he was seeing. She was here and she was his destiny.

The three adventurers stood together to face the coming onslaught. There would be time later to discuss the matter of secrets and misinformation…hopefully. As Kale's thoughts finished, the demon storm descended upon them roaring with hatred and the need for blood.

Chapter 5

Day turned to night as the three companions were encompassed by a tornado of blood and ash. The air was thick with the malevolence and hatred emanating from the storm. They could hear the demon's laughter as it made quick sharp jabs at each of them, its pleasure increasing with the racing of their hearts. The three put their backs to one another, weapons at the ready, their breathing calm and steady... almost.

"How shall I destroy you? Shall I rip you apart like tiny rag dolls or strip the flesh from your bones? Perhaps I should enter each of you and force you to battle each other or rape the female... that might be fun." Its deep laughter sent waves of terror through each of them.

Laurel's mind raced back to the horrors of that day so long ago. Doubt began to grow within her like a disease eating its way towards her heart. Could she really defeat this thing or was she throwing her life away? Her strength and courage began to waver when she felt a hand grip hers, strong and confident. She turned her head slightly to see Kale smiling at her grimly.

"Laurel don't listen to it! As long as we're together, it can't harm us! We can defeat this thing and send it back to the hell it came from! Just believe!" Kale had to shout to be heard over the roar of the winds, but when he saw her smile weakly back at him, he knew she heard him. He didn't know how he knew they would be safe... he just knew. He also knew that their weapons wouldn't work against this foe. They would need magic... powerful magic, if they had any hope of defeating this thing. Kale glanced over his right shoulder at Bane, who looked like he was about to lose his stomach, and sheathed his sword.

When Laurel saw Kale sheath his sword, she dropped her staff and linked her right arm with Kale's left arm. Then she looped her left arm through Bane's right arm nodding at him. Bane sheathed his sword and linked his arm with Laurel. If this was the end at least they would go out together.

The storm roared around them, lightning striking feet away. Red and black tendrils reached out towards each of them as they closed their eyes preparing for the worst.... Time stood still and seconds seemed to stretch out into hours. Nothing happened. As Laurel opened her eyes, she saw the tendrils striking again and again, but they never touched her. As her confidence grew, the holy symbol on her chest exploded in brilliant light encompassing the group in its protective glow. Laurel watched in amazement as a transparent shell formed around them, the golden glow of her amulet merging with the glow of something else. Looking around at their tiny group, she noticed an amulet on Kale's chest glowing brilliantly like hers. His amulet's silver glow was merging with her amulets golden aura creating a barrier the demon couldn't penetrate.

Kale watched the auric shell that had formed around them. His mother was right, the two of them were meant for each other. It would take both of them to defeat the evil consuming their country. He could feel Bane flinching with each attack from the demon, but as time went on the flinching became less and less. Kale wasn't sure how long the attacks went on or how much time had passed, but he could feel his energy draining and knew Laurel's energy had to be draining as well. Just as he thought they couldn't go on much longer the demonic storm let out a bone rattling scream of frustration before pulling away from them. As daylight returned, Kale could see by the sun's position that several hours had passed, but night had not descended… quite yet. The demon's threatening voice drew his attention like a thunderclap.

"If I cannot dispose of you in my own way then I will have to destroy you another way. Have fun playing with my new creation." The storm withdrew, its laughter echoing around the valley. A low rumbling sound began growing from the opposite side of the town's buildings. Laurel quickly picked up her staff and turned to face this new threat. She was exhausted, but there was no other choice but to fight. It was too late to run.

Laurel, Bane and Kale glanced at each other briefly before turning to face their new opponent. Cautiously they looked around wondering what new horror was coming for them. A new silence filled the desolate area. Then a thud followed by a ground tremor resonated through the valley. In the distance, a flock of birds fled the forest's protection heading north, over the ridge. Another ground rattling thud, followed by several more, jarred the three comrades as they fought to maintain their balance on the shaking ground.

The three of them watched in terror as, from behind the remains of a rather large building, a monstrously large, white creature rose into view staring at them with flaming red eyes. It was as tall as one of the remaining two-story buildings and was definitely as wide as one. As they continued to stare in wide eyed horror, a sudden realization came to them. The creature was white because it was comprised of the bleached bones of the deceased inhabitants of the town. It stood, hunched over, on its two hind hooves. Its front clawed hands held a large bone sword long enough to sweep through the three of them in one swing. Its head had two large boned horns protruding from either side and instead of eyes it had flaming orbs. Its mouth contained several rows of razor-sharp teeth that gleamed in the late afternoon light.

Glaring at the small group, the monstrous creature bellowed out a roar that sent a shockwave towards them, nearly knocking them from their feet. Its breath smelled like the stench of several rotting corpses. Laurel could feel her heart racing and the blood draining from her face. How could they possibly defeat this demonic creature? She lightly touched her amulet hanging against her chest. Her holy symbol felt cold and spent against her skin. They would have to defeat this abomination by some other means than the goddess.

Kale pulled the mage book from his pack and began flipping through it. There was no way they would be able to fight this thing with the weapons they had. It was too large, too strong, and most likely immune to mundane weapons. The pages of the book filled with countless runes line after line. He scanned page after page listening to the heavy breathing and snorting of the creature and the stomping of its hooves. Time was running out. They would need a miracle if they were going to survive this day. Then the book flew from his hands and started flipping through its pages faster than they could ever be read, settling finally on one page near the back. Kale grabbed the book out of the air and quickly read the spell in front of him.

"Kale, what are you doing?! Grab your sword man! It's charging!" Bane loosed two arrows at the charging bone monster. Both just bounced off its hardened exterior. Kale ignored Bane's shouts and focused on the runes, then facing the creature and raising one hand in front of him, he focused on the outcome he wanted.

"Contris deruvick grantis!" His shout echoed through the valley as a wave of energy exploded from his hand and surged towards the oncoming monster. Kale sank to the ground, exhausted, as the creature was blown into a thousand pieces, bones scattering everywhere.

"What was that?! Kale… what did you just do?" Bane looked fearfully at his lifelong friend. Kale could only look back wearily, feeling exhausted after this last expenditure of energy.

"Magic…that was magic forbidden magic. Kale… you've just signed your own death certificate. If the death squads discover you…"

Kale weakly smiled at the concern and compassion filling Laurel's voice. She was his destiny, and she was safe... that was all that mattered.

A rattling from the pile of bones made them look up and gasp. They could only stare wide-eyed, their feet frozen to the ground as the bones began putting themselves together again. Shaking the ice from their blood, the three grabbed their bags and ran from the town. Laurel led the way with Bane half carrying Kale away from their certain death. If they could make the tree line at the base of the mountains they should be able to find a place to hide, at least until Kale was strong enough to continue. Laurel would have to plan a new route out of this area. One that would lead them away from that thing, avoid the dangers of the mountain, and then the soldiers that would undoubtedly be waiting for them back in town. This would be a long night... a night where failure meant death and the only way to survive was to keep running until they found safe passage away from this nightmare. Laurel had failed in avenging her family and town, but she wouldn't fail in getting them safely through the mountains. She had come to far to yield now.

As the sun began to sink below the peaks of the mountains Kale, Bane and Laurel reached the edge of the forest. Behind them, in the distance, they could hear the enraged roar of the reassembled creature. Laurel shuddered as she listened to the creature's angry rampage and final destruction of her home. A single tear slipped from her eyes as she ushered the boys into the deepening darkness of the forest. Once inside the shelter of the trees, she took a moment to gain her bearings. If they continued in this direction they would run into the mountain's swamps and the lands of the lizard people. If they moved to the right they would enter the stronghold of the goblins, an area filled with traps, sink holes, and war parties. If they headed to the left, they would be heading back the way they had come. That direction would now be heavily guarded and the sounds from the battle from the town would have probably drawn more attention and higher patrols in the region. That way would also take them back near Vale Ridge, the town they left from, which was currently overrun with the King's soldiers and most likely a few death squads.

Laurel sighed; they would go left. If they went past their original trail, they could follow the mountain peak west and come back down a day's travel from Kern. It would mean traveling through areas heavily patrolled by the goblins and it would bring them dangerously close to the Beserkers, but there really was no other choice. She motioned for Kale and Bane to follow her as quietly as possible and began heading deeper into the forest and towards the west. They would have to travel through the night if they wanted to put enough distance between them and that thing.

As darkness encompassed the group, their progress seemed painfully slow. The dark had made it more difficult for the two humans to see well and the thick underbrush was constantly pulling at their legs and tripping them up. Laurel took to moving further ahead and then circling back around continually scouting the area. Behind them, the thunderous roars of the beast could be heard as it began crashing through the forest trying to find them. Kale had recovered most of his strength which allowed for both him and Bane to move more quickly, but it was still a snail's pace compared to what was crashing through the forest behind them. They were exhausted, but the constant reminder of what lay behind them, caused energy to course through their bone-weary limbs and propel them ever onward toward some hope of salvation.

"Hey, where are we going? Shouldn't we be heading more up the mountain side and less along it?" The exasperation in Bane's voice was exceedingly evident as he stopped and leaned against a nearby tree.

"We have to keep moving or that thing will catch us! Would you like to try facing it again?" Laurel tried to keep the frustration out of her voice, but she was so tired.

"No, but I also want to know what you have planned for us!"

"Bane, quiet down. We don't need to give that thing any clues as to our whereabouts…" Kale put a hand on his friend's shoulder and tried to reassure him before looking at Laurel and continuing. "But Bain is right. Laurel, I think some answers are in order."

"I know, but not right now. I'm taking us the only way that may give us a chance of escaping that thing and getting us out of here. It's risky though. We will have to dodge several goblin patrols and encounters with Berzerkers. I know I'm asking a lot, but if we don't move quickly and quietly, we're going to get boxed in and it won't matter if that thing finds us, because we'll already be something else's dinner." With a sigh she started moving again, searching desperately for the marker she used to find her way. It had to be here somewhere.

"So, wait… we're heading into more danger?! Isn't there a path out of here that doesn't get a person killed?" Bane reached out and grabbed Laurel by the elbow; she pulled away sighing with exasperation.

"NO! I warned you this would be dangerous! I do this trek every year, and it never gets easier…. Bane, I know you're scared and exhausted, I am too, but we have to keep moving or we are dead."

"Kale… if we make it through this the first thing I'm going to do is take a nice hot bath. Then I'm going to find myself two buxom tavern wenches and have myself an amazing night, and guess what? You're paying for it!" Bane slapped Kale on the shoulder before trudging off in the direction Laurel had walked. Kale shook his head smiling to himself.

"If we make it through this Bane, I'll pay for as many buxom beauties as you want… you know I didn't mean for this to happen. I just needed to know… I needed to…"

"I know, I know… so did you find what you were looking for?"

"Yeah, I think I did. I think I'm a mage…"

"Kale don't say that! We're already in enough trouble. The last thing we need is the death squads after us!"

"Don't worry Bane, I have no intention of letting them know I can use magic… at least not yet."

"Kale, I know that look…. What are you planning? That look always means trouble, and usually for me." Bane felt his stomach do flip flops at the sight of the smile crossing Kale's face. He was definitely not going to survive this adventure… definitely not.

"If you two are done, can we get moving a little faster… or would you prefer to wait around for that creature to catch up to us?" Both men shook their heads and began trudging along at a slightly faster pace behind Laurel.

It seemed the creature's roars and destruction of forest was keeping the goblin patrols away, at least for now. At least they had that one consolation for all their exhaustion. Laurel could feel the last bits of her energy ebbing away. She had to find the marker and quickly. Once she found her marker, she would be able to lead them up the mountain at an angle that would take them very near the Berserkers. With any luck the creature's noises would draw the Berserkers towards it and the two monsters would attack each other. It was a long shot, but it was the only plan she currently had. The only problem was that they would have to come perilously close to the Berserkers and wait for the creature to pick up their trail enough to follow into that land.

Finally, she spotted her marker and nearly cried for joy. She quickly gathered Bane and Kale and showed them what she had been looking for. Then she led them quietly and quickly up the mountains side. The moon was now high in the sky, its broken light shining down through the forested canopy casting eerie shadows everywhere. As they approached a rocky outcropping, Laurel paused to catch her breath and urged them to do the same. The bone creature wasn't far behind them. It seemed to sense their exhaustion and weakening condition and was now determined to catch up to its prey. In a hushed whisper, Laurel told Kale and Bane her plan.

"Very near here lives a group of creatures called Berserkers. They were created by the same magic that created these mountains. They will attack and eat anything that comes within their borders, sometimes even attacking and eating each other. I want to lead the bone creature towards them and, using us as bait, lure out the Berserkers so that they will attack the creature. I'm hoping in the chaos that ensues we'll be able to escape further up the mountain and out of their territory." Both men looked at her, mouths partially open and eyes heavy with exhaustion. Bane was the first to speak.

"Well… that is probably the craziest plan I have ever heard. We become bait and hope that our exhausted bodies can get us out of the way before they rip us to shreds getting to the creature. It's insane… I like it. It's just crazy enough that it might work. Besides, I don't have any other ideas and I don't think I could even lift my bow right now." With a resigned shrug he leaned against a tree and slid to the ground. Kale thought a bit longer, listening to the crashes and howls of fury coming ever closer, before commenting.

"It's a sound battle plan. I don't think I could pull that spell off again if I tried and there is no way we could possibly fight that thing… not with the weapons we have." Kale took Laurel's hand in his and squeezed it reassuringly. He wanted to do so much more, like take her in his arms and protect her. He wanted to lay down with her and feel her body drift into sleep while he held her close to him. He wanted to give her a life without pain or suffering. He wanted…. No, he had to focus on the now. There would be time after they escaped this death trap. He would take her to his home and introduce her to his father. Somehow, he would make everything right again.

Laurel smiled as Kale squeezed her hand. He truly believed in her. How could he believe in her after she had deceived him and brought him so much trouble? Their confidence in her was reassuring, and hopefully she would now be able to get them out of here without getting them killed. Their progress slowed as they started climbing the mountain's side. Quickly and quietly she led them past caves, and up a particularly steep embankment overlooking the side of the mountain. From there they could see at least ten caves and they could see the trees falling where the creature was crashing its way through.

Laurel waited nervously until she could see the white of the creature's head as it clawed its way towards them. She turned to Kale and Bane, holding up her five fingers, slowly dropping one at a time. As the last finger dropped, Laurel began screaming and yelling like a lunatic. Bane and Kale looked at each other for only a moment before joining in the cacophony. The creature stopped clawing its way forward and whipped its head up in their direction. Its blazing eyes froze them to where they were standing. Its roar shook the very foundations of the mountain. Then another sound was heard. From the caves issued countless bestial howls, grunts and screams, and the ground began to shake from the force of the stampeding Berserkers as they surged from their caves. At first the creatures were confused searching out their prey, then they focused on the three interlopers to their territory. Laurel, Bane and Kale froze in terror of the grotesque creatures standing just below them. They had multiple heads, each of a different creature, each dripping a black bile from their mouths. Some had three or more arms ending in sharp claws. Others had the warped bodies of men and beast combined, their size far beyond that of any normal creature. Some had spikes sticking out of their backs like porcupines or instead of legs they had the bottom of a snake. There was no way these terrifying creatures were natural.

The bone creature roared in defiance at these trespassers that were interrupting its hunt. This drew the Berserkers' attention as they turned in unison towards this new interloper. As one they roared back at this giant creature, before charging towards it, their enraged screams driving the frightened trio to the ground. As the bone creature clashed with the Berserkers the noise was so loud that it deafened the three allies as they kneeled on the ground in a huddled ball. For one short instant the world was deathly quiet. Then the surrounding forest and mountain shook and screamed with the chaos of battle. Laurel dared to look up and watch the battle rage below them. Tears fell freely down her face as she watched the destruction of this beautiful area.

Kale watched silently as the Berserkers threw themselves at the bone monster ripping it apart and crushing the bones. Some started ripping into the bones, crushing them and devouring the pieces. Other Berserkers attacked their own fallen ripping them apart even as they continued to rip bones out of the demon's creation. He watched silently as Laurel cried for the death and destruction happening around her. How could she cry for these monsters? How could she feel pain for them? Kale realized he had a lot to learn about her, but not now… there would be time. Gently, he put his hand on her shoulder and squeezed.

"We need to go, before they remember we're here." Laurel nodded and the three companions rose quietly to their feet and walked away from the slaughter happening behind them. They walked through the rest of the night in silence, only taking a couple of short breaks to pull food from their packs before continuing on. As the sun peeked over the horizon, Laurel led them down a small embankment and towards a rocky overhang that could be used as a shelter. After pulling some shrubs together to further hide them, they laid down inside their new enclosure and fell into a dreamless sleep.

Chapter 6

It was midafternoon by the time Kale had woken up. His mind was still reeling from everything that had happened. Was that thing still after them? What about those other creatures? How had Laurel managed to make this journey every year and why did she hide her identity from them? How could he use magic and was his mother a mage or had that ghost been a demon in disguise? He had so many questions and more were mounting by the second.

Kale took a deep breath and looked around their small, sheltered camp site. Bane was still sleeping, if fitfully. Bane... he was like a brother to him. He could trust him with anything, including his life. Bane was the son of his family's cook; she had been a second mother to him after his own mother had died. Now they were off on this suicidal adventure and Kale couldn't imagine anyone he would want more by his side, except perhaps Laurel.

She was sitting with her back against the cliff face, her knees drawn up under her chin and her arms wrapped around them. She looked so fragile... so alone. Kale quietly moved to her side, resting his back against the cliff face as well.

"That was one hell of a night. I honestly didn't think we were going to escape with our lives." He tilted his head towards her and smiled weakly. She met his gaze with a look of despair.

"We still haven't escaped. I've heard three goblin hunting parties pass our camp. They were out of sight range, but I could hear them. We still have a long way to travel, and we can't go back to Vale Ridge... unless you would like to surrender to the Death Squads that are probably swarming the place. I for one do not want to give the death squads any more free entertainment." Laurel paused, waiting for his reaction. Kale breathed deeply as he thought about her words.

"I know... so where are you guiding us?" Kale tried to gaze into her eyes as she stared into the distance.

"I'm taking us towards Shadowvale. It's a couple of days further West, but we should be able to avoid the Death Squads that way and get both of you to safety. After that... we'll say our good-byes and we can head off in our own directions." Kale stared at her in disbelief. There was no way he was going to lose her now that he had found her. He turned directly towards her.

"Why don't you come with us? We seem to be stronger together than apart and I have a feeling we haven't seen the last of that demon cloud. Besides... we need each other. Laurel... I remember... before the storm.... I remember my parents bringing me to your family's bakery. Our parents were friends... I think they wanted us to meet. I think they would want us together. If the magic is freaking you out, I understand. I'm not sure I'm totally comfortable with it either, but... I can't just let you go off on your own... I won't!" Kale stared intently into Laurel's eyes as he grabbed her arms, forcing her to face him. She returned his look steadily, even though he could feel her breathing quicken and her body tremble slightly. As they stared at each other, Kale saw tears begin to well up in her eyes, as a look of fear and concern enveloped her face.

"I remember too… but Kale… I'll only bring pain and disaster to your life. That thing was after me. I'm the one that must stop it! I can't…" Laurel dropped her head, no longer able to look into Kale's eyes, so full of strength and passion. "I can't put your life in danger. You need to go back to your life… hide your magic, get married, have a family, lead your lands. I must face that thing and most likely die destroying it…. I've accepted my fate, but it's my fate and I can't bring this trouble down on you… I can't." Laurel could feel tears slip from her eyes and the emotions of the past few days finally overwhelmed her. She couldn't let Kale pay for her existence.

"Laurel…" Kale gently grasped her chin and lifted her face up towards his. "Laurel, I'm not going anywhere. I'm a mage, for better or worse, and we are meant to be together. I'm staying with you whether you want me to or not. I'm not going to let you face that demon alone. Besides, in your village… I saw my mother's spirit. It said we had to face this together. It's going to take both of us to destroy it. You don't have to do this alone…" Kale pulled her into his chest and just held her, letting go of all the frustrations and questions that were spinning in his mind. For now, they could just be. When Bane finally woke up, they would have to continue their journey, but for now… they could just be.

As Kale sat there stroking Laurel's hair and holding her gently to his chest, he noticed something for the first time. Laurel's ears were slightly pointed…. Only elves had pointed ears… or perhaps… had her father or mother been an elf? Was Laurel a half-elf? Half-bloods were forbidden. Mixed race marriages and unions were forbidden. Was this why Soldar was attacked? Had the King discovered that Laurel was a half-elf… but then why destroy the whole town? Kale looked down at the top of Laurel's head and glanced off to the side where he had smoothed her soft hair away from her one ear. It was definitely pointed… not as much as an elf's would be, but noticeably more than a human's ear. How had he not seen that at the tavern? Did the people of Vale Ridge know?

"Laurel… how many people know that you're a half-elf?" Kale felt her stiffen beneath his arms. He waited patiently as they sat rigidly for several moments.

"No one. At least, not that lives in Vale Ridge anymore. The old inn keeper and his wife knew, but they passed on a couple years ago." Her answer had been barely a whisper. "My father was an elf, but I didn't know that until the end. My mother was human. I've hidden it for so many years now…" Kale continued to hold her as her hand went up to her ear and lightly touched its tip. What could it have been like for her to have lived her whole life having to hide what she was? He needed to reassure her… to let her know that he wouldn't leave her.

"It's ok, you know… I think your ears are beautiful…" Did he really just say that? Kale felt like hitting his head against the rock wall behind him. "I mean… I think it's fine that you're a half-elf…" Really!? What was he doing? "I didn't mean it that way… it's just… ugh… I'm trying to say that I don't know… I'll keep your secret and…" Kale could feel her shoulders shaking in his arms. Oh, by all the Gods, did he make her cry again!? "I'm sorry… I was just trying to say that… I'm an idiot." Kale hung his head in defeat as Laurel pulled away from him. Then he heard the most beautiful sound he had ever heard. It sounded like music, but lighter and full of mirth… Laurel was laughing. Slowly, Kale looked up and saw her face glowing with mirth, her eyes twinkling with light. He could only smile and join in her laughter.

"Kale… thank you. I know what you were trying to say, and it means a lot. I like you too. I see you are still as articulate as ever." Laurel watched as Kale's face reddened in embarrassment.

"Actually, I'm only this tongue-tied with you. How did you hide it for so long?"

"I use a skin toned putty to shape rounded tips to my ears. It must have fallen off when we were running last night."

"Well… I hope you don't feel you have to hide your ears in front of me. I think they're beautiful… like the rest of you…. I guess what I'm trying to say is… Laurel come with us. I've just found you again… I'm not ready to let you go." Laurel felt her heart skip a beat at the look of hope and desire that burned in Kale's eyes. How could she say no to him? How could she even think of leaving him now?

"Ok… I'll go with you… but you realize… we'll be putting your family and friends in danger… right?"

"I'm apparently capable of using magic. They're already in danger. Plus, I left Vale Ridge in the middle of the night. I'm sure the King's guards and Death Squads are already looking for someone with my description. So, are we good?"

"Yeah… we're good…. So how long does sleeping beauty over there usually need before he gets going?"

"Hey! I heard that and for your information I was just faking it so that you two love birds could have some time alone. Shit… how could anyone sleep after the last couple of days? So, you guys met when you were kids huh? Guess that's the time your parents took you away for a time… wasn't that the year before…. Sorry Kale, didn't mean to bring up bad memories."

"It's fine Bane… and yeah, that's when we met. Somehow this is all linked together… we just need to figure out how. I think our best place to start is back home. I think I have a few questions for my father." Kale stood and offered Laurel his hand, helping her stand up. Bane stood brushing off his back side and stretching out his back and neck.

"Well, no time like the present. Shall we make our way down the rest of this forsaken, death mountain or set up more permanent residence?"

He looked back and forth between Kale and Laurel, his eyebrows raised questioningly.

"Let's get going. If we make good time and don't run into any more obstacles, we should be able to make it down to the foothills, and tomorrow we should be able to get to Shadowvale, or at least within spitting distance of it." Laurel grabbed her pack and began leading Kale and Bane down the side of the mountain and West towards Shadowvale.

It had taken them two more days to reach the outskirts of Shadowvale. By the time they were in view of the small city, their supplies had run out and they looked like three very bedraggled and exhausted travelers who had run into some very bad luck. As they entered the town, locals gave them a wide berth and avoided making eye contact. The three continued down the main street for several blocks before Kale spotted an inn he was comfortable with and ushered Bane and Laurel towards its front door.

As he entered the tavern, the room went silent and a half dozen pairs of eyes looked up to stare at the spectacle that had just entered. Kale sighed and then motioned for the inn keeper. After some quiet discussion, Kale handed Laurel a key and then ushered them up the stairs towards their inn rooms. Laurel was both happy and relieved to see that her room was clean and fresh with one bed near the window, a wardrobe against the left wall and a dressing table and washstand against the right wall. A small table and two chairs were positioned near the middle of the room. Laurel gratefully sat in one of the chairs and let her pack slip to the floor next to her. She let her eyes close as she rubbed the back of her neck with one hand and stretched her legs out in front of her.

A sudden knock at her door made her nearly topple out of her chair. Shaking the drowsiness from her head she walked to the door and opened it a crack. Outside, stood two men and a large tub.

"My lady… um… we were told to bring this tub up to your room. The maid will be up in a minute to fill it with hot water. If that's ok?" Laurel sighed inwardly as she opened the door to admit the two men and the beautiful wooden tub. After a few minutes, three maids showed up carrying several buckets of hot, steaming water. Within thirty minutes Laurel was soaking up to her neck in luxurious, clean, hot water, allowing all of the anxieties from the last week to melt away. She wasn't sure how long she had been there or if she had fallen asleep while in the tub, when a gentle rap at her door caused her to lift her head and realize that her water was now cool and her fingers were turning into prunes.

"Yes?" Laurel called to whoever was on the other side of the door as she reached for her towel and began drying herself off.

"Hey, you ok in there?" Laurel smiled at the sound of Kale's uncertain voice on the other side of the door.

"Yes. I was just finishing up. Let me get dressed and I'll be down in a minute." She winced as she looked at the filthy clothes she would have to put back on, but she hadn't been able to return to her apartment to get any other clothes and she hadn't planned on never returning when she had left. She would have to find a way to get some more clothes, or at least some material to make herself some more clothes in one of the towns they were traveling through.

"About that... I have something for you... can you open the door and I'll hand it through?" Laurel smiled at the nervousness in Kale's voice. She could tell he was fumbling for words again.

"Hold on a minute." Laurel wrapped the towel tightly around herself and, standing behind the door, she opened it just enough for something to be handed in. As she did, Kale's hand poked through holding a wrapped package. Laurel took the package from his hand allowing their fingertips to touch briefly. She felt a thrill shoot through her at the momentary contact. "Thank you." She could hear her own voice shaking slightly from her own embarrassment and nervousness.

"No problem.... Um.... I wasn't sure what you liked to eat so I ordered the house stew and some wine... when you're ready of course." Kale could feel his face reddening as he stood talking through the door while standing in the hallway. He felt so foolish! In his time at the military academy, he had seduced and bedded at least a dozen girls... so why was Laurel so different. Why did she always make him feel like a nervous, twitchy, dolt. "Well, I'm going to head back down... see you down there." He shook his head as he walked away, not even waiting for an answer.

Laurel quietly closed and latched the door biting her lower lip as she listened to Kale's footsteps fade down the hallway. Walking over to her bed she opened the package and held up a beautiful light blue dress with satin laces to adjust the waist. There was also a chemise and appropriate undergarments to match. As she slipped the clothing onto her body, she relished the soft, smooth feeling of its touch. After tightening the laces, she brushed out her hair and arranged it so that her ears didn't show. She would have to be careful until she was able to buy some more putty for her ears. Making a few more adjustments she stood in front of the mirror, hanging on the inside of the wardrobe door, examining her reflection. The blue of the dress matched her eyes perfectly. She couldn't believe the woman she saw in the mirror. In her reflection, she could see her parents gazing back through her. She quickly brushed a stray tear from her eye before closing the door and heading downstairs to join Kale and Bane.

Bane smacked Kale in the arm and nodded his head towards the stairs. As Kale looked up his breath caught in his chest. Laurel stood at the bottom of the stairs, her long blond hair cascading down her back like a waterfall of spun gold. The dress was perfect, its blue bringing out the brilliant blue of her eyes. She stood tall and strong, with a regal air about her that harkened to the royal lines of old. He felt his heart leap as she smiled, her eyes glancing downward before walking over to them. Kale quickly stood up and pulled a chair out for her, before retaking his seat.

"I'm glad the dress fits… I wasn't sure on size, so the shop keeper suggested this style… do you like it?" Kale could feel his palms sweating and his heart racing. Why was Laurel so different from all of his past conquests?

"It's beautiful… thank you…. So, after we eat and get a good night's sleep, where to next?"

"We'll head towards my family's estates. I have some questions that I believe my father can answer and perhaps then we can figure out what to do next."

"Your family's estates, alright…. This stew is delicious. It's nice to have a cooked meal after days of travel rations." Laurel stuck another spoonful into her mouth to give her time to think. She remembered that her father had planned to take her once, but things happened and the planned trip never occurred.

"Yeah, personally I'm looking forward to getting home and having some of mom's venison sausage and herb potatoes." Bane smacked his lips and smiled dreamily. "I am completely ready to put this adventure behind us and find a nice, pretty tavern wench to settle down with…. Never thought I would say that."

Dinner was a relaxed occasion, to anyone in the tavern that evening they were three friends catching up after a long separation. They talked about years gone by, life at the military academy, working in a tavern, adventures, hopes and dreams. Kale avoided looking too often into Laurel's eyes.

It was just too easy to lose himself in their warm gaze and right now he needed to stay focused. They should be out of danger, but he wouldn't feel completely comfortable until he had reached his family's estates in the northwest.

After a couple of hours, Laurel rubbed the back of her neck, and sighing said her goodnights to Kale and Bane. Kale watched as she went up the stairs to her room, fighting a growing impulse to follow her. She was a commoner and by law he had every right to take her to his bed with or without her consent, but… he couldn't. There was something different about her… something he wanted to understand and protect.

Shaking his head he looked back at Bane to see his friend wearing a knowing smirk on his face. Kale sighed and ordered another ale. Bane was never going to let him live this down, but perhaps he could forestall the ribbing with a bribe.

"So… see any ladies that look appealing for a night's company?" Kale watched as Bane perused the room before slyly smiling back at him.

"Not really… but I think you've found one that you wouldn't mind keeping warm with. Why don't you go up there and sweep her off her feet? You know you want to."

"Bane, stop. Laurel's different… there's something about her. I think… you're going to laugh…"

"No, I won't. Just say it." Bane gave him a knowing smile as he waited for Kale to continue.

"I think she may be the one. I don't know why, but I… I'm drawn to her, in every way possible. It makes absolutely no sense." Kale winced as Bane let out a bark of laughter.

"Sorry, I'm not laughing at you... well, actually, I am. How can you not understand? Your parents introduced the two of you when you were children, and your mom wanted you to come back and find her. Kale, don't you think it's possible that the two of you were promised to each other as children. You've already figured out that your parents were friends. I say just be happy your parents apparently picked you out a beautiful, soft, and daring wife to be. Although you won't catch me getting ready to tie that noose around my neck any time soon. Why if I had it may way..." Bane's thought was interrupted as a large commotion was heard outside and a frantic man came running into the tavern, a look of terror on his face.

"The death squad is here! They're getting everyone out of their homes and dragging them into the streets! They say they're looking for traitors to the King and a half-blood!" As soon as the man finished, he ran through the inn and out the back door fleeing what was to come.

Kale and Bane looked at each other in shock. The death squad had found them. Their time had run out.

Chapter 7

Kale and Bane took one quick look at the door and then the chaos of the room before casually making their way towards the stairs. As they reached the top, they heard the door to the inn slam open and patrons screaming as the death squad began its round-up.

"We have to get Laurel and get out of here before they start dragging sleepers from their beds." Kale moved swiftly down the hallway until he came to Laurel's room. He tried opening the door, hoping she had left it unlocked. The door rattled softly but didn't open. Kale looked at Bane and shook his head.

"Bane, go get our things from our room and I'll try to get this door open."

"No problem. Just hurry… I have no desire to save your ass from a bunch of death squad barbarians."

Kale turned towards the door and raised his hand to knock. As his knuckles came down to rap on the wood, the door silently opened. Laurel was standing in the doorway dressed in her travel gear with her pack on her shoulders and her staff in her hand. She looked towards the stairs, a terrified look on her face.

"I was hoping it was you. I heard the commotion downstairs. When I looked out my window, I saw a death squad moving down the street followed by an accompaniment of soldiers. Kale, how are we going to get out of here?!" Kale took her arm in one hand and motioned for quiet with the other, then he led her further down the hallway and away from the stairs. Within moments Bane had joined them and was handing Kale his gear and sword.

"Ok, there's a set of servants' stairs back here behind this panel. I checked it out earlier… just in case. We can make our way down these and then out the back way. With any luck we can get out of town without being seen."

"Sounds great, but you forgot one thing… they have horses and we don't. No offense, Kale, but it won't matter if we get out of town if they catch up to us on the road." Kale rubbed his forehead straining to think.

"Well, we'll just have to take some horses and do the best we can. There was a stable on the edge of town. If we can get there, we can grab some horses and ride out of here. Regardless, we need to get moving or we're dead!" Kale could hear the shouting and screams that echoed through the building and town, nearly drowning out their own harsh whispers.

Without any more words the trio raced down the back stairway as quickly and quietly as possible, straining their ears for any hints that they were being pursued. In the distance they could hear more screams from the townspeople and the sound of doors being smashed open.

As they rushed out into the cool night air, they paused to find some cover to run behind and catch their breaths. It was a clear night, the full moon and sparkling stars lighting the surrounding area almost as if it was early morning. They searched the area for any cover they could find. The bright night was not going to be their friend tonight. Bane grabbed Kale's arm and pointed to a low wall that ran the length of the inn's yard. Kale grabbed Laurel and sprinted towards the low-lying wall. If they stayed low and moved quietly, they should be able to make their way down towards the edge of town and reach the stables.

They managed to reach the wall and duck behind it just as two death knights burst through the back door of the inn. Kale, Bane and Laurel froze on the other side of the wall, their backs firmly pressed against the cool stone. Barely daring to breath, they sat against the wall listening to the two men argue. Bane and Kale slowly and quietly checked their swords in their scabbards, making sure they were loose and ready to be pulled.

"There's nobody out here, Craig. Let's get back out front and have some fun. I saw some pretty faces I wouldn't mind bedding and if we take too much more time we'll miss out on the choosing."

"Dammit Jarrold, someone came down those back steps… I know it! If they get away it's going to be our heads!"

"Fine, I'll check the alleys and you check the wall. Yell if you find anyone."

"Sure."

Kale and Bane carefully removed their swords from their scabbards readying themselves to strike. Kale motioned Laurel to stay down and hide. Then they listened as the death knight approached. Kale could feel every muscle in his body tensing in preparation to strike. They would have to be quick, striking instantly with a killing blow so he would be unable to call out for help.

Death squads were the most deadly and skilled warriors in the country. With no morals or honor code, they served the King until their deaths. They killed, raped, tortured and stole whenever the mood struck them. Kale despised them and had argued on a number of occasions with his father about the destruction they deserved. His father had told him such a thing was impossible and it was his duty to ensure that, should they come to their town, the people were taken care of properly afterwards. To go against the riders was to invite the King's wrath. Kale hadn't understood, until years later, how helpless his father was when it came to the death squads.

Kale shook his head and refocused on the sound of the death knight's footsteps coming closer. He could just hear the heavy breathing of the man as he came nearer to the wall. Kale glanced at Laurel and saw the fear and strain in her eyes. Seeing her, strengthened his resolve and he tightened his grip on the sword hilt. He glanced up to see the man put his hand on the edge of the wall and then he struck.

In one quick swift movement he thrust the tip of his sword through the death knight's throat, the one area in their armor that was open. It was quick, clean and silent. With Bane's help he pulled the dead knight over the wall and out of sight. Then they hid once more and awaited the return of his friend.

They didn't have to wait long before they heard the other knight coming back. He strode into the yard with a heavy gait chuckling to himself. Kale took a deep breath and prepared for the next attack. Hopefully they could take him out before he called an alarm.

"Hey Craig, you should see what's going on in the street. The boys are really having a good time with the shop keep's daughter. If you're.... Hey Craig..." Bane raised the hand of the dead knight over the wall, making it appear as if the dead man were waving from laying down. Kale listened as the other man began chuckling again. "So, found yourself some fun of your own, huh? Well, I hope you're planning on sharing whatever little pretty you happened to find." Kale looked at Laurel hoping she would get what they were doing. Laurel grimaced, but let out a muffled whimper, as if a hand were over her mouth to keep her from screaming.

Kale could hear the other coming over to get a better look. The screams and cries from the town still rang through the night and he knew from experience that some of these people would be dead by morning… unless…. Kale felt more than saw the other knight reach for the wall. He glanced up towards the edge of the wall waiting to strike. As soon as he saw the other's face, Kale lunged with his sword, aiming once more for the throat. This time, however, the knight was faster and dodged out of the way. Kale leaped over the wall striking out with all of his skill. The death knight dodged and backed away trying to free his own sword from its scabbard. Bane quickly ran to Kale's aide, his sword flashing in the light of the moon. The death knight was outnumbered and outmatched. Freeing his sword, he tried to push back as he let out a cry of alarm. Kale and Bane wasted no more time. They both lashed out at the same time spearing the knight through the throat.

The alarm had been called leaving them no time to hide the body. Kale and Bane quickly leaped back over the wall and, grabbing Laurel, they ran down the length of the wall sticking to the shadows and hiding behind what barriers they could find. Luckily, the noise from the death squad's activities had apparently drowned out the cry of alarm. They made their way into the stables and searched for three horses that could carry them away from here. Kale quickly found two large stallions in good condition, probably belonging to visiting nobles or soldiers. He handed them off to Bane to saddle and then searched for one more that would carry Laurel.

"Have you ever ridden before?" Kale turned Laurel to look at him instead of the doors to the stable. Laurel jerked her head in a quick no.

"There was never any need to. I've always walked where I needed to go." Kale felt his hope plummeting. She would have to ride with one of them on their horse. It would be hardly ideal, but she could fall off her own mount if she rode alone.

"Ok. You'll ride with me, just hold on tight and we'll get through this… I promise."

"Kale…if we leave without them seeing us… this town… these people, I can't leave them to suffer because of us." Kale smiled mischievously at her as he motioned her towards the now saddled horses.

"Don't worry, they'll know we're leaving, and we'll give them one hell of a chase. It's going to be dangerous though. How are your fighting skills?"

"You've seen how I am with my staff, and I'm also good with a bow, but that's it."

"That will do. We can't let them live to report who we are. We must kill them before we head towards my family's estates." Laurel sighed deeply, biting her lower lip as she thought about his words.

"Fine… as long as we lead the death squad away from here before we finish them. May the Goddess have mercy on us." Kale squeezed her shoulder and nodded reassuringly before helping her up on the horse. Bane was already mounted on his.

"So, I know that look… what's the plan?" Bane drew his horse around and loosed his sword. Kale smiled at Bane and nodded.

"First, we bust out of these stables. Then we make enough of a ruckus to grab their attention. Perhaps we can ride right through their revelry and out the other side of town. That should grab their attention. We'll only have a couple of minutes head start while they mount their horses, but at least they're already down two knights. That means there should only be three to four more for us to deal with." Bane shook his head and laughed.

"Well, who wants to live forever? Maybe I can shoot an arrow into one of them on the way through. Never have been one to do things the easy way. Let's get this ride through hell on its way. I have a tankard of ale waiting for me back home and maybe a tavern girl to wed… On second thought, you sure you don't want to just fight them all here and go down in a blaze of glory?" Bane mischievously smiled at the two of them and gave Laurel a wink. "Nah, didn't think so. No time like the present." Bane kicked his horse's flanks and launched out of the barn at a gallop. Kale was close behind with Laurel holding tightly onto him.

Kale had chosen well. The horses were strong and swift. They sped through the town like lightning. Bane had already pulled his bow and had set an arrow in place. Kale kept an eye on their surroundings to call out any warnings that may be necessary. As they closed in on the gathered crowd, they could see a young girl being passed around by the four remaining death squad knights. Her clothes were torn, exposing her breasts to their rough groping. Kale watched as Bane took aim and loosed his first arrow.

The arrow sped through the air silently seeking its target. Bane's aim was slightly off as the arrow grazed the lead death knight's exposed neck. The townspeople screamed in terror; Bane whooped in triumph. The knights threw the girl to the side, drawing their weapons as they ran to confront their would-be attackers. Kale could feel Laurel's arms tighten around his waist as they prepared to run straight through the group of armed knights. The townspeople scattered in all directions heading for the safety of their homes. Kale drew his sword preparing to fend off any attacks as they sped by.

As they urged the horses on, the death squad knights stepped to the sides attempting to stab at them as they sped past. Kale easily countered their thrusts, knocking their swords to the side. Bane loosed two more arrows in quick succession, which found the flesh of one death knight's shoulder and another death knights knee joint. Even Laurel got in a few knocks with her quarter staff. Then they were racing out of town, whooping cries of triumph as they fled. Kale looked back only briefly to ensure the squad was planning on following. He could just make out in the distance their forms racing for their horses that were tethered to a rail outside of the inn.

Into the night they fled, knowing that soon the squad would catch up to them, and they would have to stand and fight. Kale and Bane began looking for an area that would be suitable for the battle, preferably one with a good hiding spot. If they could get there first, he would be able to let Laurel down and have her hide until the battle was over. There was no way Kale would be able to fight on the horse with Laurel holding on behind. Desperately he scanned the moonlit landscape as it sped past.

"Kale! Over there!" Kale looked towards where Bane was pointing and saw a rocky outcropping and several bushes and trees. That was as good a place as any.

"That'll do." Kale guided his horse towards the area and then lowered Laurel towards the ground. "Laurel, find a place to hide until it's over. Whatever happens stay hidden unless you hear one of us call you. Do you understand?" Laurel looked at him with exasperation.

"Kale, I'm perfectly capable of taking care of myself!"

"Laurel, please don't argue. I need to keep you safe. Just do as I ask." Laurel sighed heavily at the pleading look in Kale's eyes and shook her head.

"Fine, I'll hide like a good girl, but we're going to discuss this later." Kale beamed at her reassuringly, while inside he groaned at her words. She was not going to be an easy woman to manage. Still, she was worth it. He watched as she ran towards the rocky outcrop and ducked behind it. Then he turned his attentions back towards the road and the oncoming death squad. He could just make out their forms in the distance.

Bane checked his sword, then pulled his bow back out and knocked another arrow. Kale watched as his friend put three more arrows in his mouth, then he checked his own sword and pulled his crossbow out, setting a bolt in place. They waited silently, staying seated in their saddles so as not to give up that advantage. As the knights came within range, Bane and Kale took aim and fired. Kale's bolt dinged off the armor of the knight he was aiming at, as did Bane's. Kale quickly drew his sword as Bane rapidly fired off three more arrows before drawing his own sword. Two of his arrows struck flesh turning the one knight into a pin cushion, but still the knight raced towards them.

The knights' horses encircled the two, ringing them in. The horses kept them from getting too close to effectively attack in pairs. Kale and Bane kept their horses next to each other dancing in a circle taking their strikes when they could. Most of the time, they were defending against the onslaught from the knights, as they struggled to look for their openings. The death knights taunted them and questioned where the third rider was. They were certain it was a girl, and they made several suggestions as to what they intended on doing with her once they were done with the two of them. Kale knew they were just trying to anger them, get them to jump, making them easy targets. He took a deep breath and ignored their taunts focusing on their movements, searching for an opening to strike.

As their deadly dance continued, Kale noticed that his horse and Bane's were beginning to become restless and uneasy. If something didn't change soon their horses would most likely rear up and throw both of them. Kale was becoming desperate, and the knights could sense it. Their taunting grew along with their smugness and arrogance... perhaps Kale could use that to his advantage. Kale began glaring at the knights as they circled, responding to their taunts with venom. Bane caught Kale's eye and gave him an imperceptible nod. Both started acting as if they were succumbing to the stress of the situation. Then suddenly the taunting stopped as one of the knights fell from his saddle, the head of an arrow protruding from his throat, a look of shock on his face.

Everyone turned to look in the direction from which the arrow was loosed. They found the shooter too late. Another arrow flew true and embedded itself in the throat of a second knight, taking him down in one stroke. Now with the numbers even, Kale and Bane launched into their own offensive attack, throwing themselves at the two remaining knights. The battle raged on, swords clashing and ringing though the otherwise silent night. In a final lunge the four remaining fighters fell from their saddles. Struggling to their feet the warriors resumed their desperate fight.

Now the taunting had ended. Both sides were completely focused on the eradication of the other. Time seemed to stand still as the men continued their deadly dance. Laurel watched on from the tree, unable to get a clear shot. She could only hope that Kale and Bane would overcome the death knights.

After what seemed like an eternity, Kale finally found his opening and took it. With a few quick thrusts, Kale had penetrated the knight's armor in several places and wounded him gravely. As the man fell to his knees, Kale finished him off with a slice across his throat. Bane wasn't far behind him, finishing off his opponent a few moments after Kale. When his battle was done, Bane collapsed to the ground exhausted and wounded. Kale rushed to his side as Laurel climbed down from the tree and ran to Bane's other side.

She quickly looked Bane over, removing his armor, with assistance from Kale. Bending over his body, Laurel took her holy symbol in her hands and began praying to the Goddess. A soft glow emanated from her hands as she laid them onto Bane's chest. Within moments Bane's wounds were gone and he was opening his eyes and looking around groggily.

"We won, right… I'm pretty sure I killed the guy… right?" Kale laughed and clapped him on the back.

"Yeah Bane, we won… thanks to Laurel and her bow shots… I thought I told you to stay hidden!" Kale looked at Laurel reproachfully. She smiled back innocently and shrugged her shoulders.

"You were outnumbered, and besides… who was it again who got you both safely through the mountains, a place not even the King's soldiers will go? I'm not helpless, Kale! I know how to fight, and I know how to defend myself. If we're going to get through this, you need to realize I am not some damsel in distress." Kale shifted back slightly from the fire in her eyes and put his hands in the air defensively. How did this turn into an insult to her?

"Ok, ok, you're not helpless… but do you know what they would have done to you if they had gotten hold of you?! They didn't know where you were, and they weren't even sure you were a girl. If they had won, after you showed yourself… Laurel… you would have suffered a slow torturous

end. I can't let that happen, Laurel… I can't!"
Laurel watched him, her heart aching for the pain
and emotion contorting his face. She wanted to
hold him, to reach out and put her arms around him
and reassure him. She wanted to take his pain
away, but the truth was right in front of them. If
they were caught their ends would not be quick.

Laurel reached out and took one of his
hands in hers, squeezing it gently. Their eyes met
and for that instant everything seemed right, and
then a cough brought them back to the present.
They looked down and saw Bane watching both of
them, a smirk on his mouth.

"No offense, but if you two are done than I
think we should get out of here or at least do
something about their bodies and their horses….
Not that lying here with Laurel's hand on my chest
isn't nice, but I have no intention of sleeping
among four corpses."

Chapter 8

They spent the rest of the night burying the death knights and stripping their horses down. Once the horses were free of their saddles, harness and travel burdens, Kale and Bane slapped their rear ends and sent them off into the wild. Eventually they would find their way back to a town. By the time anyone realized who the horses belonged to, there would be no way to trace them back to their group.

It was far into the night by the time they finished their task, and dawn would soon be approaching. They decided to ride their horses a little further up the road and then seek shelter in the small mountain range to the west. It would be morning by the time they stopped, but if they took their horses far enough into the shadow of the mountain, they should be able to avoid detection. It would mean sleeping on rocky ground, but after what had just happened none of them had any intention of traveling into another village.

Kale and Bane knew there were two more villages and one city on the road towards his family's city and estates. Avoiding those areas would mean traveling through the Elven lands to the West of the road, or unprotected and open country to the right of the road. They would also have to cross three rivers and the only bridges over those rivers were within view of the city and one village.

Kale thought about their options as they road through the surrounding hillside. Kern would be the next inhabited town. Really, it was more of a small city than a town, but the lord there wasn't keen on his area being called a city. If he could help it, they would avoid spending any more time than necessary there. After Kern would be a two-day ride to the city of Anwar. They would most likely have to stay there for at least one night to avoid any suspicion. There could potentially be death squads in Anwar, and if the knights had acquired a reasonable description of them, there could be wanted posters as well.

After Anwar they would travel through Keb, a rural farming village that supplied food to most of the western towns and cities. Keb was near his home and shouldn't pose too much difficulty. Still the roadways posed the threat of death squads and soldiers. The forests posed the threat of Elves, which could kill them on sight for trespassing on their land. The open land to the East would leave them too exposed and fair game for thugs and bandits as well as soldiers and death squads.

Kale rubbed his forehead at all the variables that were just not in his control. His commander had always told him when you were overwhelmed by the differing variables in a war, concentrate on the ones in your control. If you focused on what you could control, then you could react to the ones out of your control. So, what could he control? He could choose the path they took. He could limit additional variables by taking certain paths. He could control when they traveled and how far they traveled in a day. He could also control what information they gave out. The forest had too many unknown variables, so that way was out. The open country had less variables than the roadway, but it also posed a greater vulnerability. If they stuck to a simple story and avoided too much attention, they could travel the roadway and get lost in the crowds.

When they woke several hours later, Laurel felt refreshed and clearer of mind. Before sleep, Kale had insisted they discuss their plans for the rest of their journey. Laurel had been so exhausted and drained from the past several days of exertions that she had not been very willing to listen. However, now that she'd slept away most of her fatigue, she had to admit to herself that Kale had made some very good points. Her father had wanted her to go to the elves when she was old enough, so she doubted they would harm her as Kale thought, but she wasn't sure how they would react to two humans entering their realm. The countryside to the east was also problematic. With death squads, bandits, goblins, trolls, and who knew what else was roaming around out there, they would be sitting ducks. They had already been forced to fight so much and run from so much that Laurel wasn't sure they could keep up the pace. Eventually their luck would run out. That left the roadway, city and towns as their final option. This was also not ideal, but beggars couldn't be choosers. They would need to come up with a plausible story for why the three of them would be traveling together.

Laurel didn't look like either of them, so she couldn't pass as either one's sister. There was one possibility, but she was too embarrassed to even suggest it. Maybe one of them would suggest it. Laurel decided to let them decide on the story… after all they're the ones that knew more about this land than her. She, after all, had only been hiding right under the King's nose for the past several years. She smiled and shook her head ruefully before moving off to the side of camp to perform her morning prayers.

After her prayers, Laurel readied some food while Kale and Bane packed gear and discussed possible strategies. From the sounds of it they were making things much more complicated than they needed to be. She went from being the daughter of a second cousin twice removed to being the sister of a friend of a second cousin twice removed who was being escorted to her wedding by the two of them as a favor to the father of the second cousin who owed a favor to the father of the friend. Laurel shook her head and started to chuckle softly to herself.

"Hey, what are you laughing at?" Bane's voice sounded offended and accusatory as he looked at her with his arms across his chest. "If you have a better story, we'd love to hear it."

Oh damn, now she'd done it. How would she get out of this one? She did have a better and simpler story, but it would be humiliating to even suggest it. Laurel quieted her laugh and moved away, but Bane wasn't going to let this one go.

"Laurel, get back here. You think our story is bad, then you come up with a simpler one!"

"Bane, she doesn't have to. I'm sure we could simplify this if we try. It does sound rather convoluted."

"For crying out loud, Kale, it's not like we can say she's family! She looks nothing like us!" Bane ran his hand through his hair as he turned to finish strapping his belongings to his horse.

"Laurel, do you have any better suggestions?" Kale looked at her questioningly, almost as if he were imploring her to create a better story. Laurel dropped her eyes, feeling her face flush under his scrutiny.

"We could always say you're escorting me to my wedding… or *our* wedding…." Laurel felt her voice falter and glanced quickly up at Kale's face gauging his reaction before continuing. His eyes were wide with surprise, but a smile was slowly spreading across his face. She quickly hurried on with her explanation before he could laugh at her. "I mean, if we said I was betrothed to one of you, then it would make perfect sense that you had traveled with a trusted friend to fetch your bride and return with her…. I know it's ridiculous, but it is a simple story that people would be willing to believe, especially if my parents had passed, so there wouldn't be a proper escort." Laurel let out a breath she hadn't known she was holding as she turned away to gather up the rest of her belongings. She then looked around for a place to get changed that was out of view of the guys. This whole situation was uncomfortable enough. There was no need to add any more embarrassment to it.

Quickly she walked off behind a rocky outcropping and changed into the dress Kale had bought for her in the previous town. Once she was changed, she worked her hair into a style that would hide her ears, but still keep her hair out of her face. When she returned to the camp site, Kale and Bane were talking quietly over by the horses. They were doing some sort of hand pumping motion, banging their right fist into their left hand three times and then sticking out a differing number of fingers at the end of it. Bane stomped his foot and cursed after they showed their fingers, then said "best three out of five!"

When they realized she was watching them, they quickly brushed off their attire and cleared their throats before walking over towards her as if nothing had happened. Laurel waited nervously for the teasing that was sure to come over her earlier comments. Regardless of what they said, it had been a good idea, she would take their joshing good-naturedly. Preparing herself for the first round of jokes, Laurel's eyes went wide in shock as Kale dropped to one knee in front of her and took her left hand in his.

"Kale, what are you doing?" If this was a joke, it was too cruel. Laurel could feel tears beginning to build up behind her eyes. Why would he do this? It wasn't her fault she was born a half-blood.

"Laurel, Bane and I talked about it and your idea makes the most sense, but since I'm not that great of a liar I have an idea to make this work the best for all of us. So… for the rest of this journey… would you consent to being my fiancé?" Laurel couldn't believe what she was hearing. Her voice locked in her throat as she tried to catch her breath. Was he serious? Laurel looked at Bane expecting to see him trying to hide a laugh behind his hand, but instead he had an intense and somber expression on his face.

"Kale… um… yes?" Kale smiled at her as he took a ring out of his pocket and slipped it gently on her finger. Turning her hand over she saw the leather cording that had been wrapped around it so the ring would fit. Laurel began wondering how often he proposed to girls he barely knew. As they walked towards their horses, he whispered into her ear.

"Bane's a little upset he didn't get to ask you, but he'll get over it. The image on the ring face, is my family's crest… the standing lion with a crown in case you were wondering. Legend has it, the crest was designed for my family's ancestor as a royal wedding gift, but the wedding never happened. A war happened instead, and a new monarchy took over. The crest, however, remained a symbol of my family to remind them of what they lost. That ring has been handed down from one generation to the next and someday it will be handed down to my son."

Laurel looked down at the ring on her finger and then back up into Kale's smiling face. Was his proposal real or just a ploy for their journey? The way he was talking… it felt real… but how could he ever want to be married to a half-blood? No, Laurel decided, it had to be just a ploy for the journey. She shouldn't look more into this than what is right in front of her face. Laurel smiled back pleasantly, hiding her true feelings deep within her. This was going to be a long journey.

Bane walked behind them, head down, kicking random stones that crossed his path. Why did Kale always get what he wanted?   Why did he feel like he was always the one being kicked to the side? Bane mounted his horse, anger and resentment growing inside him.

Chapter 9

Kale and Bane had been discussing the story they wanted to use since they woke up. The story they really wanted to use was Laurel being betrothed to one of them, but there was no way they were going to suggest that to her. She was much too proud and strong willed to accept that as a story. So, they made a plan, before she woke up, to come up with the wildest story ideas they could, hoping she would suggest the betrothal idea herself.

Kale had been so relieved when she had suggested it, although he had been surprised by how shy she had been about it. He had expected her to look at them like a pair of idiots and take charge of the whole thing. Instead, she had suggested the idea with a rosy flush to her cheeks and a quiver to her voice. The look in her eyes had made Kale's heart skip a beat and forcefully swallow past a lump that had suddenly appeared in his throat.

When she had gone to get changed, Kale took his signet ring off his finger and pulled out some leather strapping to tie around it, making the hole smaller. Bane, however, had other ideas and voiced them rather vehemently. Kale had been taken aback. Bane had never acted like this before. They had never competed over a girl before. He had no idea where this resentment and anger had come from. Bane had always been like a brother to him and now this....

Kale had suggested their old childhood hand game to settle the difference. Bane had agreed and they set about playing sword, net, shield. Both players held their left hand out and their right hand in a fist. They then hit their right fist into their left hand three times. After the third hit, each player holds out a certain number of fingers; one finger for sword, palm towards opponent for shield, and clawed fingers for net. In the game sword beats net, net beats shield and shield beats sword. Kale won the first round and Bane wanted to go best two out of three. On the second round, Bane had won and then Kale had won the third one. It was settled… or at least Kale had thought it was, but Bane glared at him and demanded best three out of five. Kale was at a loss, until he noticed Laurel watching the two of them questioningly. Quickly he nudged Bane and the two of them tried to compose themselves like two children who had been caught sneaking tarts from the kitchen.

Bane had grudgingly yielded, but Kale could still sense a great deal of anger and resentment from him. He tried to shake it off as he turned back towards Laurel, but the feeling still lingered even now. Kale remembered the way she looked, standing there in the center of camp. Her hair was loosely pulled back away from her face, small tendrils framed the sides. He knelt before her and took her hand in his. When he looked up into her face, he was taken aback by the storm of emotions that had begun to war inside him. In her eyes he saw more beauty, strength and courage than he had ever seen before, but he also saw a gentleness and frailty he had not been ready for.

He couldn't believe how amazing he had felt when she said yes. He knew it was only for the journey to his city, but with any luck, he would be able to make it permanent in the near future. After she met his father, and Kale told him who she was, there was no way his father would object. Now he just had to convince her, but what would work... not the usual flowers, poems, dashing stories of his heroics, or expensive presents. This would take something more... something special... something...

"Kale, we're coming up on the city. Think you can bring your mind back to the present." Laurel's voice in his ear snapped his attention back towards the city walls quickly approaching.

The gates were open, but they were bordered by several guards, armed to the teeth. They were stopping everyone that passed, checking faces and stories. Kale cautiously observed the head of the line as guards roughly pushed and pulled people through the gate or off to the side. Some travelers were yanked out of line, their hands bound behind their backs as they were led off to a holding area. Each time someone was apprehended, the head guard had glanced at a parchment in his hands first. The slow-moving line meant they wouldn't get in until much later, and most likely they would be stuck here for the night. Kale quickly assessed the change in their situation. If that parchment held information about them, then he would have to take a different tact to get them through safely. With a grimace, Kale realized he would have to use his family name and station to dissuade the guards from considering them a threat.

As they approached the gate, Kale sat a little taller in his saddle and hooked his right arm around Laurel's waist as she sat in front of him. The guards approached cautiously, their weapons drawn. The head guard glanced at a parchment in his hand and then back up at Kale, Laurel, and Bane.

"What business do you have here?" The head guard looked up at him, annoyance and boredom clearly painted on his face. Kale took his time as he haughtily glanced at each of the guardsmen around him.

"If you must know… I am taking my bride back to my family's estates for our wedding. You should be happy I don't report you to your lord for negligence, making us wait in this accursed line with peasants. Now out of my way before I have all of you sent to the stockades for laziness!" Kale tapped his horse's flanks causing the horse to jump forward, Bane was right behind. The men jumped out of the way giving their apologies and wishes for a happy marriage.

Once they were past the front gate, Bane pulled up alongside Kale and gave him a withering look. Laurel looked up from her docile pose and glared at him furiously.

"What happened to keeping a low profile?" Bane's voice was barely above a hiss.

"I had no choice. If there wasn't a line, we could have passed unnoticed, but with the extra guards and time they were taking, I couldn't give them a chance to second guess those posters they were holding. The less time they had to think about it the less likely they were to make any connection." Kale looked at both of them pleadingly.

"Well, what's the plan now… your greatness?" The exaggerated tone of Bane's voice sent chills down Kale's back. He would have to have it out with Bane sooner rather than later if there would be any hope of salvaging their friendship. It just didn't make any sense. Why would Bane change his mood so quickly?

They rode through the city streets in silence. Kale noticed that posters were pasted to the outside of every tavern. The posters were of two men and one girl wanted as traitors to the crown. They dismounted in front of a posh inn, called the Golden Swan, it was a tavern and inn that catered to the needs and desires of nobility. A groom quickly stepped forward and took the reins of their horses and led them to the well-kept stables.

As they approached the door, Kale and Bane both noted the posters and the descriptions of the supposed traitors. According to witnesses the men were short and stocky with black hair and brown eyes. The apparent leader had a scar going down his right cheek and wore several golden rings. The girl was a pretty thing with long black hair and green eyes, slight of build with a large bosom and tiny waist. She was last seen in their company and is thought to be a captive.

Bane started coughing as he tried to hide his laughter. Then he went in and arranged rooms for the three of them, playing serving man to Kale, as would be expected. Once the inn keeper had arranged for their rooms, serving girls were sent to escort them up and assist them with whatever they needed. Kale immediately sent for a seamstress and tailor to bring an assortment of attire for them to choose from. After all, he couldn't have his new bride arrive home without a proper wardrobe… that would be unthinkable. He also sent for a carriage hawker, since this was the new story… they would need a carriage to take them the rest of the way home. Their two horses would be fine to pull the carriage and then he would just need to hire a driver. He doubted Bane would acquiesce with being a coachman for the remainder of the journey.

After he had bathed and changed into a clean suite of clothes, Kale summoned in the tailor and seamstress and informed them of his bride's need for proper attire. The seamstress quickly rushed off to Laurel's room and the tailor quickly took Kale's measurements and went about pulling different suits and materials out of a trunk that his assistants had brought up. After Kale had selected several pieces and ordered several new pieces for himself and Bane, he sent the tailor to Bane's room to get his measurements before sending him off to begin the new outfits.

He informed the tailor that they would only be staying for two nights and the tailor was quick to assure him that the outfits would be ready by tomorrow evening. Kale paid him half of the fee plus some extra in gold and then dismissed him from his presence. Shortly thereafter Bane entered his room fuming from head to toe.

"Would you like to tell me why we are ordering an entirely new wardrobe and staying for two nights instead of getting the hell out of here tomorrow?"

"The story I told the guards won't be believed if we rush onward. We came into town on two horses with a girl sitting in front of me on mine. Laurel is clearly a commoner, or at the very least merchant class. They'll assume I took her by force, which is my right by law, but if I don't provide her with proper attire and a more appropriate form of travel from here on out…"

"They'll cry a warning, and we'll have the death squads breathing down our necks, again. Ok, fine, another wardrobe it is. My mother is going to start thinking I'm more interested in clothes than girls. That doesn't bode well for me." Bane tried a forced smile, but failed.

"Bane? Can I ask you something?" Kale looked at his long-time friend questioningly.

"Sure, as long as I don't have to answer."

"Ok… what happened back there? We've been friends a long time… I consider you my brother. By all the Gods, we took a blood oath when we were eight! Do you really desire Laurel that much?" Kale watched as Bane sank into the nearest chair and put his head in his hands.

"I don't know… It just seems that you always get what you want. You have everything going for you and now you have this girl… I always thought she was some fantasy out of your dreams. She's beautiful, smart, skilled with a bow, and her hands are warm and soft as silk. Why can't I find someone like that? Why do I always seem to be the odd man out? It's just frustrating ok.... The two of you share something between you that's so magical and it was instantaneous. I guess I just want what you have."

"Bane, we're brothers and you are never odd man out. There is no way I could have dealt with those death knights without you. We have always fought together and been there for each other. Hey remember that red-head in Saunder? She was the hottest filly I had ever seen, and you sauntered right up to her, pulled her in and kissed her hard on the lips. I thought you were a dead man for sure, but nope she slapped you once and then returned the kiss whole-heartedly. I didn't see you the rest of the night." Kale chuckled at the memory. They had both been students at the military academy and had earned a leave for the weekend. Kale had been dumbstruck by the girl's smile, but not Bane. He had been the most notorious wencher at the academy.

"Yeah, I remember. She was something. I guess I did have a way with the ladies back then." A smile slowly spread across Bane's face as he remembered all their escapades. "I even gave you a few pointers!" Both of them laughed as memories of a better time rushed through their minds.

"Yeah, you sure did. I have to say that I don't think I ever became as good as the master."

Kale bowed his head to Bane in acknowledgment. "Laurel though is different. I don't know what to say to her or how to say it. I don't think the techniques for wenching are going to help with seducing her. Then again… I'm not sure I want to seduce her. I think I want to win her completely, and I have no idea of how to go about that." Bane slapped him on the back squarely.

"Well, I guess I'll have to have your back on this one too. Just promise me that the next damsel in distress we rescue will be mine."

"No problem. The next damsel we rescue can most assuredly be yours."

They sat down to dinner in the dining room waiting for Laurel to appear. Finally, after what seemed like hours the seamstress and her assistants scurried down the stairs, curtseying to Kale and Bane before hurrying back to their shop. Minutes later, Laurel came down the stairs dressed in an elegant gown that showed off her exquisite form perfectly. She was a jewel and every man's eyes in the inn turned to watch her descend the stairs. She moved with such liquid grace that it was almost as if she were floating down towards them.

The room seemed to stop, and everyone parted for the beautiful lady to glide to her table. Bane stood and held her seat out for her as she sat down delicately. There was no doubt Laurel knew how to play this part, but how? She had been raised the daughter of a baker… yet she carried herself as if she were royalty.

Laurel sat down silently; her eyes lowered towards the table in front of her. She ate in silence thinking about all that had happened. Kale had sounded so arrogant at the gate. She knew it had been an act, but still… weren't they supposed to be keeping a low profile. Now they were staying in a very high-end inn and he had just ordered an entire wardrobe for her. The seamstress had been nice enough, but she guessed after receiving the amount of gold Kale had given her… she would have been nice to anyone. Laurel hated this…. She hated feeling like property, like a doll to be dressed up and put on display. She hated being on such uncertain ground and she hated not knowing her own feelings.

Kale had her head spinning. She glanced up a few times during dinner, always through her eyelashes and always trying to see Kale's reactions. He seemed so at ease, so calm, when they could be facing another death squad at any moment…. Almost as if her thoughts had summoned them, two death knights sauntered into the inn. Laurel felt her heart begin to race and her breath catch in her lungs.

The knights walked around the room looking at everyone's faces and dress. The room had grown quieter as the varying nobles in the dining room watched the knights saunter around the filled tables. The inn keeper quietly approached them and asked if there was any assistance he could offer them. They spoke in hushed tones before the inn keeper motioned in their direction and stepped away. The knights walked purposefully towards their table and bent to speak with Kale. Laurel watched through her lashes, horror gripping her heart. She knew better than to make any sudden movements. At this point there was no escape... only death.

Kale stood and walked to a side room with the knights, never once looking back. He had been gone for several minutes. Laurel glanced at Bane several times, but Bane just kept eating his dinner and acting as if nothing was happening. Laurel wanted to kick him, she wanted to make him react... do something, anything instead of just sitting there eating.

Finally, Kale returned to the table and sat down. He said nothing as he sat and finished his meal. After the meal he ordered some drinks for himself and Bane and suggested that she go upstairs and retire for the evening.... After all, she needed her beauty sleep.

Laurel was seething. How dare he order her around! How dare he act so nonchalantly towards everything that was going on! When she reached her room, she slammed the bolt in her door home and plopped down into the oversized, upholstered chair near the fireplace. With effort she calmed herself down and then readied herself for bed.

Just as she slipped under the covers, she heard a soft knock at her door. Groaning she got out of bed and opened her door slightly. Kale was standing outside, a casual smile on his face. Laurel opened the door further and let him in. Once inside he closed the door behind him and turned to face her, the smile gone from his lips.

"Are you all right? I know that situation downstairs was pretty intense. I thought I was going to choke on the pheasant I was eating." Laurel just stared at him and waited for an explanation. "Well…I just wanted to tell you what was going on. They wanted to know from the inn keeper which patrons had only just arrived today. When they had me back in the side room, they showed me the wanted posters that have been pasted up everywhere. They asked if we had seen anyone fitting those descriptions during our journey and, if we had, where was the last place we saw them. I told them Bane and I had seen three people matching those descriptions while we were hunting in the mountains south of here. They seemed to be heading south through the mountain range. We had just assumed they were peasants trying to avoid any road taxes on their way to their destination." Kale imploringly looked at her as if he were begging her for forgiveness. Laurel continued to stare at him, arms crossed. "So… well… they thanked me for my time and offered to escort our carriage the rest of the way to my family's estates. I …."

"They what? Tell me you said no and sent them on their way." Laurel desperately searched his eyes for his confirmation… there wasn't any.

"I… well… I told them we would be pleased to have the added escort, especially considering these new bandits on the roadways…" Kale winced as Laurel sank to the floor, a look of terror on her face.

"Kale, we can't keep this up for two weeks. What happens if we slip up? What happens if they discover the truth? Are you out of your mind?!" Kale bent down and put his arms around Laurel.

"We'll just have to be extra careful. We'll be riding in an enclosed carriage for most of it. That should give us some breathing room. Besides that, the posters and descriptions are nothing like us. We're going to be ok. Tomorrow I'm going to hire a driver for the carriage, and we'll be getting on the road the next morning…. If they are escorting us, then they're not suspecting us. We'll be hiding right underneath their noses. Maybe we'll get lucky, and they'll get called away on some other business…" Laurel could only look at him in shock. She had spent her whole life avoiding the death squads and now she was going to be riding along with them?! This wasn't possible! Kale gently lifted her face towards his. "Laurel, it was the only way… if I had refused their offer, they would have suspected something. Please try to understand. I've dealt with the death squads all my life. I know how they think and what they do. Please, trust me." Laurel looked into his eyes and felt herself falling into their liquid blue depths.

"Kale, I'm frightened. I've spent my life hiding from them, and now…"

"I know… I promise I won't let anything happen to you. Laurel…I…" Kale pulled her close and she felt his arms holding her tightly to his chest. There was so much strength there… so much warmth. This would work… it had to work. They would get through this… somehow.

Chapter 10

By the evening of the next day, their carriage had been brought to the inn along with their new traveling trunks and wardrobes. They had eaten their dinner quietly, Kale occasionally taking Laurel's hand in his and smiling at her sweetly. It was all an act... at least that was what she kept telling herself.

The following morning saw them readying to leave the inn. Bane had made sure their luggage was securely fastened to the carriages bumper board before climbing into the lavish interior. Laurel and Kale were already inside awaiting their departure. As the coachman made final preparations and took his seat, Bane sat down across from Kale.

As they pulled away from the inn, the death squad knights fell into formation around them. The streets emptied before the carriage, people bowing to whoever was riding inside. As far as they were concerned whoever was inside the carriage was someone of great importance, either high nobility or royalty. Laurel understood their reactions, it hadn't been long ago that she would have been bowing and scraping before a passing carriage of such opulence.

The carriage ride was long with so much jouncing and bouncing that Laurel felt like her insides had become mush. She was really beginning to miss riding in front of Kale on his horse. That had been uncomfortable, but this.... The death squad accompanying them also lent to the tension. None of them could talk freely. Most of the conversation revolved around Bane and Kale's supposed hunting trip and how poorly it had gone. They blamed the cursed magic of the elves and bandits for much of their bad luck. They also discussed their past conquests and competitions for certain tavern wenches. Laurel could only sit there in silence acting like a submissive, docile trophy. With every passing comment her anger rose a little bit higher inside of her. She could feel it getting ready to boil over.

The first two nights they camped by the roadside, the death knights, coachman and Bane set camp up for everyone. Laurel, being a woman and prize of High Lord Kale, was able to spend her night sleeping in the carriage, while the men slept outside. By the third night they had arrived in a quaint little town with only one inn. They were allowed to grace the inn with their presence once the death knights had made absolutely sure it befitted a high lord and his betrothed. Their dinner had been delicious, and Laurel's room had been beautiful and perfect. Kale and Bane had spent most of their time playing cards with the knights and talking about the few, but important uses for women. Not one civil word had passed by any of their lips and Laurel was very close to letting them all have it.

The only thing that stayed her hand was the knowledge that it was all an act. She knew Kale's and Bane's performances were most likely keeping the knights from suspecting anything out of the ordinary. Those thoughts were the only ones keeping her silent. She would endure, because to do otherwise would get them all killed.

The next two days were more bumping and jostling around inside the carriage and camping by the road at night. Laurel's backside hurt from all the bruises she was growing on her hips, buttocks and thighs. She spent her days silent and observant, watching for any signs of suspicion from the knights. The sixth night of their never-ending journey found them in a small, poor village. The inn was declared to be unfit for their personage, so the death knights found the finest home in the village, the manor house of the mayor. For a manor house it was small, but for this town it was palatial.

Laurel watched in horror as the death knights barged into the home and kicked the entire family out onto the streets. When the husband had objected the captain of the guard had struck him about the head with his metal gauntlet. It took his wife and two sons to half carry him to the inn. The coachman removed their luggage from the backboard and carried it into the house. Kale went inside with the captain laughing at the stupidity of backwoods peasants. Bane escorted Laurel into the house and up to a suitable room where he left her and locked the door on his way out.

Laurel was beginning to wonder if they were still acting or were they enjoying their parts a little too much. She threw herself across the bed in the room and began crying. She had given up so much and now she felt like prey trapped in a cage. She was exhausted from lack of a decent night's sleep, furious and terrified. What if this wasn't all an act? What if the Kale and Bane she had met before was the act and this was the real men? How was she going to get away from them? How was she ever going to find freedom again?

She wasn't sure when it happened, but somewhere in the middle of her sobbing, frustration and fear, Laurel fell into a deep and dreamless sleep.

Kale punched the wall, putting a hole in the plaster. How was he going to get through the rest of this journey without killing these bastards? He was absolutely sick from having to play up to these assholes, and his plans for seducing Laurel…. Those plans were completely destroyed. He could feel his stomach hurting from the knots building up inside. Between trying to keep his own cool and continually keep up his act, and worrying about Laurel doing something irrational, Kale felt like his nerves were going to explode.

At least he had been able to get Bane to go look in on the family and father that the knights had brutalized. The cover had been that Bane needed to be sent out to get some supplies for the rest of the journey. Kale just knew he would have to mend things with Bane when they reached home in more ways than one. Bane was still acting strangely, even though he had said things were fine. Kale sat in the nearest chair and ran his fingers through his hair. He would have to fix things with Bane, and then find out what was going on with Laurel.

Laurel had been acting strangely ever since the city. In truth, it was a good thing she was playing so submissive and docile, but it unnerved Kale. This was not the Laurel he had grown to know and adore. This was some other kind of quiet, subservient, twisted version of his Laurel, and he didn't like it one bit. He had expected her to act out, to scream, shout, or even attack one of the death knights. In fact, Kale and Bane had been primed for a fight the entire journey. They had just been waiting for Laurel to break under the strain of the travel, conversation and company.

Instead, Laurel had been nothing but silent and beaten down… almost as if she truly had been taken from her family and forced into this situation. Kale didn't like it one bit. He hated this serene, sad and beaten woman that sat with him in the carriage daily. He wanted his Laurel back, the one that cracked jokes off, slapped him upside the head when he was being stupid and joined a fight regardless of what he said. He missed that strong, independent, intelligent and beautiful woman he had come to know.

Kale closed his eyes and tried to calm himself further. He couldn't go to her, not here and not now. He would have to wait until they were home and able to talk freely. He would just have to wait, it would only be a few more days by carriage… about five. Then he would be back home in his city, at his estates. His father would thank the knights for their service before sending them on their way with a suitable reward for their assistance. Something else his father and he disagreed on. It disgusted him the way his father always catered to the death knights. Kale would have to talk to his father and hopefully garner his support, but there was always the chance that his father would side with the King and his laws. If that happened Kale would need to move quickly to get them out of there. So, before the conversation with his father, Kale would have to make sure that certain provisions were packed and ready to go in a moment's notice.

What had started as a simple quest for answers, had become an ongoing nightmare that wouldn't end. Kale sighed deeply before standing and kicking off his boots. He would get cleaned up and then continue his duties downstairs with the captain of the knights. Thankfully, Laurel was locked in her room, so, for tonight at least, Kale wouldn't have to worry about her safety. Now if he could just get through the rest of this journey....

Before heading downstairs, Kale made a promise to himself and all of the people that had suffered at the hands of the knights. He swore when he came into his position and power fully, he would kill every death knight who crossed his path. He would make them all suffer for the pain and death they had caused.

The next five days went similarly to the previous days on the road. Bane had informed Kale that the father would live, and the family was grateful for the assistance offered. Kale continued his sadistic and demeaning conversations with the knights each night before sleep. Laurel continued her silent vigil in the carriage and had even taken on the look of a frightened rabbit whenever Kale or one of the knights looked at her. Bane joined in with his own dark, fictional stories and often played cards with the knights after Kale had gone to sleep.

Thankfully the rest of the journey went uneventfully. By the evening of the fifth day, they had arrived in Lyrenvale, Kale's home. The city looked beautiful with its colorful rooftops and decorated roadways. The gates were still open for travelers to enter the city and the local guards were there to provide information to new visitors. The captain of the gate guard stopped their carriage as they approached the gates to look inside.

"My lord Kaleford, welcome home. Your father will be happy of your return. Would you like me to send a message ahead to inform him of your arrival?" The captain motioned a young recruit over.

"Thank you, Captain, and let him know that I have brought a potential bride with me."

"Of course, my lord." With a few quick words the young recruit was off running, and their carriage was moving once more into the city.

Laurel gazed out the window of the carriage as the city slowly moved by. She was amazed at the sheer size and beauty of the place. The marble and stone fronts of homes and stores were elaborately decorated in carved scenes of forests, glades, and mountains. It was as if every building had a life of its own. Adding to the wonder and beauty were the flowering trees and bushes that lined the streets and framed the homes. Baskets of flowering vines hung from the upper stories of the buildings creating cascades of color down the sides of the buildings. It was almost as if they weren't in a city, but instead were traveling through a magical woodland.

The carriage moved through the streets slowly, allowing for people, carts and other carriages to move out of the way. It took almost an hour to travel through the congested streets. The entire time the knights were grumbling and trying to shove people out of the way. Laurel gasped as they approached a set of golden gates crafted in the form of leaves and vines. The gates stood open with two city guards flanking them. On the other side of the gates stood a courtyard and the most beautiful castle Laurel could ever imagine.

The castle appeared as if it had been made of snow-white crystals that shimmered in the evening light. Its towers reached towards the sky in elegant spirals. It was as if the entire place had been built by the famous elven artists of ancient times. Her father had often spoken of the elven artists of old. They supposedly had created buildings and art that resembled the natural world. Laurel's breath was taken away by the exquisite artistry of the entire city. This was where Kale grew up and lived? If Laurel had grown up in a place like this she would never have wanted to leave. Then again, if Laurel had grown up here... it probably wouldn't still be standing.

Laurel turned in the carriage to see Kale smiling at her reaction to the city. His smile was knowing and warm… and she wanted to slap it off his face. She quickly turned her back on him and looked back out the window. In the distance, the doors of the castle opened and a tall, well-built man resembling an older Kale stepped out and approached the carriage. A servant dressed in blue and silver livery quickly approached the carriage and opened the door. Kale moved around Laurel and stepped out of the carriage, followed by Bane. Once they were outside the carriage the servant extended a hand into the carriage to assist Laurel in stepping out. Laurel watched as Kale approached his father and embraced him warmly.

"Hello, father, we were unable to kill any game on our hunting trip, but I did happen to capture another prize instead. Overall, not a bad catch, don't you think?" Kale motioned towards Laurel and then stepped aside. Laurel swallowed hard as his father approached her solemnly, looking her up and down. She didn't dare move as he circled around her, sighing to himself. Finally, he turned back towards his son.

"She is quite lovely, Kale. I take it this is the maiden I was informed of?"

"Yes, father."

"Very well, I'll inform the temple a test is in order to judge her suitability as a wife or… as a consort." His father looked towards a servant standing to the side and motioned him over. "Edward, escort the young lady into the house and to suitable quarters. Make sure she has what she needs to freshen up and make herself presentable."

"Yes, sir. My lady, if you will please follow me." Laurel glanced briefly at Kale and Bane before following the servant towards the castle. As she left, she could hear his lordship talking to the captain of the knights and thanking him for his escort. A quick glance backwards showed the lord handing a purse to the captain and the two of them shaking hands. The captain quickly made his congratulations and then led his knights away. Laurel turned back and followed the servant to her new quarters, all the while wondering what she had gotten herself into, and how would she ever escape.

Chapter 11

Kale followed his father into the elven designed castle. His home had been built centuries ago by the elves that used to live and rule this area, or at least that is what his mother had always told him. Coming back after all this time felt strange. So much had happened since the last time he was home. He knew he would have to answer to his father for his recent actions, but it had been necessary, and he wasn't a kid anymore. Silently he followed his father into his study and waited for the yelling to start.

"Kale… take a seat." His father walked around his desk and sat down, folding his hands on the desk. Kale sat in the chair opposite him and steadily gazed back at his father. "Perhaps you would like to explain to me why you left military academy with the excuse of returning home to fulfill your duties and then disappeared into oblivion. I would also like to know who this girl is and why you saw fit to bring that poor creature here! You are not a child anymore, Kale, and there are certain responsibilities you need to be made aware of. First and foremost, you are betrothed, and I need you to go and retrieve her and bring her back here. Secondly, you need to learn about your responsibilities to your people and how to deal with the other lords. After all, I'm not going to be here forever, and you will have to assume the position you were born to." Kale swallowed hard and fought the urge to yell. He was betrothed… to who?!

"Father…. First, I needed to leave the academy to find some answers. Answers about a town called Soldar. I know you don't like talking about it, but…"

"Kale, never mention that place again!"

"Father listen to me! Soldar is real and it's the place that mom saw in her last vision! I saw it too. I went to a town near there and found someone to take us there. When we got there… I remembered when we went there before. I remembered Laurel and her family! Bane, our guide and I faced off with some demon blood cloud and then a skeletal monster, before racing through the mountains dodging goblins, berserkers and that skeleton monster. By the way, our guide ended up being Laurel, who happens to be the girl I brought home!" Kale took a breath, slamming his fist on the arm of the chair before continuing. "Father, I couldn't leave her there… I couldn't leave Laurel behind once I knew who and what she was. Did you know her father was an elf or that she's a half-elf? Are they the reason you don't want me to talk about Soldar or is that demon cloud the reason? One more thing… did you know I can use magic?" Kale desperately looked at his father praying he wouldn't call for the guards. His father just sighed as he rubbed his head with one hand and looked down at his desk.

"You retrieved Laurel? Excellent, that will make things easier. I'll have to arrange the proper papers and we'll have to speed up some of the preparations, but we should be able to have everything ready within a couple of months. First, I'll have to talk to the high priestess at the temple and have her perform Laurel's test of virtue. That way if her virtue has been compromised the priestess will be able to fake the results. Then we'll be able to…"

"Stop! Haven't you heard anything I've said?!" Kale stood, his hands firmly on his father's desk, staring at him in shock. He couldn't believe what he was hearing. His father looked back at him calmly, his eyebrows raised. He wore that look that always made Kale feel as small as a lost puppy.

"Kale, sit down. I guess you're old enough now to know… although I have my doubts after you took off from the academy…" Kale sat down with a sigh and waited for his father to continue.

"Yes, I know you are a wizard. You inherited the gift from your mother. She used a spell on you, when you were an infant, to hide your magic ability. I also know about Soldar and Laurel. We were very good friends with her parents, so yes, I knew about her being a half-elf and I knew about her father. When we went down there, it was to sign the betrothal contract with her family. We knew the King would eventually find out about Laurel and her family, and when he did, he would send the worst thing he could at them." His father stood and walked over to his liquor cabinet. He grabbed two glasses and poured some brandy into each. Then he walked back to his desk and handed one to Kale before sitting back down and continuing.

"Laurel's father and I became members of the resistance when we were barely old enough to be called men. For years I have hidden those with magical talent and sent them to live in a hidden fortress. We work to thwart the death knights where we can and gain information on the King and his allies when we can. The resistance has also kept the secret of the true heir a secret since she was born…" His father gave him some time to let that information sink in. "Yes, Laurel is that descendent. She descends from the original royal line of our country. That is why the King wants her dead. That is why he will stop at nothing to destroy her. A seer told the King that a half-blood would someday sit on his throne, and in his greed and fear, he condemned all half-bloods to death.

The vision you shared with your mother, on that final day, connected you and Laurel together forever. Together, the two of you hold the key to destroying the tyrant and freeing our country from the evil that is choking it. Everything I have done, everything you have been put through, all of it, was to prepare you for what is happening now." Kale stared at his father in disbelief. Was this the same man who played up to the death squads and had always told him to not create any waves?

"Wait… so, Laurel and I are betrothed, and you're part of a resistance against the King? Why didn't you tell me?"

"Kale until now you weren't ready. Quite honestly, you've been too much of a hot head. You're impulsive, reckless and you take far too many chances, but with recent developments… our time has run out. You will have to be ready if our country has any hope or survival. I'm quite impressed you were able to maintain your self-control while dealing with the death knights for so long, perhaps you have grown into the man you need to be. That was quite some story you came up with… little did you know how much of it was truth." Kale drank down the drink his father had handed him in one gulp. It was a good brandy… probably the best brandy he had ever had. He looked at his father with bewilderment and saw him chuckling softly to himself. "You may want to be careful drinking that down so quickly, Kale, it is elven brandy after all."

"Elven brandy… How closely do you work with the elves, father?" Kale gazed at his father, High Lord Kellen Kingsford, steadily as he tried to collect his thoughts and absorb everything he had been told.

"Is that really the question you want to ask me right now?" He paused tilting his head to one side. "Very well… yes, I work with the elves very closely. As I said, Laurel's father, Toren, and I were very good friends. The elves are not the monsters our Kingdom believes them to be. Those are rumors spread by the royal court to prevent any intermarriages between the races. Kale, the elves are a magical people, who under normal circumstances live a very long time. They have knowledge and understanding that far exceeds our own. After your wedding, you will have to take Laurel to the elven lands. There you will learn about your magic and more about Laurel's destiny.

They can help the two of you discover the information you will need to be successful…. This is a lot to take in, I know. I'm asking a great deal of you and her…. more than I have a right to ask, but this is our world, Kale. Everything I have done has been to get you and Laurel to this point. The two of you are our future. Do you understand that?" Kale could see the look of desperation and hope that lay in his father's eyes. Could he understand? It was a good question. He needed time to think… time to come to grips with what he had just been told. Somehow, he and Laurel were supposed to save their country. Somehow, they were supposed to overthrow the King and take the throne. Somehow, they were the answer… somehow.

"I need time to think about this…. Time to try and understand, to let things sink in… if that's alright." Kale saw his father nod.

"You have time. Why don't you go get cleaned up, have a talk with Bane and Laurel… sort through things. Take some time, nothing must happen tomorrow. There are arrangements to be made before the wedding, anyway. I wish I could give the two of you more time to get to know each other and let things happen more naturally, but… we just don't have the time for that. If things had gone differently… you both would have grown up knowing each other, but…"

"But the demon cloud changed all that, I know. I think I may go have a couple of drinks with Bane and talk some stuff out. We had a bit of a disagreement on the way back and I think we need to sort some things out."

"Good. Don't forget to stop into the kitchen and say hello to Martha. She's been worried sick about the two of you." Kale smiled weakly at his father as he stood and walked towards the door. His mind was still spinning from everything he had learned, and he really needed to talk some stuff out with Bane and Laurel. How was he going to tell her they were betrothed? How would either of them react to all of this? Should he even tell them everything or should he tell them only part of what his father imparted?

Kale made his way to his quarters and slipped into the hot bath that had been drawn for him. After getting cleaned up, he would go to the kitchen, say hello to Martha and then find Bane. Maybe after he talked things out with him, he would have a clearer idea of what to do.

Kale found Bane sitting with his mother, Martha, in the kitchen. When Martha saw Kale, she squealed with joy and bustled him over to a chair near the counter, where she then plied him with a large roast turkey sandwich, roasted potatoes, onion tarts, and cake. He couldn't even get a word out, with Bane's mother complaining about how worried she been and how horrible they were for not sending word of their whereabouts. She spent every moment scolding them for their callousness and cruelness. How could they not think about how worried she'd be?

Kale tried not to laugh, but it was hard. Martha always picked at the boys and harassed both of them for their behavior, appearance and eating habits. If it hadn't been for Martha's constant interference while they were growing up, both boys would have turned out very different than who they were now… at least that was how Kale felt about it. Bane, on the other hand, looked like a child who got his hand caught in the cookie jar. Kale could tell that Bane had been getting the brunt of his mother's scolding and his frustration was going to take over soon.

With a soft chuckle, Kale stood and swept Martha into a spin and hug, kissing her cheek gently and telling her how much she meant to them. He flattered her as he danced her around the kitchen, and she called him a rogue and scoundrel. Before long, Martha was shooing them out of the kitchen with a couple of handfuls of berry tarts to eat along the way. Kale clapped Bane on the back as they headed out the back door and towards the practice yard they used when they were younger. As soon as they were out of sight of the kitchen windows, Bane pulled away from Kale, walking at a brisker pace.

"Well, you handled that easily enough." Kale was taken aback by the sharp tone in Bane's voice.

"It's never bothered you before when I've flattered your mother to get us out of her scolding…. Bane, what's going on? You've been pissed at me since that town. This isn't like you." Kale put a hand on Bane's shoulder to stop him from walking away, but Bane shrugged it off and rounded on him, anger in his eyes. He punched

Kale squarely in the jaw with a sharp right hook, sending Kale spinning into one of the fences. Kale shook his head to stop the ringing in his ears as Bane let loose with a shouting tirade directed at him.

"Why do you always have to get the girl? Why do you always have to save the day and be the leader? Why do you always have to be in control of the situation?! Do you think I'm stupid?! Or maybe, I'm not good enough for your high and mighty ways!" Kale looked at Bane in shock. This was not the conversation he was hoping to have.

"Bane… is this about Laurel, or something more? If it hadn't been for your skill with the bow and sword, those death knights would have destroyed us… we would have been dead. I have never thought less of you. You're the one who excelled at battle training at the Academy. You're the one who saved my ass more times than I can count. I thought you understood that. I thought you understood how important you are to me. I would never have gotten through the loss of my mother or the training at the Academy if it hadn't been for you. By the Gods, Bane, you would make an amazing general or commander in any army. If it hadn't been for my decision to run off to Soldar, you would probably still be there earning top rating for your performance."

"You know I would never get to be a general or commander… hell I wouldn't even be allowed to become a captain. Those positions are reserved for nobles only… which I'm not. I'm just the son of the family cook, only useful as cannon fodder. In the meantime, you get the girl, the fame, the riches and the title." The heat had left Bane's voice, but the bitterness still remained. Kale realized this must have been building in Bane for some time, and his connection with Laurel had been the final straw sending Bane into an angry tirade.

"Bane, if the military system bothers you… then help me change it. Help me change our country and how things are done here. You were the top cadet at the Academy when it came to battle command and military strategy. I need you to help me lead a revolution. I need you to lead an army. Help me ignite a rebellion. We can…"

"Kale, are you listening to yourself?! You could be put to death for less than what you're talking about. What the hell are you thinking?" It was Bane's turn to look at Kale in shock and concern.

"Bane, I spoke with my father…. Laurel and I are betrothed… that time I went to Soldar with my parents… our fathers signed a marriage contract for the two of us. He only just told me about it. Apparently, Laurel descends from the original royal line of our country and there's a resistance group that's been waiting for her to come of age to start a rebellion. Problem is from what my father said… they're not too organized and they're scattered all over the land. We need to get them united and find a way to confront and destroy the King. We'll also have to gain the support of the elves and perhaps a few of the other races that live on the borders of our land. Perhaps if we…"

"Kale, stop! Give me a minute to take this in. Laurel and you are betrothed… officially, and your fathers did this when you were both still children? Now, your father's told you that it's up to you to start a rebellion and overthrow the King and you want me to lead the rebel army?"

"Yeah, that's pretty much it in a nutshell. There's a lot more I need to talk to you about, but first I want to make sure we're good. Bane… you're my brother, and I don't know what I would do without you. I'm sorry if I ever made you feel less than me. I never meant to."

"I know… it's just… sometimes a guy wants to hear he's awesome by someone other than himself.… So have you told Laurel about the betrothal yet?"

"No… I'm honestly a little nervous about it. Am I sure I want to marry her? I don't even know who this girl is. The way she acted in the carriage… I spent the whole trip figuring out ways to keep us from getting killed and she just passively sat there. She wasn't anything like the strong and independent girl we met in Soldar. I don't know what to make of her. What if the girl in the carriage was the real Laurel? What if that wasn't an act?" Kale sat down on a low bench at the edge of the practice ring running his hand through his hair. Bane sat down next to him leaning forward on his knees.

"Well, you won't find any answers sitting down here. I don't think you're giving her enough credit. Think about it Kale, she's spent her whole life hiding from the King and death squads. I think what you saw was an act, just like your behavior was an act. You both behaved in a way you knew would be expected. I'd say it took a hell of a lot of courage and strength for her to pull that off. She probably wanted to put arrows into the lot of them and wack a few on the head with her staff. She's stronger, tougher and braver than you give her credit for." Kale looked at Bane in wonder as he finished talking. When did Bane get so wise?

"Wow, Bane, when did you get so deep and understanding of people and especially women?" Bane choked on a laugh and looked at Kale comically.

"Kale, no one understands women. If some guy tells you he does… he's lying. As far as the insight… it's just good tactics. A commander has to be able to read his soldiers and know how they're feeling and thinking. That way you can head off any doubts or dissension." Bane looked at him with a small smile before looking back at the ground.

"So, does that mean you'll help? Are you going to join probably the most dangerous adventure we've ever encountered?"

"Stop being so dramatic or I'm going to start calling you Kallie. Yeah, I'll lead your army. Who wants to live forever… right?" Kale clapped him on the back before standing and looking up at the castle towers.

"Right…. Well, I guess I better go talk to my bride to be and let her know the situation. Hopefully, the courageous and independent Laurel is back." Kale looked at Bane as he heard the other begin laughing ruefully.

"Kale, be careful what you wish for… you just might get it." Kale sighed and rubbed his jaw where Bane had punched him.

"Thanks for the advice. By the way, nice right hook. It feels like you dislocated my jaw." Bane laughed again before standing and clapping Kale on the shoulder.

"I only dislocated it? Well, a dislocated jaw is better than a broken jaw, right? I must be getting rusty." Kale grumbled to himself as he watched Bane walk towards the front gates, whistling merrily to himself. Then he turned his attention back to the castle and walked slowly to Laurel's quarters.

Kale found himself standing outside of Laurel's rooms about thirty minutes later. He stood there staring at the door, his heart pounding in his chest. Whether he liked it or not, Laurel was going to be his wife. Was this what he wanted? It was before the carriage ride from hell, but now… what did he really know about her? She was the daughter of a baker, or if his father was to be believed, the daughter of someone much more important. She was the rightful heir to the throne and a half-elf. She was a priestess of Gaia, the Goddess of Nature, and a skilled tracker and archer. She was highly capable in a battle with death knights, but he could also see the terror in her eyes when they were around. Kale had so many questions about her and her family… and none of them would get answered standing here. Kale stepped forward and knocked on the door softly.

From the other side of the door came the soft sound of Laurel's voice telling him to enter. Well, it didn't sound like Laurel was angry or upset in the least, the bath and time alone must have done a great deal to relax her. Kale opened the door and strolled into the room with a broad smile on his face… and was promptly hit in the head with a brightly colored vase.

"Owww! What the hell!! Laurel, what are you…" Kale's question was cut short by a hard punch to his right jaw. Kale jumped away from his assailant putting his hands up in front of him to block any further attacks. As his vision cleared, he saw a furious Laurel stalking towards him, the fireplace poker waving threateningly in the air. "Now, Laurel, just calm down and put the poker down. Let's talk about this like mature rational adults. I'm sure this is all some big misunderstanding and…" Kale shut his mouth and ducked as the poker came swinging dangerously close to his head. Ok, so he would have to subdue her before talking to her. The bath and time alone had apparently only served to fuel whatever storm of anger was broiling inside her.

Kale focused on her movements and waited for her to make her next move as he cautiously moved around the room. When Laurel took her next swing, Kale grabbed the poker pulling Laurel towards him. As he did, he twisted her arm, forcing her to drop the poker to the ground. Kale then pulled her in towards him, holding her tightly and letting her beat at his chest until her fury was spent.

"You bastard!! How could you betray me like that?! You monster!! You have no right to keep me here!! I am not going to be your personal whore to play with as you like!! I hate you, I hate you, I HATE YOU!!!" Kale continued to hold her as Laurel finally collapsed against him, worn out and sobbing. So, she believed what he had said in the carriage... how could he have been such a fool. She knew as little about him as he knew about her. How could she possibly know that it had all been an act? And now she believed he meant to make her his consort instead of his wife. Well, what did he expect? For the last couple of weeks now, all she had seen of him was a monster who catered to the death knights and laughed at their jokes and tales. Bane was right... he was going about this all wrong.

Gently, Kale smoothed Laurel's hair and lowered them both down onto the small loveseat that sat facing the fireplace. He held her like that for what seemed like forever, neither of them saying a word. She obviously didn't hate him, or she would still be fighting and trying to get out of here... but how did she feel towards him? Kale lifted her chin so he could look at her eyes, wet with fresh tears and red from those already shed.

"Laurel... it was an act... if I hadn't done that... they would have suspected something. I just behaved how they expected. I'm guessing you were doing the same, behaving like they expected.

I'm sorry. I never meant to hurt you. I guess we should have talked about this at the inn or some time before we left with them. It was an oversight on my part and … it was stupid. I shouldn't have been so careless. Can you ever forgive me?" Laurel looked into Kale's warm and welcoming eyes and felt her heart melting. Of course it was an act. How could she believe that the man who fought by her side and risked so much would be such a monster?

"Yes… we were both foolish. I should have known it was just an act, but you were so convincing… I started doubting what I knew. How's your head and jaw?" Kale smiled ruefully.

"Well, I have the beginnings of a pretty major headache and now my right jaw matches my left jaw."

"What?" Laurel took his face gingerly in her hands and began examining every inch of it. Kale chuckled at the shock and dismay on Laurel's face.

"Yeah… Bane has a mean right hook. I think he may have dislocated my jaw." Laurel ran her fingers gently over his injuries.

"Don't be an idiot. If your jaw was dislocated, you wouldn't be able to talk. Let me heal you quick." Kale held still as Laurel closed her eyes, whispering a prayer to her Goddess. Within seconds, Kale's jaw felt as good as new, and his headache was gone. He shifted his jaw around smiling before coughing and sitting back on the couch. He still had to tell her about their betrothal and about what his father had told him.

"Laurel, there's something else we need to talk about. My father told me about his relationship to your father. Apparently, they were good friends… actually our parents were really good friends and that day in your father's bakery… they signed a marriage contract… for us. We're actually betrothed, and my father was getting ready to retrieve you from the town for our wedding." Kale tried to judge her reaction, but she just silently sat there, her eyes looking everywhere but at him.

"We're betrothed… but how… why? If we're betrothed, then why didn't your father come and get me after Soldar was destroyed? Why did he leave me there… alone? I had no one, nothing. You don't know what that was like… what I went through." Kale took her hands in his and held them for a long time before continuing.

"Laurel, there's more. My father told me you descend from the original royal line of Kallihan, you're the rightful heir to the throne. Your father wasn't just a baker or a wizard, Laurel, he was much more and so are you. My father said we're the hope of Kallihan… we're our country's only chance of being free from the King's tyranny." Kale watched as Laurel absorbed what he was saying and then met his gaze, determination burning in her eyes.

"Alright… where do we begin?"

Chapter 12

Kale and Laurel spent the rest of the night talking about their lives, their losses, their fears and their hopes. They had tried to avoid the topic of their betrothal and the fate everyone seemed to have planned for them. After a while, though, they were unable to avoid the topics that haunted their thoughts. The idea of being forced into a marriage was repulsive to both of them, and the desires that had filled their thoughts only a couple of weeks ago faded with this new information.

They talked about what Kale had learned from his father, and what they were going to do with this new knowledge. Things seemed so complicated, and it still felt like they were missing a great deal of information that would help them figure things out. At least they knew they weren't alone in this… they had allies. Now they just had to figure out how they would shift their position from pawns to leaders.

They weren't sure how long they talked or when they had fallen asleep. It had to have been some time in the very early morning, because they didn't remember seeing any sign of morning light. When they had woken up sometime during the late morning, they found themselves wrapped in each other's arms. They both shifted quickly away from each other, shock painted on both of their faces colored with a hint of embarrassment.

Laurel's mind was reeling. How could she have let this happen? Wasn't she furious with him just last night? She ran through her memories of the previous night and what they had discussed. She had been so open with him… so trusting. She had told him things about her that she had never spoken to anyone before. Like the last time the death squad had come to town. That night had been a never-ending nightmare. The captain of the squad had taken a liking to her and had insisted on her company for the night. She still remembered the pain and torment of that night. Kale had held her as she spoke about it. She could feel the muscles in his arm tightening and flexing as she spoke of that night. She hadn't dared to look at his face. She had also spoken of happier times with her parents when she was younger. So many things had been spoken of, so many secrets had been told. What would he do with the information he now had? How would he react to her now that he knew everything? She didn't want to be forced into a marriage with him, but… would be married to him be that bad? She wasn't falling in love with him… was she?

Laurel watched Kale as he quickly jumped out of the bed and began pacing around the room, his hands running through his hair. He said nothing, just looked down towards the floor and avoided her eyes. The look on his face was worried… or shamed, Laurel couldn't tell. The one thing she was sure of was he did not look happy, he looked… was he disgusted by her? All she could do was shamefully hang her head.

Kale felt his heart racing as he looked at Laurel lying in bed next to him. Her body was so warm, and her hair carried the scent of wildflowers.

She was beautiful… and she wanted nothing to do with him or their betrothal. How could he blame her after everything she had been through? After his ploy with the death knights, how could she ever trust him? Kale knew enough about the tastes and actions of the death knights to understand her torment, without the details.

He paced around the room, shame and frustration flooding his countenance. Why, after the destruction of her town and family, had his father left her there to suffer alone? There was a marriage contract… she should have been brought here…they should have grown up together… so why?! His father had much to answer for… they needed to talk to him and get their answers.

Kale glanced at Laurel, still lying on the bed, and froze. Her head was down, a stray tear traveled down her left cheek. Kale felt his heart ache for her. He wanted to help her… to take away her pain and suffering. Could she ever forgive him? Was there even a chance she could ever love him? Kale moved towards her, wanting to comfort her, to express his love, but he stopped. Would she listen? Clenching his hands into fists he stormed out the door, briefly stopping once to memorize her face.

"I'm going down to get something to eat. When you're ready, meet me down there. We'll speak with my father and get all the information before making any decisions…" Kale began to open the door then paused, turning once more. "Laurel, we'll make them pay for what they did to you… I promise you."

Laurel silently watched as Kale disappeared down the hall. Did he still care for her? Could he overlook her past? Laurel dried her eyes as she contemplated Kale's words. A small smile began spreading across her face as a glimmer of hope began to burn inside. Maybe all wasn't lost... maybe everything could work out... maybe...

Kale stormed into his father's office, slamming the door behind him. His father calmly looked up and met his son's gaze expectantly. Kale threw himself into the nearest leather chair. Leaning forward and raking his fingers through his tousled hair, he tried to organize the chaotic storm of thoughts raging through his mind.

"How could you leave her there?! When you knew her town was destroyed, why didn't you bring her here? She would have been safe here! She would have been with me... not being brutalized by death knights and living in absolute terror that she might be discovered! We could have grown up together. We would have had a chance. Now..." Kale buried his head in his hands. He heard his father stand up and walk over towards him. He could feel his father's presence as he pulled a second chair over and quietly sat down.

"Kale, if I had brought Laurel here, the death knights and the King would have been tipped off. For her safety and ours, she had to stay where she was. I did the best I could with what was available. The captain of the guard, who led the recovery force, was a friend and ally. He retrieved her while his soldiers were sleeping. He took her to the town you found her in and hid her there with an inn keeper and his family, who are part of the resistance." His father paused as he placed his hand on Kale's shoulder. "I'm sure they kept her as safe as possible, considering the circumstances. She's alive and sane, that's what matters. Does the fact she's not a virgin make her any less worthy of a wife in your eyes?" Kale glared at his father. How could he even ask that? Then Kale thought about that morning, in Laurel's room, and the look of shame on her face. How had his actions looked to her? Kale closed his eyes, mentally kicking himself for the way he had behaved. Did she think he found her unappealing because of her past? He smacked himself in the head as he grimaced painfully.

"Oh Gods, I'm an idiot. Last night, Laurel and I talked through the night about what you had told me. We fell asleep next to each other. This morning when we awoke… I was storming around the room looking like a trapped wolf. I barely said anything to her! If she didn't hate me before… she definitely will now." Kale despairingly looked at his father who was shaking his head ruefully with his eyes closed.

"Kale, while things might look pretty bad right now… I'm sure you'll figure out a way to make it up to her. Perhaps you could start by telling her how you feel?" How could he confess his feelings after the last couple of weeks? He would just have to think of something else. Kale sighed deeply as he tried to devise a solution to his predicament.

"Thanks for the advice, father, but I think I'll have to contrive my own solution. I don't think words will mend this wound." Kale grimaced as his father chuckled softly and shook his head.

Lord Kingsford returned to his desk as a soft knock was heard at the study door. Both men turned towards the door expectantly as it quietly opened. A servant entered announcing Laurel's presence in the hallway. Kale's father motioned for her to enter as he resumed his chair. Kale wondered how his father could be so calm with everything, but after years of hiding the truth, he supposed his father had developed coping strategies.

Kale briefly met Laurel's eyes before turning in his chair and staring grimly at his father's desk. He didn't dare look at Laurel as she quietly took her seat. He couldn't trust his own emotions. His father smiled warmly at the two of them. Kale wasn't sure who should start.

"Lord Kingsford, Kale has told me a great deal about the conversation you both had. I don't think I understand how we could be betrothed. Why would you have signed a marriage contract for the daughter of a baker?" Kale watched his father smile knowingly.

"Laurelie, your father was one of my closest friends, and though he may not have told you… he wasn't just a baker. Your father was an elven high noble, and an important person to his people. In truth, both of your parents were very close friends of ours. The marriage was arranged for many reasons, but mainly to save our country. The King, as you know, has been on the throne for a very long time, much longer than would have been normal for a human. As you can see from your journey here, he is also a monster. If he is allowed to continue as the King of our land, our country will perish."

Lord Kingsford silently stood and walked over to a display cabinet standing in the far left of the room. Opening one of its lower drawers, he took out one rolled scroll and one large, rolled parchment. Returning to his desk he carefully unrolled the scroll and laid it out on his desk facing Laurel. "Perhaps you would like to see this. I have kept it safe all these years. It is the marriage contract your father and I signed."

Kale watched as Laurel took the scroll from the desk and began reading it in silence. Her eyes widened a little more with each line she read. He could only imagine what thoughts were racing through her mind at this moment. He had always known he would most likely have an arranged marriage, but Laurel had grown up the daughter of a baker, and then an orphaned tavern girl. An arranged marriage would be a foreign concept to her.

Laurel read through the document, shock coursing through her body. How could her father have done this to her? Why wouldn't he have told her? All the anger and frustration of the past few weeks surged through her like a tidal wave threatening to drown her. She took several deep breaths trying to still her mind. She needed to think about this clearly and not allow emotion to cloud her judgment. The signature was definitely her father's hand… there could be no question as to the validity of the contract or what Lord Kingsford had told her. Her father was of high nobility blood as was her mother. Why hide then … the King… He would never have allowed an elf to marry a human. Such a marriage would result in the creation of a half-elf… something forbidden by his laws. Everything made sense, but she refused to be forced into a marriage… especially with someone who would be ashamed of her. Laurel looked up at Lord Kingsford and smiled sweetly.

"I still have one more question, my lord." Kale cringed as his heart thudded harder in his chest. Laurel's voice was too sweet and her face too angelic for this to go well.

"Of course, my dear, ask whatever you desire. We will soon be family after all." Kale winced at the reassuring smile his father gave Laurel.

"My lord, if Kale and I were promised to be married… then why did you leave me stranded, in a strange town with no parents, no family and no protection? Why did you leave me to be raped and tormented by soldiers and death squad captains?" Kale closed his eyes, grimacing at Laurel's dulcet tone. He heard his father cough and clear his throat before answering.

"Well, Laurel, we really didn't have a choice in the matter. If I had brought the daughter of a baker here, after what had happened, it would have raised a great deal of suspicion. The captain, who carried you from the wreckage, was an ally. He assured me you were ensconced with a good innkeeper and his family… that was the best we could do. To do anything else would have brought the King, and his death squads, down on all our heads. Then there would have been no escape for anyone, including you. I wish it could have been different, but… the innkeeper was the lesser of the evils. I'm sorry for what you endured, but it could have been much worse…"

"MUCH WORSE!?!   Years of being a sex toy to monsters who would just as soon kill me as bed me! Trying to hide my ears and what I actually am! Knowing every moment that if they discovered my identity, I would suffer a slow torturous death that could take days!!! I've seen what they do to those they discover have a gift for magic. I've had to stand with the rest of the town as the death squads beat and tortured their victims, regardless of age, and then…." Laurel paused trying to catch her breath, tears streaming down her ashen face.

Kale felt his heart torn in two as he watched Laurel rant at his father, the pain of the past years pouring out of her in a tidal wave of emotion. Kale couldn't take it anymore, regardless of what she thought of him. He quickly rose and went to her, putting his arms around her and holding her close. It was like a dagger to his heart when she pushed him away.

"Stop it! I'm not a child… not anymore!" Laurel turned her glare towards Lord Kingsford. "Do you have any idea what it is like to stand by helplessly and watch innocent people burned alive because some crystal glows, revealing magical talent? I have witnessed countless friends die painfully and there was nothing I could do… nothing! I could only hide, like a coward, and hope one day I might avenge them. And now you are telling me I must continue to hide and play a happy wife… waiting for some mysterious organization to *finally* show themselves and rise up against the King!? I won't do it! I don't care what my father signed, or you signed! I don't care what your resistance wants or what kind of a symbol I'm supposed to be! I'm not going to sit quietly in some safe hold and wait for it to be over! You want the King dead… fine, but I'll be the one to kill him, just like he killed my family and friends! I am done with being manipulated by people like you!" Laurel stormed out of the room, slamming the door behind her. She didn't know where to go, she just needed to get away from him. She raced out the back doors of the estate, fleeing into the fields and orchards beyond the garden wall. Why did she ever come here? She should have gone her own way long ago, but could she really leave Kale behind? She just didn't know her own heart anymore…

Kale stood stunned in his father's office, staring at the door Laurel had run out. She hated him. He had lost her, somewhere along the way he had pushed her so far away, he could never get her back. Slowly he turned towards his father sitting calmly in his chair, carefully rerolling the scroll he had shown her. After putting the scroll away he returned to his seat, unrolling the second parchment.

"Well, that went better than expected, wouldn't you say?" Lord Kingsford smiled as he looked at his son's stricken face.

"Father... I..." Kale couldn't even form a cohesive thought at the moment. He glared at his father when he heard him chuckle softly.

"It's all right Kale, she'll come around given time. Laurel has been through a great deal. It will take time for her to adjust to her new reality. Honestly, I'm glad that outburst happened so soon. It means she'll be able to move on much sooner than expected. Now, as to this parchment before you... it is a map of the elven lands. After the wedding, the two of you will travel to the elven capital and present yourselves to the high elven council. You will have to go through an elven ceremony to make the union permanent. After which, the council will grant Laurel her title and estates. Their High Wizard will teach you to control your magic, the elves are the best ones to teach you control. That will take some time, but we have waited this long, a few more years won't matter that much. Once your training has been completed, the elves will tell you what the next necessary step will be. There are different parts of the resistance, you will have to visit all the groups to gain the knowledge you need to defeat the King. Now are there any questions?" Kale looked at the map, overwhelmed by his father's information.

"Father… I don't think Laurel will become my wife… not now… and you expect me to lead a rebellion against the King?"

"Of course, why do you think I've worked so hard to get you the very best training? Kaleford, you have been raised to be a King, and liberate our country. As far as the wedding goes… in time, Laurel will realize it was her parents' wishes and it's for the best. You must learn to prioritize your concerns. The wedding will fix itself. The priority is getting both of you to the elves without anyone noticing. That will require careful planning. For now, why don't you spend some time practicing your skills and discussing plans with Bane. I'm sure the two of you will be able to develop some reasonable strategies for the coming war."

"Very well, father, but I think you are underestimating Laurel's reaction and overestimating my skills as a leader." Kale sighed deeply as he left his father's study. Kale had a feeling he would be needing that map sooner rather than later. As he headed down the hall, a servant informed him Laurel had been seen running towards the orchards and fields beyond.

Kale hurried down to the stables and saddled his stallion, Thunder. Within moments he was racing through the paddock and out towards the orchards. Regardless of how much Laurel hated him, he was responsible for her safety… he had made her a promise, and now he had to keep it.

It wasn't long before he spotted her, curled up on the banks of a pond at the edge of his family's estates. Kale halted his horse under a large oak tree nearby, removing Thunder's halter so he could graze at his leisure. Slowly he approached her, silently sitting on the grass next to her. They sat in quiet contemplation for a time before Laurel finally spoke.

"He has no right telling me what my parents wanted." Kale glanced at her, concern growing in his heart.

"I know… Laurel, he just doesn't understand. He has a set goal in mind, and he just can't see past that. I'm sorry… I never should have brought you here. I thought…" Kale sighed deeply and looked out over the pond. "After everything you've been through… I wouldn't blame you if you never wanted to see me again. But Laurel… he is right about one thing… can we really stand by and let this King continue to rule? I must do whatever it takes to liberate the people and overthrow the King, but I don't think I can do this alone." Kale looked over at her, the sun made her hair glitter like gold, and his heart began to skip a few beats. "I'm not saying we have to marry, but can we work together long enough to figure things out? Laurel, I need your help if we're going to succeed. Then you never have to see me again… I promise." Kale could feel his heart ache with those words, but he wasn't going to force her to stay with him… he couldn't.

Laurel gazed at Kale as he sat there stammering out apologies and asking for her help. Did he not realize how she felt? How could he think she hated him? Laurel's anger began dissipating with every stupid word he spoke. Every barrier she tried to erect crumbled with his words. Of course she could forgive him... there was nothing to forgive. Laurel reached out and gently took Kyle's hand in hers.

"Of course I forgive you... you big dolt. It's just... everything that has happened... I shouldn't have yelled at your father, but I was so angry. I don't want to be a pawn. I..." Kale grasped her hand tightly, his eyes locking on hers with a desperate intensity that made her breath catch.

"I know... he never should have left you there. He can be such a bastard at times. What you went through was a nightmare, but Laurel... I... we can make sure it doesn't happen to anyone else." Kale took a deep breath before going on. He couldn't let himself get carried away. Perhaps if he was careful and took things very slowly, she would still consent to be his wife when this was all over... maybe. "My father has a map of the elven lands in his study. I think we should take it, talk to Bane and the three of us should head to the elven lands now before any wedding can take place. We'll have to leave in the next few days... and it will have to be before dawn, but I think if we're careful we can get far enough away from here that my father won't come after us."

Laurel smiled at Kale and squeezed his hand in return. Tears stung the back of her eyes. He just wanted her to help him with the resistance and fulfill her duty. For a moment, she thought he would say more... maybe proclaim his love.... Laurel quickly squashed such thoughts before they could overwhelm her. How could anyone love a half-blood like her? Still, she couldn't leave him... even if his heart wasn't hers, her heart was his.

"It's a plan... the three of us. We'll find the elves and discover what information they have. Then we'll figure out where to go from there."

Kale and Laurel rode back to the stables and spent the afternoon locating Bane and filling him in on the plan. Bane listened intently before adding some suggestions of his own. By dinnertime their plans were finalized. They would wait a few more days to make sure the death squad had left the city. Then they would sneak out of the estates a few hours before dawn with horses and supplies. In the meantime, Kale would teach Laurel to ride... or at least teach her how to not fall off the horse. Bane would take care of supplies and stash them in the stables until they were ready. Kale would acquire the map from his father's study and put on a display of courting Laurel, while Laurel behaved as a proper daughter would, apologizing for her outburst and accepting the marriage contract.

The days passed at a snail's pace, and Laurel could feel her nerves shredding with each passing day. Kale behaved like a man in love, bringing Laurel bouquets of flowers, chocolates, and gifts of jewelry. Each day he would take her on picnics or rides through the orchards and fields. He wrote her poetry, and demonstrated his prowess with a sword in bouts against the family guards. Kale's attentions were so convincing, it was difficult for Laurel to restrain her emotions. His attentions, along with the knowledge it was a ploy, were tearing her heart to shreds.

Bane became scarce, supposedly heading into town to carouse with the tavern girls, drink and gamble. Actually, he was gathering supplies and information about the death squads and any rumors from the southern cities.

Finally, the morning of their escape arrived. In the cover of darkness, the three friends slipped into the stables, saddled their horses, gathered their supplies and disappeared like ghosts into the stillness of the night.

Chapter 13

Dawn found them several leagues south of the city. They had crossed the river just before first light, avoiding any potential witnesses to their departure. They rode in silence, having agreed to ride until they reached the edge of the forests. Their meals were taken on horseback, not daring to stop and rest. The sun was sinking in the horizon as they arrived at the forest's edge, marking the boundaries of the elven lands. Once they passed within, they would be under the jurisdiction of the elves and at their mercy.

Kale dismounted his horse and gazed into the forbidding darkness of the forest. The trees created a nearly impenetrable wall of darkness. Laurel stepped closer to him; Kale tightened his hand in a fist to prevent reaching for hers. He had to take things slowly. Bane stepped past them, cautiously approaching the forest. Gently he laid his hand on the trunk of one of the towering giants.

"Well, this is it. You're sure about this, right? Your father said we had to go to the elves?" Bane paused to glance nervously at the darkness engulfing the forest. "By all accounts they're not very friendly with visitors. We could be walking to our doom." Kale and Laurel glanced at each other with resignation, before nodding to Bane and leading their horses over to the side where they could hobble them for the night.

"Yeah, the elves are the only ones that can train me and protect Laurel." Bane grimaced at

Kale's pronouncement, before grabbing his horse's reigns and leading him over to join the others.

"Hey, I know the two of you have some kind of mystical connection, but could you let me in on the silent conversation!" Bane grimaced as he began helping set up their small camp for the night.

Kale and Laurel worked without speaking, only the occasional exchange of glances demonstrated their awareness of each other. It was a solemn night as the small party sat around a small fire eating rations in silence and glancing over their shoulders at the menacing presence of the forest. With few words spoken they decided to each take a watch through the night. No one wanted to be caught unawares and vulnerable. By the time the sun was peeking over the horizon the three companions were packed up and staring at the ominous wall of wooden giants before them. With one last look back at the world they knew, Kale, Laurel and Bane entered the dark embrace of the forest.

They walked through the closely packed trees, carefully leading their horses through the dense foliage. Night seemed to rule within the forest's embrace. The canopy was a thick interwoven ceiling of branches and leaves which light could not penetrate, yet richly colored flowers and bushes abounded. Laurel gazed around in wonderment. How could so much life thrive in such a dark and foreboding place? Carefully, she stepped around raised roots and tangled undergrowth, attempting to maintain her balance.

As they walked, an irritating tickle ran the length of her spine, someone was watching them. Laurel stopped as she searched the dense foliage for any sign of a spy. Kale walked back towards her, gently putting his hand on her arm. She gave him a brief smile before resuming their journey. They continued walking through the looming forest in single file, the trees standing like silent sentinels guarding their passage. Uneasiness crept through Laurel's body. She just couldn't shake the feeling of being watched.

Kale walked in silence, speaking seemed almost sacrilegious in this place. He also didn't want to give their silent guards any reason to attack. So far, their escort remained hidden, but he knew that could change in a moment's notice. Kale hadn't said anything to either of his companions, but he could tell from Bane and Laurel's actions they were well aware of those watching them. Kale was unsure how much longer they would be allowed to continue unmolested, but he would accept whatever time they had. Once they were in the hands of the elves, their fates would no longer be their own.

Every so often, he would catch the glimpse of something moving behind the trees and bushes, but he couldn't be sure. They seemed to continue their slow trudge through the dense undergrowth for hours. Occasionally, they would stop to untangle their horses' legs, and their own, from the vines and plant life wrapping around them, attempting to trip them.

Branches and vines covered in thorns grabbed at their legs, arms and hair. It seemed like the forest itself was trying to keep them out and make them turn back. In the distance, birds of prey could be heard taunting them with their screeches. A couple times the horses tried to rear up and bolt. The only thing stopping them was the tightly packed surroundings.

It was impossible to tell the time of day. The growling of Kale's stomach was the only indication of how long they had been traveling. Finally, he saw a glimmer of hope in the distance. Calling a halt to their exhausting march, Kale made his way back towards Laurel as Bane moved forward to join the discussion.

"I see a brightening in the forest up ahead. It may be a small clearing or a path, either way we should aim for it and hope we get there." Their voices were barely above a whisper as they huddled together talking. Bane glanced knowingly at the trees around them and nodded silently before answering.

"You know they're never going to let us get that far. I think they've been closing in on us, though I don't know how we haven't seen or heard them yet." Kale nodded his agreement.

"I know, but if we can make it to a clearing, that should give us enough room to defend ourselves. I think if…."

"Wait a minute… Kale, isn't the point of coming here to find the elves and gain their support and assistance? If the two of you start drawing weapons and acting aggressive, we'll never get close to one of their cities. We can all agree we are being watched…so, maybe we should let them know we are aware of them and see what happens." Both men stared at her in shock, as if she had just suggested running into an encampment of trolls naked. She glared back defiantly, her arms stubbornly crossed.

"Laurel, what you're suggesting is hardly a strategic move. We would be their prisoners instantly. We need to get ourselves to an area where we can negotiate from a position of power, not weakness. Then we can talk to them about why we are here." Kale placed a hand on Laurel's shoulder to reassure her, but only received a cold glare in return.

"I think you are both being fools. Not everything needs to be solved with force!" Kale and Bane winced at the harshness of her whisper. Glaring at them one last time, Laurel stormed to the other side of her horse, away from them.

"Um… Kale… do you think she's got a point?" Bane looked at Kale questioningly for a long moment. Kale thought about what Laurel said. Could it be that easy? After a long pause they looked at each other smirking and shook their heads. Warriors only understood force and strength in combat.

Laurel stood on the other side of her horse fuming as she glared at the surrounding darkness.

That sensation of being watched had been growing steadily since they stopped. Her instincts screamed at her to do something before Kale and Bane could draw their weapons. If that happened, Laurel suspected it would be kill first and ask questions later. They needed the elves' support and she hardly believed fighting them would be a great way of gaining that support.

Laurel glanced once more at the surrounding forest before striding resolutely into the encompassing forest. She deliberately moved her hand through her hair pulling the bulk of it into a loose ponytail, exposing the delicately pointed tips of her ears. She glanced back only once at the boys before addressing their surroundings.

"We know you're there. We mean no harm and only wish to speak with you. My name is Laurelie, my father's name was Toran. Please, we need your help. I've been told the elves will help us in our quest to free these lands from tyranny. Without their assistance, we will most assuredly fail in our task." Her voice was carried away by the wind, fading into the darkness beyond. Kale ran towards her, grabbing her arm and dragging her back towards the horses. Bane and Kale placed themselves between her and the surrounding trees, their weapons at the ready.

For a long moment they stood frozen, watching and listening intently for any response. Nothing could be heard. It was as if the entire forest was holding its breath in anticipation, as if time had stopped. Suddenly the horses stamped the ground restless and anxious. As they turned to grab their reigns, shock gripped their hearts. Somehow the forest had opened a path for them. It was as if the trees themselves had uprooted and moved out of their way, revealing a clear and uncluttered path before them.

Slowly they mounted their horses, glancing around nervously before nudging them forward. They traveled down the new winding path for an endless amount of time. Only once did Laurel look behind them and quickly faced forward again with a shudder. The path behind them was gone, the trees tightly packed together once more, preventing any chance of escape. Was the forest magically enchanted or were the trees themselves alive and capable of moving themselves? Laurel shivered at the idea.

After what seemed like an unending journey, they came to a small clearing next to a brook. The path seemed to stop here. The three of them dismounted and Laurel led the horses towards the brook to drink and refresh. Kale and Bane looked around the clearing. It didn't take long, it wasn't that large of a space, just enough room for the three of them and their horses. Near the brook was a lean-to with a stone ring for a fire. There was wood already set up in the little circle and there were two fishing poles with bait leaning against the side of the shelter. Bane and Kale looked at each other and shrugged, shaking their heads in wonderment.

Laurel glanced around the glen searching for any sign of movement. Everything seemed peaceful as the sky darkened above them.

Stretching her aching muscles, she quickly tethered the horses within reach of the brook so they could graze and drink at their leisure. As she made her way towards the lean-to, she noticed a basket sitting just inside filled with different kinds of fruits and edible plants. There was also a wire rack for grilling and a small pot for tea. She glanced around again, before cautiously sitting down on the layers of soft moss and fabric carpeting the lean-to's floor.

"Are we sure this isn't someone else's camp site? Everything looks like it's ready for a camp out." Laurel looked at them questioningly as Kale and Bane grabbed the fishing poles and sat down next to the brook to begin fishing. Kale turned towards her and smiled ruefully.

"Well, if it is someone else's, we'll get the fishing and cooking done for them. Then everyone can enjoy a good meal and warm fire…. Besides, I think if someone was going to be camping here besides us, they would have already been here readying their own meal. It's strange, but perhaps this is a way of saying welcome, or maybe this is always set up like this for travelers in need. I just know we need to eat and rest and that path led us here and stopped. I think this is meant for us… somehow." Bane shrugged and leaned back against his pack as he waited for the fish to bite.

By the time the sun had set, they were enjoying freshly cooked fish, fruit and hot mint tea. Laurel leaned back under the lean-to and felt her head come to rest on Kale's shoulder. Quickly she sat up, hiding her face so he wouldn't see the blush coloring her cheeks. Most likely she would die when she faced off with the demon cloud, so regardless of what anyone thought or wanted, she couldn't marry or get involved with anyone. It would just be too cruel. Carefully, she shifted herself over and laid down. She rolled onto her side as her eyes began to close and dreams of a future with Kale flooded her mind. A smile blissfully stole across her peaceful face.

Kale felt full and content as he leaned back into the shelter of the lean-to. Bane was already snoring with a smile plastered on his face. He was probably dreaming of some tavern wench or two. Kale smiled ruefully as his eyelids grew heavy with sleep. He felt Laurel's head come to rest lightly on his shoulder, before jerking swiftly back up. A sharp pain struck his chest as she moved away from him, but he couldn't find the energy to open his eyes or argue. Something was wrong. Sure the last couple of days had been long and hard, but he shouldn't have felt this tired. He should be able to open his eyes… move… speak, but he couldn't. Too late he realized the site had been a trap. One they had more than willingly walked into. He felt the drugged sleep take over as he wondered if they would ever awaken again.

Chapter 14

He could feel the bed beneath his body, soft and warm. He could hear voices and sounds in the distance... the sounds of a bustling village or town. He could feel a dryness in his mouth, as if it had been stuffed with cotton. He could feel his limbs gradually coming back under his control.

Kale slowly opened his eyes and glanced around the room he found himself in. He was lying in a four-poster bed, where the posts appeared to be living trees whose interwoven branches formed the canopy above him. There was a fireplace in the far wall that hosted a cheerfully warm blaze. On the left side of the room were two windows with a tall, carved wardrobe between them. Light shimmered through the windows creating small rainbows that danced around the room gaily. The door to his room was against the right wall. The image of a majestic stag was carved into its surface. The whole room was done up in natural earth tones giving the feeling of the outdoors.

Kale sighed and rubbed his temples as he slowly tried to sit up. His head was still spinning and his stomach lurched in protest. Ignoring his body's complaints, he swung his legs over the side of the bed and took several deep breaths before attempting to stand. He had to discover where he was and what had happened to Laurel and Bane. They had to be somewhere nearby... if anything had happened to Laurel.... He wouldn't think about that right now. First, he had to find his clothes and armor. Then he could find a way out of here and obtain some weapons. Right now, though, he had to stand up without falling.

Just as he placed his feet firmly on the smooth, wooden floor, Kale heard the sound of voices at his door. Maybe if he was careful, he could trick his captors and take one of them hostage. Then he could get the information he needed and possibly bargain for Laurel's and Bane's freedom. Quickly, he slipped back into bed and closed his eyes pretending to sleep. He concentrated on his breathing, making it slow and steady.

He heard a faint click of the door's handle just before it opened with barely a whisper. Kale could barely make out the sound of soft footsteps coming around the bed to stand next to him. He fought to control his heartbeat as it banged in his chest. Then he heard a voice talking quietly to someone else in the room…

"I was sure he would be awake by now. The drug we used should have only lasted a day… I'm sorry your highness… I'm not sure what has gone wrong. We've used this drug several times before on intruders without any ill effects… I'll fetch the healers immediately." Kale listened as one set of footsteps hurried out of the room.

Kale couldn't believe his luck. This would be easier than he had expected. Not only was he left with only one person to deal with, but that person was a royal. With a royal for a hostage, he would have no problem gaining the location of Laurel and Bane. Then they would just need to get out of here quickly.

Kale listened as the royal poured something into a glass and set it on the table next to his bed. When he felt the light, soft touch of a woman's hand smoothing his hair from his forehead he acted. In the blink of an eye he grabbed her wrist, spinning her around and pulling her against his chest and onto the bed. With his other hand he quickly muffled any attempts at a scream. Once the royal was immobilized, Kale began whispering harshly in her ear.

"Look, princess, I'm not too keen on the idea of being a prisoner and I'm sure you would like to get out of this unharmed. Here's the deal, you tell your guards to set my companions free, return our belongings, and we leave here without any incidents. Nod if you understand what I'm telling you." Kale had been hoping for a nod or agreement… possibly expecting a whimper of fear or tears… but he was in no way prepared for the mirthful giggles threatening to explode from behind his hand. Was she delirious with fear, or just insane?

With some shock and trepidation, Kale relaxed his grip on his prisoner, who immediately spun around in his arms to face him. Kale could only stare in wonderment as Laurel's mirthful, angelic face looked back. Gently, her hand traced down the side of his face sending sparks of energy coursing through his body. He knew he had to look like an idiot, but he just couldn't stop staring at her in awe…. She was resplendent in her delicately crafted tiara. If there had ever been a doubt, it was gone. He loved her completely. In that moment,

Kale knew he would go wherever she went… even if it meant going into the depths of Hell.

Laurel had been too shocked to say anything when Kale had spun her into a tight hold against his chest. When he started whispering in her ear, she had closed her eyes as his words tickled her ears. When Kale had asked if she understood, she couldn't prevent the laugh from escaping her lips. The look of shock that overcame him was priceless, and only made her laugh all the more. Once they had both regained their composure, and Laurel had sent the healer and attendant away, she sat down next to Kale on the bed and related everything that had been happening.

She explained how they had been drugged with the tea and fruit. She described how the elves had brought them to their capital city of Laurendale, a city named after her great grandmother. After the elves had woken her, she had explained who she was and who Kale and Bane were. She had also told them why they had traveled into elven lands and about her own father and the attack by the storm demon. Upon hearing her renditions of events, the council of elders had convened and summoned their high wizard to ascertain the truth of her story. She had submitted to the spells, with some apprehension, but the result was the support of the high wizard and the council. After her identity and lineage had been verified with the help of her father's amulet and magic, the council had welcomed her home with open arms, restoring her rightful title and estates. Kale was now in one of the bed chambers of her family's estates, and Bane was down in the kitchen challenging the cooks with his large appetite.

Kale had listened to everything in silence as he stared at the floor deep in thought. When Laurel had finished talking, he rubbed his eyes slowly and then ran his hand through his unkempt hair. His mind was a jumble of thoughts and questions. At least Laurel was safe and the elves would apparently help them. With any luck, they would be able to teach him more about his magic.

Laurel handed him a cup of watered wine, which he accepted and drank gratefully. Kale watched as she walked to the wardrobe and pulled some clothing out for him to put on. His armor was still nowhere to be seen, neither were his weapons, which was a touch unsettling. He would have preferred to be dressed and ready for battle, but for diplomatic purposes he accepted what she handed him.

After she left him, Kale washed and dressed in the new attire. The clothing was strange and smooth against his skin. It was almost as if he was naked. In addition, the fit was rather tight across his chest, which was a little embarrassing. As he came out of the room, a couple of girls, standing in the hall, stared at him in shock before running away giggling. A man, he could only assume was a servant, nodded and motioned for Kale to follow him down the hall. The whole place had an ethereal feeling to it, almost as if the home was grown into its form instead of built.

Downstairs he met up with Bane, who seemed disturbingly peaceful with this strange world they found themselves in. Kale nodded to him and then took a seat next to Laurel at a large oak table set with a feast. They ate in silence, each one keeping their thoughts to themselves. As they finished, an older gentleman walked in and bowed to Laurel before walking over and whispering something in her ear. Kale watched as she smiled and nodded, a glimmer of mischief in her eyes. The servant went out of the room and shortly after a young elven woman entered dressed in ranger attire. She smiled to Laurel and took a seat across from Bane at the table.

"Well, it looks like everyone is up and around now. Have you had a chance to look around the city yet… or has our returned princess been keeping you boys all locked up?" She spoke with a quick lilt to her voice and mischief in her eyes. He could already tell by the looks exchanged between Bane and this newcomer; they had already met.

"I'd have to say, I haven't seen much of anything yet. After all I only just awoke from being drugged." Kale couldn't keep the resentment from his voice when he spoke. As he glared around the room, he noticed Bane's eyebrows raise in surprise as Laurel sternly glared at him. If he had been expecting a reaction from this newcomer, he was sorely disappointed. She didn't so much as flinch.

"That's too bad. We'll have to get you out and about now that the council has determined you're not a threat." Kale wanted to smack the smirk off her face. He took several slow breaths, carefully controlling his features and containing his frustration. Two could play this game.

"Well, perhaps you would like to show me around… if you're not too busy. By the way, I don't believe I caught your name." Kale smiled ruefully as he coldly watched her.

"Oh, no one told you yet… I'm Islaura. Most people just call me Isla though. I'm one of the captains of the forest guard…. I must say our clothing does look very fetching on the both of you." Kale barely prevented the heat from rising to his face at the backhanded compliment. Bane rescued him from further embarrassment by interrupting the stand-off between them.

"Well, I wouldn't mind seeing the archery ranges. From what I've heard since waking, they're beyond compare." Isla quickly turned a beaming smile towards Bane.

"Do you know how to use a bow?" Bane smiled at the challenge in her voice.

"Haven't met my equal yet." Kale knew that was true. He was the best archer at the academy, even outshooting their instructor. A glimmer of amusement sparked in Isla's eyes as she continued to smile at Bane.

"Then it's a match. I'll let our archers know and we'll see if we can't find you some reasonable competition." Isla smiled with a confident, playful smile that should have left both men quaking. Instead, Bane barked out a laugh and slapped the table.

"I look forward to it. Perhaps we can make a little wager of it. Let's say if I win, you'll have dinner with me…" Kale choked on a laugh as Isla's jaw dropped at Bane's wager. She quickly recovered, though, as her look of amusement turned to one of excitement and anticipation.

"Very well, but if I win… you'll clean the stables in a dress." Kale couldn't contain his laughter any longer. Laurel even joined in on the merriment. Everyone looked towards Bane in anticipation of his response.

"Agreed!" Bane spit in his hand and extended it across the table towards her. To Kale's surprise, Isla spit in her own hand and firmly grasped Bane's in a strong handshake.

"Very good. Tomorrow morning I'll come and take you to the range."

"Why wait until tomorrow?" Bane mischievously smiled at her as she playfully smiled back.

"Because… I need to go pick out the perfect dress to match your eyes. In fact, I better get going if I'm going to find enough challengers." Isla blew a quick kiss to Bane and then Kale before nodding towards Laurel and departing the room.

Laurel sighed and shook her head as she wearily looked at the two of them. With a small chuckle she gracefully rose from the table.

"Was that really necessary, Bane?"

"Hey, don't look at me. Kale was getting ready to explode. I was just being diplomatic. Besides, you two are betrothed… I didn't think you would want another girl flirting with your man."

"BANE!!!!" Laurel and Kale simultaneously yelled his name in exasperation, before all three burst into laughter. Kale knew Bane had been right, he had been about to lose his temper. It felt good to laugh and let go of all the stress and tension that had been building, too.

The next morning found the three of them, and Islaura, at the city's archery range with one of the largest crowds Kale had ever seen. Several elves were standing around with their bows slung over their shoulders talking and laughing jovially. No one spoke of fights or war. There were no arguments happening and the air wasn't filled with tension and anger. It was almost like a festival.

Bane walked over to the other archers and began shaking hands and greeting them enthusiastically. The elves responded with a tepid greeting, as if they were humoring a naïve child, with little talent or skill. Kale hoped Bane would teach them a lesson in humility.

The competition was organized into several rounds with the best shots advancing on towards the final. Kale and Laurel watched from a raised platform giving them an excellent view of the range. Kale noted, with vexation, several elven men maneuvering themselves into more desirable positions around Laurel. With difficulty he swallowed his jealousy. After all, the two of them had agreed they were going to ignore the betrothal contract. She wasn't his... not yet at least.

Kale focused on the competition, trying to ignore the encroaching elves. Bane was performing well in the contest, advancing through the rounds steadily, never being the best, but just doing well enough to move on. As the finals commenced, Kale noted that Bane was in last position, while Islaura was in first position. The three finalists looked at each other and exchanged handshakes. Bane had apparently gained the admiration of at least some of the elves gathered.

Islaura shot first, her arrow hitting the target dead center. The next to go landed his arrow just to the right of hers. Then it was Bane's turn. The crowd went silent. Every face was turned to watch what the human would do. Bane walked up to the line and took his position. He glanced at the target in the distance then closed his eyes and breathed deeply. Kale knew what he was doing. He had done it a thousand times before. As Bane drew his bow, he opened his eyes and locked them on his target. Taking a slow deep breath, he released the arrow. It was almost as if time had slowed down. Everyone held their breaths as the arrow whizzed through the air, splitting Islaura's arrow right down its shaft.

The crowd exploded in a burst of shouts and cheers as Islaura acknowledged Bane's win. Elves rushed the range, clapping Bane on the back, laughing and congratulating him. Kale smiled at his friend's success; it was well deserved. Turning towards Laurel, he saw she was laughing and talking with several of the men around her. Kale closed his eyes and bit back a harsh comment.

Quietly he stepped off the platform and walked away from the area.

As he headed back towards the palace, an older elven gentleman came up to him and matched his pace. They walked that way for several minutes, neither saying anything. Finally, Kale's curiosity got the better of him.

"Is there something you would like to talk to me about?" Kale stopped walking and turned to face the gentleman. The elf chuckled and met his gaze calmly.

"You are rather impetuous, aren't you? My name is Lysander, Elder Lysander, and High Wizard of this city. I was told you possess some skill with magic. I was also told your father is High Lord Kingsford. I believe the two of us have a great deal to discuss, and possibly more to begin working on." Kale looked at him dumbfoundedly.

"You can help me? You can teach me about magic and how to use it? I have so many questions about my abilities... about what has happened..."

"Slow down young man. We have plenty of time to go over everything, but first... let's get some tea and see exactly the amount of skill you have. Then we will begin looking for the answers to your questions." Lysander placed his hand on Kale's shoulder and smiled warmly. Kale felt a sense of awe and respect for this man. Here was someone who could teach him and tell him what he needed to know... a mentor, at last.

Chapter 15

Over the next couple of weeks, Kale spent every waking moment with High Wizard Lysander, going over spell runes, learning to read ancient texts and speak ancient elven. Every day Lysander tested Kale's abilities and skills, pushing him to his limits and beyond. There were days when he didn't retire until well after midnight. On those nights, Kale would fall into his bed still dressed for a night of dreamless sleep. His head hurt and his body felt as if he had fought dozens of battles.

Kale learned about the energies that surrounded everything. He learned about nature and about the balance that had to be maintained. He studied the history of the Elves and the war that tore the country apart, separating it into the different nations. He also learned about the prophecy that foretold of the half-blood who would sit on the throne. Laurel was the half-blood in the prophecy. She was the descendant of the original royal line, an elven line. Laurel was their hope for the future, the one to restore equality and balance to the lands.

What Kale didn't have time for, was Laurel. There wasn't a day gone by where Kale didn't think about her, but he was just too busy. Either she was stuck in meetings with the council, or she was busy dealing with potential suitors or visitors. Not that he was available during the day anyway.

As promised, they did tackle the numerous questions Kale had. As to why his powers didn't manifest until now… his mother had placed a binding on him. The binding wore off once he returned to Soldar to find Laurelie. This also answered the question of how he was a wizard. His birth mother must have had magical talent. It wasn't until a week and a half later he learned the elves believed him to be the son of his father but not the woman he had always known to be his mother.

"Master Lysander, why does everyone believe me to be the bastard son of my father?" Kale looked at him quizzically as he waited for his answer.

"Bastard is a rather harsh word, Kale, but if you must know… it's because of his wife, Sarafina." Kale shook his head in confusion.

"Master, I don't understand… Sarafina Kingsford was my mother. She is the woman that bore me." High wizard Lysander looked at him with a look of pity and sympathy that made Kale's stomach tighten into knots.

"Kale, come sit down with me. There is something you should know. Sarafina could not have been your mother…. She was elven, not human, and you are most definitely human." Kale closed his eyes, trying desperately to make sense of what he was being told. His mother was an elf? She must have hidden her identity similar to Laurel's father.

Kale thought about all his conversations with Laurel and about what had happened in Soldar. Laurel had said her father had put an illusion on her as a child so she would appear human. Her father had only removed it just before his death. Could his mother have done the same for him?

Kale searched his memories, trying to remember a day he longed to forget. She didn't think it would kill her until the end. Her last words to him had been to find Laurel. She didn't have time to remove any illusions. If she had been able to cast a binding that would fool the death squads, then a lasting illusion should have been simple.

Kale could feel his heart racing. What if he was like Laurel? What if they were both half-elves? Would that change anything… would it matter at all? Kale looked into High Wizard Lysander's eyes hopefully.

"Master Lysander, will you look to see if there is an illusion on me? I know it may only be wishful thinking, but I need to know for sure." The high wizard looked at him thoughtfully for a long moment before nodding his assent. Kale could feel his heart pounding as if it were trying to break out of his chest. It seemed like an eternity before he had gathered the necessary components for the spell.

When he was ready, he had Kale stand in front of a tall mirror as he cast the incantation. It seemed like time stood still as he waited for the results. As Kale stood staring into the mirror, a strange bluish glow began to encompass his reflection.

High Wizard Lysander stopped casting and looked at Kale's reflection curiously. He placed his hands on Kale's shoulders and turned him around to look into his eyes. Kale could see concern and hope warring in the older wizard's eyes.

"How could she have done this? Kale, there was only supposed to be one half-blood… one half-elf. With two of you… there is no guarantee you'll both survive what's to come." With a heavy sigh Lysander sank into the nearest chair and rested his head in his hands. "Kale, come sit. Let me tell you a story of four friends that were determined to change the world."

Kale sat and listened for several hours as Lysander related the story of their parents' lives. He learned how Laurel's father, Toran, was originally betrothed to Sarafina, and Laurel's mother, Lillianna, had originally been engaged to Lord Kellen Kingsford. The couples had switched betrothals to ensure the birth of a half-elven heir to the throne. That's why the four had been such close friends. That's why they had arranged for their children to be married. In that way all four would be united in the union of their children.

Kale absorbed everything carefully, taking in all Lysander had to tell him. When he finished, Kale stayed seated for quite some time pondering the consequences of their actions. The prophecy spoke of only one half-blood. With two in existence, it meant that Laurel was not guaranteed to survive the coming adventure. Kale couldn't let that happen. If a sacrifice had to be made, then he would be the one to make it.

Laurel found her time consumed with the attentions of the council and numerous suitors. Her days were spent learning about the history of her family and the elven people. Each day she met with one council member after another, who taught her about traditions and customs, politics, economy and diplomacy. When she wasn't with the council members, she was entertaining several elven suitors. It seemed to her that each meal she had was with a different man trying to win her hand. It appeared, to Laurel's chagrin, everyone assumed she would choose a husband almost immediately… it was ridiculous.

Mealtimes became exercises in patience and tolerance, and her meetings with the council members became tedious and frustrating. How were any of these lessons going to help her with the task she faced? How was any of this going to help her destroy the demon or overthrow the King? It was laughable. They spent their days safe and content in their little world, with no real understanding of what was happening out there. They didn't know what it was like growing up in Vale Ridge, knowing your death was one misstep away.

All Laurel wanted to do was have time with Kale and Bane to discuss what they had learned so far and plan their next move. Unfortunately, Kale was being kept busy by the High Wizard, studying magic and lore. Bane was busy pursuing Islaura and meeting with the captains and generals of the elven forces, discussing strategies and learning about their capabilities.

Laurel had only seen Bane once since they had been here. He had excitedly told her about the military capabilities of the elves and how he was getting closer to Isla each day. Laurel had been happy for him, but she also wanted to talk about what they were going to do next. They couldn't just stay in Laurendale. How much more time did they have before the demon cloud found them again? It had to know they weren't dead, and that they would find a way to destroy it. There were also death squads looking for them and a King that would want them dead. Time was running out and they didn't seem to be getting anywhere.

Kale was gone most days, with High Wizard Lysander, and sometimes didn't return until well after dark. On those nights, Laurel would go to his room after him and make sure his boots were off and his blankets were placed over him. Sometimes she would smooth loose strands of hair out of his face. Sometimes, during those nights, she would imagine what it would be like to spend her life with him. Everyone assumed she would live through the coming battles, but Laurel knew differently. She was planning on taking on a demon... the likelihood of her surviving such an encounter was almost nonexistent. Let them believe what they would. She would have her dreams to get her through to the end.

Bane spent his days with Isla learning what he could about her world. Isla was amazing. During their first two weeks, they had become very close, and their relationship was starting to lean towards a more intimate direction. When he wasn't with her, he spent his time discussing military strategies with the captains and commanders of the elven people.

Initially, they had only humored Bane as a child needing to learn, but as their discussions continued a new respect blossomed. Over the weeks, Bane learned from the experience of the elves while they, in turn, learned from Bane's experiences in the military. He had been amazed with their military capabilities. Their battle strategies tended more towards quick, jabbing attacks, leaving enemies confused and disoriented. They used the woods to their advantage, hiding in shadows and striking when least expected.

Bane shared the strategies he had been taught and the ones he had learned from studying the great commanders of the past. Their collaboration allowed them to develop solid strategies for dealing with the death squads and King's army. As their meetings continued, they began to lay out plans for moving their army against the King and his forces.

During their last meeting, Bane had rubbed his hands through his hair frustratingly. They just didn't have enough people. They would need to gain more allies, but how would they get races who feared and hated each other to work together as one army?

When Bane had brought this up to the elves the generals had laughed heartily. They had already spent decades collaborating secretly with

the dwarves and their human allies, like Lord
Kingsford. Bane felt chagrinned, but he was
greatly relieved for the illusion they had created.
Perhaps this was a war they could win.

It was the end of the fourth week when
Bane made the time to meet with Laurel and Kale.
There was much they needed to discuss and even
more they would need to plan. How he went from
being a mischievous troublemaker to organizing an
army, he would never know, but this was the path
he had chosen, and he wasn't about to let it go.

Laurel sat in the west sitting room patiently
waiting for Kale and Bane to arrive. They had all
agreed to meet tonight and discuss what they had
learned and their plans for the future. Laurel, for
one, wanted to leave. She wanted to find a way to
destroy the demon and, so far, the elves didn't seem
to have any information on the subject.

Laurel looked up as Bane entered the room
and nodded to her. He walked casually over to the
drink cart and poured himself a glass of wine
before throwing himself in a chair across from her.
Laurel smiled and shook her head reproachfully.
Bane was one person she could count on to never
change. They both sat quietly as they awaited
Kale's arrival. One of the house servants entered
the room with trays of cucumber sandwiches, bite-
size cakes, and fruits. Laurel set a couple
sandwiches and some fruit on her plate, while Bane
piled his plate high with everything.

As they finished eating the doors opened and Kale strode in... or at least Laurel thought it was Kale. His ears were now slightly pointed like hers and his frame, although still muscular and large, was slightly smaller. Laurel couldn't stop herself from staring openly, her lips barely parted in surprise. It was Bane's voice bursting out of the silence that shook her back to reality.

"Kale?!? What the hell happened to you? Did you mess up a spell?" Bane stood and circled Kale appraisingly, as if he were assessing a newly designed weapon or armor. Kale laughed heartily at Bane's reaction before shoving him back and walking towards Laurel.

"My mother was an elf. She hid it with illusions, just like your father did, Laurel. She didn't expect the visions to kill her. By the time she realized the truth... it was too late to remove the illusion. High Wizard Lysander had to cast several incantations to remove the layers of illusions she had placed on me. It took about half a day to undo all the illusion and binding spells that were on me. Laurel, our parents were closer than we knew. That's why they wanted us married. They wanted us to have what they couldn't have. I've been so stupid. There is so much I need to tell you." Laurel smiled at Kale in amusement and wonder. He was so excited and boisterous.

"Kale, slow down, you're not making sense. What happened to not wanting to marry and deciding our own fates? I thought what our parents wanted didn't matter to you... I mean why would you want to be with a half-blood cast off?" Kale looked at Laurel as if for the first time. She thought he didn't want to marry her?! Kale could have hit himself. He had been so caught up in trying to keep her safe and not force her into anything that he had pushed her away. He shook his head in amazement and pulled her into his arms.

"Laurel, I love you. I have loved you since we were children. I thought you knew… I'm sorry, I was trying to let you decide what you wanted. I didn't want to force you into anything, because that had been your whole life. All I wanted to do was protect you and keep you safe." Kale looked into her eyes, mirth, compassion and love filling his soul. Then he shook his head and quickly continued. "Back to what I was saying though, your mother was betrothed to my father and my mother was betrothed to your father. They switched so we would be born, so there would be two half-elves, not just one to carry the burden. That's why the demon cloud couldn't hurt us. The combination of both our powers, our connection to each other, protected us. It's going to take both of us to destroy that creature."

Kale held her tightly to his chest. Laurel could hear his heart beating steadily and strong. He loved her. She could have cried in that moment from the joy she felt. Kale loved her and wanted to be with her. She stayed in his arms, not wanting to leave. She looked up at him as he loosened his hold and began speaking to Bane.

"Bane, we are going to really need your help. I've heard about what you've been up to and we're going to need you to organize the army and assemble the different pockets of resistance members. We'll be traveling to the dwarves to discover the information they hold." Kale walked over to the couch, still keeping Laurel close to him.

"That all sounds well and good, Kale, but how am I supposed to locate all these members? It's not like I can snap my fingers and... poof... they appear. I don't think it is going to be as easy as you think." Kale nodded his head in agreement.

"I know, but I believe High Wizard Lysander has a way to contact them all. There is also a conclave of wizards somewhere in the northern part of the country near the border. The elves aren't sure where they are exactly, but apparently the dwarves will direct us... after we've passed their test and acquired a special weapon to destroy the demon."

"Well, it sounds like the two of you have had a productive couple of weeks. I've been stuck in princess lessons and been ogled at like a prime cut of meat. No one will tell me anything, at least, anything useful." Bane and Kale started laughing, and Kale put his arm around Laurel's shoulder and rubbed it comfortingly.

"I think they're a little too excited to have their princess back, and besides, they have no intention of letting you fight in any battles or have any adventures. I think they would prefer you stay safe and sound, locked away in your palace." Kale smiled at her sympathetically.

"Yeah, they want you to be the pretty little princess in the proverbial tower." Bane choked out a laugh just before Laurel threw a pillow at his head. "Hey!"

"I am not about to stay locked up in this palace while you two go off to have all the fun and adventure!" She glared at both of them with her arms crossed over her chest.

"I don't expect you to... which means, we're going to have to be a little sneaky as to how we leave here. Bane, do you think Islaura will help us get Laurel out of here?" Bane leaned back against his chair and thought for a moment.

"Yeah, I think..." Everyone turned towards the windows as screams and shouting filled the air. Bane was the first to reach the windows and look outside. He turned back to Kale and Laurel, a dark look clouding his face. "It's found us. We're under attack."

Chapter 16

"Quickly grab what you can. It looks like you will be leaving sooner than you thought." Bane loosened his sword in his scabbard before grimly smiling at them. Kale grabbed Bane's arm.

"You mean we're leaving." Bane shook his head regretfully.

"Sorry, Kale, not this time. Islaura's out there somewhere. Besides, I need to stay and raise an army…. Don't worry, we'll see each other again. This isn't good-bye, yet." Bane pulled Laurel into his arms and gave her a hug. "Take care of him, Laurel. He's my best friend, and you won't find a more honorable man in all the world." Laurel could feel tears forming in her eyes.

"Take care of yourself, Bane. Be safe." Laurel quickly ran from the room to gather her things and change into more appropriate attire.

"Bane, I expect you and Isla to dance at our wedding, so you can't die before then." Kale grabbed Bane's hand and squeezed it tightly. Bane returned the squeeze and nodded his head.

"No problem. Now get going. We'll hold them off as long as we can." Kale watched as Bane ran out the door, drawing his sword as he went.

Kale bolted up the stairs past oncoming guards and armed servants rushing to defend their princess and people. Laurel ran out of her room dressed in her traveling gear, with two packs on her shoulders, just as Kale arrived in her hallway. Quickly, she motioned him to follow her as she tossed him one of the packs. Together they fled down the hall to a set of stairs hidden behind a tapestry. Down they ran through dark stairways and hidden corridors until they came to what appeared to be a dead end.

Laurel ran her hands over the stone wall until she found what she was looking for and pushed a stone into the wall. In front of them the door slid back and to the side revealing another passageway. Kale grabbed her hand and pulled her with him down the dark tunnel that seemed to go on forever. Finally, they came out into a clearing far from the city. As they exited the tunnel, two guards stepped out from behind the trees. As soon as they saw the panicked look on Laurel's face they stepped up and quickly led them to a shelter with horses corralled nearby.

"Your highness, these horses will carry you where you need to go. They can handle any terrain you may come across. If you continue heading in that direction you will come out north of the forest, near Lord Kingsford's lands. If you need aid, he will lend it. The goddess' speed be with you and carry you to safety. Now go your highness. We will stay here and prevent any chase." Laurel nodded to both of them gravely.

"Be careful. Your enemy will be demons, if they come through. Do not risk your lives unnecessarily, you are too important." Both men placed their hands over their hearts and bowed to her before turning to guard the tunnel and attack anything that would follow.

Kale grabbed Laurel's arm and led her to a horse, before mounting one of his choosing. Then they were off, racing through the trees at speeds that would have never been safe on their other horses, but these seemed to know the trees and paths intimately. They rode through the night never looking back and never stopping. The screams and shouts of the city still echoed in their minds, driving them forward.

By morning, they were exhausted as were their mounts. They slowed to a walk and finally stopped by a river's edge. They were out of the forest and Kale knew they were not far from his family's estates. He also knew they couldn't go there. If the demons were following them, then they would only bring death to whatever town or city they passed through. From now on they would need to stay off the roads and avoid populated areas. With any luck they would lose the demons and find the dwarves quickly.

Kale dismounted and walked over to the edge of the river to join Laurel as she sat by the banks. Their horses drank their fill and then walked a few steps away to graze on the nearby grass. Kale took his pack off his shoulders and sank to the ground next to her. Laurel looked into his tired eyes as he looked back into her frightened and exhausted ones.

"Kale, how are we going to get through this? We have demons chasing us now and death squads hunting us. Where do we go that won't endanger everyone else?" Kale could see the pain in her eyes. He shared her worries and her fears, but how could he reassure her, when he had so many doubts himself.

"Laurel, I don't know. I do know we have to travel to the dwarves in the mountains east of here. They supposedly live in a stronghold deep within the mountains. They have the weapon we need to destroy the demon. After that, we'll find a way to drag out that monster and we'll kill him. With the demon dead the armies will be able to invade the capital and take down the King." It sounded crazy, even to Kale's ears. Laurel stared sleepily back at him and tried to smile weakly. Kale closed his eyes briefly and then pulled her close to him.

With the sun still rising, Laurel laid her head on Kale's shoulder enjoying the warmth of his body and the sound of his heart beating. Kale tried to keep his eyes open, but the exertions of the past night after a full day of training had taken their toll. Exhaustion swept over them, wrapping them in a cocoon of deep, dreamless sleep.

Kale was woken by the sharp point of a boot in his side. With a jolt, he realized Laurel wasn't in his arms anymore. Springing to his feet, he quickly glanced around, assessing their situation. The desperate flight of the previous night rushed back into his mind as he tried to grasp their current dilemma. They were surrounded by five men in worn, damaged armor. One of the larger ones had Laurel held against his chest by her throat. Terror and rage warred in her eyes as she met his glance. The men had their swords out and were laughing dangerously.

"Let her go!" Kale growled the words out, his wrath storming inside. A dozen different spells were swarming his mind. He needed one he could say quickly before he was skewered by one of their swords.

Kale could feel his body go cold as they laughed even louder and the one who appeared to be the leader tightened his grip on Laurel's throat. Kale's hands went into fists as the leader licked the side of her face, while his other hand grabbed her breast and squeezed hard enough to make Laurel wince in pain. Kale could feel his rage building inside and with it the power he would need for the spell. As the men began closing in, Kale gathered his energy and focused his mind.

"Domin entracta lucidea!" Kale felt the energy burst from his body as it surged toward the men surrounding him. In moments, they were writhing on the ground screaming in agony. Kale then directed his attention towards the man holding Laurel. Kale narrowed his eyes at him and repeated the spell. The man released Laurel as he crumpled to the ground in torment. Kale continued focusing on the men and their suffering as Laurel ran towards him.

"Kale, stop! What are you doing? You're killing them! Please, stop!" He could feel Laurel pulling on his arm trying to break his concentration. Kale glared at the men and closed his eyes one last time. With a final surge of power, he ended it.

"Extractain!" As soon as the words left his mouth, the five men stilled. Laurel ran to the nearest man and knelt beside him.

"Kale, what have you done?" Kale met her pained expression with coldness in his eyes. Laurel couldn't believe what she saw in his face… he was a complete stranger, dangerous and cold.

"I did what I had to. They would be able to identify us to the death squads. It's them or us." Laurel felt a chill shudder through her body as Kale delivered his judgment in an icy tone.

"We don't have to become like them! Kale, we can't let ourselves become like them! You didn't just kill them… you made their deaths agonizing." Laurel choked on her last words as she looked into Kale's eyes pleadingly.

Finally, Kale looked into Laurel's eyes as the coldness melted from his demeanor. He took her hands in his as concern swept across his face.

"Laurel…" Laurel watched as he closed his eyes and sighed deeply. "Alright… I may have let my anger get the better of me. I'll try to keep things under better control… but I won't let anyone hurt you." Kale paused and glanced around the clearing. "Come on, we should get moving. We have a long way to go before we reach the dwarves, and I doubt we've seen the last of the demons."

Kale grabbed their belongings and quickly mounted his horse. Laurel quickly followed and soon they were crossing the river and hurrying on their way further northeast. By mid-afternoon they arrived at the second river on their journey and found a safe place to cross. After crossing, they turned their horses and began heading east along the foothills of the northern mountain range. Forests and hills covered the landscape as they carefully made their way just out of sight of the road. Their heads were on swivels, trying to look everywhere at once as they crossed the unfamiliar landscape.

Every sound heard from the darkening forests made them jump in their saddles and urge their mounts into a faster pace. As the sun began to set, Kale brought a halt to their journey for the day. A small clearing in one of the valleys looked like a reasonable place to set up camp for the night. So far, they hadn't run into any more problems as they made their way further east, but Kale doubted their luck would last much longer. It was almost as if their flight were going too perfectly.

As they dismounted, an eerie howl echoed in the distance. The surrounding forest froze in silence as the first howl was answered by several others. Laurel looked at Kale questioningly. He held his finger to his mouth as he listened for more sounds. The howl repeated, sending a shiver of terror down their spines. This time the responding howls were closer. Kale quickly mounted his horse, as it launched into a flight of terror. Turning briefly in his saddle he saw Laurel silently riding on his heels.

The bone-chilling howls intensified in frequency and horror as the pursuit went on. Instinct told Kale they weren't the howls of a wolf pack… they were something sinister and deadly. On they raced through the night, breaking from the forest as they searched for an easier path. Their horses raced on heedless of what lay ahead, Kale and Laurel giving them their heads.

Screams now joined the howls as their pursuers broke from the woods and saw their prey ahead of them. Kale risked a quick glance behind, but in the growing darkness all he could see were the heat signatures of the dark, monstrous creatures that pursued them. He needed to do something, but what would stop so many creatures? He knew there were spells he could call on, if only he could remember any of them at that moment. The demons were steadily gaining on them, their howls and screams becoming relentless as they closed in on their prey.

Without warning, Laurel spun her mount around and pulled her holy symbol from under her shirt. Holding it aloft, she cried out to her goddess beseeching her aide.

"Gaia, aid us in our time of need! Cast these demons back into the dark abyss from whence they came!" A thunderclap echoed through the mountains as time seemed to stand still. Kale watched in horror as the demons swarmed towards Laurel, reaching for her with their sharp claws.

Just as the demons were about to tear into her, a bright glow ignited the night emanating from Laurel's amulet and spreading across her body. For a brief moment the darkness was banished, forcing Kale to shade his face with his arm. As the light faded, it became clear the demons were gone. Kale bolted to Laurel's side, reaching her just as she began to slide from the saddle.

Her porcelain skin was glistening with beads of perspiration. Kale gently pulled her onto his horse. The demons were gone... for now, but Kale refused to stop... not yet. He urged his horse onward, trusting Laurel's mount to follow in his wake. By dawn of the next day, they were in sight of the dark mountains, home of the dwarves. Exhausted, Kale urged the horses back into the woods and towards the shadowy mountains in the distance.

When he found a safe and sheltered hollow to rest in, he stopped his horse and carefully dismounted, gently taking Laurel in his arms and carrying her towards the hollow. Instead of lighting a fire, Kale pulled Laurel close to him, wrapping their blankets around them, to stay warm. With a last glance at the horses, exhaustion dragged Kale into a deep sleep.

That day, his sleep was restless and fraught with nightmares of demons and monsters stealing her from his arms. He woke suddenly as Laurel tried moving out from under his arm. Jolting awake he drew his sword pulling her tightly to his chest as he lunged out with his weapon.

"Kale! It's ok, it's just me. I just woke up and was going to get some things from our packs. It's ok… we're safe, for now." Kale looked around wildly before taking a few deep breaths as he allowed Laurel's words to sink in. He looked into her concerned eyes, relief washing over him.

"I'm sorry. You were unconscious and… I thought we were in more trouble." Kale rolled his shoulders and stretched out his sore tight muscles as he released Laurel from his grasp. She looked at him smiling as she moved to gather up their belongings and tend to the horses.

"So how much farther did we get… while I was unconscious?"

"The dark mountains are within view, northeast of where we are now. We'll have to cut through the forest and then travel over some hills before we reach them. Once we're there we'll have to wander around until we find a dwarven town or, more likely, they find us. Let's just say, I doubt we'll have a magical path to guide us to them."

"I guess we should probably get moving then… if you're ready… we can always stay here longer and let you rest more… I'll keep watch." Kale smiled at the hesitation and concern in Laurel's voice.

"No, that's fine. Let's get moving… time isn't exactly on our side, and I would really like to be closer to the mountains and further from the road by nightfall." When Laurel didn't move right away, Kale sighed and walked over to her taking her hands in his. "Laurel, I'm fine. When I went through military training, I had to adjust to much less sleep than this. I'll be fine. Honestly, the most energizing thing right now is seeing you awake and doing well." Gently, he leaned down and kissed her silky lips before grabbing his pack and mounting his horse. Laurel quickly mounted her horse and they resumed their journey towards the mountains.

By nightfall, they had found the northern edge of the forest and the beginning of the foothills that would eventually lead them to their destination. They made a quick makeshift camp and small fire to warm their dinner before settling down for the night. It wasn't long before they were both sound asleep and dreaming of different times and places.

Kale wasn't sure how long he had been asleep when he was woken by the sense of danger approaching. Cautiously he glanced around the surrounding forest. Nothing made a sound, nothing was moving. Slowly, he extended his arm towards Laurel and gently squeezed her hand to wake her. She silently returned his squeeze letting him know she was awake and alert.

Extending his night vision, Kale searched the looming forest, discerning the heat signatures of five large individuals. Quietly, he motioned for Laurel to move as stealthily as possible out of the clearing. Silently he watched her heat signature slip across the forest floor and into the sheltering trees. Kale reached for his sword slowly as he cautiously moved towards the nearest tree. Silence was not his strong suit, and it wasn't long before a snapped twig brought their attackers storming into their campsite. Kale had only a moment to raise his sword in defense before the first attacker's sword was driving down on him, clanging against his own.

Kale fought, his back against the tree, like a man possessed. He knew it wouldn't be long before he would be overwhelmed. He could already feel his strength ebbing as two of the death knights boxed him in. Where were the other three? In the distance he could hear Laurel cry out as the clanging of metal against metal echoed through the forest and nearby hillsides. Her cries fueled his fighting. He wouldn't lose her... not like this. He wracked his mind for useful spells, but he couldn't focus his thoughts. One of their blades slipped through his defenses, slicing into his side. Burning pain lanced through his side, but his blade never faltered. He managed two cuts of his own, before another hole in his defenses allowed one of them to slice into his right thigh.

As the battle wore on, Kale could feel his life bleeding away along with his strength. Where was Laurel? What were they doing to her? He could still occasionally hear her screams in the darkness as she fought against her attackers. Everything began going dark and Kale felt a blade pierce his left shoulder as the other thrust into his right hip. Kale fell to his knees, knowing his end was near…

Chapter 17

Kale stared hopelessly at the ground waiting for the end to come. He had failed… failed in protecting Laurel and in saving his homeland. In the distance he could hear thunder rumbling. He felt so cold. Perhaps they were going to leave him here to die… alone. He felt four rough hands grab his arms and maneuver him onto his back. Kale squinted, trying to see the faces of the men hovering over him. They seemed stockier than he remembered. They were talking gruffly amongst themselves, but Kale couldn't understand them. He knew the sun should be rising soon, but everything was growing darker.

Laurel's face came into view, hovering just inches from him. She was trying to tell him something, but he couldn't make out what she was saying. He felt her hands press down on his chest as her eyes closed. Warmth radiated through his body starting from the point of their contact. He was so tired and the warmth was so comforting. Kale could feel every muscle in his body relax as darkness enveloped him.

The dwarves had swarmed over the rise of the surrounding hills and descended upon Laurel, Kale and the death knights like a pack of ravenous wolves. Laurel had been so relieved to see them, and even more relieved when they destroyed the death knights without question. Quickly, she had scanned the area looking for any sign of Kale.

When she saw him slumped on the ground near a tree she had rushed to his side, hoping he was still alive. Two of the larger dwarves had carefully grabbed a hold of him and were lowering him to the ground. As she approached, they moved aside so she could kneel next to him.

Laurel could feel unshed tears burning behind her eyes, but she couldn't allow herself to yield to grief. Carefully she studied Kale's body, finding all his injuries as she checked his breathing and heartbeat. Dear Goddess, please let her still be in time to save him. She immediately began her prayers, willing the energies and power of Gaia to channel through her and into Kale. Slowly, she could feel his breathing strengthen and his heartbeat grow stronger. Sitting back on her heels, she studied his sleeping form. He had lost a lot of blood, but he would live.

While she had been healing Kale, the dwarves had made a litter to carry Kale's body on. Laurel watched in amazement as they made short work of cleaning up the camp site, disposing of the bodies and readying Kale for transport. Silently, the dwarves helped Laurel stand and then proceeded to head off in the direction of the mountains. It was a long hike through hilly terrain, made even more arduous because they had to drag Kale on the litter and lead the horses.

Laurel had tried to engage some of the dwarves in conversation a couple of times, but each time they would motion for her to be silent. By mid-afternoon they began their climb into the mountains. Laurel had been worried about the horses, but there had been no need. The dwarves had chosen a hidden path with few obstacles and sure footing. As evening began to fall across the mountains, the lead dwarf called a halt to the traveling party. He silently moved over to an alcove in the side of the mountain and disappeared into the shadows. Laurel couldn't see what he had done, but within moments a part of the rock face slid away to reveal a grand hallway leading into the mountain.

The dwarves led Laurel deep within the heart of the mountain. The hallway opened into one grand hall after another. She couldn't stop herself from gazing around the cavernous rooms carved out of the very rock of the mountain. The carvings were beautiful, intricate and, at times, almost life-like. Rich tapestries and masterly designed weaponry graced the stone walls. Large chandeliers hung from the towering ceilings, casting a warm glow over everything. Laurel could hardly breathe from the beauty of it all.

She was so entranced by the sights greeting her that she was unaware of being suddenly alone in a gracious side chamber. A fire was blazing in the hearth beckoning Laurel to sit in one of the large comfortable chairs facing it. A bowl of stew and warm bread sat on a table next to one of the chairs, along with a mug of ale. Laurel gratefully sank into the enveloping chair and began devouring the stew and bread. She hadn't realized how hungry she was until the smell of the stew assailed her nose.

Within moments her meal was consumed, and she sank back into the chair with a contented sigh. She must have dozed off, because when she opened her eyes a stout, burly dwarven man sat in the chair across from her, smoking a pipe. Laurel quickly sat up straighter and tried to look more confident and calmer than she felt.

"Relax princess, you are safe within these walls. I am Aldric, leader of the dwarven people." His gruff voice was warm and pleasant like a crackling fire. "Your friend is resting in one of the halls guest rooms. Our healers are tending to him, although it looks like you managed to heal most of his most grievous injuries."

He paused to take a gulp from a tankard that sat on the table next to him. Then with a satisfied smile and crack of his neck he settled back into his chair and resumed puffing on his pipe. Laurel didn't know if she was meant to say something now or not. Thankfully, the dwarf resumed speaking after a second gulp of the dark thick liquid in the tankard.

"I don't suppose you would like a tankard yourself… some dwarven spirits?" He motioned to his tankard and then chuckled at the look of uncertainty on Laurel's face. "That's alright lass, our spirits are a bit of an acquired taste. They're also a bit stronger than that light elven wine you've probably been getting. I'd have to say the two of you are a might bit lucky the elves found the time to send a messenger bird warning of your arrival and the trouble following you. If it hadn't been for that, you both might have ended up disappearing into the night or worse." Aldric took another gulp of his drink before continuing.

"According to some of the resistance's spies the King has it in his head to take you as his bride. Seems you're worth more to him alive than dead. Can't say the same for your friend. The price on his head is rather high." Laurel stared at the fire crackling in the fireplace, dread creeping into her heart.

"Now don't you be worrying about it. I know what you've come for…. You're looking for the sword, Demons Bane. Unfortunately, it's not something I can just give you. That sword has a mind of its own and will only accept a certain master. When your friend is feeling better, the two of you can run the trial, and see if you are worthy of the sword. If you are… we'll help you get to the wizards' conclave. From there you will discover how to achieve the next part of your quest. For now, rest and recover from your ordeals. Soon your friend will awaken and then we'll discuss the trials you must overcome."

"Thank you… for coming to our aide and for your assistance now." The dwarf smiled reassuringly as he stood and walked towards the door.

"Don't thank me yet princess. You may wish you had never come here by the time all is done." He opened the door and called into the hallway for someone called Rhinn, before turning and beckoning her forward. Laurel could hear someone rapidly running towards the door. They spoke quietly and then he turned once more towards Laurel. "This is Rhinn, my daughter. She will show you to a room where you can rest and clean up. If there is anything you need, just let her know. Now there are matters I must attend to, good day highness." With a bow the dwarf stepped out of the door and disappeared down one of the many long corridors leading off the main hall.

Laurel smiled at Rhinn and was happy to see the young girl smile back. Rhinn couldn't have been more than thirteen years old, but then again dwarves aged differently than humans. Laurel had to remind herself that Rhinn could be much older than she appeared. Still, she was only just growing the beginnings of her beard, a pretty strawberry-blonde, by what Laurel could see. Her father's beard had been a deep vivid red, full and long. Rhinn's green eyes were bright and lively as if she were always up to mischief and fun. Laurel couldn't help wondering what would happen to this girl if they failed in their mission. She smiled once more at Rhinn, trying to force dark images from her mind.

"Well, Rhinn, I'm placing myself in your hands. Which way do we go?" Laurel smiled at the childish giggle that spilled out of Rhinn.

"You sound so dramatic. Are all elves like you? I've never met an elf before. Father says they are silly, flighty creatures who prefer magic and gossip to honest work with their hands…. Oh, I'm sorry, I shouldn't have said that. Your rooms are down this hallway." Rhinn quickly began walking down one of the corridors silently with her head bowed. Laurel smiled at her honesty and impetuous nature. After several twists and turns, Rhinn finally came to a stop before a set of double doors. With a strong, grunting push, she managed to open the doors and show Laurel inside.

Laurel gasped at the grandeur of the room before her. A large four poster bed sat against one wall with a waterfall, surrounded by lush greenery, cascading down into a pool of clear water sitting adjacent to it. On a third wall was a large fireplace already lit and cheerfully blazing and crackling away. Bright tapestries hung from every other part of the walls and a chandelier of glowing crystals hung from the center of the room, casting a warm, cheerful glow throughout the room. Thick, plush carpets covered the floor around the bed and piles of pillows were heaped in front of the fireplace for sitting and lounging. It was a room fit for royalty, not the daughter of a baker... then again, she was now considered royalty. Laurel was brought back to herself by the sound of Rhinn's uncertain voice.

"Princess... princess Laurel... is the room to your liking? If not... I might be able to find something else that may please you more." Laurel turned and looked at Rhinn's nervous and uncertain face.

"Oh... Rhinn, this room is beautiful... it's a room fit for royalty, not the daughter of a simple baker. I'm not sure I deserve a room like this. After all, I haven't done anything yet to earn such respect and honor." Laurel smiled at the gleeful giggles and excitement that exploded from Rhinn.

"I told father you wouldn't be like a normal elf. He didn't believe me. He thought you would scoff at the room and consider it inadequate, but he was wrong. He owes me an ale and new ribbons for my hair and beard." Laurel couldn't help laughing as Rhinn danced around the room in triumph. Then she suddenly stopped and looked at Laurel with a look of much more wisdom and intelligence than she had shown yet. "Your past will serve you well when you are queen. I know everyone expects so much of you and the young man with you, but you will succeed, because your heart is true. Trust in yourself and in each other.... I have to go now. I'll bring you dinner when it is ready, and I'll let you know how Kale is doing. For now, you can bathe in the pool and rest. There are clothes for you in the wardrobe through those doors. I'll see you soon."

After the doors closed, Laurel took Rhinn's advice. The pool of clear water was warm and soothing and the clothes in the wardrobe, while a little big for her, were soft, clean and deliciously comfortable. Between the soothing bath and crackling fire, Laurel sunk into the soft bed and drifted quickly to sleep.

She was woken several hours later by a hand gently brushing some strands of hair from her face. With a stretch and yawn Laurel opened her eyes expecting to see Rhinn. She jumped back with a start of surprise when the person looking at her was not Rhinn, in fact it was a man she had never seen before. His icy, blue eyes looked at her from a stone chiseled face. He smiled coldly, before touching her face with icy hands that were too soft to have ever done an ounce of work in their lives.

"Hello, my beautiful princess. I wondered what you looked like, and now that I've seen you...." He smiled cruelly at her. "Let us end this foolish game of cat and mouse, shall we. Come to me in the capital and I will let your friends live. I would hate to destroy two entire races of people, but I will have what I desire. Come to me, become my wife and queen, and I will allow the elves and dwarves to continue their miserable existences. Refuse me and I will bring all my power down upon them, wiping them out completely." Laurel shivered as he took her hand in his. Her mind was spinning wildly as she tried to process what was happening. She had to buy them time, but how?

"I need time. I can't decide something like this so quickly. I'm just a baker's daughter, nothing more. I don't understand any of this. Please..." She hoped letting her own fear and desperation slip into her voice would convince him to allow her some time. From the tilt of his head and slight shifting of his eyes, Laurel thought he was considering. When he smiled at her again, she felt her heart nearly leap from her chest.

"Why did you go to the dwarves?"

"I don't know... this is where they sent me, I don't know why." He stared at her in silence for what seemed like eternity.

"You have been thrown into such chaos, haven't you? You don't even realize your own importance or who you are. Well, let me explain...

Many years ago, there was a prophecy about you. Now many, mainly the elves and dwarves, have used this information to create a revolution to remove me from the throne. Because of this I have had to take many drastic measures to protect our beloved land. Don't let them fool you, Laurel. All they desire is power and to control you. They even went so far as to send an abominable, demonic creature to destroy villages and attack our poor law-abiding citizens. My only recourse has been to institute death squads and send out as many soldiers as I can to fight off such monstrosities."

He paused and moved to sit on her bed next to her, pulling her into his arms. Laurel didn't dare pull away. Any attempt to fight him, would undo whatever tiny illusion she had managed to create. She had to continue to look helpless and confused, in need of comfort and protection.

"I have spent years looking for you. I knew your father. He was a good man and not just a baker. He was a descendent of the original royal line that had ruled in this country. They had stepped down, because they believed a ruler should not be able to use magic and their descendants had begun to develop magical abilities. Your father was one of them. He hid the magic from you in hopes you would not develop such abilities. We had spoken many times about you and what would happen when you were grown. He wanted to wait until you were of age to send you to the capital. After the village was attacked, I sent three regiments to Soldar to check for survivors and dispatch any creatures they might find. The general who led them found you, hidden in a room under the house terrified beyond reason. Unfortunately, he betrayed me and hid you away somewhere, but I never gave up hope of finding you. Now that I have, it is time for you to join me in the capital and take your rightful place at my side." He paused, lifting her face to look into his eyes, now filled with compassion and lust. "I will send a regiment to Kerrington. It will take them two weeks to get there. I will also have my most trusted squad camp at the foot of the mountains on the eastern edge. Come to the eastern edge and my men will escort you to Kerrington. From there, the regiment will bring you home, where your father wanted you to be. Do you think you can get to the mountain's eastern edge?"

"I think so, but it will take some time to convince them to let me walk around freely."

The King nodded his head slowly as if knowing that would be the answer she would give. Then he smiled once more.

"I will visit you again in five nights. If you are unable to get away from them, let me know and I will send my squad and regiment into the mountains to free you. Trust me my dear, we must not let those vile and treacherous creatures manipulate us into destroying our land. In five nights time I will see you again. For now, good night my sweet." With those words he pulled Laurel to him and kissed her passionately, his hands sliding over her body which was now naked and vulnerable to his touches. She couldn't pull away, she couldn't escape. She could only pray to wake up before anything more happened.

Chapter 18

Laurel woke screaming, sweat running down the sides of her face. Three armed dwarven guards rushed into her room, axes raised. A crash echoed from the hallway and Rhinn came running in wielding a short blade in each hand. Laurel could only stare as the dwarves rushed around her room looking for an intruder that didn't exist. It had been a dream, but a very real one. After a few moments, Rhinn dismissed the guards and came over to sit on the bed near Laurel, who was still shaking uncontrollably from her nightmare. Gently she laid a hand over Laurel's arm.

"Laurel, what happened? Are you all right?" The concern in her face touched Laurel deeply, but she still couldn't bring herself to speak. All she could do was shake her head and cry, hopelessly.

As they sat there, Rhinn smoothing her hair and trying to calm her down, the door to her room opened and a servant brought in a new tray of food and drink. Following closely behind her, was Aldric, a look of deep concern on his stern but warm face. He looked at Rhinn and then at Laurel, sighing deeply.

"Rhinn, leave us." Rhinn glared at her father stubbornly

"But father…"

"Rhinn… I need to speak with Laurel alone. Go check on Kale and his recovery. I think we will need him awake and ready sooner than anyone would like." Rhinn looked back and forth between her father and Laurel, concern, curiosity, and frustration warring on her face. Finally, she sighed deeply and bowed to her father before leaving to tend to the duty he had assigned her.

Once she was gone, Aldric handed Laurel a robe and beckoned her over to a couple of chairs Laurel hadn't noticed were sitting in the one corner. Pulling them out, Aldric waited for Laurel to sit in one of the chairs before he grabbed two glasses and filled them both with drink. Then he took the other chair, handing her one of the glasses and taking a large gulp of his before he began speaking.

"Tell me what has happened. While it may seem insignificant to you, with current happenings everything must be examined."

Laurel took a sip of the thick warm liquid from the glass in her hands. The drink warmed her throughout and seemed to revitalize her a bit. After a moment's pause, she nodded to Aldric and began telling him all about the nightmare that had frightened her so badly. She told him everything she could remember about the words spoken, how the King appeared, what he had done. When she approached what had happened to wake her so violently Laurel had to pause and take a long drink from her glass before she could finish. After a long pause she finished her retelling and sat in silence with her head down. She could feel tears of anger and humiliation burning behind her eyes as they tried to escape.

Aldric sat in silence for a long time slowly drinking from his glass and then refilling it. Finally, he took something from his pocket as he looked at her with the compassion she used to see from her father. Taking her hand in his warm, large hand, he turned hers over and placed a crystal on a chain in it.

"Wear this around your neck at night when you sleep and he will no longer be able to enter your dreams. These crystals protect us from being detected by magic. It should protect you from such invasions in the future." Aldric stood and purposefully strode to the doors of her room before turning to look at her once more. "I am sorry princess. You do not deserve the pain and torment you have had to endure and will still endure. It is a great burden we ask you to take upon yourself…. Rhinn, I know you're there. Come in and help the princess dress, and then you may take her to see her friend." He turned once more to Laurel, bowing in his formal way. "Princess, I must see to my people and army. We must prepare for war. I will come see you both when Kale has recovered enough to face the trials."

Laurel watched him go and tried to smile as Rhinn came in to keep her company and help her get herself back together. It took some time for them to go see Kale, because Rhinn wouldn't let Laurel do anything else until she had cleaned her plate and had a couple more glasses of the warm drink. Then she quickly dressed, and they journeyed through the labyrinth of hallways that made up the dwarven Kingdom until they reached Kale's room. His room was near the healers' rooms so they could tend to him as needed.

Quietly, Laurel entered his room and stepped towards his bedside. He looked so pale and weak. What if he didn't wake up? What if he couldn't recover from his injuries? What if she hadn't been fast enough in healing him? Laurel could feel tears running down her cheeks warm and salty. She didn't try to stop or hide them. She just let them flow and with them all her frustration, anger, pain and stress flowed out of her. When her tears were spent, she slipped into the bed next to him and held him close. Maybe it wouldn't help, but... then again... what if he could feel her presence? Maybe she could give him some comfort.

Laurel wasn't sure when, but at some point Rhinn had left the room, leaving her to be with Kale for one peaceful moment. She placed the crystal around her neck and then gently laid down again and held him. No one tried to move her... no one disturbed them all night. Her dreams ran a gauntlet that night, everything from beautiful and joyous to terrifying and tragic.

By morning she felt as if she hadn't slept at all, but when she looked at Kale energy filled her. His face had more color in it and his sleep seemed less tormented. Rhinn entered shortly after with a tray of food and drink for her. She didn't comment on Laurel's appearance or exhausted state. She just sat there in silence as they ate breakfast and kept vigil over Kale.

Throughout the day, healers came in and out of the room discussing his progress with her and talking about possible remedies to speed his recovery. When Laurel wasn't in consultations with the healers, she was talking with Rhinn and learning more about her life. She was a little surprised to discover that Rhinn was about the equivalent of her age. Her protected life had left her time to dream about love, parties and friends. She hadn't endured any of the torment and suffering that would have made her mature before her time. Aldric had done an excellent job of allowing his daughter to grow up in a safe and normal life.

Laurel learned of Rhinn's desire to travel the world and see new places. She also learned of her fascination with humans and their crazy manic ways. Laurel appreciated Rhinn's honesty and forthright nature. She also greatly appreciated her company as she sat vigil over Kale.

As night approached Kale's condition improved, but he still hadn't woken up. Laurel hoped he would awaken soon. Otherwise, she would need to remove the amulet and meet with the King again to try and buy them more time. She wasn't sure she could survive another night like that. His touch made her want to scream. How could she continue that charade another night? Her dreams were tainted by the many worries and fears that plagued her.

By morning her hair was damp with sweat and her muscles were sore from the tension she had been carrying. As she stretched and tried to rise from the bed, arms encircled her and pulled her back down. Laurel couldn't stop herself from tensing and trying to jump away. The arms just pulled her in closer, sure and strong. Laurel turned slowly in the embrace, fear gripping her heart, to look into the face of who held her. Kale's clear piercing eyes looked back into hers, concern flooding his features.

"Laurel… it's just me. I'm here now. It's all right. You've sat vigil long enough. It's my turn now. Just lay back and rest. I won't let anything hurt you."

"Kale…" Laurel sank into his arms tears of relief dampening his shoulder as she buried her head in his shoulder. He was better. He had woken up and now they could finish what they started. Laurel laid there letting him smooth her hair and hold her tightly to him. Occasionally, he would kiss her forehead and rub his cheek against the top of her head. Soon all the nightmares and concerns faded into distant memories as she melted into his embrace.

She wasn't sure how long they stayed that way, perhaps she had fallen asleep, because when she opened her eyes again Rhinn was entering the room with a tray of food that resembled lunch or dinner rather than breakfast. She smiled at the two of them as she set the tray down. Laurel regretfully pulled herself from Kale's arms and sat up. She noticed that Kale smiled back at Rhinn as she prepared to leave.

"Thank you Rhinn. I think we could both use some lunch. You didn't happen to bring in any more of that warm, thick, dark drink, did you?" Rhinn giggled at Kale's question before nodding her head and slipping from the room. Laurel looked at Kale sternly as they rose from the bed. Kale looked back at her, his hands raised defensively in front of him, with a shocked expression that said what did I do. Laurel just shook her head and smiled ruefully at him.

"So, I slept through breakfast, huh?" Kale's look changed quickly from playful to concern.

"You were exhausted. When you laid down next to me that first night… I could feel you… sense you. I could feel the fear and anguish you were experiencing. When you slept… I experienced your nightmares. I am so sorry, Laurel. I should have been here to protect you." Laurel looked at him with disbelief.

"Kale, you had been run through by several swords. I'm just happy you're still alive. I thought I was going to lose you. I couldn't… I just… I love you Kale, and I don't know what I would do if…" Kale quickly moved to her side and took her in his arms once more.

"It's all right, I'm here now. I love you too. It's going to be all right. We'll get through this… somehow."

They ate their meals quietly, just watching each other in the silence and smiling occasionally at each other before lowering their eyes and looking away. After they both ate and took turns bathing, they stepped out into the hallway to find Aldric. Turning a corner, they nearly ran into Rhinn quickly striding towards them.

"Good, you're both up and looking well. My father wishes to see both of you. He is in his war room planning the defense of the mountains.

Follow me." Rhinn quickly turned and moved down the hallway at a quick step for dwarves. Kale and Laurel followed quickly behind, keeping pace with little effort. It wasn't long before the three of them were standing in front of the doors leading into Aldric's war room.

"I'll let him know you are here." With a quick smile, Rhinn opened the doors and stepped inside, leaving Kale and Laurel standing in the hallway unsure of what to do next. It was only a moment before Rhinn returned and showed them into the room. Then with a nod to her father and his generals she quickly took her leave.

"Princess Laurel, Kale…come, sit over here by the fire. We have much to discuss and very little time to accomplish a great deal." Pouring three drinks, Aldric handed out the mugs and took a seat near the fire. With a stern expression he addressed the two young half-elves.

"It would appear the demon King has discovered the princess's whereabouts and is determined to have her brought to him in the safety of his capital. You need to obtain the sword, Demons Bane. We will give you as much time as possible. We should be able to defend the mountains for quite some time, but even then, his magic and demons will eventually find their way into our cities. The princess was brave enough to keep her head about her and buy us some time, but even with the extra time we will probably be able to only hold the mountains for a couple of weeks. After that my people will have to flee to the Elven lands and prepare for war. I have already sent a message to the elven council. In dark times such as these we must all forget past disagreements and unite." Aldric took a long drink from his mug before continuing.

"Kale, the sword you seek may only be obtained by the one it is meant for. This changes from age to age. I do not know if you are its master or not. Only the sword can determine that. Deep within the mountains is a complex labyrinth of tunnels. This will be your first challenge. Navigate the labyrinth correctly and you will find yourself at the second challenge. Navigate it incorrectly and… well, let's just say you won't have to worry about the King or demons anymore." Aldric paused to let this information sink in.

"Well, that sounds encouraging." Kale turned to look with concern at Laurel. "You are staying here. I'm not going to risk losing you."

"I don't think so! I'm going with you, Kale. Remember… we said we would get through this together. I'm not staying behind while you risk your life."

"But… this is going to be dangerous." Laurel could feel herself wanting to yield to the pleading look in Kale's eyes. She shook her head slowly, his concern mirrored on her face.

"When have our lives been anything but dangerous. Remember it was me who got you through the mountains around Soldar. I can handle myself." When Kale closed his eyes in submission, Laurel knew she had won this argument.

"Very well. Alright, Aldric, what else can you tell us about these tests?"

"Not very much. We are merely the gate keepers of the labyrinth. We do not know what lies beyond. I do know that you will be judged on your courage, honor and honesty. I do not know how this will happen or how many tests you will have to pass. If you succeed, you will receive the sword and shown your path. If you fail... death awaits you. Take some time to prepare yourself, but not too much. When you are ready, I will escort you down to the labyrinth's entrance."

Kale looked at Laurel for one more long moment and saw the determination in her eyes. There was no need to put this off any longer. Either they would be successful here or they would die. That seemed to be the way of their lives as of late. With a nod, Kale turned back to face Aldric.

"Show us the way, Aldric. We are ready to face this challenge." Kale smiled as Aldric's bushy eyebrows raised up a fraction with surprise, but he nodded in acknowledgment.

Soon the three of them were traveling once more down the long and twisting corridors of the Dwarven city. Kale wasn't sure how long they had been walking, but it seemed as if the day was quickly melting away as they continued their track deeper into the mountain's heart. Finally, they reached a pair of heavy metal doors sculpted and carved with images of demons battling the different races in what looked like a massive battlefield. Aldric paused and turned towards them.

"Are you both sure you are ready to proceed with this? There is still some time allotted us before it becomes dire." Kale and Laurel looked at each other, their faces mirroring their determination. Kale turned to face Aldric, looking deep into his eyes.

"No, we will not put off what must be done. It is better to move forward than wait until it becomes imminent. Open the gates, please." Aldric nodded knowingly at the two of them and then produced a key from a chain around his neck. With a sure hand he slid the key easily into the lock and silently turned it. A faint click was the only sign that anything had happened. Then the heavy gates ominously swung open. The tunnels within were lit with an eerie glow that sent shivers down Laurel's arms. For Kale, every muscle in his body tensed as a strong and overpowering urge drew him forward.

Kale nodded once to Aldric before taking Laurel's hand in his own and leading them into the labyrinthian tunnels beyond.

They walked onward for what seemed like hours to Laurel. Kale never seemed to tire. Laurel found the driven pace he was keeping exhausting and difficult to keep up with. If she stopped, however, she would become lost within the twisting and turning tunnels that surrounded them. She was left with no choice but to continue following him, even though her feet ached and her body begged for a break. They had brought no food with them. Which probably hadn't been the best of ideas, but with Kale's trance-like state, they probably wouldn't have been able to stop and eat anyway.

On they walked turning right occasionally and other times left, twisting and turning. Their path was so convoluted Laurel knew she would never be able to find her way out of the labyrinth without Kale's help. She wasn't even sure if he would be able to find their way out of here. He moved as if being guided by something or someone, blindly being drawn forward. Beads of sweat trickled down the sides of his face. The one time she was able to catch a glance at his eyes she had gasped in shock. His eyes were clouded over, no longer the vivid blue she remembered, but a frightening milky-white.

The further into the mountain they went, the harder it became to breath. Almost as if they were being cut off from the pure air of the surface. Laurel's concern only grew as she watched his breathing become ragged and gasping. What if this power guiding him was leading them to their deaths? What if they never made it past the first trial?

Suddenly, Kale slumped against the nearby wall, his breathing harsher and thinner than her own. She rushed to his side and tried to support him. Milky eyes stared back at her unseeingly. With her support they continued onward, even deeper into the mountain's heart.

After what seemed like several more hours, they finally came to a stone archway standing sentinel over another set of heavy-looking metal doors, twice their height and with more inlays of demons battling the armies of races. Strange runes were carved into the stone archway and as they approached, the runes began to glow with the same eerie light that had lit their passage so far. Kale stepped forward placing his hand on the cold stone of the archway and closing his eyes. He breathed deeply several times, a calmness coming over him. Laurel took a couple of steps back as she watched the glow of the runes descend down the archway and into Kale's hand, moving quickly up his arm and through his body.

"Venta incribus sorla entrista!" Kale's deep voice echoed through the tunnels reverberating off the rock and making Laurel shiver from the wave of power that flooded the passageway.

Silently, the metal doors swung open, inviting them to enter the inky darkness beyond. Kale calmly reached his hand back towards Laurel, never once turning to see where she was. Hesitantly, Laurel accepted his hand and stepped forward to join him at the foreboding entrance. Kale turned smiling at her in his typical mischievous way. His eyes were once again the piercing blue she had come to trust and love. With a tension releasing sigh, Laurel smiled back at him reassuringly. With a squeeze of her hand Kale stepped forward into the darkness pulling her after him.

The darkness was absolute. If Laurel hadn't been holding Kale's hand, she would have thought their existence had ended. Even her heat vision, normal to those of elven blood, was useless in this choking darkness. She could feel Kale pulling her gently onward, deeper into the unending abyss. Finally, he stopped and pulled her closer to him.

She felt his mouth near her ear, moving as if he was trying to say something, but no sound issued forth. When she tried to respond… no sound emanated from her. How was that possible… magic? Laurel gripped Kale's hand tighter and felt him pull her more tightly into him. She could tell by the movement of his body and the deep breaths he was taking that he was trying to shout, but still she could hear nothing. Was this the next test? What would they have to face in this seeming death?

When the doors opened, Kale was amazed by the brilliant light that greeted him. He could feel the warmth and power that beckoned him onward. It called to him like a welcoming old friend. He reached back taking Laurel's hand in his before stepping through into the radiance beyond. It was only once after they had walked into the room that Kale realized Laurel had a death grip on his hand. When he turned to look at her, he could see fear and worry in her eyes as they quickly darted around the room. It was almost as if she couldn't see anything. Kale squeezed her hand in reassurance and pulled her closer to him. By the look on her face, she really couldn't see him.

Kale quickly led them further into the room until they stood in the center. He glanced around and at the countless perfect crystals that lined the walls and ceiling. Each one reflected their image back at him a thousand times, like hundreds of mirrors, and in each one Laurel's eyes were blacked out. He looked quickly back at her, but could see no difference in their appearance, yet each reflection showed them black and empty.

"What sort of trickery is this? I thought I was here to be tested, not played with!" He could feel anger building in him, and he could also feel fear building in Laurel. Gently he pulled her towards him and wrapped his arms around her. Gently he whispered into her ears to comfort her, but she only shook her head.

"Kale, I can't hear… you. Oh my Goddess, I can't hear anything." Kale pulled her into a tighter embrace as her breathing quickened and fear began to grip her. His anger quickly became overwhelming. Laurel had been through enough. This was cruel and unacceptable.

"Release her from this! Your test is for me, not her! She doesn't deserve this… she has been through enough in her life!" Kale breathed deeply trying to control his temper.

"Are you sure you want her to see what will be shown? It may change how she feels towards you. You could lose her once she sees what you will be shown. She is blinded to protect her and you from the secrets you keep. The choice is yours… of course." The voice emanated from nowhere and everywhere all at once. It was the sound of crystals clinking into each other and dozens of voices in one. It made him second guess his thoughts and turned his blood to ice. He looked down at Laurel shivering in his arms, and his mind was made up.

"Release her from this magic! I hold no secrets from her, and I will not allow her to endure this torment to protect myself!"

"Very well, we shall release her. Remember war wizard, this was your choice." The sound of glass fracturing echoed throughout the cavern and then Kale heard Laurel gasp in wonderment. He looked into her face and saw the awe with which she surveyed the room.

"Can you hear me now?" Kale smiled as she nodded and then leaned into his chest.

"What happened? Where did this all come from?" Kale breathed deeply and then looked down into her questioning eyes.

"There was a spell put on you by my testers. It would seem they didn't want you to see what would happen, but I talked them into letting you see and hear what was happening. Feel better now?"

"Yes, most definitely. Kale what will happen now?" Kale glanced around the room uncertainly before answering.

"I don't know, but I'm guessing that we're going to be shown things about me. Perhaps some things I'm not too proud of." Laurel took his hands in hers and looked compassionately into his eyes.

"Whatever they show us... we'll get through it together. I love you and that will never change." Kale smiled warmly at her words. He only hoped what she said was true.

"We shall see if your love is so strong. The two of you have come here to obtain Demons Bane. You, Kaleford Kingsford, have come here to prove you are worthy of Demons Bane. We shall see. Do not try to fight what is about to happen. Do not try to hide your soul from us, for we see all. Are you prepared to be judged?"

"I am. See what you will." Kale motioned for Laurel to step back. With uncertainty painted on her face, she took three steps back and away from him.

"Very good. Then step forward into the circle on the floor." Kale did as the voice commanded and waited for his judgment to commence.

All at once the crystals around the room began flashing and glowing. Each one represented a different moment in his life. Some were moments of bravery and courage. Some were moments of compassion and comfort. Still others were moments of cowardice and cruelty. He had not always believed the way he did now. There were moments of lust and desire, moments of humility and humbleness. Moments when he had lied, tricked and betrayed those around him, and other times when he went above and beyond to be honest and truthful. The room contained every moment in his life. All the moments that test and teach a young boy and take him from childhood to manhood. It was a vivid representation of how he grew into the man he was now... but would it be enough to earn him the sword?

The entities brought forth one of the many images from the room and Kale watched in shame as it played out before him. It had been when he was at the Academy. He had gone to a local tavern with several other noble sons and they had made a game of tormenting one of the serving girls. One of them had purchased time with her and then set about yanking her blouse off and exposing her bare chest to the rest of them. They had all taken turns pinching, kissing, biting and touching her. It had been the first and last time Kale had taken part in such an activity. Afterward he had been filled with shame and disgust. Bane had been furious with him, punching him squarely in the jaw. When he had gone back to check on the girl she had cowered from him in terror. He had left feeling like the cruel monster he was.

The next image his tester had pulled forward was from a year later. He had been sitting in a tavern with Bane when a group of cadets came in and began tormenting another young serving girl. She couldn't have been more than fifteen years of age. Kale had made a deal with the owner who quickly pulled the girl away from the others and brought her over to him. She obligingly sat on his lap, although Kale could feel her fear. Bane had glared at him sternly but said nothing. After a time, he had taken the girl upstairs to one of the taverns rooms.

At this point Kale heard a shuddering gasp emanate from Laurel. He didn't dare turn to face her. He had done what he had to. The scene continued to play out. Once he had the girl in the room, she began undressing. Kale gently put his hand on her to stop her actions. He pulled off his boots and just laid down on the bed motioning for her to join him. She did and they laid there, fully clothed for the rest of the evening. He had told her to keep their secret. She had agreed and that was the end of it.

The next scene was a time when a death squad had come to the town near the Academy. He had stood by and watched as they pulled everyone outside and began testing the locals for magic. Each time the crystal glowed they would grab the victim roughly, tying and gagging him or her. Sometimes it was an adult, but most times they were much younger. Kale had stood and watched in horror, not daring to act. He had been terrified. It had only been his first year at the Academy. What could one young boy do against people that powerful? He had chosen to stay quiet.

The next scene was his last year at the Academy. A death squad had come to the town again and had pulled everyone out, as usual, but this year… only one was found with magic, a baby. The soldiers had laughed as they dragged the screaming infant from its mother's arms. The lead soldier had put the baby in a sack and walked off out of town towards the forest. Kale had waited until the others were distracted and then followed the soldier into the woods outside of town. He took the babe to the river's edge and prepared to dunk it into the icy spring river. Kale acted without thinking. In moments he had crept up behind the soldier and ran him through with his sword. Carefully he had picked up the child and turned to go. He had been stopped however by several men who appeared from the trees. After a rather quick discussion he had given the baby to them and described the mother to them. They had agreed to rescue the mother as soon as they could and get them both to safety. That had been Kale's first and only experience with the resistance, and now it appeared as if he might end up leading it.

Hours seemed to bleed into each other as scenes from his life played out evoking every emotion he had ever experienced in his life. Lies told to protect himself and, later, lies told to protect others. Punishments he had allowed Bane to take in his place and later punishments he had taken in Bane's and others' places. Women he had saved from abuse or rape. Women he had loved and been with. The scenes showed friends and enemies he had made, the enemies outnumbering the friends. Every detail of his life etched out perfectly in the presentation from the crystals.

Finally, the scenes of his life stopped, the crystals going blank. Kale felt exhausted and emotionally spent. How would they judge him? Would he be allowed to wield Demons Bane? Kale took a deep breath and slowly turned to look at Laurel standing silently behind him. Her eyes were glistening with unshed tears. Her hands were clasped over her heart as she stared at him with compassion and love. How could she still love him after what she had seen? How could she still love him after seeing how many times he had failed to do the right thing?

"Oh Kale… I didn't know… I didn't…" She ran into his arms holding him tightly. Her warmth and touch were more reassuring and strengthening than any words or magic could ever be. She was his world now. He would die a thousand deaths to keep her safe.

"Kaleford Kingsford, you have been judged. You are a man of imperfections, passions, rage and love. You have proven your courage, strength and heart. You are judged... worthy of Demons Bane. Step forward and claim that which is yours." Several steps in front of Kale a column of blue fire rose from the floor and stretched upward to the ceiling. Kale nodded to Laurel and then walked towards the column of blue flame. "Kaleford reach into the fire and pull forth the weapon you seek."

Kale reached into the fire prepared for searing pain, but none came. His hand reached down into the flame until he felt his hand encounter something solid. Carefully he grasped a firm hold on the hilt and pulled forth the sword, Demons Bane, from the fire. Holding it aloft, he examined the blade in awe and wonderment. The hilt and blade were a shimmering black, like obsidian, with veins of deep blue shooting through it. The pommel was a smooth round sphere glowing with the fires of Hell. The hilt was wrapped in leather braiding crisscrossing back and forth, creating a solid grip and the cross guard ended with two smaller orbs matching the pommel. A blue light seemed to emanate from the blade as if its power could not be contained.

He could feel the power of the sword pulsing through him. The light in the room seemed to dim, as if the sword were trying to suck all the light into itself. The sword made him feel strong and indestructible. There was nothing he couldn't

accomplish. That demon lord was as good as dead.
Nothing would stop him in his quest now. Kale
looked at Laurel, pride, confidence and
determination suffusing his features. She was
looking beyond him at the wall to his back. He
turned around to find a new archway standing
where once was a wall of crystals.

"You have gained your sword, war wizard,
now go and face your enemy. Let nothing stand in
your way of defeating the beast." Kale glanced
back at Laurel and extended his hand towards her.
She looked at him with determination and stepped
forward to take his hand. Together they walked
through the archway and into another world of fire,
darkness and evil.

Chapter 19

Kale and Laurel had been down in the labyrinth for ten days. Aldric sat in his war room staring at the map in front of him. The map displayed the entire layout of the mountains and all their exit routes, should they need them.

Yesterday, Aldric's scouts reported that the King was sending two regiments and two death squads into the mountains to rescue his bride. He rubbed his forehead wearily. He had hoped a battle now could be avoided. They would need as many of his people as possible in the coming war. A battle now would only deplete the number he could send.

Many of his subjects he would send North into Evard, the country bordering Kallihan. He would only take his soldiers, scouts, weapon smiths and engineers with him. If it wasn't for the importance of the two half-elves, Aldric would take his people out of here now, but they had to succeed... they had to. It was Aldric's job to hold the mountains until they returned. Then he would have a group of his best take Laurel and Kale North, to the wizard's conclave. Until they returned, he would just have to hold the King's forces at bay with as few casualties as possible.

He had already ordered the first group of his people to leave for the safety of Evard. Tomorrow he would send the next group. By the end of the week all his non-combatant people would be well on their way to safety. Hopefully, by then, Kale and Laurel would have returned, and the rest of his forces could slip through the King's grasp and join with the elves in Laurendale. Aldric looked up as one of his generals coughed to attract his attention.

"I'm sorry Korg. I was lost in thought." His best general and friend nodded knowingly. He knew all too well the thoughts going through Aldric's mind. "Have the engineers finished rigging the rock falls and ledge drops?"

"Yes, Lord Aldric, everything is ready. They will find the mountains are not so easy a place to enter or exit alive."

"Excellent. I know it is against our nature, but we must avoid direct confrontation as much as possible. It may not seem honorable, but in these dark times we can scarcely avoid any honor at all. As soon as Kale and Princess Laurel return, we will leave to join the rest of the united army in the elven lands. When the last dwarf is safely out, we will set off the final traps and bring the mountains down about their ears. If we can take out two of the King's regiments and two death squads we will be helping the coming war out considerably." Aldric took one last look at the men standing around the table. He had known most of them since childhood and by the time this war was over, he will have, most likely, said good-bye to most of them. With a nod, more for himself than anyone else, he put both hands on the table and stood.

"Korg, I want scouts reporting in regularly on the movements of the enemy. Also remind them to keep a wary eye out for signs of demons. I wouldn't put it past the King to use his demon allies to acquire his reluctant bride. Alright gentlemen, you have your orders. We hold until further notice."

"Aye, Lord Aldric!" Their unified voices echoed through the chamber. Then as one they turned and left the chamber. Aldric sat back down in his chair and rubbed his forehead once more. May the Gods have mercy on their souls, for the enemy most certainly would not. His only comfort was that he had sent Rhinn north with the first group. At least she would be safe.

Down a dark, side hallway, Rhinn pulled her cloak further over her head. She had exchanged her garments with one of the other girls heading North yesterday. She had spied, with some measure of guilt, her father sighing happily as he watched the first group leave the mountain. She knew she would be safer with the others in Evard, but she hadn't been practicing with sword and ax for the majority of her life, to run and hide at the first sign of battle. She had also been practicing with the scouts for the last three years, learning their tricks and strategies. Now she would put all her training and skills to use, helping her people defeat a monster. She just had to stay out of her father's sight until they were too far from the mountain for him to do anything about it. With a devious smile, Rhinn crept down the passages to spy on their enemies and find something useful to tell the others.

Kale and Laurel walked through the devastated and burning landscape. They were surrounded by black and burning spires, glowing with red embers. They had to step carefully across the rocky terrain avoiding the pools of glowing red liquid that bubbled and steamed. Kale wasn't sure what the thick red liquid was, but he knew he didn't want to touch it. It had the smell of rotten eggs and the heat rising from the pools was searing. The sky was black with ash and ominous clouds that rumbled and flashed.

Small lizard-like creatures scurried here and there across the rocks, occasionally stopping to hiss at the strange trespassers in their land. Kale held Demons Bane in front of him and at the ready. Laurel walked closely at his side not daring to stray further than a couple feet from him. The sword hummed with energy, as if it knew its enemy was waiting just ahead. Kale could feel the sword pulling them one way and then another as it searched out its prey. He let it guide them through the smoke-filled surroundings keeping his eyes on the rocky outcroppings and spires around them for any sign of demons.

In the distance a black, ominous structure rose up from the surrounding inferno. Kale could feel the sword pulling them towards that structure. As they came around a high pile of rock and bones, they were attacked by three demons. Kale felt the sword flare to life as his mind and the swords desires became one. He moved with a grace and swiftness he had never possessed before. Demons Bane was an extension of himself and he was an extension of it. They had become one and the same. As he sliced through one demon after another, the sword's power grew. It was as if the blood of the demons and their life force fed and fueled the sword.

The battle was done in moments. Kale could feel his body being flooded with energy and strength. He searched the horizon for more demons to destroy and fuel the sword and himself more. The power was delicious and intoxicating. He could feel the smile that spread across his face as he searched for another victim. He hungered for another kill, and then... he saw Laurel, a look of horror on her face. Confusion flooded his mind. Why was she looking at him like that? He had just saved them from three demons! She should be congratulating him and thanking him for saving them... shouldn't she? He looked down at the sword and saw his reflection in its black surface.

The sword dropped from his hands as a shudder ran through his body. The face that had stared back at him was crazed and wild, hungry for power and death. Kale fell to his knees as his recent feelings came rushing back to him. Then he felt Laurels arms around him, holding him close.

"Kale... Kale... please tell me you're all right. Please say something." Shame and self-loathing filled him as he listened to Laurel's desperate and sobbing voice. He could still feel the energy and draw of the sword, but now he saw the precipice he was so close to falling over. Was that the price he would have to pay? Would he become a monster to destroy a monster? Would he have to lose himself completely to the sword? Slowly, he met Laurel's pleading eyes and returned her embrace.

"I'm better now. I'm not sure what happened. It was like I was losing myself and becoming part of the sword. I can't explain it any better than that. It was addicting… all I wanted was more… more power… more blood. When I saw you… when I saw my reflection… Laurel, what's happening to me?" Laurel took his hands in hers as she stayed kneeled beside him.

"I don't know… but that sword is evil, Kale. You should get rid of it. We'll find another way. There has to be another way. I won't lose you to… that thing. We'll face the demon another way." Her eyes pleaded with him, but he knew there was no choice. If she were going to survive this then he would have to use the sword.

"Laurel, if we don't use the sword, we could both die. I'm not willing to risk that…. I'm not willing to risk you. I know what I'm dealing with now… better than I did at least. I'll be better prepared for it. We need to go forward. If we don't do this now, we may never get another chance. If we don't destroy the demon lord then everything will have been for nothing. I love you, but we need to take the chance and opportunity given to us." Kale looked at her, willing her to understand and accept his decision. Laurel slowly and regretfully nodded her head before standing and helping him up.

Kale reached for Demons Bane tentatively. He hesitated only for a moment before grasping the hilt in his hand and raising it once more at the ready. Immediately he felt the power and pull of the sword flood his mind and body. With one more glance at Laurel he turned and focused his attention toward the demon lord he could now feel, awaiting him in the looming fortress.

Their progress seemed quicker now as they came closer and closer to the black, towering fortress ahead of them. The nearer they approached the more powerful the pull of the sword became. Kale tried to focus his thoughts on Laurel and how he felt about her. He tried to focus his thoughts on their love and how he wanted to take her as his wife. He focused on the life he wished he could have with her and knew he probably wouldn't.

Soon they were standing at the gates of the fortress. Nothing stirred outside of the towering walls and spires. From beyond the gates, they could hear the sound of tormented screams and demented laughter. Kale touched the tip of the sword to the gates and watched as they exploded inward with a thunderous boom. Cautiously, they proceeded to enter the dark fortress prepared for battle. The sword pulled him ever onward toward the object of its desire.

Kale heard Laurel gasp and followed her gaze upward, toward a cage suspended over a throne made from the countless bones of the dead. Inside the cage were dozens of humans, trapped and terrified. Kale's eyes traced the path of the chain, holding the cage aloft, until he found where the other end was. He motioned for Laurel to look over by the wall to the right. The chain was attached to a wheel and crank system sitting on the floor.

After a quick glance at Kale, Laurel rushed to the wheel and crank and began lowering the cage slowly towards the floor. Just as the cage touched the stone floor a cruel and cold laugh broke through the silence.

"Aaah, little half-elves, did you think I would let you come into my domain and take my little toys. They are so fun to play with. It seems, wizard, you have brought me a new toy to enjoy. That silly puppet King wants her for his bride, but perhaps I will play with her first. What do you think my pretty one? I could show you things beyond your most terrifying imaginings."

Kale leaped forward as a large demonic form stepped from the shadows and lifted Laurel off the floor in one fluid motion. He smiled wickedly at Kale as he stepped away from his thrusting sword and leapt to his dais. Kale spun around and moved to attack once more. He only hesitated when the demon touched one of his talons to Laurel's throat and drew a single drop of blood.

"Good boy, it would be such a disappointment if I had to slit her throat. Now I can be reasonable. You want her back and from the look on your face you also want the villagers to go free. Let us see what kind of agreement we can reach, shall we?" Kale looked at the demon with scorn and hatred.

"What do you want demon?" Kale nearly spat the words out. He watched cautiously as the demon tapped the talon of his left hand on his chin.

His other hand held Laurel by the throat, his talon still pressed against her exposed skin.

"There really is nothing you can give me, but some entertainment could be enjoyable." It paused to smile a bloody, malevolent smile. "You decide who goes free. I'll let you walk out of here with either the villagers or the princess, but not both. Only two groups will leave here. Who will it be?" Kale closed his eyes and allowed himself to sink into the essence of the sword.

He could attack the demon, but it would mean losing Laurel. If he got the demon to release Laurel, an opportunity would present itself. Through the sword, Kale saw the way to attack and save both Laurel and the villagers. He would have to give himself completely to the sword. If he did, he would be able to destroy the demon without yielding the lives of the villagers or Laurel. There would only be one life lost… his. He knew Laurel would make a great queen. He only hoped the man who sat at her side deserved her.

His mind was decided. Without any more thought, Kale released control of his mind to the sword allowing it to pull his life force into itself. Then with cold determination he met the eyes of the demon one last time.

"Very well, demon, release Laurel and we'll leave your lands." Kale grimaced at the demon's dark and foreboding laugh and waited for his moment.

"So, the great hero chooses his whore over a village, how delicious. Here take your whore and leave my lands."

The demon shoved Laurel down the steps towards Kale, and in that moment the sword took hold of him. Kale felt his body move of its own accord, swiftly flying up the stairs. Kale and the sword moved as one, slicing and stabbing at the demon lord. With each movement Kale felt more of his life energy leaving his body. Spells flew from his mouth of their own accord as Kale continued to slash and stab with Demons Bane.

Finally, with one last jolt of energy the sword point hit home driving deep into the demon's heart. As the sword fed on the blood and life of the demon, draining it of all it was, Kale sank to the ground. Laurel rushed to his side lifting his head into her lap. Tears streamed down her cheeks as she looked lovingly into his eyes. She never looked more beautiful. Kale smiled at her as his heart slowed. She was saying something, but he couldn't hear. He let her radiant image fill his vision completely as his heart and breathing came to a final stop. This was a beautiful way to die.

Chapter 20

A bright, white light filled Kale's vision as his body began to feel light and airy. All of his pain and exhaustion faded away and was replaced with a peaceful serenity. He had defeated the demon and saved Laurel. She would now be free to become queen of Kallihan. Kale knew she would rule wisely, with compassion and understanding. A sudden, disturbing thought struck him, who would become her King? Who would Laurelie choose as her husband? Would she marry at all? She would have to for the sake of the throne and stability of the country, but would she marry for love? Would she fall in love with someone else?

Kale was gripped with feelings of frustration and jealousy. She was supposed to have married him. They were supposed to have a life together, and now.... He mentally slapped himself. He was dead, she should go on with her life and find happiness where she could, not mourn him forever. Warmth returned to him almost as if someone were holding him. He knew he needed to open his eyes, but he didn't want to. He just wanted to stay in this peace.

Slowly, Kale opened his eyes and looked around, only to be immediately consumed by confusion. How was this possible? He was back in the crystal cavern, surrounded by glowing crystals all reflecting him. Laurel was sitting beside him crying and shaking as she cradled his head in her lap. Kale slowly raised his hand up and caressed the side of her tear-streaked face. She gasped as she opened her red, worn eyes to look at him. Kale immediately sprung to his feet and pulled her into his arms. He was alive, somehow, he was alive!

"Laurel, are you all right? How did we get back here? Where are the villagers?" Kale smoothed her hair as he kissed the top of her head, deeply breathing in her familiar scent. "Laurel everything is fine, we're alive… all of us. Now that the demon's destroyed we can take the army and face the King. He won't have his demonic allies to help him this time. We're going to win… we're going to save Kallihan, you'll see…." Kale paused and looked around again. Where were the villagers? Shouldn't they be in this room as well? A sinking feeling began growing in his chest and stomach. How did they get back here? "Laurel, tell me what has happened?"

Laurel leaned against his chest, slowly regaining control of her emotions and tears. She looked into his eyes as she tried to contain her anger, frustration and pain. How could they have done that to him? How could these entities have tortured them both like that? How was any of this right?

"Kale… it was all a test… none of it was real…. You didn't kill the demon… it's still alive and hunting us….There were no villagers… none of it…" The fury growing in Kale's eyes choked off the words Laurel was going to say. She could only shake her head as she looked at him, lost for explanation. She watched as Kale stood and walked to one of the crystals in the wall. She closed her eyes as he pounded his fists against the cold, hard surface, screaming his rage.

"WHY!!!! Why would you do this to us? How could you do this to us… to her?! You have no right to torture people this way!!! Is there even a sword that can fight that demon or is that a lie as well!?!?" Kale's furious voice echoed back at himself as he stood there heavily breathing, his anger spent. The chamber was silent as a grave. Then the barely audible sound of chiming crystals played through the cavern.

"You seem angry. This was unforeseen. You came here asking to be judged. We have judged you. Words mean very little. A person's oaths are just vibrations and wind. It is their actions that tell the truth. We needed to be sure you would use the sword for good. We needed to be sure you would not let the power of the sword corrupt your heart. As for the girl… we warned you she may see and experience things that you would wish she didn't. We warned you what she saw and experienced may change her. It was your choice to remove the protections we put in place.

Now you both know what you are made of. Now you both know what you face. Now you both have paid the price for saving your Kingdom. What you seek to do is not going to be easy. You will face true evil and darkness. Now you know both of you will be able to face it. Such knowledge is rare. You should be grateful for acquiring such knowledge of yourselves." Kale laughed bitterly. This entity had no understanding of human emotions. It only saw logic. It only saw the end result. How could it possibly understand the pain, fear and frustration they both felt? It served only one purpose... ensuring only one worthy would wield Demons Bane. It had been right about one thing... they now knew what they were willing to do to save their Kingdom.

"I apologize. You are correct... such knowledge is valuable, but humans, elves, dwarves, and all the other races don't just base our lives on knowledge. We also base our lives on emotions... love, anger, joy, sadness. We feel all these things, sometimes to extremes, and you have just put us through the extremes of all these emotions. It is a lot to endure and survive in only a short time."

"This is an interesting development. Perhaps this is something we should study and include in future tests. We will think on this... for now, you have been found worthy of Demons Bane. You have proven that you will do what is necessary to destroy the demon without sacrificing innocence. Through the doorway you will find a crystal case. Open it and take Demons Bane as yours."

The light in the crystals faded as Kale took Laurel's hand and they approached the new doorway that appeared in the far wall as one of the crystals slid sideways. Cautiously they walked through and into a smaller chamber with a stone altar at one end. Upon the stone altar was a long crystal case that glowed faintly in the darkness.

Kale apprehensively approached the case and carefully lifted the lid. Inside was the most exquisite sword he had ever seen. He knew of no forges that could have created such a weapon. It could only have been created by the Gods. Kale carefully lifted the sword out of the case to admire it better. As his hand touched the silver wrapped crystal handle a pure light and warmth filled him. Everything seemed clearer, his thoughts, his fears, his confusions… everything had come clear, and understanding was his for the knowing.

As he lifted the sword into the air, he admired the pure, clear crystal blade. It shone with a radiant light that chased the surrounding darkness away. The edge of the blade was honed to a perfect cutting edge. The sword's weight was nothing in his hands. It was almost as if he held a feather instead of a lethal weapon. There were no carvings, no etched designs, no intricate patterns. The sword was shear perfection, no embellishments necessary. Whoever crafted Demons Bane was a master of masters to have created such a beautiful blade.

As he looked once more into the case, he saw a scabbard for the blade made of simple leather, also without embellishments. Carefully, he removed the scabbard, slipped the blade into the protective case and belted it around his waist. Everything fit perfectly, as if it had been made for him. Kale smiled wryly at Laurel and then rejoined her by the door.

Kissing her forehead, he took her hand in his and they began walking out of the chamber and back towards the world they had left behind. Kale led the way as they made their way up and out of the heart of the mountain. They knew they were working with very limited time, and Kale only hoped they weren't too late returning.

As they approached the gateway they had originally entered, a dwarf hurried towards them, desperation coloring his eyes. He motioned for them to follow, only glancing back once to ensure they were following. Quickly they made their way through the deserted tunnels, screeches and screams echoed down to them from the mountain's surface. The King had wasted no time in coming for them. Finally, they reached Aldric and several of his generals quietly discussing their options. When he looked up and saw Kale and Laurel, sword in hand, relief swept over his face and that of his generals.

"Thank the Gods you've both returned safely. You know what to do my friends. Keag, take your group and lead Kale and the princess to the wizards' conclave. Once you have seen them safely through, join us in Laurendale. Men, let us bring the mountains down on their dark hides so that they never see the sun's light again."

Keag nodded to Kale and Laurel and then began walking down a long corridor they hadn't seen before. He stopped at a side room and motioned them inside. In the room were five other dwarves, all armed to the teeth and looking ready for anything, including an army of demons. Kale nodded to them as he looked around the room. On a table nearby were their packs loaded and ready to go. There were also a variety of swords along with Laurel's bow and staff.

"Lord Kale, Princess… our job is to get you safely through to the wizards. It's said the two of you will bring an end to the King's union with a demon. By the King's reaction in trying to obtain the two of you, I would guess that's not rumor. I know you carry Demons Bane, but that sword shouldn't be used in normal combat. Pick your weapons of choice quickly and then we will be off. We have little time to lose and much ground to cover." Keag quickly went to work strapping on his own weaponry and armor. Kale quickly approached the table and began checking each of the swords. Two of them felt right in his hands and he quickly strapped them on along with some leather armor the dwarves had managed to make for him in the time they were gone.

"Keag, if you don't mind my asking… how long were we gone. It was difficult to tell time while we were down there." Keag and the other dwarves laughed heartily.

"I imagine it would be. When you left the labyrinth, you left our world. Where you went to only the Gods know, but you have been gone for two weeks now." They all paused to watch Kale and Laurel's reactions. Kale swallowed hard; Laurel sat down in a nearby chair. A stunned expression had swept over both of their faces. The dwarves laughed heartily once more and Keag slapped Kale on the back good naturedly.

"It's all right boy. We dwarves aren't that fond of that magic stuff either. Would have thought those with elven blood in them would find it more comforting though." Keag laughed again. "Guess not. Better get used to it. Soon you'll be at the Wizards' conclave and that's all they have there… magic, that is…. Let us go. Time is wasting and the enemy is closing in." With that they went as a group into the hall keeping Laurel in the center.

Quickly and silently, they moved down one hallway after another. Before long they reached what looked like a dead end in the passage. Keag, however, quickly pulled on a lever to the left of the door and the wall slid silently to the side. Within moments they were outside near the base of one of the mountains. Keag motioned the group to follow as he moved forward into a twisting and winding, narrow path. They could only travel single file and the screams and howls that echoed through the mountains made the hair on Kale's arm stand up. He glanced twice at Laurel and could see the same fear mirrored in her face. They knew what made those sounds, the demons that served the King.

At every turn, Keag would send a scout to report back on the path ahead. With each pause in their flight, the screeches and howls gained on them. Were the demons chasing them, or were they still trying to find their trail? Kale hoped it was the latter, but as time went on and they were still in the mountains, his hopes faded. As night approached, a distant rumbling could be heard on the south side of the mountains' edge. As they turned to look smoke and explosive rubble shot into the sky. Aldric hadn't been kidding about bringing the mountain down on their heads. Kale only hoped their new friends had made it out alive.

Keag continued to lead them on through the mountains even as the moon rose in the distance.

Kale could feel his body tiring and knew Laurel had to be exhausted as well. Finally, around the middle of the night, Keag allowed them to sit and take a quick break to eat and rest. No one spoke. They just listened to the continual howls and screeches in the distance. Laurel leaned her head against Kale's shoulder, her eyes closing from exhaustion. Kale placed his arm around her and felt the coolness of her skin. When he tilted his head to look at her, he noticed how pale she had become. How much longer could she keep this up? How much longer could any of them keep this up?

A howl close by caused everyone to jump and become alert. Keag motioned quietly for everyone to continue forward. Two of his men gripped Keag's arm and pulled him close. Their whispers were desperate and harsh, but Kale couldn't make out what they were saying. After a brief dispute, Keag nodded to them. With a brief salute to them, he turned and led the rest of the group onward while the two warriors turned and prepared for battle. As they approached the foothills the small company could hear the triumphant screams of the demons behind them. Each of them bowed their heads in a moment of grief for their fallen brethren. Up ahead the land seemed to stretch on forever. Where was this wizards' conclave? Kale desperately searched the fields for any sign of the conclave but saw none. His fears were mirrored in the eyes of the dwarves with him.

The howls and screeches signaled the demons' approach again. Keag unwaveringly moved the group forward into the grasslands. Kale checked his sword, making sure it was loose in its scabbard. Several others did the same with their weapons. The screeches and howls were almost upon them now. The sound had grown to a cacophony of enraged and hungry screams. Kale wanted to cover his ears and curl into a ball on the ground, but he stood his ground. If he could face a demon lord, or at least the illusion of one, he could face whatever was coming for them.

Keag called a halt and ordered everyone to turn and prepare for battle. It was better to face the enemy head on than with your back turned, running away. The demons must have realized their quarry was near, because their dark desires echoed through the mountain drowning out all other sounds. Kale grabbed Laurel's arm and pulled her behind him. If all else failed, perhaps Laurel would be able to find the strength to banish these demons once more. It had nearly destroyed her last time, but he knew she would attempt to save them all again if she could.

"Laurel, only try if there is no other option. We may be able to defeat them ourselves. Just promise me you will wait until there is no other choice." Kale had to almost yell to be heard over the growing cries. He looked at Laurel in earnest and felt his heart wrench as she smiled back at him darkly.

There was no more time for discussion. The screams of the demons rose to a crescendo and then vanished. After the constant howling and screeching, the sudden silence was deafening. Kale grabbed an arrow from his quiver and nocked it in his bow as lightning flashed in the sky followed by a low rumble. He tried to look everywhere at once using the flashes to aid in his search for his query. His heart thudded in his chest as his breath quickened and every muscle in his body tensed for battle. From which direction would they come?

Nothing moved… nothing made a sound. Everyone stood tensed and unmoving as statues. Kale could hear Laurel beginning to pray to her Goddess and ask for the strength to once again banish these terrifying creatures. The dwarves readied themselves to take the brunt of the assault, their axes at the ready. Keag looked at his fellow dwarves and smiled darkly.

"My friends…. Today is a good day to die!" The dwarves roared, sharing his sentiment. Kale even found himself echoing their enthusiasm. He dropped his bow and pulled his spare sword from its scabbard. Raising it high, he prepared for the onslaught.

Every muscle tensed as several shadows moved towards them, growing in height and form as they came closer. Kale waited for the signal as he watched Keag squint into the darkness. Suddenly, Keag raised his hand and shouted "Hold!".

Kale cautiously lowered his weapon as he directed his eyes back towards the oncoming forms. Striding towards them across the hills were dozens of men and women wearing long embroidered robes. Kale felt his heart rejoice in relief and jubilation at the sight of them. They had found the wizards… or at least the wizards had found them. Finally, they were safe… for now.

Chapter 21

The conclave was actually a surprisingly large manor house surrounded by high walls constructed of stone, steel and magic. Beyond those walls were vegetable gardens, areas for livestock, workshops, temples, a tavern, inn, and shops for everyday goods. It was a completely contained town filled with mages of different genders and races. They lived here in peace, studying their magics.

The entire place had been concealed with a mass illusion spell. It must have taken several wizards working together to cast it. After the dwarves had seen them safely in and made introductions, they quickly resupplied and left to join the rest of their people in the elven lands. Kale had been surprised by their choice to walk instead of magically travel, but Keag had told him he didn't want to show up on the other side with his head where his ass should be.

Kale and Laurel had said their good-byes and hopes to see them again soon. Once the dwarves had left, seven wizards gathered at the gates of the wall and began casting the illusion to cloak the town. Kale watched in fascination as the magic took hold. Could he do something like that? Would his magic be that powerful after he had learned to master it better?

A young girl, by the name of Leona, showed them into the manor house and the council chamber. Here they would meet the wizards who made up the high council and be able to speak with them about their mission and plans. Kale and Laurel sank wearily into two chairs that sat around the table. Soon Leona returned with a tray filled with food and two steaming mugs of mulled wine. They gratefully accepted the hospitality, eating and drinking their fill as they waited for the high wizards to arrive.

"Kale, I don't think I would have been able to banish those demons regardless of how hard I tried. They were stronger than the ones that attacked us in the forest. If it hadn't been for the wizards..." Laurel's voice caught in her throat, as a shudder shook her body. Kale reached over and took Laurel's hand in his own, squeezing it reassuringly.

"I know. We were all in a great deal of trouble. I think it's only going to get worse from here on in. They don't know we have the sword yet, but it won't be long before they figure it out. Then... the demon lord will most likely do everything possible to stop us." Kale paused to gather his thoughts. He looked down at their hands joined together... unified... strong... unbreakable. "Laurel, about what happened in the caves. I didn't know... I didn't think beyond the moment. If I had known what they were going to do... I never... I never would have put you through that. I'm so sorry." Kale felt tears come to his eyes as he continued to look at their hands. He couldn't meet her gaze. How could he after the torment he had just put her through. He felt her other hand brush softly alongside his face.

"Kale... that wasn't your fault... what happened... if you had known it wouldn't have been a test. We're both probably going to face worse... though I can't think of much worse than losing you." Kale's head snapped up at those words, his eyes locking onto Laurel's... searching for a deeper meaning.

"Laurel, will you marry me? Before we go after the demon.... Will you become my wife?" Kale searched her eyes as he waited for her answer.

Laurel felt her heart pounding against her chest as she tried to find the breath to speak. Was he really asking her? They had already professed their love for each other... and there was no other she would rather spend her life with. Was this all a fool's hope though? Would they even live long enough to enjoy their marriage? Did she care? Don't wait, don't let time pass you by until you miss everything. Didn't she deserve happiness, even if it was only for a moment? Laurel felt her breath come to her and she took several slow deep breaths. Kale's eyes searched hers longingly, seeking her answer.

"Kale... I would be honored to become your wife." Kale smiled broadly as he took her into his arms and kissed her passionately. She said yes! It didn't matter what came next, they would be together, their souls united forever.

"Sorry if we are interrupting a moment, but we thought you would be eager to discuss what is yet to come. Perhaps we should give the two of you some more time instead?" Kale and Laurel looked up shocked and embarrassed by the sudden interruption. Several wizards, both male and female, had filed into the room looking rather amused at what they had stumbled upon. Kale cleared his throat and sat up straighter in his chair as the wizards took their seats and smiled at the young couple in turn.

"Now is fine for the conversation, high wizards… we were just…" Kale's words caught in his throat as he tried to come up with an excuse. The wizards all chuckled good naturedly as they watched him struggle for an explanation.

"Do not trouble yourself, Lord Kingsford. We are not so old as to forget what it is to be in love. That you are here suggests that you were successful in obtaining Demons Bane. Is this true?" Kale looked at Laurel and then returned the wizard's questioning gaze with resolution.

"Yes, we were successful in obtaining Demons Bane… and… some important lessons." The head wizard nodded knowingly.

"The heart can be harsh, but it does what is best for all, not what we desire." The wizard paused as he took the two of them in. Kale and Laurel felt as if they were prize turkeys at the butcher's shop. "Princess, it is good to see that your ordeals haven't destroyed your spirit. Perhaps now is the time to tell you what this is all about. You know that you are part of a prophecy, but I'm not sure you know or understand the prophecy as it stands. Years ago a seer was asked by the King to judge his reign and tell him of what was to come. He had been a good King once, but years had passed, and life had taken its toll. Rumors were spreading of deals with demons and sacrifices. His own allies were beginning to turn on him. He wanted to know if there were any threats to him and his reign. The seer told him that she saw a half-elven child sitting on his throne. The King went into a rage. Long time fears of the elves and their magic along with his own secret insecurities caused him to potentially misinterpret the prophecy.

"He took it to mean that he would be usurped by a half-elf and killed. He so feared this prophecy that he killed the seer and made a pact with a demon to protect his throne. He immediately set about separating elves, dwarves and humans, instilling fear and hatred between them. At least this is the way we had always thought the events of history had taken place. More recent research has led us to believe that a demon had seduced the King and earned his trust. The demon then warped the King's mind, sowing seeds of doubt and fear within him. These fears caused the King to seek out the seer, but the demon was there, hidden in shadows, whispering fears and threats in the King's ears." The wizard paused to allow them to absorb all he was telling them. He glanced at the others and then with a nod of resignation, continued his story.

"The seer had tried to warn him that prophecies can be taken many ways and that it was not an exact magic, but the King would not listen. His bargain with the demon is what destroyed your village. This bargain is what haunts you even now. This is why the King wants you. If you sit on the throne at his side the prophecy is fulfilled, and he can continue his demonic reign. He will not accept the other option that has always been available to him. He could have taken an elven bride and their child would have inherited the throne after him. Unfortunately, his mind is now too far gone to even consider that option. The third option is the revolution, in which his greatest fears will come to pass. He will be overthrown and the two of you will sit on the thrones, ruling our country as King and Queen." Kale shook his head at the ludicrous nature of what he was being told. He had always known the King was a madman, but this... How old was he?

"High Wizard..."

"You may call me Wizard Zebulon." Kale nodded to him in appreciation.

"Wizard Zebulon... I know this means that the King is probably much older than he appears, by what you are saying, but I'm not sure I understand why any of this is important. Our mission now is to destroy him, so what does the rest matter?" Wizard Zebulon smiled at him and nodded his head.

"The impatience of youth, I remember it well. You are correct about the King. He is much older than he appears. From what we have learned he is around two hundred years old. His bargain with the demon keeps him young and strong. That is why you will need to break the bargain by killing the demon lord who made it. As to why this is important... it is always good tactics to know your enemy. Understanding why he has done these things may give you a weakness you can exploit… such as buying time while considering a proposal." Kale saw his eyes shift to Laurel as he said those last words. Kale nodded in understanding.

"That's all well and good, but we'll be going after the demon. You wouldn't happen to have any useful information about that adversary, would you?" Zebulon smiled again, mischief twinkling in his eyes.

"As a matter of fact, we do. The demon lord you will be facing is called by many names, but the one we know him as is Svecknar. He likes causing suffering and chaos, but most importantly he has a talent for seeing people's inner most fears. He enjoys exploiting those fears and driving people insane. His weaknesses are truth and courage. You must remember that courage isn't the absence of fear but going on in the face of it. Truth, on the other hand, is one of the most difficult things to confess and can be terrifying in itself. The heart showed you truths… truths that could be twisted into fears to plague your mind. You have already gained all the tools and preparations you need to deal with Svecknar. Now all you need is the key to enter his domain… and that, we have." The wizards solemnly looked at the two of them, sorrow and resignation painted on their faces.

Kale grabbed Laurel's hand and felt her squeeze it in return. Kale knew what they must be thinking. How could two individuals, as young as them, defeat such a creature? Kale was wondering the same thing, but the cavern, or heart, showed him they could defeat it. Kale glanced at Laurel to find her looking steadily back at him. She knew this could be a suicide mission, and yet she was still determined to follow through with it. She was their courage. Kale glanced down at the crystal sword sitting in its plain leather scabbard at his hip. That was their truth. They weren't perfect. They weren't heroes of legend. They were a young couple that had found each other by chance and... maybe a little magic. They had made mistakes, and they would probably make more, but they were willing to learn and give everything. That was their strength and truth. Kale stood and looked around the table meeting each wizard's gaze steadily.

"Well then, it doesn't sound like time is on our side. In fact, it sounds like we shouldn't be sitting here wasting any more of it. I suggest we discuss strategy, for the resistance will need your help and magic if it will be successful, and we will need that key." Kale nodded to each wizard in turn and prepared for a long session of planning and discussion.

The hours flew by as they sat in the chamber discussing the capabilities and skills the wizards could lend to the resistance and war. There were a few priests that had taken up residency with the wizards. They were more than willing to lend their healing talents and powers of faith to the cause as well. With the number of wizards at the conclave, and those they knew of still in hiding within the country rescuing those who were scheduled for death, the resistance would have plenty of magic to combat the King's demonic powers.

The key they spoke of was a spell that several would have to work in unison to cast. Once cast it would open a gateway into the demon's dimension. It would then be up to Kale and Laurel to make their way through the demon realm and find the stronghold of the demon lord. Once there, they would face the demon together, and kill it.

The exit strategy was the most difficult part of the plan to figure out. After much discussion and debate they decided on creating a totem that they would have to carry through the realm. Once their job was accomplished, they could use the totem with a few words to activate a gateway out of the demon realm.

As the sun kissed the horizon, the council broke apart for the evening. Laurel and Kale joined in the celebratory dinner that the fortress held. The night was filled with singing, dancing, music and games. Children ran around demonstrating their burgeoning skills, while adults laughed and spoke of the promise of a future without hiding. They wandered through the crowds trying to reassure people and sharing in their hopes for the future. Inside, Kale felt a tension building that he couldn't explain. Laurel felt dread fill her heart as she smiled and laughed with these people who believed so much in them.

As Kale grabbed another drink from a nearby table a woman approached him, a small child trying to hide behind her skirts. Kale could tell she was nervous by the way she bit her lower lip and kept shifting her eyes between him and the ground. Cautiously she approached him and brought the child gently to her front. The little girl looked up at him with big wondering eyes. Fear and excitement danced in their depths as she stared up at him.

"My lord, I don't know if you remember me... you were much younger then, but you saved my daughter from being drowned. The resistance told me about you and how you killed that death squad soldier to save her. We wanted to say thank you. The wizards say she will be a powerful summoner when she comes into her magic fully. Right now she likes calling squirrels and chipmunks to eat out of her hand." The woman looked down at her daughter lovingly, causing Kale to feel a pang for the loss of his own mother. As if on cue the little girl bent down and a small chipmunk scurried into her hands and up to her shoulder. Kale smiled as she giggled and spoke to the chipmunk. Kale looked at the woman in earnest. He knew he needed to say something, but what?

"I remember the action and I remember describing you to the resistance... but I apologize for I do not know your name. I was still growing myself at the time and learning what it meant to be a man and noble." The woman's smile filled her face adding a twinkle to her eyes.

"My name is Sasha, my lord, and this is my daughter, Cassandra. If I may say my lord... you have grown up well, your father must be very proud of you." Kale nodded and smiled at Sasha and Cassandra. What did his father think had happened to them at this point? He should get word to him before they left. It might be his last chance to speak with his father… ever.

"Thank you, Sasha. It means a great deal to see you both well. If you will forgive me, there is something I must tend to." With a parting nod he waded through the crowds until he found Laurel. He gently pulled her into an alcove where they could talk without extra listeners.

"Laurel, I have to speak with my father before we go. It may be my last chance and…" Laurel put her hand lightly on his arm and shined her warm smile on him.

"I understand. Well, we said we would marry before entering the demon's realm. Why don't you invite him to the Elven territory and we'll have the wedding there. That way everyone we care about will be there and you can see him again without endangering him." Kale looked at her with pride and relief.

"Do you know how much I love you? Thank you for understanding." Kale pulled her into his arms feeling her warmth and taking in the scent of her. Laurel laughed and shook her head.

"Well, I figure he's due an 'I told you so' after the way we left things." Laurel spun out of his embrace and smiled warmly, the terrors to come forgotten for the moment.

Kale had completely forgotten about all of that. Had it only been a few weeks since they left his father's house? It seemed like a lifetime ago that they were making their way to his family's home and trying to sort out their own confusing feelings and thoughts.

Sometime during the night, Kale and Laurel had turned in while the celebration continued outside. The next morning, they met with the council once more to finalize plans. By mid-morning everything was set and those that would be joining the battle gathered their supplies and belongings, gathering in the central courtyard. It was shortly after lunch when everyone was ready to go. The council had spent all the time since their meeting creating the totem that would allow Kale and Laurel to return to this realm after defeating the demon. No one spoke of any chance of failure. Failure meant their world would be doomed and everyone would perish. Failure was not an option.

Several wizards gathered at the front of the group and opened a gateway into the realm of the elves. Laurel and Kale went first, followed by the council and the rest of the wizards willing to join the war. In total, there were over one hundred wizards joining the resistance. Kale only hoped it would be enough.

As they entered the gateway a bright light enveloped them as they continued to walk. In moments they stepped out into a clearing at the center of Laurendale. The sight that greeted them, stunned everyone.

Chapter 22

The peaceful city of Laurendale no longer existed. In its place stood a military encampment filled with elven, dwarven and human soldiers. Where once there had been open gardens and flowerbeds, there now stood tents, weapon smiths, bower fletchers, armorers, practice fields and food tents. Kale, Laurel and the wizard council had to step aside quickly to allow for the others to come through. With the arrival of each new group the surrounding soldiers took more notice. As the last group entered the diminishing space the crowd of surrounding soldiers parted, and a familiar face stepped forward.

"I wondered when the two of you would show up with my wizards. Took your sweet time didn't you." Kale smiled and laughed as he stepped forward to embrace Bane.

"Well, we would have been here sooner, but we ran into some problems with demons. They gripped arms and then parted giving Kale a good look at the surrounding area and a better look at his friend. Bane now had a scar running down the right side of his face. He also looked harder, more tempered. The jovial attitude he had always taken had been replaced by a commanding presence that demanded respect and attention. "You've been busy since we left. I see you've gained a new medal of honor." Bane touched the side of his face and smiled riley.

"Yeah, led a group out to test the waters. We took on three death squads that were harassing a nearby town. Most of the townspeople are now here in Laurendale assisting where they can with the resistance. We've had recruits streaming in for the past couple of weeks from all the neighboring towns and villages. The magic of the forest prevents any spies from getting through. It seems it can tell the true intentions of those that enter the woods and only allows those that wish to help get through. I don't completely understand it, but I'm grateful for it."

Bane clapped Kale on the shoulders before turning to take a long look at Laurel and sweep her up in a hug. With a smile on his face, he ordered some of his captains to show the wizards where they could bunk down and set up an area for their magics. Then he led the two of them off through the crowds of curious onlookers towards the inn at the heart of Laurendale.

Once inside, Bane ordered some drinks for them and motioned for them to follow him into a side room. Inside a table was set up with maps and, what Kale could only assume, were piles of scout reports. Leaning back in a chair with one booted foot pressed against the tabletop as she looked through one stack of reports was Islaura. When they came in, she glanced up briefly, a warm smile spreading across her face as she motioned for them to sit down in one of the available seats.

Kale watched as Bane quietly walked over to stand next to her and look over her shoulder at the report before kicking the legs of the chair out from under her causing her to tumble to the floor. The chair clattered to the ground, but Islaura sprung to her feet and swept Bane's legs out from under him causing him to lose his balance for a moment before sweeping her into his arms and spinning her into a kiss. Things had definitely changed in the time they had been gone.

Kale cleared his throat as he looked at Laurel, who was trying not to laugh and failing miserably at the scene playing out in front of them. After a second throat clearing from Kale, Bane and Isla separated and smiled nonchalantly at them as if this was just another day. With a free hand, Bane righted the chair and then pulled a second over for Isla to sit in.

"Sorry about that, but we don't get much time together these days. Isla is one of my best scouts and archers, so she's hardly here. Actually, I didn't know she was back yet." Isla lowered her eyes and gently took Bane's left hand in hers. Kale recognized the look that had passed between them. It was one he had experienced all too often lately with Laurel. It was a look that said this may be our last day together, we should embrace it while we can.

"Believe me, Bane, I know all too well what you mean." He grabbed Laurel's hand, squeezing it gently, without taking his eyes off Bane.

"I guess you would. The dwarves have said that you were successful in obtaining the sword, Demons Bane. I'm going to assume this means you'll be going after the demon lord that works with the King. I don't suppose I could talk you out of that..." Kale shook his head slowly with grim determination. "I didn't think so." The King has started attacking many of the outlying villages and smaller cities. I've taken the liberty of sending word to your father and warning him. He's on his way now with all his soldiers and all the townspeople. They should be here tomorrow. The only dwarves that are missing are the ones that escorted the two of you to the wizards, but we've sent a wizard to meet them on their way and gate them back here. Our army is mixed, but working reasonably well together. The forges have been working overtime creating armor and weaponry for everyone. We've even been creating backup armor and weaponry and some interesting projectile weapons that will come in handy when we face the King's mass army." Kale looked at Bane, trying to read his face like one would read a book.

"Bane… things are never going to be the same, are they?" Bane lowered his eyes and looked at the maps and papers spread across the table.

"The things I've seen over the past few weeks… the horrors that have been visited on the people…. I guess I had to grow up at some point. We've even had deserters from the King's army join us. They've been integral in finding weaknesses in his defenses and squads. Now we just have to get the army to the city without losing too many of our numbers." Bane paused and looked at one of the reports in front of him before rubbing his hand across his forehead and closing his eyes. Islaura put her hand reassuringly on his back, concern and love coursed across her features. Bane took a deep breath before continuing. "Kale… there are reports of demons everywhere.

We've already lost three scouts to these things!"
Kale could see the strain and toll his position was
taking on him.

"Bane…" Bane's head snapped up and a
mixture of determination, fear and frustration
flooded his face.

"NO, Kale! Don't tell me it will be all
right! It won't be! I'm sending these people to
their deaths and there is nothing I can do about it! I
want to tell you not to go, but if you don't kill that
damnable demon… we're all dead. You may very
well be going off to face your death and there isn't
a damn thing I can do but say good luck! Do you
have any idea how hopeless I feel right now? I
can't save them all! I've already lost some! Every
day I look into their faces knowing it may be the
last time I see them. Every day I make sure to
memorize their names, so someone will remember.
The elves have an ancient tree in the center of
Laurendale that now bears the names of those we
have lost. By the time this is done the tree may not
have any bark left, it will be so carved up with
names." Kale put his hand on his friend's shoulder
squeezing it in support.

"I know… believe me, I know. The burden
of leadership beats you down every day. You must
make decisions for the greater good and hope you
don't get everyone killed in the process. I'm sorry
I put you in this position. I'm sorry I cursed you
with this horrible burden." Bane met Kale's gaze
and their looks spoke volumes. These two brothers
by choice understood in that instant everything that
had come before. In their matching looks was the

understanding that they may never see each other after these few days. It had been a good adventure… but every adventure must come to an end.

A knock at the door interrupted their thoughts. As the inn keeper brought the food and drink in, conversation resumed. The four friends ate, drank and filled each other in on everything that had happened since they parted. As the day waned it began to almost feel like old times, before demons, blood storms and death squads. Kale and Laurel told them of their plans to marry before heading into the demon dimension, which started Islaura talking about arrangements, dresses and decorations. They may only have a few days to prepare, but for such an occasion as their princess getting married… it would be all hands at the ready. Laughter and jokes replaced worries and stress, and for just a moment they were as they had always been.

A commotion outside the inn drew their attention as a scout burst through the doors gasping for breath. Bane was immediately out of his seat urging the young man into a nearby chair and handing him a mug of ale.

"Take it easy, Jonus. What news have you?"

"General…. We found the dwarven party that had escorted the princess and Lord Kale…. They were slaughtered… every last one of them. It had to be the work of demons. Their bodies… there was so much blood… I… it… all we could do was bury what remained… General it was…"

Bane put a reassuring hand on the young man's back as Jonus began crying into his mug of ale. Bane closed his eyes for a moment, taking several deep breaths. When he opened them, Kale could see the pain and anger that suffused them.

"It's all right, Jonus. You did your best. There was nothing more you could do. Get yourself something to eat and go join some of your comrades for a drink. You shouldn't be alone tonight. The good news is the princess and Lord Kale have arrived. In fact, we will all be witnessing their wedding before they journey into the demon dimension to destroy that monster. We'll win this Jonus, and those that have tortured the people will pay for their crimes with their lives." Kale watched as Jonus raised his head, his tears no longer coming. Instead, a new hope and strength had filled his eyes. When he saw Kale and Laurel standing together on the one side of the room courage filled his features as he turned towards his general.

"Yes, General Bane. Sir… may I spread the word about the wedding?" Bane smiled at the young man and nodded, clapping his shoulder as Jonus stood.

In moments the young man was out the door racing to spread the word of the princess's wedding to Lord Kale. Bane turned with a grim expression towards Kale and Laurel.

"Well, don't think the two of you are going to be allowed to sneak off and avoid this wedding. It's too important to the army's moral now." He tried to laugh, but he only managed a rough chuckle. "I'm sorry guys, but I have to go speak with Lord Aldric and let him know what has happened. Then I'll need to send out new orders and prepare the army to move out in waves. We're going to be taking three approaches to the capital to try and hide our approach. The hope is the demon will be so busy trying to track the two of you down he won't be keeping track of our army. If we move in small enough groups, we should be able to get most of the way there without being detected." With a sigh, Bane rubbed his temples one more time and looked at his map. I'll try to catch up with you both later, but I have to deal with this now." Kale gripped his friend's forearm and met his eyes with determination.

"Bane, I don't know how, but we're going to get through this. We'll see each other again before we leave. Besides, you need to be my best man." Bane forced a smile that didn't quite reach his eyes.

"You know I wouldn't miss that for anything. I'll see you later."

Islaura escorted them out of the inn and began walking with them to Laurel's estates in Laurendale. They walked in silence as they passed by one group after another. Everyone whispered and stared as they walked past. Many bowed or saluted them as they passed by. Laurel and Kale tried to acknowledge them as much as possible as she walked by. The further they walked the more people joined in watching their progress. Many began chanting or calling out "long live the rightful Queen" or "long live Queen Laurel".

By the time they reached the estates Laurel was on the verge of tears. The tension within was almost causing her to burst at the seams. They were all putting their faith, trust and hopes in her. They were here because they believed in her and what was about to happen. These men and women were going to fight to the death for her and for a dream that may never come true, and all she could do was smile at them and try to look confident.

As the doors closed behind them, Laurel sank into the nearest chair overwhelmed with emotion and exhaustion. When was the last time she had slept peacefully through a night. She still wore the amulet that would prevent the King from entering her dreams, but that didn't stop her own fears and doubts from manifesting unchecked nightmares. She just had to focus on what was right… what was good. Right now she would focus on their wedding. Islaura placed her hand gently on her shoulder and looked compassionately into her eyes.

"I know… it's a lot. You're being asked to be so much to so many. It doesn't seem fair to continue asking more of you… either of you. I know it must seem silly to ask everyone to drop everything and prepare a wedding, but it will help the people find hope. A celebration gives them something to look forward to, and most of those here would never be allowed to attend a royal wedding. Now they'll get to tell their children that they were present when the Queen and King were married. It gives them something to fight for and to believe in." Laurel looked at her and smiled.

"I know… it's just…" Laurel sighed as she tried to put words to her feelings and thoughts. "How many of them are going to die before this is all over? How can I ask them to fight this battle for me? I had always envisioned this battle being mine and mine alone, and now…. How much of their blood will be on my hands by the end of this?"

"Laurel, they are not just fighting for you…. They're fighting for their own futures as well. They are fighting for freedom and a chance at happiness. Yes, you are at the center of that, because you are the rightful heir, you're a symbol to them… but they are doing this for themselves as well. Until word spread of your existence, these people had no hope. Now there's a chance for a better life and a better Kingdom. They believe that's worth fighting for. Don't take that away from them." Laurel swallowed hard. Was she really being so self-centered? She looked over to see Kale looking out the window a small smile spreading across his face.

Laurel went to join him and as she approached the window she could hear singing from the groups of soldiers. It was a song of hope, of a bright future where magic wasn't outlawed, and people were no longer persecuted. It was a song about a dream… a dream they all shared, and all held dear to their hearts. Tears came unbidden to Laurel's eyes as she listened to their unified voices.

"You're right, Islaura. This is everyone's fight… and if this is everyone's fight, then our wedding should be a day of celebration for everyone. It should be a sign of things to come, and I think I just found the song that should be sung as I walk towards my husband to be. Do you think we can have everything ready for three days from now?" She turned with a smile to look at Isla, who was returning her smile with one full of mischief and light.

"I don't think it will be a problem at all. Do you think the two of you could talk Bane into a wedding? He's refusing until after the war. He says I'm too young to be a widow, as if I wasn't eight times his age. He's lucky I love him and put up with his stalling tactics." With a chuckle she turned and headed to the front door. "I'll get the ladies on the dress, flowers and decorations. We'll get the innkeeper and other cooks on the feast. Until tomorrow… sleep well and trust in fate and the Gods to see you through."

That night, Laurel and Kale retired to the same bedroom and slept in each other's arms. In three days, they would be married and then they would face the demon together… united body, soul and heart. In four days, their war for freedom would begin and the King's end would come.

The three days went by swiftly as Laurel was fitted several times for her dress. The ladies of Laurendale had wasted no time in creating a gown fit for a queen of the elves. Kale's father had arrived with the entire city in tow, and many had already taken up arms and joined the army. He had been elated to learn of the wedding and of their success in obtaining the sword. What he wasn't thrilled with was their plan to enter the demon realm and face off with the creature on their own.

Arguments had abounded, but in the end he conceded to the need for the offensive approach. He had gone over the battle plans with Bane and had been very impressed with his strategy and maturity. He had told him he couldn't have been prouder if Bane was his own son and he hoped that he would always consider himself part of their family. Bane had been struck speechless and had only coughed roughly a few times and went on to explain some other minute details of the planned attacks.

Finally, the day arrived for the wedding and the army camp had been turned into a cathedral of trees, flowers, streamers, lanterns and music. Kale stood under a canopy made of flowering vines and small lit globes. Bane stood silently at his side solemn in the festive atmosphere. Everyone gathered around the clearing trying to get the best view of the ceremony and the royal couple.

Suddenly the entire clearing fell into a hushed silence. The whole forest held its breath in anticipation of Laurel's arrival in the clearing. Then some minstrels began playing softly and everyone in the clearing began singing the song that they had only heard a few nights ago. Kale could feel his heart trying to beat out of his chest. Every muscle seemed to tighten, making it difficult to breath. This was it... the moment he had been waiting for. The crowd began to part and Islaura walked through the cleared path towards the canopied altar. Kale heard Bane take in a sharp breath as he stared at the image coming towards them. Kale turned to him and smiled.

"You know… we could make this a double wedding." Bane punched him in the arm jokingly as he coughed and cleared his throat. Kale just chuckled as he went to turn back towards the assemblage. As he turned around, his breath and voice caught in his own throat. For a moment he thought his heart had stopped. Even the crowd had lost track of the words they were supposed to be singing. Everything had paused as Laurel had stepped into the clearing. It was as if time itself had stopped for her entrance.

Laurel had been awe-struck by the beauty of the gown the women of Laurendale had made for her. The fabric was softer and lighter than anything she had ever felt. The gown was an icy pale blue that floated around her, giving her the appearance of a goddess. The bodice was accented with tiny crystals and silver braiding. Small, gathered bands of the fabric wrapped around her arms leaving her shoulders and neck bare. She had chosen to wear her hair down with only the sides twisted and pulled up exposing her ears. On her head she wore a crown of blue and white flowers that had been freshly picked that morning. Around her neck she had chosen to wear her family crest, close to the nape of her neck.

In that gown she felt like a queen… actually, more like a goddess. She had never owned a gown so delicate and beautiful before and now she was wearing this one as she went to join

Kale under the wedding canopy. As she passed through the crowd everyone fell silent and all eyes turned towards her. Laurel could feel the tips of her ears burning as everyone stared at her in awe. She tried to only look forward towards Kale, and almost barked out a sharp laugh at the dumbfounded look that was plastered on his face. Instead she smiled and started forward once more. As soon as she began walking the song picked up once more and with some oohs and aahs accompanying it.

As she approached the canopy Kale reached out and took her hand in his. Once her gaze met his, she was lost to everything else. She remembered answering a question or two and she did repeat something although she wasn't sure what, but then everyone erupted in cheers and Bane and Isla were nudging the two of them and telling them to kiss. Laurel had never been so happy, or dazed, in her life. From the look on Kale's face, he was just as dazed and elated as herself.

Music filled the clearing and surrounding forest as everyone sang, danced, ate and made merry. It was a night to remember. Maybe it wasn't some formal, fancy to do like the nobles and royals would have anywhere else, but it was perfect for them. From all the revelry happening around them, it was exactly what everyone else needed as well. The celebration went late into the night, but Kale and Laurel retired early to their home.

Kale carried Laurel up the stairs to their bed chamber and gently set her down on their bed. He gently removed her hair piece and ran his fingers through her hair, allowing all her hair to cascade down her shoulders. They didn't speak... they didn't need to. They had been waiting for this night for what seemed like forever, and he had no intention of letting it be anything less than perfect. Kale wanted to be a patient and tender lover, taking his time to work her into a heated passion. His patience was rewarded as Laurel returned all of his tenderness and affection tenfold. It was a night like no other and one they knew might be their last, though neither shared their worries.

When morning forced its way into the world unbidden and unwanted, the time for revelry and celebration had ended. The forest had once again been drowned in the foreboding sounds of battle preparation. Troops assembled and reported to their commanders. Bane busily organized the wizards, archers, swordsmen and pikemen into their units. Everywhere people were rushing around making last-minute preparations. Families said good-bye to one another, and tokens of love and hope were given. Prayers were said for the safety of all as wagons were loaded.

Kale and Laurel dressed in silence. Kale donned his silver armor, emblazoned with the royal crest of old, and checked his weapons. Laurel dressed in a set of armor created just for her, a mythril breast plate and skirt that fell mid-thigh. Under this she wore leggings and high boots that matched the silver of the breast plate. She checked her bow and quiver, making sure everything was in good repair. Her staff she hooked into a loop on her back. Laurel carefully tucked the small, crystal totem, that would be their only way of return, into a special padded pouch that had been attached to the inside of her breast plate. Lastly, she placed her holy symbol of Gaia around her neck and worked her hair into a tight braid.

The future Queen and King exited their home, heads held high. All eyes turned towards the couple as they walked to the center of the clearing. Kale and Laurel walked to the top of a small knoll and faced the on-looking army. Silence and anticipation greeted them. Bane joined them on the rise and strongly embraced Kale's forearm with a nod. Then Kale turned towards the crowd and cleared his throat, taking Laurel's hand in his own.

"I know you are frightened, we are as well, but we are also angry. For too long a tyrant has sat the throne, torturing and murdering our people. For too long we have lived in fear of the coming days and the demons that haunt the shadows. I say no more! Today we take back our Kingdom, our lives and our souls!" Kale paused as the soldiers cheered and raised their swords. He glanced at Laurel with grim determination as he loosened Demons Bane from its scabbard. In one smooth motion he pulled it free and raised it to the morning sun. Light shone off the blade and bathed the clearing in a brilliant, warm glow. "Today, your Queen and I will travel into the heart of the demon's realm, where he hides! Today we will take vengeance for all he has tainted and destroyed! Today you must take the fight to the capital where that cowardly tyrant hides safe in his castle! Today you must take back what was stolen and cut our enemies down where they stand! No quarter will be given to any who stand with the tyrant! No mercy shall be shown to the death squads and traitors of the people! We will no longer sit in silence! Today we shout our rage! Today we take back our future… for ourselves… for our children… for our country!"

The clearing erupted into a cacophony of shouts and swords banging against shields. Weapons were raised into the air and the people rose to stand and fight. It was time. Today the war would begin. Their fight for freedom would be decided in the next few days. Kale's and Laurel's eyes knowingly met. With a final pump of Demons Bane in the air, Kale smoothly sheathed it and they turned to walk towards the area set up for their gateway. The continued shouts and cheers of the people followed them to their destiny and possible doom.

Chapter 23

Seven wizards, standing in a circle, awaited them as they approached. Laurel checked the gate-crystal in its pouch one more time, making sure it was secure. Kale checked to ensure Demon's Bane was securely in its scabbard. The high wizard nodded to each of them as he motioned them to the center of the circle.

"Once the spell is cast you will be transported to the demon's realm. We believe the demon's stronghold will be respectively near the King's stronghold in this realm. Unfortunately, we can't transport you directly to the strong hold… the demon's power is too strong there. You will have to make your way across the demon landscape and find its stronghold on your own." The wizard paused and sighed deeply. "Kale, the moment you use Demons Bane, the demon lord will know where you are. You will need to travel to his keep without the sword's assistance…. I'm sorry, if there were any other way…" Kale gave the wizard a grim smile.

"There is no other way, I understand. I still have the magical swords given to me by the dwarves. Those will have to do. We also have our magic and faith. We will succeed Zebulon. The demon lord will be destroyed, even if it cost us our lives." High wizard Zebulon smiled sadly at them.

"I pray it does not come to that. Do your best to return to us… the country needs a good King and Queen." Kale and Laurel nodded their heads, tight smiles on their faces.

The high wizard returned to his position and motioned for everyone to ready themselves. Bane rushed up and called to Kale before the casting began.

"Hey, Kale, Laurel... the two of you better meet us in the capital. If you don't come back I might just crown myself King." Kale chuckled hoarsely

"Then we definitely better come back. I'm not sure the country could survive such a rowdy and insane King.... Hey Bane, take care of yourself... and good luck." Bane brought his gauntleted fist to his heart and nodded his head.

"Good luck to you too. See you in the capital." Kale nodded as he put his gauntleted fist to his heart bowing his head.

As the wizards began their spell, Kale and Laurel took one last look at their world and the people depending on them as the energy grew around them. Then within the space between seconds the world shifted and changed. Instead of the welcoming forest of trees and animals, they were now standing in a dark realm of twisted bodies, impaled on tall spikes, torturous screams frozen on their twisted faces. The sky was red with black clouds thundering across it.

Kale took Laurel's hand in his own and they began their long trek across the barren and terrifying landscape. After a few steps, Laurel gasped, grabbing at her holy symbol. Kale turned to her and saw panic and shock fill her eyes.

"What's wrong? Laurel, what happened?" Laurel looked at him with tears in her eyes.

"I can't feel her presence anymore. It's like I've been cut off from Gaia. There's an emptiness where her presence used to be. It hurts…" A choking sob cut Laurel's words. Kale put his arms around her and pulled her towards him.

"Laurel, it's going to be all right. As soon as we return to our realm, you'll have the connection back. For now, just feel the connection between us. Hold on to that and we'll get through this." Kale could feel Laurel's breathing slow down and steady itself. After a few moments she looked into his face, a resolute smile brightening her features.

"I'm all right now. I just wasn't prepared for that. Her presence has been with me since I was a child. It was a shock to have it suddenly gone. We can keep going, I'll be fine." Kale smiled back at her and, squeezing her hand, began walking once more.

Onward they walked, through a landscape of scattered bones and black, rocky spires. Dark storms raged around them as they stepped carefully across the uneven terrain. Scattered across the land were cesspools of bubbling black and red liquid. The air had the constant smell of rotten meat and eggs, making it difficult for them to breathe without gagging. The screams and howls of otherworldly monsters echoed across the plains sending shivers up Kale and Laurel's spines. Above them, black clouds continually thundered and sparked with lightening, always threatening but never actually raining.

They seemed to walk forever, their heads constantly swiveling and searching for any signs of danger. A few times in the distance they saw the twisted shapes of creatures fighting and tearing into each other, but none looked their way. Everything about this place was dark and depressing, almost as if it were sucking the life from them.

After some time they came to, what appeared to be, a river. However, this river was not like the clear blue waters of home. This river was a tumultuous, torrent of raging, red liquid the consistency of blood. It bubbled and roared as it swept by them. It was impossible to see anything past its threatening surface. They looked around hoping to find a way across, but none presented themselves.

"We could walk along the river for a ways and see if we can find a narrower place to cross. Perhaps we could find somewhere shallower or even a bridge of sorts." Kale looked at Laurel hopelessly. "I just don't see any way for us to cross here."

Laurel wandered around the area looking everywhere for anything they could use for a boat. All she could see were the bleached and broken bones of creatures long dead. Bleached bones… some of them were quite large… could they… did they dare…. Laurel began pacing off one of the larger bones and then looked back at the width of the river. She gave Kale a look of resigned disgust.

"I can't believe I'm saying this, but… what if we drag some of these larger bones to the river and try to push them across. Maybe we could create some kind of bridge or dam. If we work together maybe we can pivot some of them all the way across." Laurel roughly swallowed the bile rising in her throat. Her stomach turned with what she was suggesting, but what other choice did they have.

Kale looked at the bones scattered around and then back at the river. He understood the revulsion Laurel felt about this idea, but it was a good idea. Better to work and create a bridge now, then get trapped later between the river and any possible enemies. At least, right now, they were still undetected in this realm. They didn't know how much longer that would last.

"It's a good idea, but if we're going to do this, then we should get started now. Once we've crossed, we should destroy it. I've been thinking… if this realm mirrors our realm, then this river will lead us to the demon's stronghold. It also means we will have to cross this river once more to reach its lair. We should stay near the river and look for anything we could use as a boat or crossing. We still have a long way to go, and I doubt we're going to get all the way there without any challenges." Laurel nodded her agreement as she took a sip from her flask. They had brought only essentials with them, which meant water, dried rations, flint and steel and their weaponry.

Together they began dragging the larger bones over towards the river. Once they had a large pile of giant bones they began positioning them so they could lift them end over end, dropping them over the river's width. The first couple splashed into the river's depths getting caught up on some rocks further downstream. While they worked, they began to hear the screams and howls of demons over the ridge. The sounds only encouraged them to quicken their pace. The next several bones followed suit, crashing into the first two and creating a shuddering, temporary bridge.

Kale and Laurel quickly approached the bridge. Behind them, the sound of screams and howls grew louder. The bones shuddered and quaked as the river of blood crashed into them. Kale took Laurel's hand as they cautiously began crossing their make-shift bridge. With each step the surface below them creaked and groaned. Their steps became swifter as the shuddering and cracking became louder. From around the rise behind them, fanged and twisted monsters bounded hungrily towards them.

Kale and Laurel leapt the last few feet to the other shore. Without hesitation, Kale took Laurel's staff and used it to pry some of the bones free of their rocky bracers. As several demons attempted to cross the bone bridge, a loud crack echoed across the plain and the bridge along with the demons were swept away downstream. The demons that were still stranded on the other side howled and screamed their frustrations at losing their prey.

Laurel pressed her hands to her ears to block out their cries as Kale returned her staff to its holder. With a final glance at the monstrous vestiges howling at them from across the river, Kale and Laurel turned their backs and began walking once more towards their destination. They decided to keep near the river hoping to avoid most of the demons.

As the sky darkened with heavy clouds, they made camp near the river's shores. They didn't dare start a fire, not that there was anything lying around they could burn, besides their own belongings. Huddled together, they pulled out some of their dry rations and began slowly eating. They had no idea how long it would take them to reach the stronghold, so they rationed their food preparing for the worst.

They had decided that Kale would take the first watch and then Laurel would take the second. Hopefully that would allow both of them enough sleep to keep up their strength and energy. As threatening thunderheads blanketed the sky and land, silence encompassed everything. The only sound they heard was the rushing and bubbling of the river near them.

Laurel tried to sleep, but her sleep was restless and tormented. Nightmares plagued her mind and showed her a world ruled by demons and monsters. Kale sat up watching the surrounding terrain for any signs of movement. Every so often he would smooth Laurel's hair trying to calm her tortured mind. He doubted either of them would get much sleep here. The sooner they found the stronghold the better.

As the end of his shift drew near, Kale stood to stretch his sore and weary muscles. Nothing had moved all night, but his instincts had told him they were being watched. Still nothing moved across the jagged peaks and rocky hills.

Everything was quiet except for the constant bubbling of the river… the river!

Kale whipped around just in time to see a long tentacle reaching for Laurel's sleeping form. Quickly he drew his swords and slashed at the slithering appendage. As his blade cut into the slimy flesh a scream erupted from the depths of the swiftly flowing river. Laurel awoke with a start, scrambling backwards on her hands and backside barely avoiding the thrashing arm.

Several more tentacles erupted from the river's depths, along with a monstrous demon whose lower half resembled an octopus. Its arms whipped out, reaching to grab Kale and Laurel in their deadly grasp. Kale's swords moved with unseen swiftness as he cut into one arm and then another. Laurel leapt to her feet and began shooting one arrow after another into the chest of the monster. Still the beast slithered towards them, its towering form hungrily glaring down on them.

Kale continued hacking at its limbs trying to slow it down, but the demon continued to slither closer undeterred by his attacks. Laurel's arrows impaled themselves in its chest time and time again, and still the creature came on backing them towards a rocky wall. Kale suddenly noticed that its limbs were regenerating with every cut he made. He would never be able to defeat it this way.

Re-sheathing his swords, Kale grabbed Laurel's arm and began running down the valley. He didn't dare travel any farther inland, but he also knew he had to put some distance between them and it. His only other option would be to use

Demon's Bane, and he didn't want to give away their location yet. He had to think of another plan, but what? Was the sword his only option? What about magic? Laurel's wasn't going to work here, but maybe his would?

After he judged that they had put enough distance between them and the creature, Kale stopped and caught his breath. Turning around he couldn't find the creature anywhere on the land. He doubted that it would have given up, which meant it had returned to the river and was waiting to attack again. Laurel looked at Kale, desperation in her eyes, as she tried to catch her breath. She nervously watched the river for any sign of the demon that had nearly caught them.

"Kale, we can't… stay here. If it's back in the river…we need… to get as far… away as possible." Kale squeezed her arm reassuringly.

"I know… but we can't keep running… like this… either. I think… I can kill it… with a spell…but that means… getting it to… come out… of the river." Laurel nodded her head in acceptance.

"Ok… I'll get it to come out… you get the spell ready."

Kale closed his eyes, centering his thoughts. When he opened them, he saw Laurel cautiously approaching the river. His heart raced with worry and fear for her, but he knew this was the best choice they had. If they didn't destroy this creature now it might follow them all the way to the stronghold and kill them when they tried to cross the river again. Kale fixed the spell in his mind and the effect he wanted it to have. Then he waited.

Laurel stood near the banks, bent over as if she were trying to catch her breath. She took her canteen from her hip and acted like she was drinking from it. Still nothing happened. She sat down on the bank and leaned back on her elbows. After a time she stood once more and began pacing back and forth along the bank. Everything remained quiet.

Finally, believing the creature was gone, Laurel turned away from the river and began heading back towards Kale. She shrugged her shoulders in bewilderment as she walked back.

"It must have given up or gone after easier prey than us." Kale didn't believe that. He kept his eyes fixed on the river, waiting for it to strike.

As Laurel drew further away, the river's waters began churning and bubbling. Every muscle in Kale's body tensed as he prepared to attack. Laurel must have sensed his alarm because she whipped her head around, her staff at the ready.

The creature surged out of the river, rising out of its watery depths and landing with a bone-jarring crash just a few feet from Laurel. Its impact sent her sprawling across the ground as she rolled out of the way of its flailing tentacles. Kale extended his hand towards the monster and cast his spell.

"Contris deruvick grantis!" As it had before, a wave of energy surged from Kale towards the demon threatening Laurel.

As the wave hit the beast, it was thrown into the air and across the river. It landed with a thunderous crash against one of the many black, stone spires that dotted the landscape. Kale fell to his knees as Laurel rushed to his side. The demon let out a roar of frustration as it slowly pushed itself upward and slithered towards the river's edge. Black blood oozed from its many injuries, but still it came on.

Kale wracked his brain in frustration and desperation, trying to think of any spell that may be useful against this unstoppable creature. Kale and Laurel could only watch in horror as it oozed closer and closer with each passing moment. One of the bubbling pits near its path suddenly exploded with gasses and flame. The demon reared back and screamed as some of the fire burnt its quickly mending flesh.

Kale noticed that it didn't seem to be as capable of regenerating the fire damage as it was the slashing and cutting damage. An idea quickly came to him, and with Laurel's help, he stood once more to face their foe. This time, Kale envisioned fire and poisonous gasses enveloping and engulfing the demon. The words he needed came to him unbidden and hungry for their use. Once more Kale raised his hand towards the approaching monster.

"Contris ignateous lucidea!" A wave of exhaustion flooded through Kale as the last words left his lips. Fire burst from his fingertips, surging and swirling around the demon.

They could no longer see the creature that was now encased in a cocoon of fire and agony. Its screams echoed across the hills and valley. Kale and Laurel pressed their hands to their ears as its howls of torment sent ripples of pain through every fiber of their beings. When its cries finally died away, they lifted their heads and looked at its charred remains. Nothing moved… not one of its limbs twitched. Kale was in no mood to take any chances though.

Drawing his swords from their sheaths on his back, Kale cautiously approached the demon's charred remains. With one quick motion, he sliced through the demon's neck, severing its head cleanly off. He quickly wiped off his swords and sheathed them before returning to Laurel.

"Now it shouldn't be able to regenerate. Let's get going, I doubt it will be long before more denizens of this world come running towards the smell of roasted flesh." As if on cue howls and screeches echoed across the valley and hundreds of demonic creatures swarmed to the top of the surrounding rises.

Grasping hands, Kale and Laurel began running East, following the river downstream and, hopefully towards the demon lord's keep. Behind them they could hear the demons begin to fight over and devour the dead predator. Only once did Kale turn around to look at the grotesque scene behind him. What he saw only made him run faster, pulling Laurel along with him.

"Not all of them are eating….we're… going to have… a long night… of running… ahead of us.

The ones that aren't feeding… are on the hunt… and we're the prey." Laurel glanced back briefly and then redoubled her efforts in running.

In the distance they saw a jagged ridge, rising up from the horizon. If they could make that ridge, perhaps they could escape their pursuers. It was a risk, but it was all they had. Behind them, the frenzied howls and screeches grew as their pursuers began closing the distance between them and their prey.

Chapter 24

Bane rubbed the back of his neck as he sat at his travel desk studying maps of the country and reading through the new scout reports that had just arrived. The desk had been a gift from Islaura's brother. He was a master carver and had created a desk that easily folded up for transport. Now it served as his writing desk, discussion table and dinner table. Today, it was a good, hard surface to bang his head against.

The scouts had reported demon signs everywhere. Farmhouses had been razed to the ground, their inhabitants remains shredded and scattered everywhere. Now that Bane had the use of wizards, he had ordered several transportation crystals created. Every scout carried one when they went out. The crystals were similar to what Kale and Laurel had taken with them, except these didn't transport people to different dimensions. They transported people back to the army's base. They were only to be used in emergencies, but lately there had been a lot of emergencies.

It had only been a couple of days since they had left the elven lands, and already they had encountered five death squads and a couple hundred soldiers. His forces had dispatched them quickly. He had lost only a few of his men from their carelessness and overconfidence. He had given the order that none of the King's allies would be allowed to live. No quarter was to be given… not even to those that surrendered. It had been one of the hardest orders he had given, but it was necessary. Any enemies left alive could wreak havoc later as the army moved eastward.

Bane rested his head on his arm, squeezing his eyes shut. When was the last time he had slept through a full night? He couldn't remember. He also couldn't remember when the last time was that he had shaved. A full beard was starting to cover his jaw line and top lip. Islaura had said it made him look older and more distinguished. He thought it made him look like a wild man.

Islaura…thinking of her made a smile creep across his face. It also made him want to pull out all his hair. She was several hours overdue with her report. Bane sat back in his chair, rubbing the back of his neck yet again. He was a man of action… not one who sat on his ass while others did everything. Frustration and impatience flooded every part of his mind and body. Slamming his hands down on the desk, he resolutely stood and began walking towards his tent opening. Grabbing his sword and scabbard, he began belting it on and then stopped.

He couldn't go look for her… he wouldn't even know where to begin. He also couldn't leave on any solo missions; he was the commanding general of this army. Everyone in his camp, and the other two squadrons, looked to him for leadership and confidence. Kale had asked him to lead these men and women in battle… in a war they may not win…damn him. Bane didn't want this position, nor did he deserve it. He was only twenty years old. There were men under his command that were old enough to be his father. They were men with much more life experience and knowledge, but they still looked to him to lead.

Bane paced the length of the tent like a restless tiger. Islaura was his best scout. He had to use her. Besides, she would kill him if he tried to keep her tied up in camp… although… the idea did have merits. Annoyed with his own wandering thoughts, he kicked a stone on the ground towards the entrance of his tent.

"Whoa there, general, are you trying to knock me out with rocks? If so… I suggest you aim higher." Bane spun around, a broad smile spreading across his face as he watched Isla saunter into his tent. Remembering himself, he hardened his expression and prepared to give her a stern lecture on procedures and protocol.

"Now you listen here, Islaura, I will not have you prancing in whenever you feel like it! You were due in over four hours ago! Where have you…" Isla stopped his words with a passionate kiss, before stepping back and smiling mischievously.

"You were saying?" Bane wanted to scream with frustration. Instead, he took a different tactic, yelling never worked with Isla.

"You do realize there is a war going on and I'm trying to keep as many of my people alive as I can? You are hours overdue with your report. Islaura, this isn't a game. We either win or die trying. Even if we win, many of those men and women out there are going to die… and there is nothing I can do about it." Bane sank onto his stool and rested his head in his hands. He took several slow breaths and then looked up to see Isla watching him, concern and compassion flooding her eyes. "Isla... I already hate sending you out on these missions. I can't afford to be constantly worried about you. I thought something had happened... that maybe one of these demon parties had caught you... I thought..."

Isla was at his side in a second, her arms wrapping around him. She buried her face in his neck, and he felt the warmth of her breath against his skin. Bane put his arms around her pulling her closer to him. She looked into his face, and Bane could see all the words they left unspoken in her eyes. She kissed him again, but this time it had a tenderness to it that Bane had rarely felt in their kisses.

"Bane, I will always return to you. It was more difficult getting back this time than a few others, but I was alright. There are more demon parties about. I saw three on my way back. I don't think we're going to make it all the way to the capital before we run into the army. I traveled as far as I could and... what I saw... villages burning in the distance, bodies strewn across fields, left to rot. I'm not sure having the army split is such a good idea. If we weren't facing demons, it would make sense, but now."

Bane closed his eyes. It was as he feared. The demons were being used to pick off any hope of supplies and reinforcements. The demons would also be able to begin picking off the three forces without much trouble. Was there any way he could keep to the original plan? No, his teachers had taught him well enough. A good commander was flexible and could change plans as the situation called for it. He needed to change plans now. He looked back down at the map in front of him. He had the location of all three forces. He could consolidate everyone at Welford. The Lord in charge of that city was an ally. If they could reach the city quickly then they could bring all their forces to bear against the enemy.

The area was a vast plains area with a river running down the middle. On the north side of the plains were thick, vast forests. They were difficult to travel through. To the south of the plains was a lake and hills. The plains acted like a funnel. That would be the place of the first battle. The plains and river would be turned red with the blood spilled. Hopefully, their sacrifice would not be in vain. Bane could only pray Kale and Laurel were successful in their mission. If they failed... all would be lost.

"Isla, can you let the captains know I need to see them. I want them here for the conference with the other commanders. Spread the word. In one week's time... we strike full force." Isla gripped his shoulder squeezing it gently. Without a word she left the tent sprinting across the ground with her message to bear.

By the time his meeting with the other commanders and his captains finished, it was late into the night. Bane knew there was only a couple hours left before sunrise, and then they would begin their march towards Welford. He knew he should get some sleep, but his mind just wouldn't settle enough to rest. Instead, he began packing up the maps, reports and his own belongings.

As the first rays of dawn fell onto the encampment, Bane had completed his packing and was breaking down his tent. As he looked around, he saw the men and women around him doing much of the same. From the looks of it, not many slept the previous night. In fact, it looked like most everyone had had similar thoughts to his own. Almost the entire encampment was packed and readying to move out. Bane chuckled darkly to himself. They were all so eager to go to war… all so eager to die. Well perhaps that was a good thing, because most likely many of them would.

By the time the sun had crested the horizon, the army was in formation with its cavalry leading the march. Bane rode in the front astride his brilliantly white stallion, Tiberious. It was just like the elves to put the commander in the shiniest armor and sit him on top of the brightest damn horse they could find. Bane smiled at his predicament. Nothing like having a bright large target painted on your front and back. The rest of the army was wearing armor and attire that was mottled and dull. As Bane looked back at the army… his army, he admired the genius of it. Anyone looking at them would have a hard time counting their numbers and a harder time figuring out where everyone was. The only one who drew the eye and stood out was him and that was the whole point.

Let the enemy's gaze be drawn to the lone shiny rider. By the time they began taking in the vastness of the army it would be too late. To add to this potential confusion, his forces were spread out across the river valley. Between the ingenious engineering feats of the dwarves and the artistic craftsmanship of the elves, their movements were nearly silent. It was as if the earth itself had risen up and was rolling in a vast tidal wave across the countryside.

Onward they marched, through the morning. Bane had assigned small groups to the task of burying the ravaged dead they came across on their journey. Yes, he was in a hurry to reach their destination, but he would be damned if he allowed the dead to be left to rot. He had also made sure each group had a priest that could perform last rights for the departed. The last thing he needed was fields of angry ghosts and specters roaming around and causing more problems.

Shortly after lunch they reached the river stretching across their path. Quickly, without being told, elven and dwarven craftsmen and engineers laid temporary bridgework for the army to cross. The frameworks were another example of these two races genius. They were able to be laid out, across the river and then once everyone was across, they could be retrieved and folded up into easily transportable sizes.

It blew Bane's mind to watch their ingenuity and skill. How much had his land been denied by the separation between the races. With everyone working together they were accomplishing and creating more inventions and advances than had been seen in ages. As horrible as war was, it was bringing people together in a way unseen for over a century. Bane only hoped that the cooperation would continue after the war was over. With Kale and Laurel leading the country, it probably would… if they survived.

Bane quickly pushed the dark thought to the back of his mind. He had other things to worry about right now. He could just make out the dot on the horizon that was Welford. Tonight they would camp outside of the city and in three days the other two divisions would hopefully be joining them.

By mid-afternoon, the city was plainly in sight. Bane eased the army into a slower march as they approached. A strange prickling sensation was growing in his stomach and up his spine… something was wrong. Raising his hand, he called a halt to their movement. He rode forward a short distance to get a closer look. Two of his captains rode forward to join him as he continued his inspection of the looming city.

"Commander… what is it?" Bane didn't respond right away. He wanted to make sure his instincts and observations were correct first. Slowly he gazed across the surrounding fields and ground. He stared at several places for long moments barely daring to breath. Finally, he saw what he was looking for. The city was a trap.

"Captain Daniel, tell everyone to ready themselves. Our enemy is hiding in the fields and grasslands surrounding Welford. Try to be inconspicuous as you pass the message. I want everyone to proceed like we don't suspect anything. Captain Marcus, I want you to ready the cavalry. We're going to approach down the road and when I give the signal, I want all horses kicked into a full gallop half going to the left of the town and half riding towards the right. We're going to trample as many as we can. Tell them to draw their weapons at the last moment."

"Daniel, have the archers ready their bows. When the cavalry takes off, I want them to rain as many arrows as they can down onto those fields before we get there. Captain Marcus, you will lead the left charge and I will lead the right. Have the rest of the army follow in after us and cut down whatever's left. Have the wizards launch as many spells as they can. They know what will work in this type of attack better than I do. Once the fields are cleared, we'll regroup and turn our attentions towards the city. If anyone is still alive inside, we'll do what we can… and men… remember, we could be dealing with demons not humans. Tell everyone to show no mercy. No quarter is to be given. Understood?" Bane looked to his two captains who nodded their assent and then turned to see to their troops.

So today would be the first real test of the army. Bane only hoped the Gods were with them on this day. Hopefully by the end of the day, his soldiers would prevail and the enemy would be crushed. As the cavalry came forward Bane nudged Tiberious into a slow walk. He wanted the enemy to think they were all tired from their long day of marching. In truth, he had no idea how tired his troops were, but sleep would come soon enough. Hopefully the thought of battle would give them renewed strength and energy.

All his forces moved with slow trepidity toward the town. As they drew closer, Bane kept his eyes on the fields that surrounded the town. The enemy was becoming more restless as they could see and sense their prey approaching. Bane closed his eyes and breathed in the clean, fresh air. He cleared his mind of all emotion, focusing solely on the coming battle. When he opened his eyes, it was as if time slowed down. Everything appeared brighter, clearer. Sounds seemed crisper, louder. A light breeze gently caressed the surrounding fields causing soft ripples to play across their surface.

With a quick glance out of the corner of his eye towards Marcus, Bane flicked his left hand as if swatting at a fly. Without hesitation the cavalry kicked their mounts into a full gallop, splitting off and racing across the fields on either side of the city walls. There was no more time to think. Bane led his men across the field, sword raised to the sky. Dozens of arrows arched across the sky burying themselves in the fields a few yards in front of the riders. Screams and howls erupted from the grasslands and hidden demons, goblins and soldiers sprang up like monstrous flytraps hungry for their prey. Bane raced into the thickest of them bringing his sword down onto one and then another.

The sound of battle split the peacefulness of the afternoon as the foot soldiers and archers rushed to join the fray. The ground quickly became stained with the blood of the fallen. Balls of fire, lightning and ice tore through the enemy. Bane kept swinging his sword from left to right, striking at whatever foe was nearest. Tiberious kicked and bucked, slamming his hooves into one attacker after another. There were so many of them.

From somewhere in the distance, Bane could hear the sound of a horn calling across the chaos. He didn't know if it was an ally or the enemy calling reinforcements and he couldn't spare the time to figure it out. He had no idea how the battle was going. He was just trying to survive the moment and win out the day. Frustration and anger at his own foolhardiness drove his sword and he became a blur of movement as he struck out again and again.

Finally, he surged through the mass of bodies and found a clearing. He spun Tiberious around and quickly assessed the field. From this vantage he could only see his side of the town, but if his side was any indication of how things were going then they were in trouble. Again he heard the clear piercing sound of the horn and spun in his saddle trying to locate its source.

Spinning Tiberious in a circle he saw a young man standing on the top of the city's wall blowing the horn. Suddenly the gates of the city opened and riders and foot soldiers poured from the openings. In their lead was Lord Welford, his sword raised to the sky as he shouted a call to battle.

Several of Bane's cavalry struggled to his side, regrouping and preparing for another run.

Bane patted Tiberious's neck reassuringly. In response, Tiberious snorted and stomped his hooves eager to return to the battle. Bane smiled grimly and nodded his head. "Ready men… this time we don't leave the battle until it is done. TO VICTORY!!!"

Bringing his arm down, Bane kicked Tiberious into a charge straight down the middle. The cavalry surged once more into the fray, trampling more of the demons, goblins and soldiers. Bane slashed and stabbed at one demon after another, his sword never dulling. His blade hummed with the music of battle as one after another of his enemies fell to his sword.

The enemy continued to fight on, never running, never trying to escape. The added support of Lord Welford's forces helped to turn the tide of battle and soon all that was left were the demons, a handful of goblins and a few scattered soldiers of the King's. Bane had long since left the safety of Tiberious. It had become too tiring to try and keep his balance while both he and the horse continued to fight.

Bane cut through the enemy like a man possessed. He lost track of time and everything else. The goblins and men began backing away whenever they saw him, choosing any but him. The demons began focusing their attacks on him. Even with the weakening light his armor and sword gleamed with the light of dawn. His soldiers rallied around him becoming a solid mass of swords and shields.

As the sun fell below the horizon, the last demon fell to Bane's blade. He shouted with his rage and triumph. Taking several deep breaths he slowly looked around the field of battle assessing their losses. His captains were still up, if injured. Marcus seemed to be cradling his right arm and Daniel was limping slightly. Lord Welford was making his way towards him… probably to ask who was in charge. He would most certainly be surprised when he discovered it was Bane. His men were looking at him in awe and respect, something Bane had not been expecting to see considering his disastrous plan. Most likely they would all see him as an incompetent fool by morning. Might as well use his authority while he still had it.

"Thomas, Alexander, Selwin and Oleg… come here." Bane stretched his neck and back as he waited for them to arrive. "I need you to organize teams and search for any survivors. If they're ours get them some help and healing… if they're not, kill them. I'm not going to deal with prisoners. Make sure you have some of Lord Welford's men with you, we don't need to accidentally kill our allies." The men saluted him before heading off and organizing their groups.

Bane slowly began making his way towards Lord Welford. It was better to get this over with sooner rather than later. Captain Marcus was approaching as well. Hopefully with a more positive report on how the battle on the other side of the town had gone. Bane felt every muscle in his body relax as he saw Isla directing soldiers who were able, to set up the tents and get food cooking. Bane would have to ask if Lord Welford had any extra tankards of ale available for his men. The Gods only knew how well they deserved a small celebration. Bane raised his hand, in greeting towards his lordship, as he stepped over corpses and body parts.

"Lord Welford... well met. Thank you for your timely assistance and aid. I'm not sure we would have prevailed without it." The Lord stepped towards Bane and offered his hand in friendship.

"Well met commander. Your captain told me where to find you. I must say... you were very thorough in your destruction of the enemy." Bane could feel his eyebrows rising with dark amusement. What did this lord expect? Did he think that war would be soldiers sitting down to tea and cake with the enemy over a game of chess?

"This is war, my lord... a war for our very survival. If you don't mind, we have need of your city and its services. Many of my soldiers are injured and in need of healing. Also, if you have any barrels of ale or rum lying around, I will gladly pay for them so that my soldiers may have a small celebration to raise their spirits." Bane hurried on to prevent any protests. "I assure you, my lord, my soldiers will remain outside of your city walls. We will only be here for a few days and then we will be moving on towards the capital. If any of your soldiers would be willing to join our force, we will welcome them, but rest assured, my lord, we do not force enlistment." Bane smiled at the choking cough that his lordship issued forth.

"Of course... commander, my city would be more than happy to assist your men in whatever way they need. I would like to know, commander... is it true?" Bane quirked his eyebrows as he looked at the lord curiously.

"Is what true Lord Welford?" The nobleman glanced around looking unsure and hopeful.

"Has the true heir been found? Is he truly as great as rumors have said?" Bane barely choked down his laughter.

"It is true, Lord Welford, the heir has been found and she is quite amazing. In fact, she is battling her way through a demon dimension right now to destroy the demon lord who is allied to the false King." The surviving men around them gave a hurrah and cheered to the Queen's health, while Bane laughed heartily at the shocked look on the lord's face. "Don't worry, my lord, I won't inform her of your misgivings."

"Misgivings... of course not. She is the true heir and we welcome her wisdom, strength, and... power... on the throne." Bane clapped him on the back and started guiding him back towards the city and tents being set up.

"Come my lord, why don't I fill you in on the truth about our future Queen and King." The relief at hearing that there would be a King as well, made Bane laugh all the harder.

"That sounds excellent, commander, let me have some of my men fetch food and drink for all our men. I think everyone could use a celebration after today."

It wasn't long before the city and armies were celebrating the destruction of the false King's demonic army. As the night wore on, stories of the day grew and exploded as events became blurred by drink and pride. After a hearty dinner and long discussion with Lord Welford, which cured the lord of his delusions, Bane retired to his tent to rest and read through the reports of the dead and injured.

The healers had only been able to tend to the most severe of the injured that night. Tomorrow they would tend to everyone else. The dead had been gathered up and carefully taken to the city's cemetery for proper burial on the morrow. The enemy's dead would be burned in a mass grave the next day. Some of the city's citizens had volunteered for the task of digging and burning the monsters. Bane supposed it would give them some closure, although the war was far from over.

Looking at the losses, Bane was surprised to see how well they had faired. In total, he had only lost twenty men... twenty men who would never see their families again. Twenty men who would never see the country they were trying to create. Twenty men who would never see another dawn. Bane slammed his fist into the table as he stood and began pacing the area.

He had informed the other commanders of what had happened that day and their losses. He had expected them to strip him of his leadership... instead they congratulated him on a job well done.

How could he still lead these men and women? He had nearly gotten them all killed! He would punch Kale, when he got back, for getting him into this... him and his damnable prophecy.

"Good evening, commander." Bane spun around to see Isla standing quietly in the entrance to his tent. Her arms holding her cloak tightly around her. She tilted her head watching him with concern in her eyes. Bane motioned for her to enter.

"So...how goes the celebration?" Bane mumbled as he watched Isla approach. She smiled as she pulled him from his chair and drew him towards his bed.

"It's going well. Your men can't stop talking about your skill on the battlefield. All of them swear the day would have been lost if not for you. They say you fought as if guided by the Gods... as if you are their weapon." Bane closed his eyes, sighing deeply. Leaning back on his forearms he looked up towards the ceiling of his tent, hopelessly.

"Isla... I got twenty men killed today.... How many more will die because of my decisions? I don't belong here... I'm not a leader of armies. I should be..." Isla put a gentle finger to his lips silencing him.

"Bane... you don't see your own greatness. You have always been surrounded with those who you were told were your betters. You're more than you think you are. I saw you fight today. You fought with blinding speed and accuracy. No one on that field was your match... not even the demons. Your sword and armor glowed with a holy light as you fought... even when there was no light. People die in war. You only lost twenty... twenty out of how many? You know every man's name and story. How many generals and commanders do you think would do that? These men will follow you into the pit of darkness, because they believe in you... not Kale, not Laurel... you... and so do I." Bane met her eyes and was surprised to see a single tear running down her cheek.

"Isla... stay with me tonight." Her smile warmed his heart and eased his troubled mind.

"Always."

The next three days were spent recuperating from the battle and resupplying. Lord Welford proved to be a very valuable ally. He had stored up cellars of supplies waiting for this day to arrive. Almost his entire force joined Bane's army to continue on to the capital. Lord Welford would stay behind with a small force and enough supplies for the city to survive a month within its walls.

Bane only hoped that would be enough time to end this war. On the second day, after the battle, the group from the north, led by Aldric, arrived. They had also been forced to face an army of demons and men one day after speaking with Bane. Aldric had used similar tactics to Bane's with a few modifications to account for his group's makeup. He had lost forty-five soldiers in all, but had gained thirty in their travels. He had also discovered his daughter among the injured. She had apparently disguised herself as a man and slipped into his forces. Bane was never having children... especially daughters.

By day three, the southern army had arrived, led by Kale's father, Lord Kensington. They had encountered a demon army two days after they had spoken with Bane. Lord Kensington had been forced to use very different strategies because of the hilly terrain they had been forced to fight on. Thankfully, they had been able to secure some high ground and fight from a more defensive position. They had lost fifty soldiers, but their losses were offset by the number of villagers and adventurers who had joined the fight.

That night they sat around the table pouring over the maps and scout reports trying to discern their enemy's next move. After a long night of discussion and debate, it was decided. They would continue forward as one force and prepare for the worst. With the entire army together, there would be no way to hide their actions. The plains leading to the serpent's tongue, which is what many called the fork in the river, would most likely be the sight of the next battle. It would be the place where the war would be won or lost.

The next day was a solemn day as soldiers busied themselves with repairs, improvements and honing their skills. That night songs of home, hope and a brighter future filled the night air. Isla stayed with Bane... something that had become natural and welcomed. The following dawn brought the army to its feet as it began its march towards the rising sun and war.

Chapter 25

Kale and Laurel had run for hours. Their bodies were exhausted and weak. They no longer knew what time of day it was, let alone how many days they had been in this horrible place. Every time they tried to catch their breath, the demons would be there, ready to sink their slavering jaws into Kale and Laurel's soft flesh. Howling and screeching hounded their flight as they bolted down one chasm after another.

The sloping valley had been replaced by tall spires and sheer cliffs towering over them. Kale wasn't sure how long it had been since they lost sight of the river. He only knew they couldn't stop. His head constantly swiveled searching for somewhere to hide… somewhere to escape. They were beginning to lose their balance and trip over rocks and bones as they fled their pursuers. It wouldn't be long before their bodies surrendered, and they would be left to the hunger of the demons.

Twice, Kale and Laurel had needed to turn and fight. Twice they had barely escaped with their lives. Now Laurel's arrows were gone and Kale could barely hold his sword. Still they continued to run, battered, bruised and bleeding. The howling surrounded them as they clambered over bones and fallen rocks. It was almost as if they were being herded… but towards what?

The darkness suddenly went silent as if the creatures had called off their pursuit. Kale didn't trust any of it. They continued to run scanning the canyons around them for any sign of demons. As they rounded a corner Kale spotted a fissure in the cliff face. As they approached, they could see it was just large enough for them to slip into. Laurel and Kale looked at each other for only a moment before squeezing their bodies through the tight crack.

As they inched themselves further in, the darkness filled with the angry and frustrated howls and screams of the demons. Laurel continued to push herself further back into the crevice. The further back she went the larger the gap became until she fell out into a large cavern. She only just managed to move out of the way before Kale tumbled after her. The cavern resembled a vast greeting hall in a castle. The floor was smooth and clear of debris. Against one wall was a large alcove that looked like it had once seen grand, warm fires. In the opposite walls were more alcoves, large enough for someone to sleep in.

For now they were safe. Laurel stumbled over to one of the sleeping alcoves and checked it for any signs of life. When she found none, she hoisted her pack inside and crawled in for some much-needed sleep. Her mind and body were exhausted. The lack of connection to her Goddess had taken a toll on her entire being. She glanced at Kale once more, a half-hearted smile creeping onto her lips, before slipping into a deep sleep. She just couldn't find the energy to care anymore.

Kale watched, exhausted, as Laurel's eyes closed and her breathing became regular. He knew they needed sleep, but he couldn't force his mind to relax. Every nerve and muscle in his body was taut and strained to the point of snapping. He had no idea what time of day it was or where they were. He had lost track of their location and their points of reference. Where was the demon's stronghold? How far did they still have to go? It seemed like weeks since he last saw the hint of the stronghold's spires. When was that? It had been before they entered the maze of canyons and chasms. Each step seemed to take them further from their destination.

The nightmare the crystal cavern had shown them was nothing compared to this. That had been a dream by comparison. Everything had seemed so straight forward. Here everything was so different. Every one of their steps had been harried. Every time they tried to take a stand and fight they found themselves surrounded by even more demons than before. It was as if each kill gave birth to ten more demons… each kill.

Kale shuddered with the thought. What if they were creating the demons? What if more demons were born with each death by their hands? How could they ever win? How could they ever survive? He had been such an arrogant fool to think this would be like any other mission. He was still that arrogant child who thought he could do anything and win any challenge.

He paced back and forth in the cavern occasionally stopping to watch Laurel sleep. She was so beautiful. Even with the grime and darkness surrounding her, she was a beacon of light and hope. Slowly he made his way over to her and sat down next to her on the ground. He felt like he was losing his mind, but maybe if he stayed near her… maybe he could….

A prickling, sharp feeling raced up his spine and down his arms. Panicked, he shot glances around the room, peering into the darker areas… straining to see anything in the darkness. His half-elven eyes sought out any heat signatures that would radiate from a living creature. Someone… or something was watching them. He scanned the cavern, finding nothing. Shifting back to normal vision he began hallucinating. He would catch movement out of the corner of his eyes, but when he turned to see what it was… nothing was there. Faces, fangs and claws lunged at him from the darkness… but they were only shadows.

Kale drew his sword swinging it at the encroaching darkness… lashing out at nothing. He could feel the madness gripping him… choking him. The room began to spin as his balance faltered. He heard a noise behind him and spun to attack. His foot slipped and he crashed to the floor. He felt his head hit something hard and saw something small climbing into the alcove with Laurel as darkness finally claimed him.

Laurel wasn't sure how long she had slept, but the grumbling of her stomach wouldn't let her sleep any longer. As she went to stretch, she felt the presence of another body lying tucked against her abdomen. Slowly, she opened her eyes and looked at what was pressed against her.

Her breath caught in her throat as she looked at the small form of a child curled against her. Gently she stroked the hair away from the little one's face and realized that she wasn't looking at a human child. This was a demon…a young demon child. Her long, thick, dark hair was tangled and matted with dirt, ash and possibly blood. Her skin was the color of untempered steel. Her frame was light and small… almost fragile, though Laurel doubted she was. Her face was almost angelic, the sweet face of a sleeping child.

As she looked down at her, the girl's eyes snapped open wide with fear. The girl tried to run, but Laurel held onto her and pulled her closer. This little one reminded her so much of herself when she was small… terrified, alone, untrusting.

"Shh, shh… it's ok. I won't hurt you. My name is Laurel. Who are you?" Laurel released her gently, hoping this little demon wouldn't bolt. She didn't … she stood there tilting her head and looking at Laurel with fear and hope.

"I don't have a name. I'm alone. I hide here. It's safe here. They can't get in." She looked at the ground and drew her clawed feet across the smooth surface of the floor. Laurel held out her hand beckoning the child towards her.

"Are you hungry? I have some food in here, if you would like some." Laurel saw the girl lick her lips as she slowly inched towards her. Smiling to herself, Laurel pulled some of the dried meat and bread from her pack and gave some to the child. The girl quickly inhaled the food and then sat down next to her. "Well, if you don't have a

name... we'll have to give you one. Let me see...
you're bringing some light to a very dark place
with your spirit... how about Leora, bringer of
light." Laurel watched with a smile as the small
she-demon tested out the name and a warm smile
spread across her face.

"I like it... you're really nice. You can stay
here if you like." Hope filled her voice as she
looked longingly at Laurel. With a sigh, Laurel
pulled a comb from her bag and began gently
brushing through the tangle of hair on Leora's
head.

"We can't. There is a stronghold of a
demon lord somewhere near here and we need to
get there and destroy him. After that we'll have to
return to our own world. The only problem is...
we're a little lost right now.... You wouldn't
happen to know where the stronghold is, would
you?" The girl bit her lower lip and glanced
nervously around the chamber. Laurel could tell
the child was starving for company and...
surprisingly love. She didn't even know it was
possible for demons to love.

Leora suddenly jumped off the ledge and
ran to the other side of Kale, who was still lying on
the ground nearby. She gently rolled him onto his
side and looked nervously up at Laurel. At first,
Laurel didn't understand what she was doing, but
after a moment she noticed an area on Kale's head
that was matted with blood and dirt.

"I think I scared him... he spun around and
fell. I think he hit his head when he landed."
Laurel was at his side in a moment and looking

carefully at the injury. She pulled the water from her pack and used it as sparingly as possible to clean the wound. She took a deep relaxing breath as she realized the wound wasn't too serious.

Turning towards her pack she took out an ointment she had brought with her and a bandage. Leora watched curiously as she gathered her materials to tend to Kale's wound. She frowned as she watched her clean and dress the area, looking more confused by the moment.

"What are you doing?" Laurel smiled as she met Leora's eyes.

"I'm cleaning and dressing his wound. The ointment will help it heal and keep any infection from getting in. The bandage will help protect it." Leora screwed up her face as she contemplated what Laurel was saying.

"That won't work. You need the fire water. I can get you some. It will kill the infection that has already gotten in and it will make the wound go away." Laurel looked at her curiously.

"How do you know there is infection?" Leora shrugged.

"I see it… can't you?" Laurel shook her head. "Well it's there…." Leora bit her lip again and twisted her foot into the ground. With a large sigh she met Laurel's eyes and nodded to herself. "You stay here with him. I'll go get some fire water and bring it back. I'll see if I can't find some fire berries too. They're really yummy and they give you lots of energy."

Before Laurel could say anything, Leora had taken off at a run down a dark tunnel she hadn't seen before. Once she was gone, Laurel turned her attentions back towards Kale. He should have woken up with all of their talking and moving him around, but he just laid there. She also noticed that a slight sheen was starting to grow on his skin. Without her divine healing, Laurel was at a loss for what else she could do. She would just have to wait until Leora returned and hope her instincts were right about trusting the child.

Laurel wasn't sure how long she had sat there with Kale's head in her lap waiting for Leora to return, but it had seemed like an eternity. With each passing moment, Kale's condition was getting worse, and Laurel didn't know what to do. Finally, Leora came walking back into the cavern carrying a stone bucket of red liquid and another smaller stone bucket of round red berries. Laurel quickly moved to help her carry the bucket closer to Kale. Smiling at each other they immediately set to work.

Quickly, they removed Kale's bandage and used a small stone bowl to pour some of the fire water onto his head. Laurel winced when she heard it sizzle and could only hope she was doing the right thing. She watched in amazement as Kale's wound bubbled and steamed. Leora filled the tiny bowl again and poured some more on the area. This time the fire water washed everything away and Laurel watched as the wound knitted itself back together, fading into unblemished skin. After a few more moments, it was as if there had never been a wound there at all.

Laurel glanced at Kale again. His skin was still glistening with sweat and his sleep had become restless and tormented. Leora dipped the bowl one more time into the fire water and together they managed to pour the contents into Kale's mouth. It had been a challenge and he had reflexively fought them, but after a few attempts they were finally successful. Both girls sank back against the wall as they waited for the water to take effect.

While they waited, Laurel pulled an empty water skin from her pack and dipped it into the fire water to fill it. She did the same with an empty water skin in Kale's pack before settling down and combing through the rest of Leora's hair. Eventually Kale slipped into a calmer sleep and his skin returned to its normal shade. Shortly after this, his eyes began moving behind his eyelids, as dreams took over his sleep.

By this time, Laurel had found some clothing in her pack that she could make into a makeshift dress for Leora, which delighted the little demoness. She twirled and spun giggling with delight. Laurel had managed to work out most of her snarls and had plaited her hair into several braids. While she watched Leora twirl and spin, she packed the berries into individual bags, saving out a few for each of them to eat when Kale woke. Laurel smiled to herself as a new realization came to her. She wasn't going to leave Leora in this place. Leora would come home with them. She just couldn't leave this child here alone, demon or not… she needed someone to look after her and love her. Her mind made up, Laurel sat on the edge of her sleeping alcove and waited for Kale to wake up.

Kale awoke to the sound of laughter and merriment. His mind was foggy and confused. Had the demon dimension been a terrible nightmare? Had everything been a dream? He hoped Laurel wasn't a dream. Slowly he opened his eyes, trying to get a sense of his surroundings. It sounded like a young girl was singing and laughing. Perhaps someone was playing a game nearby. Was he camping?

As Kale's vision cleared he saw the dark volcanic walls and ceiling of the chamber he was in. A warm glow emanated from somewhere to his left, but he wasn't sure he wanted to turn his head just yet. Slowly he shifted his eyes observing what surroundings he could from his position. Laurel was sitting in an alcove watching someone... a warm smile graced her face. She looked revived and full of life, something he hadn't been sure he would see again.

Slowly he turned his head to get a better view of the room and to find out where the singing and giggling was coming from. The room spun briefly, but as his vision cleared....Kale leapt to his feet, his sword instantly in his hand. Pain shot through his head as the room tilted, but he held fast, placing himself between the demon and Laurel. She must have been under some kind of spell... she had to be.

The demon leapt away from him, cowering against the far wall. A small whimper escaped its lips. It was wearing one of Laurel's tunics, the sleeves rolled up and a piece of cloth wrapped around its waist like a belt. Anger and confusion burned inside of him. He would strike this creature down and hopefully free Laurel from its spell. A gentle touch at his elbow stayed his hand. He turned to see patient and pleading eyes gazing into his.

"Kale, don't… she's just a child, alone and frightened. Please, put your sword down and listen." Every muscle in his body tensed. Every instinct in him told him to fight… this was a trick.

"Laurel, it's a demon! Whatever power or spell it has put on you… it can't be trusted." Laurel sighed with patience born from years of experience. She sounded and looked like his mother when he had pushed her to her limits.

"Kale, she saved your life. If it hadn't been for Leora, you would be dead. She knew of water that could save you and she brought berries we can eat to rejuvenate ourselves. She is smart, innocent and alone. She needs us… and we need her. Please… I'm not under any spell… I'm just trusting my instincts, and they tell me we can trust her." Kale looked at her in stunned silence. This demon saved his life? He looked once more at the creature before him. Its hair was combed and braided. It cowered like a terrified child. It… she was crying.

Kale felt Laurel's hand on his sword arm. Slowly he lowered his sword and sheathed it. How was this possible? Demons were monsters not to be trusted… but here, cowering in front of him, was proof of the opposite. She was terrified and alone.

Laurel put some red berries in his hand and he ate them without thinking. The explosion of flavor and heat in his mouth brought him quickly back to himself.

He felt the juice of the berries slip down his throat in a hot waterfall of flavor and energy. His entire body warmed and relaxed. Every muscle released its tension and he felt energy surge through his limbs. The cave was no longer so dark. His eyes began to draw what little ambient light there was and expand it tenfold. Everything became clearer... sound, sight, smells.

Kale sat down in the alcove next to Laurel and looked at the little one trying to meld into the opposite wall of the cavern. Then he looked at Laurel. His mouth opened and then closed again. He wanted to say something... but what? From the look in Laurel's eyes, she wasn't about to leave this... child, if that's what it... she was. Kale rubbed his temples, sighing deeply.

"Ok Laurel... you must have a plan here. What is it?" Laurel smiled at him and then motioned for the she-demon to come closer. Kale watched as the creature slowly inched closer.

"Kale... I think Leora should come with us. First, she knows this place better than either of us. Second, she's been hiding from the other demons her whole life. So she'll be able to help us avoid detection as well. Third, she's a child and I'm not leaving her here to be tortured and tormented the rest of her existence." Upon hearing Laurel's third reason, Leora squealed with delight and ran into her arms.

Kale was taken aback. How long had he been out? Apparently long enough for his wife to develop a fondness for a demon. He shook his head and tried to find arguments for her reasoning. It wasn't easy. She was right... they needed help, and this child was apparently willing to help them.... as long as she didn't lead them into a trap. Still, if she were going to trap them or kill them, there had been more than enough opportunity already. As for bringing her back with them...

"Laurel, I know you mean well, but... a demon in our world? How could she ever be accepted? After everything the country has gone through... she would be feared and hated." It pained him to see Laurel's face fall and sadness flood her eyes. Kale took her hand in his wishing he didn't have to cause her this pain. Leora put her hand on both of their hands, a small smile growing on her tiny face. It took all of Kale's will not to smack her hand away.

"Maybe they don't have to know what I am. I can change how I look... a bit. It might be enough." Kale watched as the demon jumped to the floor and then began altering her appearance.

Her ears became slightly less pointed and her skin shifted from ash to a creamy white. Her wings shrank and disappeared into her back as if they had never been there. Her talons shortened to look more like long manicured nails and the ridges on her face turned into dark eyebrows and smooth cheekbones. She looked like a pale, but beautiful and delicate little elven girl. Kale knew his last argument had slipped away with this revelation and with seeing the smile that spread across Laurel's face. With a sigh he threw his hands in the air in defeat and walked across the chamber.

"Fine, but this is going to be dangerous. Leora, you need to listen to us and do what we tell you. If we say run, you run. If we tell you to hide... hide. Understand?" Kale couldn't help but smile as she vigorously nodded her head and began bouncing on her toes. As if life wasn't complicated enough. "For now you should probably look like yourself. We don't need you to look like more interesting bait for the others. Now perhaps you could tell us where we need to go and what's the best way there?"

The next several hours were planning their pathway and discussing strategy. Leora ended up being very useful in this because she was able to draw out a map of tunnels and caverns that could take them very close to the demon lord's stronghold. After ensuring they had everything they needed the three of them began heading out.

Leora led them from one cavern to the next, guiding them down long winding tunnels and finding the easiest and safest paths to cross at. Kale was impressed with how seriously she took her job as guide and, as time went by, he found himself trusting her more and more. On several occasions she stopped them until the way was clear or had them back track to go a different way, avoiding unexpected dangers. By the time they reached the edge of the demon lord's stronghold, Kale found it difficult to think of her as anything other than a little girl desperate for a family and freedom.

From their spot in the crevice, they could see the towering, foreboding structure of the demon's lair. Five ebony spires spiked towards the sky, encircling the sixth largest spire. The entire structure sat on an island. To get there, they would need to cross the river of blood once more, a task none of them relished. Luckily this time there was a ferry to cross the river. Unfortunately, the ferry was on the other side of the river.

The river wasn't the only problem. Across the river was a gathering of approximately fifty demons of varying sizes and forms. Kale felt Leora cringe and hide behind him. It was obvious the demon lord knew they were coming and had prepared a welcome for them. With a glance at Laurel the three of them slipped further back into the crevice. This would take some planning if they were going to make it across the river and through the amassing army.

They crouched in a circle, Leora clinging to Laurel's arm as Kale drew a layout of the island and the fortress sitting on top. There were not many possibilities left to them. They would only have one chance and, if Kale were honest, their chances weren't good. After a very long discussion, and hopeful wishing, they decided to watch and wait. They would need to see their patterns and watches. Even demons had to sleep, at least that was what Kale was hoping.

So they waited and watched until they had a definite pattern of guard changes, sleep schedules and adjustments. Kale sent Leora off to find something they could use as rope. It wasn't long before she returned with several long, stringy vines. The three of them sat and weaved the vines together into a fairly strong rope. To the end of this Kale attached two daggers by their hilts. Then they sat and waited again.

When it was nearly time, the trio cautiously made their way to the river's edge, hiding behind rocks and small spires. Once they were in position they sat down and waited. Kale tapped off the time on his leg as he watched for his opportunity. The two demons guarding the boat shifted uncomfortably, becoming restless and annoyed with their jobs. Finally, they grunted and growled at each other before turning and heading away from the river and rapidly toward the fortress.

This was Kale's moment. Taking a deep breath, Kale made his way to the river's edge. He glanced up at the retreating demons once more before loosening their make-shift rope and throwing the daggers towards the boat. His first shot fell short and Kale held his breath as he pulled the rope back to him quickly. His second throw landed with a clank and thud inside the boats hull.

Kale winced at the sound the daggers had made, but it was necessary. Taking a deep breath he carefully pulled the rope back towards him, praying the daggers would catch. Slowly the boat pulled loose of the opposite bank and made its way towards him. As he pulled Laurel and Leora sprinted up beside him and began pulling in earnest. It wasn't long before the boat was bumping into the land and they were clambering in.

Kale and Laurel grabbed the oars and began rowing back to the other side as quickly as they could. Leora untied the daggers and put them back in the sheaths on Kale's legs while they rowed. In moments they were climbing out of the boat and moving quickly towards the fortress. As they began to climb the embankment a cry rose up from the nearest spire and howls of rage and hunger quickly followed. Laurel looked at Kale, fear and dread warring with determination.

"Kale, if there was ever a time to use Demon's Bane... I think it's now." Kale nodded firmly only once and then drew Demon's Bane from its sheath. Raising it in the air he led their pitiful charge into the onslaught of ravaging demons.

Chapter 26

Bane led the charge for the fifth time that day. His men were exhausted, but still they rallied to his call driving forward against a tidal wave of demons and monsters. The valley was drowned in the blood of the fallen. The screeches and howls of demons collided with the clanging of steel and screams of the dying. The battle raged on for hours; day turned into night, and slowly the chaos dissipated.

Bane stalked back to his command tent, sweat and blood ran in rivers down his face and armor. He had ordered all able-bodied soldiers to retrieve the wounded. The priests would be working overtime tonight healing and tending to all the wounded. Once the wounded were tended to, he would send others to try and retrieve their dead. He would be damned if he allowed the bodies of his soldiers to be ravaged by the enemy. He might not be able to save their lives, but he could damn well ensure their spirits had a proper exit.

He sat behind his desk, wiping some of the blood and sweat from his face. It had been a long, hard-fought day, and he knew he should get some rest… but he couldn't, not until he had the list of dead… not until he knew where they stood.

Lord Kingsford, Lord Aldric, High Wizard Lysander, Captain Daniel and Captain Marcus entered the tent, each appearing ready to collapse in exhaustion. Bane watched silently as these great men sank onto make-shift chairs. Lord Kingsford was a man he respected and looked to as a father.

Lord Aldric, leader of the dwarves, was a man worthy of admiration and respect. Captain Daniel was only one year older than Bane, but Captain Marcus was his senior by ten years, both were men of honor, action and discipline. These great men looked to him for leadership and strength. It was almost too much to bear… but this was the position he was in, and he wouldn't disappoint them.

"My lords, captains… before we begin, please have something to drink and eat. It seems our cooks were of the mind we would be hungry when we survived." Bane poured each man a mug of ale and brought the platter of meats, cheeses and breads to his desk for everyone to partake of. After they had drank, eaten and relaxed some, Bane resumed the meeting.

"Do we have any reports yet on the number of dead and wounded?" Bane almost cringed at the fallen looks on their faces… almost. They had lost that many… he would have to find out who wouldn't be returning to their families. Lord Kingsford was first to speak up.

"Initial reports show we have lost a quarter of our troops. At least half again that many are wounded. The priests say it will take several days to get everyone back to full health." Bane rested his head in his hands and closed his eyes.

"We don't have days." Bane went to the entry of his tent and looked around. "Kent, come here…. I need you to run and tell the healers to heal as many as they can to the point of functional. Tell them they don't need to be in perfect health, they just need to be able to hold a sword and fight."

Bane watched grimacing as the young man disappeared into the night to deliver his message. Bane returned to his seat feeling ages older than he was. How would they hold out until Kale and Laurel succeeded? What if they didn't succeed? For the first time in weeks, Bane was starting to doubt their chances of success.

Bane sat back down, moving the tray to the side so he could better study the map laid out on his desk. Direct assaults weren't working. The enemy's numbers far outweighed their own. No matter how many of the demons they killed more kept coming. It was an endless wave of demons. True they were decreasing the numbers of humans and monsters, but those numbers were only filled in with more demons. They had to develop a new strategy. Something their enemy wouldn't expect. Bane studied the map more closely, knowing the others were watching him intently. Perhaps...

"We have to hold out until Kale and Laurel can destroy the demon lord. I'm not sure how long that's going to be. So we need to prepare for the worst. Instead of trying to destroy the demon army and take ground, we're going to use a structured retreat. Something to buy us time and let them think they are winning. When the demons think they're winning, they become more reckless... more wild... we can use that. I've also noticed they don't like water. They'll cross it but only under extreme duress.

"We're going to move our encampment across the river. Not all at once, that would be suspicious. First, we'll move the civilians and wounded, then infantry and archers…. It will work. Aldric… Lysander, I need both of you to get the elves and dwarves working together to erect some of those temporary bridges. Aldric, can some of your dwarves rig them so they will crumble when the demons try to use them?"

"Yes, but they would be destroyed in the process. What are you thinking Bane?" Bane ran his hand through his hair and then scratched at his beard. An idea was starting to form… one he hoped would work.

"I'm planning on leading the demons to the river and dropping them in. The waters are high and fast right now, and from the look of the skies we'll be having more rain in another day. We're going to let the demons think we're running away, and then drop them in the river. Lysander, how many wizards do we still have?"

"We've lost about one third of the wizards. We still have enough to give them a challenge." Bane knew he must look like a wild man, but he couldn't keep the smile from spreading across his face.

"Good, how many of those wizards can enchant the new arrows being made? I want as many arrows and missile weapons enchanted as possible…. Oh, and have the wizards memorize as many of those fire and lightning spells as possible too. We're going to light up the field and burn as many of them to the ground as we can. That should buy us at least a day or two." Lord Kingsford placed his hand firmly over Bane's, causing him to look up and meet his eyes.

"Bane… slow down. Maybe you should tell us the whole plan hatching in your head. Better yet… you should get some sleep and tell us in the morning. You're exhausted and beyond spent." Bane shook his head trying to clear his thoughts. He was exhausted. He hadn't slept in days and his mind was spinning with possibilities.   Maybe Lord Kingsford was right… it would be so easy to close his eyes… so easy to surrender to his aching, tired limbs… so easy….NO! Bane took several deep breaths to focus his mind.

"No Lord Kingsford, this is war and my soldiers need their commander. I'll sleep when the war is over or I'm dead. Kale and Laurel have been gone for almost two months. We will hold out until they return or we have confirmation of their deaths. My plan, gentlemen, is simple. Sometimes in a battle you have to feint to one side before striking. We are going to do exactly that.

"We will spend the next couple of days creating a structured retreat. I will lead the remaining cavalry in sweeping assaults trying to buy our soldiers time to escape. Once our people are across, I want the bridges to collapse as soon as enough demons are on them. With the currents so high and fast, many of the demons will be carried down the river and into the ocean. Those that aren't will be enraged and try to cross of their own accord. This will cost them more demons. While they are trying to discover a way across, I want our archers and spell casters raining spells and arrows down on them until we're out. At the very least it should give them pause and decrease their numbers."

"Eventually, they will discover a way to cross, but not for a couple of days. That will give us the time we need to heal and recoup our stocks of weaponry. Now here is where things will become tricky. During the night we will move our civilian men, women and children towards the river's fork. I don't want them sandwiched between the river and army, so they'll move northeast along the river's edge and out of harm's way. Our scouts have reported no sign of demon activity on the capital island, so we should have a straight shot towards the capital." Bane met each man's eyes gauging their reaction to his plan. Their eyes widened as realization overcame them.

"Bane, that will direct the demons straight towards the capital and all the people inside." Lord Kingsford's voice was choked with disbelief. Bane knew his resignations for this plan... he had already played them through his own head a dozen times... but this was war, and people died in war.

"I know...we will lead the demons towards the capital. I know there are innocents in that city, but I can't think of them right now. I have to think of our people and our purpose. I have to do what is best for the greater good, even if that means sacrificing the capital. You put me in charge... I've tried to save as many people as I can, but I can't save everyone. I have to look at acceptable losses... and that city is an acceptable loss. If you don't like it, you are more than welcome to take over and lead this army!" Bane met their looks with determination and strength. This was his moment. They would either follow him into hell or kick him out and run things themselves. Part of him hoped they would remove him from leading.

Each man met his steady gaze. Bane could see a thousand thoughts spiraling through their brains. They all looked at each other, nodding their heads in silence. The tension in the tent was almost palpable. It was finally Lord Aldric who responded.

"We're with you lad. You're right that we put you in this position. It wasn't fair of us and perhaps it was the coward's choice. Each of us knew we wouldn't be able to make the tough decisions when it came to battle. We've spent our lives trying to save everyone, when you do that, you sacrifice the ability to condemn anyone to death. Speaking frankly, you've done a damn fine job of leading this army. You're an excellent commander. Possibly the best I've seen in ages.... We'll stand with you, Bane, we'll stand till the end, even if it damns us all."

Bane's throat constricted with emotion. They truly did believe in him. He was their leader... their commander. Looking at the map in front of him, Bane continued his plan. They would lead the demons towards the capital. By the time they reached it, the demons would be so enraged and hungry for death they wouldn't care what they were attacking. They would rip the city to the ground, and possibly take the King with them. If it came to that point... as long as his wizards were out of the way, they could destroy the city in its entirety. It was a great sacrifice, but if it freed the country, it would be worth it. He would lead the attack into the city and hopefully lure the demons after them. Although the others protested, Bane couldn't ask his men to sacrifice their lives unless he did as well. By all the Gods he hoped it wouldn't come to that. Please let Kale and Laurel succeed. Time was running out.

The next three days were a repetition of run, slash, retreat. Bane led the cavalry into battle time and time again. In between raids they would change horses to make sure the animals stayed fresh. With each charge, Bane worried for his men and their mounts. Somehow they were successful. Each raid lowered their enemy's numbers and enraged them all the more.

He had instructed his men to go for the slower moving demons and monsters. Stay away from the speed attacks and berserkers. Sometimes they would rush the right side of the demon force, other times the left side. Sometimes they would strike straight down the middle running until they broke out the other side and led the demons on a merry chase towards the swamps.

With each new strike, Bane and his men became more confident. This was going to work… it had to. The demons tried several times to attack his army, but each time they were met with a wall of blinding fire. By the time the fire cleared, Bane's forces would have retreated a great distance. As the demons raged in confusion and frustration, Bane would lead his cavalry into their heart, breaking their lines and causing more confusion. To his delight, many times the demons would turn on their own out of frustration and confusion about where their enemy had gone.

By the end of the third day, almost all his forces were across the river. All of the army's tents and supplies had been sent across and Bane was ready to lead his men in one final assault the next morning. He was brushing Tiberious down when Captain Daniel rode into camp carrying a petite scout in his arms.

"Commander, you need to hear what this scout has to report!" Bane looked up from what he was doing as Daniel carried the small scout over. It was only when they were close that Bane realized the scout was a small female dwarf. She was badly injured and barely able to keep her eyes open.

"Daniel, she needs tending, take her across…" The she-dwarf raised her hand and gripped Bane's forearm tightly.

"Commander, my name is Rhinn Stonehammer, the demons… are coming. They won't… wait… until morning…" With her last words Rhinn's eyes closed and her body went limp. Bane swallowed hard. Perhaps he had been a little too overzealous with angering the demons. Grabbing Tiberious's saddle, Bane set quickly to work readying his horse while calling out orders.

"Captain Daniel, take Rhinn to the healers, tell them to save her if they can! Take the rest of the ground troops with you! Go… now! Captain Marcus…!" Bane listened for his captain's reply before continuing. "Ready the men! It seems the demons want to continue into the night! Let's give them something to fear!" By the time he finished his orders, Bane had Tiberious saddled and ready to ride.

Quickly he swung up into his mount's saddle and swung his sword in the air, rallying his men. Was he seeing things… or was his sword actually glowing? Bane shook his head and steeled his thoughts for the battle to come. It was only moments before his cavalry were in their saddles and he was leading them once more into the fray. His last thoughts, before they clashed with the demons, were of Rhinn. He hoped Aldric's daughter would survive the night… if not… he would make sure her death wasn't in vain.

They struck time and time again at the oncoming demons, always trying to draw their attention anywhere but towards the escaping army. Two of his men went down, their bodies ripped and torn apart by the enraged demons. Bane used their deaths to strike down twenty of them. His men followed behind, striking down two or three demons as they drove on.

As the moon reached its apex, Bane rallied his men to him and they retreated to the safety of the river. The demons roared their fury and rushed after them. Some of the slower demons were trampled and killed in their haste to reach Bane. The demons had even given him a new name… Demons Bane… perhaps he would make that his surname when this was done.

His men flew through the darkness, reaching the river's edge only moments before the demons. Without hesitation, Bane charged over the makeshift bridges, feeling them shudder and crack beneath their thundering hooves. Behind them, the howls and screams of the demons surged after them.

Bane turned in his saddle and watched as the demons surged towards the bridges. As the first few touched on his side of the river, Bane gave the signal and the bridges exploded sending splinters of wood and iron careening into the surging demon force. For a moment everything was chaos, as Bane slashed into the demons that had successfully crossed, and the screams and death cries of the injured and dying demons echoed across the valley.

They had sent dozens of demons plummeting to a watery grave, as their bodies were swept away downstream. The archers and wizards now struck with everything they had. The opposite bank of the river lit up with giant rolling boulders of fire and lightning. Arrows rained down from the dark skies impaling themselves in the roiling mass of demons trampling their brethren in an attempt to flee.

Bane watched it all, a dark pride for their success in forestalling their enemy. There was no joy in their victory though, two men had died that night. Rhinn's life lay in the hands of the healers. Someone would have to tell Lord Aldric of his daughter's condition. Death surrounded him, but still he had to hold on. Bane knew he couldn't show weakness, he had to lead them… even if it was to their deaths. How cold he had become… how calculating. Would he ever be the man he once was?

As the spells died down and the arrows ran out, Bane could hear his men cheering. Slowly, he dismounted Tiberious. Patting the horse's neck absentmindedly, he handed off the reigns to a boy… the lad couldn't be more than twelve. Now he was responsible for the lives of children as well. He grabbed the boy's arm and turned him around to see his face.

"What's your name, lad?" A proud smile lit the boy's face as he looked admiringly at Bane.

"My name's Dirk, sir. I joined up after my parents were killed. I been practicing with a sword… I'm gettin good, sir. Just say when and I'm ready." Rage and disgust rose like poisonous bile choking Bane's words. All he could do was pat the boy on the shoulder and nod his understanding before turning and walking towards the healers' tents.

On his way he called a runner to find Lord Aldric and direct him to the healers. Bane would tell him about his daughter, he owed the Lord that much. As he arrived at the tent, a priestess walked out to greet him.

"Lord Bane, I assume you are here to check on Rhinn…" At his nod, she continued. "She will live. Her side had been clawed and torn open, but Captain Daniel got her here in time. She has lost a great deal of blood though and will take time to heal. For now she sleeps. Captain Daniel is sitting with her for now." Bane nodded his thanks, but still could find no words. "My lord... you need to rest. You'll be useless to everyone if you are dead on your feet."

"I know priestess Mariss, but I still have to inform Rhinn's father of her condition, and then I need to plan for the coming days. When that is done... if there is time... I will rest." As Bane turned to find a place to sit, Lord Aldric arrived looking frustrated and concerned.

"Commander, you wished to see me." Bane motioned for the stocky dwarven lord to join him.

"Aldric... sit, there is something I need to tell you. We were successful tonight because of the actions of one very brave, dwarven scout. That scout is now sleeping in the healers' tent after suffering a nearly fatal injury." Bane met Aldric's eyes trying to convey his compassion and sympathy. "Aldric... that scout was Rhinn. I thought she had retreated to the other side of the river, but... it appears she has a very stubborn streak." Aldric's face had become unreadable as he sat there mumbling to himself. Bane knew the complexity of the emotions that must be warring in Aldric at that moment. It was best to just leave him with his thoughts, but Bane didn't want him to storm in on Daniel sitting with Rhinn. An emotional father could make some very dangerous and incorrect assumptions.

"Aldric, Daniel rescued her and brought her to safety. He's sitting with her right now, so she wouldn't wake up alone. I'm sure if you would like to take his place, it would be fine." The dwarf waved his hand in the air and shook his head.

"No, let the young man sit with her. He could probably use the rest. I have weapons and traps to lay for tomorrow's assaults…. Thank you, Bane… for telling me. You are an honorable man." Bane rubbed his forehead as Aldric stormed away. He didn't envy the men he would be ordering around tonight.

As he stumbled into his tent, Isla came over to him and helped him undress. She didn't speak or taunt him. She just helped him clean up and collapse onto his bedroll. Then she joined him, fitting herself close against his side. Bane wanted to cry… to scream… but he had to remain strong. Would he ever be able to express his gratefulness for the feeling of her lying next to him…. He doubted it.

The first morning after their successful crossing, Bane had put his armor on to find a new symbol emblazoned on his chest plate, a shield with a large sword crossed over it. No one would fess up to its creation, but the priests and priestesses all looked at him with a new reverence he wasn't used to. When he strode to the edge of the river to see the progress of the demons, he was surprised to find several of them shy away from looking at him. Others fled to the back of the writhing mass. Well, if it frightened the demons, it was fine with Bane.

It took six days for the demons to figure a way across the river. With Bane's forces striking at them, it took two more to successfully cross. By then, the majority of the army was several miles downstream preparing to cross the river once more and reach the capital. Several volunteers had competed to join Bane's riders, he thought they were insane. Those who won, joined what was now considered an elite rank. The cavalry had added an embellishment to their armor, a demon's head with two swords crossed over it surrounded by rays of light. This had become the symbol of Bane's men... it had become a symbol of him, Demons Bane.

As the demons made landfall, Bane's riders struck at them mercilessly, driving them back into the roaring waters of the river. His men kept up their strikes throughout the day, killing countless numbers of demons. Still, they came on... relentless and never ending. Bane's riders never tired and never surrendered.

That night Bane called his men further back. Lord Aldric's men had laid countless traps and pitfalls throughout the river valley, and Bane did not want his men retreating through such a deadly field. Exhausted they made their way through, careful to avoid the triggers that would kill them all. They reached camp sometime around midnight. Boys, barely out of puberty, ran to take their horses from them and lead them off for water and rest. Other camp dwellers rushed to aid the riders with whatever was needed.

Bane shrugged off any assistance as he made his way to his tent. Food, drink and his council awaited him inside. He told them of their success and the difficulty facing them. They were fighting against an endless enemy. Their only hope of success was Kale and Laurel. Scouts began rushing in and out of his tent, delivering their reports and leaving to find sleep. Bane absently listened to the Lords and Captains debate as he glanced through the reports. Despair gripped his heart as the picture of what they faced on the morrow became clearer. With a raised hand he silenced all of them. Gravely he met all of their eyes, behind them all, Isla slinked into the tent pain and sorrow painting her face pale.

"I have read the reports of our scouts…. The news is not good. It seems the demons have outsmarted us… or at least their master has. Across the river, on the capital's island, is an army of demons twice as large as the one we have faced. Their numbers are almost too many to fit on the land. We are now trapped between the demon army we have enraged and the one that waits with bated breath for our demise. We have held for twelve days. We have fought harder than any army ever has. I tell you now… we will not last another three days. Tomorrow the demons will test Aldric's field of traps. They will not try to spare lives. They will throw themselves at the pitfalls and traps until they have set them all off and filled them in. This is their way. It may take them an entire day, but they will clear the field.

"The army across the river will wait patiently for their brethren to trap us. They may surge across the river or they may just watch our demise. Either way we are trapped. We are left with the choice of waiting for that demise or dying on our own terms. I choose to die with a sword in my hand. What you choose to do is up to you… I will not blame any man who chooses to run." Bane watched the faces for reactions. He wasn't disappointed. Each man's face grew more determined and grave. Bane nodded as he continued.

"Then so be it. Tomorrow while the demons throw themselves at the trapped field, we will launch an attack against the demons on the island. I want every wizard we have left throwing spells at the island. If those spells hit the city… so be it. Anything that can be enchanted tonight should be. Tomorrow we will attack until either they are dead or we are.

"The next day will most likely be an all-out assault with whatever they have left against whatever we have left. It will be the day of decision. Every man, woman and child that can wield a sword will be given one. We will face the enemy standing strong and prepared to die for freedom. Spread the word… judgment day is near."

Bane dismissed them and waited, feeling cold as ice, for Isla to approach. Her look was resolute and determined. Tonight, they would spend together… for tomorrow they could both die.

Chapter 27

Kale surged up the rise slashing through the oncoming demons, his sword singing in triumph. Demons Bane gleamed in his hand beating back the encroaching darkness. Initially, the demons had swarmed over them hungry for their blood, but now they fought to get out of his reach. The doors to the stronghold stood closed against their howls of anguish, as Kale relentlessly cut them down. Laurel held tight to Leora's hand as they followed close behind, calling out warnings of surprise attacks.

Time had stopped in shear wonderment of the destruction laid out before it. Kale was filled with exhilaration as he and Demons Bane became one and the same. It was like nothing he had ever felt before. He could see everywhere at once and anticipate every movement around him. The oppression he had been feeling since arriving in this hell hole was gone, replaced by a feeling of purity and righteousness.

Before he knew it, Kale was standing before the tall metal doors, breathless and exuberant. Laurel cautiously touched his shoulder turning him to look at her. Kale smiled confidently. Today would be theirs... if only they could figure a way past the doors.

Almost as if they had read his mind, the doors slowly swung open, revealing a long, dark and foreboding corridor beyond. Cautiously, Kale stepped forward into the threatening darkness holding Demons Bane in front of him. The sword glowed brightly chasing back the darkness and revealing the terrifying décor inside. Corpses, stripped of their skin, hung from the walls. Everywhere, they were surrounded by death and blood. The floor was littered with the bones of countless creatures… some, possibly human. Cages hung from the ceiling, filled with the dead or dying. Shadows of their grotesque forms cast about the surrounding corridor by the countless number of blazing torches.

Carefully, their small group stepped over bones and rotting carcasses. The chamber was deafeningly silent, but Kale could feel eyes watching him. When they looked away from the tortured bodies, they saw grotesque mockeries of entangled human lovers captured in black stone. The torch light made them appear to move and writhe against each other. Kale heard Leora's barely audible whimper as she drew closer to the two of them. No child should have to see such horror or depravity, but there was no other choice.

The corridor seemed endless, but they were never challenged or threatened as they made their way deeper in. Glancing behind, Kale could no longer see the doorway. In front of him the surrounding sights only became more violent and depraved. Moans and guttural grunts filled the silence as the statues now took on lives of their own. All around them scenes of orgies, rape and torture played out. Soon the sounds of begging and screams overwhelmed the cavernous corridor. Kale wanted to close his eyes against it all. Demons

Bane glowed brighter bathing the three of them in its light… warming them, strengthening them.

The cacophony of screams, howls and torture grew until it was almost unbearable. Kale glanced at Leora and saw her hands press tightly against her ears as she cringed in fear. Laurel had one hand on Leora guiding her along, while her other hand gripped her staff tightly. Fire flared not far in front of them. Kale focused on that point and led them further on.

Soon, the corridor had ended and they found themselves in a vast chamber with towering archways. In front of them, an enormous throne made of bleached bones and twisted black spikes sat upon a towering dais. Lounging haughtily on the throne was a creature that stole Laurel's breath, caused Leora to crumble to the floor, and Kale to painfully squeeze the hilt of Demons Bane… the demon lord, Svecknar.

Kale and Leora saw its spiraling horns, sharp talons, leathery black wings, and scarlet skin stretched across a broad muscular form. Kale was shocked by how dwarfed they were by this creature. It smiled arrogantly as it looked down upon them, glaring in surprise only a moment at Leora. Kale bravely stepped in front of her, shielding her from its cruel stare. Leora wept openly, curled into a ball on the floor. She didn't beg… she just waited for her death. Rage seethed through every part of Kale's being. He came here to kill this beast… and kill him he would.

Laurel could only stare at the image before her. Upon a golden throne, sat the most handsome man she had ever seen. His eyes were piercing as he gazed into her soul. Laurel could feel her heart racing. A voice in her head beckoned her forward. He wanted her to come to him… to give herself to him. His open hand extended down towards her. Almost of their own volition, her feet began moving towards this angel. All her suffering, fear and doubts faded in his presence. Was this her destiny?

A hand gripped her arm and pulled her back. The contact shattered the illusion, bringing her back to herself. Laurel turned to see Kale holding tightly to her arm, desperation flooding his features. Laurel squeezed her eyes closed and shook her head. She still felt the pull, but it was much less. Opening her eyes she saw the demon for what it was, and he terrified her. He turned his gaze towards her and smiled cruelly. Quickly she stepped back to Kale's side and gripped his arm for support. Their contact strengthened her resolve and cleared her head. She looked up glaring angrily at this monster that desired her.

"Well hasn't this been an enjoyable game. It seems you found a young succubus to assist you… surprising. I will enjoy teaching her obedience after I am through with you, little boy. Did you really think you could come into my domain and destroy me? I find the thought laughable, but you did bring me something I want… Laurel, come to me." Kale stepped forward brandishing the sword. Rage warred with reason as he waited for his moment to strike.

"Never... I will never come to you!"
Laurel tensed next to him and her grip tightened on
his arm. Kale glared at the demon and saw the
barest flinch when she squeezed his arm. Pulling
Laurel closer he whispered quickly in her ear.

"He doesn't like our contact. When you
squeezed my arm, he flinched." He met Laurel's
eyes and saw understanding there.

"Of course... like in Soldar... the blood
storm couldn't hurt us when we touched. It's the
connection between us... that's why our parents
wanted us married. It's us Kale." Hearing their
whispers, Leora haltingly stood and came closer to
them. Laurel looked down at her and stroked her
hair gently. "Kale, we'll have to keep Leora close
like we did with Bane." Kale nodded and pulled
Leora between them before turning to face the
demon once more.

"She's not yours demon, and for your
information, neither is Leora. She's coming with
us when we leave here. So, I guess I'll be robbing
you of a consort and a toy." Kale held his ground
as the demon roared his fury. When the demon
glared at him again, Kale smiled cockily and tipped
his head. "Bring your worst, you fat, lazy ass... I'll
best whatever you throw at me." Kale almost
laughed at the wide-eyed stare Laurel was shooting
at him... almost.

The demon inhaled deeply as he glared at
them. If his look could have killed, they would all
have been piles of ash on the floor. Laurel could
still hear his voice in her head entreating her. It
warred with the scene in front of her. Images

flashed through her mind of pleasures and desires fulfilled. In desperation she forced her thoughts to memories of her wedding and wedding night. The chamber suddenly went from broiling to freezing in only a matter of moments. The demon stood above them, an eerie calm settling over him.

"So be it... you dared to take what was mine... now I will destroy you and when you are gone, I will have what you covet most of all." Laurel shivered at the malevolent and hungry look he directed towards her. "VITERIN COME TO ME!"

The towering ceiling filled in with thunderous, blood red clouds. A face formed on their surface and smiled darkly. It seemed to almost bend towards the demon lord before righting and focusing its cruel eyes on them. Laurel felt Leora squeeze her arm in terror and desperation. She had time to glance at Kale only briefly and saw her concern mirrored in his face.

"Master, you summoned me. What is your bidding?" Its thunderous voice echoed through the hall.

"Viterin destroy the half-blood male... but bring me the females unharmed. I have plans for them." The cloud bowed to the demon once and then descended on them like a tidal wave of blood, claws and rage.

Laurel gripped Kale's hand firmly in hers and closed her eyes calling out to her Goddess. As the cloud tightened around them, Laurel felt her mind flooded with memories of love, peace, and joy... memories of her parents, of her journey with

Kale and Bane, and finally their wedding and love they shared. The presence of Gaia flooded her soul and body. She could feel the light exploding from her as Kale held her and Leora tightly to himself.

The howling and screaming of the storm felt distant and inconsequential. All that mattered was Kale, Leora and her. Laurel's exhaustion, fears and pain evaporated as she let the power of her Goddess flow through her. The storm raged around them trying unsuccessfully to break them. Laurel could feel its rage growing with each failure. Time stopped as Laurel opened her eyes and met Kale's loving gaze. Even in this hell the demons couldn't destroy their love, their courage or their faith.

"Kale, we destroy it together. I think..." Laurel gazed at her husband lovingly. Kale returned her gaze with a knowing smile.

"I know... always said we'd need to do this together. Count of three." Laurel nodded at him, smiling. "One... two... three..."

As the blood storm tightened around them, Kale and Laurel both gripped Demons Bane and thrust it skyward. Laurel felt the power of Gaia and the sword, combine and explode outward, piercing the cloud and destroying it. Ash rained down around them making it hard to breath and even harder to see. A cold, cruel chuckle echoed through their surroundings. The demon lord wasn't done with them yet.

"Do you think you can destroy me.... I am lord of these demesnes! I am lord over all you see! You are nothing but a bug to me! Come and face me boy or do you need to hide behind your woman?" Laurel grabbed Kale's arm warningly.

"Kale, it's a trap… you can't do this!" Kale stroked the side of Laurel's face soothingly.

"Laurel, this one is my fight. Assist where you can and keep a look out for company but let me do this. I love you… never forget that." With a smile he stepped away from Laurel and Leora and walked confidently forward to face the demon. Words were no longer necessary… he would let Demons Bane do the talking for him.

The demon lord stepped down from his dais, stalking towards him menacingly. Kale steeled himself against the growing terror in his heart. Demons Bane whispered to him, guiding his steps and movements. He knew what he had to do… he just wasn't sure if he would survive. Closing his eyes, Kale opened himself to the sword's magic and spirit, giving himself over to it completely.

Time seemed to slow as the demon lord quickly closed the distance between them. Raising his black and red sword in the air he brought it down in a swift striking motion towards Kale's head. Kale quickly side-stepped the strike and felt the wind as it passed. Spinning, he brought Demons Bane around in an arc striking for the demon's exposed leg. Svecknar brought his sword down to block and pushed Kale backwards, causing him to lose his balance.

Kale felt himself tumbling, landing hard on his ass. The demon rapidly advanced on him, forcing him to roll out of the way of several deadly blows. Stabbing upward, Kale thrust Demons Bane into the thigh of Svecknar causing him to howl in pain. Withdrawing the sword, Kale rolled away and leapt to his feet, bringing Demons Bane around to barely block another swing from the demon.

Kale knew somehow that if the demon lord's blade touched him, he would be dead. He wasn't sure if the knowledge came from the sword or something he had been told, but that sword would suck the life out of him. It was too close of a resemblance to the false sword the crystal cavern had tested him with.

From somewhere far away, Kale heard a loud, heavy banging… as if the doors to the stronghold had been thrown open. Kale mentally slapped himself, he couldn't worry about that now… he needed to focus on Svecknar and surviving. In the back of his mind, he heard Laurel cry out and saw bright flashes of light, but it was distant and unimportant. All that mattered was the battle at hand.

Again and again their swords clashed, the sound ricocheting off the soaring walls. Kale fought for every strike and block. Their movements had become a deadly dance, where one misstep would end one of them. Kale's muscles and body ached with the continual effort needed to stay upright. Even with Demons Bane's help and guidance Kale was struggling to find an opening. Without the sword's assistance the battle would have long been over and Laurel would belong to the demon.

Once more they circled each other looking for a weakness, searching for an opening. The demon limped slightly, unable to heal the wound caused by Demons Bane. That one strike was Kale's only hope of gaining the advantage, he had to find a way to push it. Kale lunged forward feinting an attack. When Svecknar swung his sword down to block, Kale spun to the right and swung Demon's Bane around to slice into its side.

The demon howled again in pain so loudly that it seemed the world was echoing with his pain. Kale didn't hesitate, he dove underneath the demon's legs and brought the sword up as he rose behind him. The sword cut into the demon's back causing blood to spray onto Kale's armor, but he didn't care. He continued his assault, trying to get the killing blow. The demon was quick to strike back sending Kale flying across the hall and into the opposite wall.

Kale shook his head, slowly coming to a stand. As his vision cleared, he could see the demon barreling down on him. He dove out of the way just barely dodging the point of the demon's blade. Their dance continued, but Kale wasn't sure how much longer he could keep this up.

Laurel had watched with terror as Kale fought the demon lord. Both fought with blinding speed, but Kale had struck first blood. Leora clung to her legs, burying her face in Laurel's tunic, too afraid to watch. Suddenly, the echo of a thunderous bang rang down the corridor. Laurel gripped her staff tighter and turned to face whatever was coming. The power of Gaia filled her as she saw the first glint of the demon eyes.

Laurel brandished her holy symbol and threw one prayer after another at the creatures. Light shot forth from her hands as an army of demons came rushing towards her. Praying to her Goddess, Laurel surrendered herself to Gaia and became a weapon.

No longer in control of her actions, Laurel struck out again and again. Her staff became a blur of light and motion as it struck at the swarm of demons. Leora stayed safely behind her as she lashed out at anything coming too close. She was still aware of the battle occurring behind her, but her focus was solely on preventing the demons from interfering in their master's demise.

Time passed and Laurel could feel her body weakening. If this didn't end soon, she would collapse and it would be the end of them. Inside she prayed that Kale would find a way to end this quickly… before all was lost.

Kale could see the demon lord weakening as their fight went on. Soon he would make a mistake and then Kale could strike his final blow. He continued to feint and spin trying to take Svecknar by surprise or knock him off balance, but his attempts continued to fail.

A crash from behind distracted the demon for the briefest of moments, but that was all Kale needed. In that one moment, Kale took his opportunity and thrust Demons Bane up and through the ribs of the demon, impaling its heart.

The scream that issued forth was deafening. Kale yanked the sword from Svecknar's chest and collapsed to the floor his hands going to his ears. It was as if the whole world were quaking at the demon's death. Everything shook as waves of pain coursed through Kale's body. He turned his head slightly and felt his heart stop at what he saw.

Laurel was lying prone on the floor, her skin pale. Leora was bent over her shielding her body from any falling debris. Kale forced his body to move. Sheathing Demons Bane, Kale crawled over to where Laurel was lying. While the world seemed to rip apart around them, he pulled her to him and cradled her in his arms. Leora cried openly as she squeezed in next to Kale's body.

Kale looked remorsefully down at his beloved. Her chest wasn't moving and her skin had grown cold. He was supposed to protect her. He was supposed to die… not her… never her.

Chapter 28

Bane walked through the tent city that had been set up between the river and the oncoming demon army. He had hoped that only his soldiers would be here, but instead it was filled with the civilians as well. Young boys and girls ran between the tents playing a morbid game of catch the rabbit, where one of them was the rabbit. They used bows with padded heads covered in red dust to shoot the rabbit. They saw it as a game... Bane saw it as training.

The older boys and girls, who could wield swords, were in a make-shift practice yard. One of Bane's best swordsmen was training them in basic moves. Those who were quick studies or naturals were quickly moved into more advanced training. It wasn't much, but what little they learned might save their lives... at least for a time. He had no intention of sticking them in the front lines, but at least this way they would stand a chance... however small... of defending themselves.

The wizards were sleeping in rotating shifts, ensuring there would always be fresh spell casters at the ready. Those who were awake were either enchanting arrows or raining fire and lightning down on the demon army awaiting them on the island. His camp had become a tent city that never slept. There were always cook fires blazing and practices or training occurring. How anyone could sleep, astounded Bane's mind. As the sun rose on that first day, Bane mounted Tiberious and assembled his riders. Staring out over the deadly field, they waited for the first wave of attack.

The first day of the demons' retaliation had gone very much like Bane had expected. The demons, enraged and hungry for blood, had thrown themselves across the field triggering one trap after another. The few who made it through were quickly cut down by Bane and his riders. The field was a desiccated mass of twisted body parts and blood. The howls of those that didn't completely die in the pitfalls haunted the battlefield.

On the river's edge, the wizards and archers were working in shifts, slinging spells and arrows at the awaiting demon army. By the afternoon of that first day, Bane went to check on their success. He was in shock at the number of demons lying dead on the other side. Their comrades devoured their remains even as the wizards rained more spells down on them. It was almost as if they didn't care.

Bane did a quick assessment of the numbers… there were about half the number of demons on the island than before. The numbers weren't replenishing… Bane ran back to the other side of the encampment and leapt onto Tiberious's back. From the higher vantage point he had a better view of the field and demon army on the other side. They're numbers had decreased as well.

Something had changed… something was now different. Kale and Laurel must have finally reached the demon lord, because he was no longer sending additional fodder to the battle. Bane dismounted and ran to the center of the camp. He needed to let his army know there was a chance… they needed to know they were having an effect.

His fevered actions must have attracted notice, because most of the camp was already assembled around the stack of crates they used to make announcements. Even the civilians had assembled to hear what he would say. Mounting the crates, Bane gazed out over the ocean of soldiers and civilians, all gazing at him with grim determination. At least this time he had some hope to give them, instead of more danger.

"Men, women and children… I have just taken stock of our situation and the state of our enemy. I have hope to give you! It seems that our future King and Queen have reached the demon lord's stronghold and are causing him no little bit of trouble! The demons we have destroyed are not being replenished! The demon lord is not sending any more of his minions to be used as fodder against our strength! The demons' numbers are half of what they were this morning! We are succeeding! We are winning this war!" Bane paused as the roars and cheers of the people nearly drowned out his voice. He waited for them to quiet down before he continued.

"This does not mean our battle is done… not yet! Though I have no right… I ask you to find enough strength and courage to finish our job! Tonight we will continue to decimate their numbers and tomorrow we will attack! We will meet their darkness with our light! We will face their terror with our courage! We will destroy them and send them back to the hell from which they came. By tomorrow night we will be beyond those walls and hunting down the tyrant who has enslaved us all! Now… who will stand with me for justice, for honor and for our victory?!" Bane was almost blown off the crates by the uproar from the crowd.

Immediately people set to work readying weapons and armor. Food and supplies were packed up as final rations were handed out in preparation of the coming battles. Priests and priestess finished their healings and placed one another into two hour comas that would allow them to awaken refreshed and ready to go. The wizards on watch returned to raining down destruction onto the island, decreasing the demon numbers even further. The archers stored up their enchanted arrows for tomorrow's final push. Everything began to move at a feverish pace now that the people knew the end was near.

Bane walked through the encampment checking on everyone, shaking hands, calming fear and tempering energies. He tried to exude calm confidence, willing those around him to feel the same. Inside his stomach was roiling and every nerve was on edge. Tomorrow would be the day they would either take the capital and destroy the demons or die trying. After a final walk-through, Bane retired to his tent to attempt sleep. As had become commonplace, Isla was already there awaiting his arrival. He flashed her a confident smile and chuckled as she raised a suspecting eyebrow. She knew his inner feelings, she knew him too well… then again did he ever want to hide anything from her?

The sun rose the next morning to an army at the ready. Gone were the tent city and any signs of civilian life. Every person that could wield a sword or fire a bow had been given a weapon and armor. Only those too small or old were evacuated during the night. Everyone else had decided to stay and fight. Bane disagreed with the children staying and forced them to prove their skills before he would allow it. Wizards had opened gateways to a safer place for those whom Bane had ordered evacuated.

Bane had split the army in two. His riders, and half the infantry, would face off with the remaining demons on his side of the river. The other half of the infantry would back up the archers and wizards as they continued their assault on the demon force entrenched on the island capital. He had spoken with Lords Aldric and Kingsford earlier that day about strategies to use against the island demons. He expected them to surge across the river and attack Bane's forces sooner rather than later. If they had any intelligence they would have already attacked instead of being picked off.

Bane however, was more than happy to take advantage of their stupidity. He had ordered the lords to keep everyone on this side of the river. There was no sense in trying to cross until the demons numbers were inconsequential. Besides, there was still the chance the demon lord would flood them with demons at the last moment. Bane didn't want to turn his people into fodder for the demons.

Sitting astride Tiberious, Bane gazed out over the bloody field. In the distance, he could just make out the lines of demons trying to push and shove others towards the front. They were afraid, for probably the first time in this war, they showed fear and a sense of self-preservation. Bane kicked his war horse into a gallop and rode down the line of cavalry, his sword drawn. Each man clinked the tip of his sword against Bane's, as he rode by. They faced the enemy with ferocity and courage as Bane took his position in the front. He patted Tiberious' neck, steadying his prancing hooves.

Bane could feel his horse's breathing. He could hear the sounds of the cavalry holding their horses in. There was a vibration of anticipation charging the air around them. Bane wanted to charge across the field initiating the attack, but a voice in his head stayed his hand. Wait, it said… make them come to you. Make them face you on your ground and your terms. Bane closed his eyes and breathed in the crisp morning air. A light breeze brushed the fetid odors of the field away, leaving the air crisp and fresh.

Opening his eyes, Bane smiled… everything had stilled, the calm before the storm. In the distance a low rumble of thunder could be heard. As if signaling the start of a race, the demons launched themselves forward trampling their dead. In their haste to cross the tainted expanse, they trampled many of their own. Those that fell vanished beneath the swarm. Still Bane held his ground. Slowly, he raised his hand as the demons grew closer by the moment.

Tiberious had become a statue, anticipating Bane's command. Behind him horses snorted and stamped their feet, feeling their riders' impatience. Bane continued to hold, his eyes focused on the coming onslaught. He could almost see their eyes… almost. He waited, the tension in his body tightening like the string of a bow before releasing the arrow. Any moment now… they were so close… Bane's hand stretched further towards the sky. The tension was palpable. Their glaring, malevolent eyes came into focus.

"NOW!" Bane charged forward, his arm coming down as Tiberious leaped ahead. The field came alive with the sounds of riders colliding with demons. Bane slashed and thrust with his sword as he galloped through the middle of the demon lines. His sword became a blinding light as it cut into one demon after another. Tiberious kicked out, crushing their heads and crippling their bodies.

The two had become one as they spun in a circle decimating anything that came within reach. Bane wasn't sure how long the battle raged, but he knew the sun was climbing high and the day was warming. Sweat trickled down his face, neck and back. He continued to battle onward screaming like a madman, trying to draw the demons towards him. Briefly he spared a glance around the battlefield, several of his cavalry had gone down. His infantry was now engaged in their desperate battle.

Bane fought his way towards the river trying to get a better view of what was happening near the island. As he burst clear of the battle field, he saw the demons flooding off the island and into the opposite line. There was nothing he could do for them now except to keep fighting. Gritting his teeth he charged back into the battle, determined to destroy as many of them as he could.

As he burst through the center of them, once more, trying to divide their lines and confuse them, he thought about everything and everyone he cared about. This would be their last stand. Laughing wildly, he dove off Tiberious into a group of demons, his sword singing through the air. Today was a good day to die....

Bane found himself surrounded by growling, ravenous demons. He laughed at their jabbing and clawing as they swarmed around him. Dozens of them were about to descend upon him when a loud clap of thunder shook the ground. Horses reared, sending their riders flailing through the air. The smell of brimstone filled the air as the demons froze where they stood. Another earsplitting crack of thunder pealed across the field forcing Bane to squeeze his eyes shut in pain.

When Bane opened his eyes the demons were gone. The field was still tainted by their dead, but there were no demons left for Bane to face. Swiftly he located Tiberious and swung up into his saddle. Turning towards the island he could still see the battle raging. Kicking his mount into a gallop, he called out to his men as he charged forward to join the new front line.

With all his army's focus in one area, Bane's hopes were renewed. He dove into the battle, his riders right behind him, giving the infantry a respite from the battle. The wizards and archers had retreated to launch attacks at the demons' back line. The battle raged for several hours more, the sun beginning to sink towards the horizon. Bane knew his soldiers were exhausted… he was exhausted, but they couldn't surrender.

Bane charged into the demon lines repeatedly, but their numbers were fresher and many were a stronger breed than what they had been facing. These demons wouldn't relent when the sun descended below the horizon. These demons would continue the onslaught without resting. If they had any chance of surviving this, they needed to destroy these monsters before darkness fell.

Squeezing the hilt of his sword, he summoned his men to him and together they fought through the demon scourge. He would not surrender… he would not yield until every last demon was dead. Many of his soldiers were wounded… he could hear their cries of torment. How many were dead? How many had he brought to this end? Anger, frustration and a strong need for justice drove Bane onward. He didn't care the size or strength of the demon. He attacked whatever was in his way.

Deep into the heart of their numbers he drove onward, hacking and slashing with reckless abandon. With a quick glance around he realized he was alone in a sea of clawing and raging demons. His riders were far behind faithfully fighting to reach his side. He spared them only a brief smile as he released all his fury into the wall of demons surrounding him. The last rays of sunlight illuminated his armor, making him a beacon in the growing darkness.

The demons were just too many. His soldiers were spent and injured. His energy was quickly diminishing. Soon they would have him… soon they would have them all. Just as the battle seemed lost, their world was wracked by another thunderous clap, shaking the very foundations of the earth. Bane was thrown from Tiberious, landing with a painful crash against the rock-strewn banks of the river. Everything had stopped.

Bane looked around in wonderment… the demons were gone. Whatever Kale and Laurel had done, it had worked. The demons had been pulled back to their demesnes… the day was theirs. Bane took several deep breaths trying to calm his racing heart. He had never come so close to meeting death before, and honestly… he never wanted to be that close again.

Captain Daniel made his way over to Bane and gave him a hand up. Stretching his back, Bane gazed at what was left of his army. Slowly he walked up the embankment and motioned for his captains and generals to join him.

"It would seem we have won… I'm guessing our win is due to the efforts of Kale and Laurel as much as to our own skills and determination. I want to rush the city, but we are in no shape to do that. Tonight I suggest we set up camp and begin healing those still alive. For the dead, we will give them a proper send off. The demons are gone… tomorrow we eliminate the King. Daniel, I want scouts and archers watching the gates to the city. Put a couple of wizards with them. I don't want the King getting out of this city alive." Bane paused to scratch his head and rub his neck.

"Oh… and Daniel… make sure Rhinn stays in camp as a favor to me and her father. Everyone else needs to rest and heal. If people want to celebrate… let them. Just remind them we still have more work to do. Marcus, post watches…. We're here to liberate the city, but they may not see it that way. I think it's best if we don't let our guard down just yet. Hopefully, by morning, Kale and Laurel will be back with us and we'll be able to attack the King together… if not… we go in at first light. Dismissed."

Bane felt like he was dragging a ship behind him as he trudged back towards camp. Already tents had been raised and people were busying themselves with cooking, tending weapons and armor, and caring for the wounded. Bane noticed several groups of men marching off to gather timber for the funeral pyres. Everywhere priests, priestesses and healers were scurrying to tend to the wounded.

Bane found his tent and gratefully dragged his weary limbs inside. Stripping his armor off, he collapsed onto his cot and closed his eyes. He heard Isla enter and cluck her tongue as she gathered up his armor and sword. He really didn't deserve her. He felt her take a damp cloth to his head and neck. The feeling was soothing and only helped him to fall into a deeper sleep. His last thoughts were of Kale and Laurel. Please, let them

be alright. Please let them be here in the morning.
Bane felt a warmth fill him as his mind grew hazy
and sleep finally took him.

Chapter 29

The throne room of the demon's stronghold was void of everyone except Leora, Kale and Laurel's lifeless body. Kale pulled her into his arms, cradling her against his chest. Tears flowed freely from his eyes as he buried his face in her hair. How could she be gone? How could he go on? Without her, life had no meaning. Was this what his father had felt when Kale's mother had died? How could Kale have been so selfish as to not understand?

He felt Leora whimpering next to him, her hand gently holding one of Laurel's hands. She was a demon, but she was also a child… a child Laurel had been drawn to. Kale put his arm around Leora, pulling her closer to him. With that action, she buried her face in his chest and sobbed openly. Kale let himself weep for his love a little longer before steeling himself for what was next. It was his duty to return to his dimension. He would take Leora back with him and raise her, like Laurel wanted. He would go on… because he loved her and she would want him to.

As Kale prepared to set Laurel's body down, a warm glow filled the chamber. Kale looked up to see a stunningly beautiful woman standing before him. She smiled down at him with love and understanding. Kale swallowed, unable to do or say anything. Was she an illusion… some kind of trick? She laughed and it was like thousands of small bells ringing. He felt Leora cower behind him, trying to avoid the woman's gaze. She motioned to Laurel's body, still lying in his arms.

"You both have fought long and hard for this victory, and you have suffered greatly." Kale felt more tears burn in his eyes, but he choked them back.

"My lady… this hardly feels like a victory… I…" Her raised hand forestalled any words that would have come next.

"You love her…that I see clearly. Laurel belongs to me, as she always has. I have watched over her and guided her through most of her life. Her spirit is with us still, in this chamber. I asked her permission to use her as my vessel and weapon. She knew the toll it would take, but she was willing to sacrifice herself for the two of you." Another melodic laugh sprung from her lips.

Kale gazed at her in confusion, but then he looked around. The area she stood in had turned to green grass with colorful flowers springing up everywhere. The longer she stood there the further her influence spread, removing the darkness and depravity. Realization struck Kale like a hammer, and he felt his jaw drop to his chest… this was the Goddess Gaia. Kale felt his mouth go dry as he continued to stare in awe.

"Come out little one, for I have seen your deeds through Laurel's heart and eyes. You aided them in their quest even though it could have meant a fate worse than death. Come… there is no need for you to hide from me." Slowly, Leora crawled out from behind Kale, inching forward with her eyes downcast. Gaia gently lifted her chin to look into her eyes. "Little one I wish to bestow a boon unto you. What is it you wish most? I can make you human or elven if you prefer. I could change you to be part of the fae, so that you may keep your wings. What do you wish?"

Kale watched as Leora bit her lower lip and glanced down towards Laurel. He saw her reach out her hand and take Laurel's in hers, tears still streaming from her eyes. Trembling, she looked back up at the Goddess and met her steady gaze.

"Thank you for your offer…but I would rather have Laurel back. She was so kind and she didn't try to hurt me. She was how I imagined a mother would be… caring… loving. Please… can't you bring her back?" Kale watched as she cringed, expecting to be struck down at any moment. With a quick glance at Gaia, he knew she had nothing to fear.

"I was hoping you would ask that. Very well, I shall restore Laurel's life and give back what was taken… and perhaps a bit more." She turned to Kale and smiled at him. "The power has always been in you, Kale. Hold her close to your heart and remember everything you can about her." Kale held her tightly to his chest. Closing his eyes he allowed all of his memories of her to wash over and through him. He could feel his arms warming, and then…she breathed… once, twice, a third time. Laurel's eyes fluttered open. As her loving gaze met Kale's, his heart felt like it would explode.

When Kale looked up to thank the Goddess, she was gone. With a grateful smile, Kale continued to hold them a little longer. They had survived. It was time to go home. Slowly standing, they gathered their belongings. Kale retrieved Demons Bane, sliding it into its sheath.

"Ok, little sprite… time to appear more human. I'm not sure what situation we're going to be walking into."

As Leora began shifting her form, Laurel pulled out the totem that would take them home. Once she was ready, they held onto each other tightly as Kale pronounced the incantation to take them home. A brief moment of blinding light, and they found themselves thrust into a world of chaos.

That morning, it had been a simple matter of breaking through the gates and charging up the main boulevard. The only defense left to the city was a handful of city guard, and they surrendered quickly… even offering to assist where they could. Lord Kingsford knew some of the guard, from his visits to the capital, and had assured Bane they were loyal to the citizenry trying to hide certain actions from the King.

Bane wasted no time in cleansing the city. He ordered several units to round up individuals whose names they had determined were a threat to the new order. He ordered several other groups to scour the city and take an assessment of the conditions of homes, number of homeless, supplies, and overall state of the different districts. He had a feeling Kale and Laurel would need that information once they were on the throne.

The last group he took with him. They charged down the main thoroughfare, heading straight for the castle. The gates stood ajar, servants and slaves running everywhere in a panic. Bane ordered half of his men to begin rounding up the servants and slaves gently. The sooner they were gathered up, the less likely the King could escape in their chaos. Taking the rest of his force he charged into the castle's entry hall. His sword was drawn. His head swiveled searching for any surprise attack. People were running and screaming in every direction, some were nobles… others were servants. Seething with frustration, Bane grabbed the nearest servant.

"Where is the King?" He knew his fury filled voice was only making the young girl more terrified, but at this point he didn't care.

"He…he… he locked himself…in…in…in the th…th…throne room." Bane breathed deeply to calm himself as he handed the girl off to one of his men as she feinted from fear.

"Men, we head to the throne room. Be on guard for anything. We don't know how much power he still has or how many soldiers are in there with him. Be ready for battle." As Bane turned to lead the way a blinding flash of light halted him in his tracks. Raising his sword, he prepared to strike.

Bane brought his sword around in a sweeping attack just as the light faded. With a shout he barely managed to redirect the blade into the stone floor before hitting the huddled forms of Kale, Laurel and… a child.

"Dammit Kale, you have insane timing! I nearly took your head off. Where have you been? I was beginning to think you were dead." Bane sheathed his sword and clapped an arm around Kale in a giant bear hug. He could feel Kale laughing hoarsely.

"Sorry it took so long. We had some difficulty with hordes of demons. We're just glad to be home. What stage of the invasion are we in?" Bane smiled as he took in the sight of the three of them.

"We're at the castle. The King has locked himself in the throne room and we're heading there now. Here have a drink." Bane handed them his flask and took a longer look at each of them. The child looked like she could have been their daughter... was she? How much time had passed in that dimension? Laurel looked pale and exhausted. Kale looked a little crazed with desperation. Bane wondered if he would ever know everything they had endured. "So you went with two and came back with a third... how busy were the two of you?" Kale gave Bane a confused look and then looked at the girl before bursting into one of his boisterous laughs.

"Bane, meet Leora... she was a prisoner we found over there." Kale rubbed his forehead and chuckled a little longer, before gazing at Laurel. "Thanks for the drink... but I think it's time to end this. Leora, can you stay here with one of the soldiers? I don't want you to see what's coming next and I don't want you in any more danger." Bane watched as the little girl glanced around nervously, biting her lower lip. Bane motioned for Daniel to come over.

"Hey, little one, this is Daniel. He's someone you can trust, ok. Daniel, this is Leora. She was a prisoner of the demons. Can you make sure she stays safe?" Daniel smiled warmly at the child and offered her his hand.

"Hello, Leora. I promise I won't let anything happen to you. Maybe you can help me calm some of these people down. If they see a brave little girl staying calm and walking around with me they may stop running and screaming. Do you think you could help me?" Leora smiled shyly, cautiously taking Daniel's proffered hand. She looked to Laurel only once and, when Laurel nodded her approval, she turned and walked off with Daniel smiling at everyone she passed.

Bane met Kale and Laurel's haunted eyes, before heading off towards the throne room. It wasn't long before they stood in front of the grand, towering double doors that would lead them to the King. Bane tested them ensuring they were locked. As he turned to give orders for a ram to be brought in Kale touched his arm and shook his head no.

Raising his hand in front of him, Kale spoke only three words. "Contris deruvick grantis!" The doors exploded inward, crashing several yards into the room. The three looked at each other as they readied their weapons and strode into the grand room.

A golden throne sat atop a raised dais at the end of the long ballroom. The grand opulence of the structure contrasted harshly with the gaudy and grotesque décor. Paintings and statues of people partaking of sexual orgies and the torture of elves and dwarves covered the walls and filled the sides of the room. They walked steadily onward ignoring their surroundings as the soldiers behind them choked and raged against the offense given. With a motion of his hand Bane sent the men to deconstructing the grotesquery around them.

As they approached the throne, their nerves taut, they could see the shrunken form of an old man cowering on the throne. A golden jeweled crown sat upon his shrunken head. As they came closer he began jabbering senselessly.

"Master.... Master... why have you forsaken me? I have always done what you wished... I'm good... I'm obedient... You promised half-elf girl to play with... you promised. Must send demons... must stop fools...fools not know power... fools... fools..." He broke into a hysterical, crazed laugh, slamming his clenched fist down on the arm of the throne repeatedly. "Squash the people... squash the fools... squash the elves and dwarves." Bane cringed at the sing-song voice as he stared horrified at the decimated form of the King.

Kale strode up the steps until he stood looking down at the crumpled form. The King looked up at him, his eyes appearing to bulge from their sockets, his laughter becoming more hysterical. Laurel joined him on the steps peering into the King's eyes. She glanced at Kale and nodded briefly. Bane watched as he drew his sword and raised it in the air, Demons Bane remained in its sheath.

"For crimes against the people of Kallihan, for conspiring with a demon lord, for the destruction of Soldar… we condemn you to death." In one swift motion, Kale brought his sword down slicing cleanly through the King's neck. As his head rolled to the ground a cheer rose up behind them. It was over… they had won.

Chapter 30

Over the next several weeks the resistance was busy apprehending those who were loyal to the deceased King. Laurel and Kale sat in judgment over their trials. Those who were found guilty of heinous acts against the people were sentenced to death. Those who had conformed to survive were given a second chance. They lost some of their status, but they were allowed to remain in the capital… more so the new King and Queen could keep a close eye on them, than any other reason.

By the third week of the reformation, Laurel and Kale were crowned Queen and King by the High Priestess of Gaia. The capital city exploded in celebration as the many changes had already been felt and the people were feeling more secure and hopeful. The castle had been purged of any remnants of the old King and was replaced by new works of art and culture. The artisans of the city began painting and sculpting likenesses of their new King and Queen. Bards were already writing songs, poems, plays and tales of the war and adventures of their saviors. For Kale, Laurel and Bane it was all very overwhelming, but it was what the people needed so they tried to encourage it whenever possible.

Bane organized the city guard and established a new army. He had been granted titles of high nobility and was also named commander of the military. With Kale and Laurel's approval he commissioned several memorials to the fallen that would be placed throughout the Kingdom. One of the first memorials to be created was a tribute to Soldar.

Reports from riders, sent to spread the news, spoke of the mountains to the south receding, opening the passageway to Soldar once more. With the opening of the mountains, the memories of the people were restored. The berserkers, created by demon magic, had vanished replaced by a multitude of normal mountain and forest creatures. People came from all over Kallihan to pay homage to the town and those lost. Laurel, Kale and Bane made a special trip there to dedicate the memorial and finally put to rest the tormented spirits of the past.

Laurel and Kale spent much of their time reviewing the laws and discarding or altering those that were detrimental to the new order. They named Lysander as the Royal High Wizard of Kallihan, and charged him with creating a wizard's academy to train all who demonstrated magical talent. He was also charged with organizing a committee to educate the people about magic and its benefits.

Kale and Laurel made an oath to themselves and their people that ignorance would not be allowed within their borders again. To that end, they put in motion the creation of several schools and academies that would train the young in basic skills and histories. Every person within their country would be able to read and write, work with numbers and understand the past. The schools and academies would help them find apprenticeships for their training and future. The teachers would be wizards, priests, elves, dwarves and humans.

The banishment of elves and dwarves was lifted, and riders were sent out to spread the news of the new King and Queen and the changes to the laws. Spies were also sent out to discover the whereabouts of potential traitors and threats. A new council of lords and tradesmen was formed in the capital to assist the young King and Queen in their rule. Laurel and Kale adopted Leora, naming her as their daughter. On the day of her presentation, a rainbow arched over the castle as the city filled with butterflies. The people took this as a good omen, celebrating their new princess.

Captain Daniel and Captain Marcus, now generals, were granted nobility titles and given lands and estates in the north and south of the country. Daniel spoke with Lord Aldric and within the year was married to Rhinn, his daughter. At the end of the first year, Bane and Islaura were finally married after being able to take a well-deserved break from cleansing the country. Bane, in conjunction with two others who had been called, opened a temple to Veerle, God of war and justice. As head paladin, he spent much time training new recruits, many of whom joined the army as officers.

Over the next couple of years Kallihan prospered. The country opened new trade agreements and partnerships with the neighboring countries. Magic flourished as did learning. The academies, placed throughout the country, became centers of enlightenment and enrichment. Prosperity and peace had finally come to the land.

Although the pain of the past couldn't be completely washed away... the hopes for the future flourished. Kallihan became a center for learning and advancement. Queen Laurel and King Kale were celebrated throughout the land and toasted regularly.

For Laurel, Kale and Bane, nightmares still plagued their sleep and the horrors of the past lived on in their hearts and minds. They only hoped that time would heal their wounds and the terrors of the past could fade into stories of adventure, becoming lessons for future adventurers.

In their fifth year of their reign, Laurel and Kale had their first child, a handsome son they named Prince Toran... in memory of her father. One month later, Bane and Isla welcomed the birth of their first child, a beautiful baby girl they named Larkspur, Lark for short. Both families were overjoyed with their blessings. One year later, it was time for Toran's presentation to the people.

The day of his presentation was perfect. The sun shone down on the Kingdom and everyone who could fit in the city was present. Leora held her new baby brother a radiant smile gracing her face. She had become a beautiful young woman, and succubus... though that was still a secret from everyone but family. As the royal family came out to the stand created for the occasion, brightly hued butterflies and birds descended on the city singing and dancing in the sky.

Music and laughter filled the air as people celebrated the day and the new royal child. Queen Laurel and King Kale stepped to the front of the stage and lifted their son into the air for all to see. Bane and Isla stood to the side holding their little daughter lovingly in their arms. The High priests and High Wizard said their blessings over the child as the citizens watched in reverent silence.

As the ceremony ended an old woman stepped out of the crowd, approaching the royal stage. Guards stepped forward to block her path, but Kale motioned for them to step aside. He was curious about this bold grandmother. She bowed respectfully to the two young families, a warm smile spreading on her face. When she looked up at the King and Queen, they noticed her eyes were milky white… she was blind. Kale stepped towards her and offered his hand. She took it gratefully as she stepped towards the two mothers holding their infants.

"My King and Queen, Lord and Lady, many blessings upon your families, for today is a day to rejoice and celebrate." Kale smiled at the old woman though he knew she couldn't see it.

"Thank you grandmother, your blessings are welcomed and appreciated. It is always good to listen to our elders, for they have wisdom we can learn from." Her smile broadened as her unseeing eyes met his.

"Wise words for one who has been through so much. I know of the pain and suffering you have endured, and I would not wish it upon anyone. I am sorry my King, for your son will know much hardship and pain before he rises to King, as will your daughter…. Their destinies are sealed in prophecy and their futures will hold much adventure, danger, and loss before they may find peace and happiness. The time of the half-bloods has arrived. One will pull allies to their side, the other will lead them to victory. Their adventures will be recorded and become known as the half-blood chronicles. All will know of the group's deeds, and they will be celebrated for their triumph. Teach and train them your majesties, for the future and survival of our world depend on them. The time of prophecy is at hand, should they fail… a darkness unlike anything you have faced will swarm over the land enslaving and destroying everything in its path."

Author Biography

After bouncing from one degree to the next and never being satisfied with the red tape and bureaucracy surrounding the different fields, J.R. Smith settled on writing fantasy to bring some assemblance of sanity to the world. She lives near Raleigh, North Carolina surrounded by her own personal enchanted forest with her husband and two daughters. When life gets too crazy it's time to read more fantasy.

To learn more and keep up to date with the goings on for J.R. Smith you can follow her at JRSmithfantasy.com